LEGENDS AND LEGACIES

Also by Lou Paduano

The Greystone Saga

Signs of Portents
Tales from Portents
The Medusa Coin
Pathways in the Dark
A Circle of Shadows
Alpha and Omega
Errant Knight

Greystone-in-Training

Hammer and Anvil
The Gifts of Kali
The Final Gauntlet

Greystone Lost Tales

Army in the Obelisk
The Last King

The DSA

Season One

The Clearing
Promethean
The Bridge
Spectral Advocate
Dark Impulses
Broken Loyalties

Season Two

The Wellspring
Foundations
The Missing
Cracked Chrysalis
Secret Histories
Terminal Point

LEGENDS AND LEGACIES

Greystone Book Eight

Lou Paduano

Eleven Ten Publishing LLC

GRAND ISLAND, NEW YORK

Copyright © 2026 by Lou Paduano
All rights reserved. This book or any portion thereof may not be reproduced or used in any manner whatsoever without the express written permission of the publisher except for the use of brief quotations in a book review.

Eleven Ten Publishing LLC
282 Fareway Lane
Grand Island, NY 14072

Publisher's note: This is a work of fiction. Names, characters, places, and incidents either are the product of the author's imagination or are used fictitiously. Any resemblance to actual events, locales, or persons, living or dead, is entirely coincidental.

Printed in the United States of America
Cover art design by GetCovers

First edition published 2026

Library of Congress Cataloguing in Publication Data
Paduano, Lou
Legends and Legacies / Lou Paduano

LCCN: 2025914440
ISBN-13: 978-1-944965-71-6 (hardcover)
ISBN-13: 978-1-944965-69-3 (paperback)
ISBN-13: 978-1-944965-70-9 (eBook)

*For Parker, Samantha and Iris,
the greatest legacy a dad could ask for.*

CHAPTER ONE

Soriya Greystone fell.

Waves of time, ripples of the infinite, swirled around her drowning form. They were deep pools of green, vacant of anything concrete. No visions of past, present, or future inhabited the Bypass' energies. There was only the fall.

How much time had passed remained a mystery to her. All that mattered was the mission—one Soriya needed to succeed.

This is a mistake.

Loren's words echoed through the void. She tried to open her eyes, to visualize his scruffy face and rundown look, but emptiness consumed her. Their last conversation, though, drove her on.

It's mine to make. I'm not whole, Loren. I can't remember pieces of my past. What I've done? What I've failed to do? I don't feel connected to this place.

In her rebirth, something had been taken from Soriya. There were cracks in the wall, holes in her mind, threatening to shatter her. Nothing made sense, not even the reason for her expulsion from the Bypass. Her memories were gone. Past victories vanished along with cherished relationships. A void remained in her heart and in her thoughts. That emptiness carried over to her city and her friends. The disconnect kept everyone at arm's length. A burning rage replaced all sense of love and hope.

Soriya refused to live like that.

I have to find out why. I have to see what is still hidden.

Yet she found nothing waiting for her. The void consumed all. It took her away from the world the second she stepped into the Bypass. The glowing infinite swallowed her whole. She continued to fall through it all, lost to everything—including her own sense of self.

Soriya snapped her eyes shut. Her fingers balled up into fists, squeezing her anxiety away. "I won't be lost."

It had been Mentor's fear. He had spoken of it often in the early days, when the Bypass was shiny and new to his young ward. Soriya wanted to know everything right from the start, but the mysteries were necessary, according to her teacher. They were for her protection. She had been meant to discover the truth in time, in her own way.

Mentor's apprehension came from experience. He had lost his teacher to the Bypass. Looking too deeply, the man who trained Mentor had been ripped from the world.

Just as Soriya had become.

"No," she whispered. Her eyes opened to the thick black void, so much darker than the Bypass appeared from the outside. Something was buried behind the light. She struggled through the shadows, yet found no clear direction and no path to follow.

"Focus," Soriya said, her voice stronger now. Her right hand ran along her hip to the hand-sewn pouch tied to her belt. Soriya retrieved the Greystone inside and held it out before her. The mysterious artifact offered no warmth, only a reminder of her failures. She tried to push them aside, squeezing lightly along the edges of the stone. "Focus, Soriya."

Nothing came. No hope beamed from the surface of the stone and no light showed her the way. The fall continued, drawing her deeper into the dark.

"Please!" she cried. "I can't be lost! I can't be—"

Soriya hit the ground with a thud. It surprised her so much she nearly dropped the Greystone at the impact. Tucking the stone away, Soriya felt the earth beneath her. Gravelly bits skittered between calloused fingers. Pavement extended to the right and left. She could see it, her eyes sparking to the dim light finally emanating within the infinite.

Standing, Soriya took in the world. It formed, brick by brick, as if years passed by in the span of a single breath. Buildings, sidewalks, roads, and cars took shape. Spires rose to new heights, blotting out the dark void.

The city formed and brought a smile to her face.

"Portents."

Soriya reached out, wanting to touch everything to ensure its reality as much as her own. She ran from the parked cars—vacant of occupants—to the brick of the businesses that made up the block. Her travels took her from one side of the street to the other, journeying across the sprawling city. It wasn't until she came to a five-point intersection that Soriya stopped in confusion.

"Where?"

She had never seen such a place in her city. Or so her memory told her at any rate, which had been less than dependable since her rebirth. Portents had become nothing more than a stranger to her. To not recognize something as unique as the five-point intersection shouldn't have been surprising in the least.

Roads converged on the location, one from the downtown spires, another from the Grove, with the others branching clearly from Grant Square, Riverside, and the Knoll. Every major district in the city flowed to this point. The buildings dotting the corners appeared innocuous enough. They carried storefront windows with signs and banners bolted to the edifice.

At least, four of the five did. One building, with cracked and weathered brick, offered no clear sign of its purpose. No windows illuminated the mystery for her. Even stranger was the absence of a door—like the building had been closed off to the world and forgotten.

"What is this place?"

"A crossroads," a voice called out. Soriya spun on her heels. A shadow approached from the far side of the intersection in slow, staggered steps. "It is a gateway. One you should turn away from."

"I can't," Soriya replied. Her feet carried her to the middle of the intersection, where she met the cloaked figure. A smirk settled across her lips. "You taught me better than that, Mentor."

He removed the hood of his cloak. Gray eyes met hers. They were the only part she recognized of the old man. His neatly trimmed white beard was overgrown and mangy. Claw marks on his right cheek and scrapes across his chin joined the scar down his left temple to his ear. Blood caked to his exposed skin—his, more than anyone else's, from the looks of it.

Mentor had clearly been through hell. Nothing, though, compared to the pain in his eyes as tears of anger and frustration filled them. "Why are you here, little one? You never should have come back."

CHAPTER TWO

At any given time during the day, millions of people flooded the streets of Portents. With over two million permanent residents in the massive metropolis, spread out across five boroughs, crowded didn't do the city justice. Add to that the three million commuters traveling the RDJ, riding the six subway lines, or sneaking through the back roads from the northern coves, there were plenty of reasons to stay home during the day.

None did, of course.

There was too much to do. Shopping and working, sightseeing and merely wiling away the hours until something better came along: these were the trappings of daily life in Portents. Whether one was taking in the latest artistic display at the Matuse Gallery or checking out the new exhibit at the Portents History Museum, the downtown streets were a cavalcade of different people, some not even from this world.

Myths and legends lived among the populace. Some people barely noticed their presence any longer, especially those able to fit in with a baggy pair of pants to hide their chicken legs or a hood to cover their horns. Hiding became their avenue of survival, even if they did so in plain sight. A lack of attention helped, but acceptance remained a long way off.

Those were the distractions of the world. They pulled away from the joy on every innocent face as they witnessed another miracle in the city—be it the shining black tower at the heart of downtown, the beauty of Heaven's Gate Park, or something as simple as a mouth-watering beef patty grilled to perfection.

"Oh, my God."

Greg Loren sat in the corner of his booth. The smile on his face grew with each passing moment. It had become a permanent staple since the arrival of Gabe Jordan, who devoured another chunk of his burger with overwhelming zeal.

"Oh, my God!" the boy of seventeen repeated.

"I told you."

Gabe held out the burger, swallowing hard on the oversized bite. "Holy crap. This is… this is…"

"Use your words."

The kid threw Loren a glare. "Why the hell have we not eaten here before?"

"Well, I thought…"

Gabe didn't wait for the response. The burger was back at his lips, and he opened wide to finish the meal. His appetite reminded Loren of a certain snake-creature he'd encountered once. His stomach churned at the image locked in his mind, and he shook it away.

"Slow down," he said.

"Not a chance," Gabe replied, small flecks of bun flying free with every word. He settled against the back of the booth, one hand on his satisfied gut and the other holding tight to a napkin to clean off his ketchup-and-mustard-stained face. A sigh of contentment escaped him. "You've been holding out on me."

"Enjoyed it?"

"You've been torturing me with so-called home-cooked meals all month when we could have been eating here?"

Loren scoffed. "They weren't that bad. The pasta—"

"Rubbery."

"The soup…"

Gabe's eyes flared. "That was soup?"

A groan escaped Loren. After years of living off crackers and flat ginger ale, Loren knew he needed to change. Gabe made the attempt necessary; the kid's metabolism was that of an Olympic athlete compared to his own. It might have come from chasing monsters in the dark as the Greystone, or Gabe simply enjoyed eating an entire bag of potato chips every day. The jury was still deliberating.

The cooking, though, had been little more than aggravation—for both of them, it seemed. Gabe had been patient through the effort, but the entire task was unnatural to Loren. He had never been the family man. Beth had always done the cooking when she'd been alive, taking his meager offerings and turning them into fine dining. Cooking was only one shortcoming Loren had failed to consider when adopting Gabe. The entire experience had opened the floodgates on Loren's terrible habits.

Gabe, though, took them in stride—resilient to a fault. He slid to the end of the bench and stood. "I'm getting another burger."

"Another?"

He was two steps away before he spun around on his heels. His hand opened in front of Loren. "Want one?"

Loren sighed. He retrieved his wallet and set it in the kid's palm. "To go."

Gabe weaved through the lunch crowd for the counter to place his order. Loren's smile remained. Days sometimes passed when all he did was watch his new ward's every action. The muffled laugh that came with watching some stupid video on the internet or the disgruntled breathing that emanated when forced to research some threat that had cropped up in the city.

He reminded Loren so much of Soriya.

Another sigh escaped him. It had been a month since she'd entered the Bypass. He'd stayed away, the protection in place as she'd requested, but his thoughts continued to linger on her. In all that time, there had not been one sign of her return, one blip on his Greystone-radar to her presence.

Part of that came from the guilt at his failure to follow through on his promise. A shadow had escaped from the Bypass when Soriya had come back to him during the knight affair. She'd sensed their arrival—feared it, in fact—yet Loren found no trace of what it could have been or what it meant for their future. He hated the idea of letting Soriya down, of not rising to the challenge of protecting the city when she needed him to.

Today, though, was for Gabe. A random Monday holiday (did they even have Superintendent Conference Days when he was in school?) had given Loren and Gabe the opportunity to shuck off responsibility for some much-needed relaxation. While he could have done without the critique of his cooking ability, he was happy to spend every second he could with the kid.

With a fresh carryout bag in hand, Gabe returned to the table. He set the bag down to put on his coat, a wary eye on Loren the entire time. Lifting it back up, Gabe jammed some fries into his mouth.

"Thinking about Soriya again?"

Loren's brow furrowed.

"Yeah, that's the look you give when you're thinking about her," Gabe continued.

"I don't have a look."

"You absolutely do," the kid said. He leaned along the table, bag locked in his grasp. "You never said what happened to her. Where she went or—"

"She needs time, Gabe," Loren answered. He stood, his coat over his arm. "After everything she's been through, she deserves that, doesn't she?"

"But when you went with her to the Bypass—"

Loren's stare stopped Gabe's sentence cold. "You were supposed to be sleeping."

"I was," Gabe said. "And then I wasn't. So, I thought I would, you know, follow you a little bit?"

"She's finding herself, Gabe," Loren said. "Like we are."

Gabe offered a nod of acceptance.

Loren took the lead, pointing to the door. "All set?"

As they reached the exit, held open by a mother of four with weary eyes and a backpack of supplies that made her appear to be attempting a ten-mile hike instead of a lunch excursion, Gabe stopped at a posted sign. He tapped it lightly and grinned.

"They have a room for rent upstairs."

Loren thanked the woman for holding the door, then rolled his eyes. "Ditching me already?"

Gabe squeezed the top of his carryout bag. "For deliciousness like this? In a heartbeat."

Loren shook his head. "I'll work on the cooking."

"And the driving."

"And the driving," Loren grumbled. "Anything else?"

"Well…"

Loren stopped. His hands fell to his hips.

Gabe laughed. "I'm kidding."

"You better be."

"I am."

The winter wind whipped up the lane. Loren slipped his coat on and zipped it up to his chin. Digging his hands deep into his pockets, he peered up and down the Knoll. "Where to now? Movies or shopping?"

"What's playing?"

Loren retrieved his phone. He scrolled through the search results. "Let's see," he muttered. "Superhero movie, superhero movie, animated film, animated superhero film... Are there no comedies anymore?"

A hand lowered the screen from his face. "Shopping it is," Gabe said. "You could use a new wardrobe."

"What's wrong with my wardrobe?"

Gabe cocked his eyebrow. "You can't wear Superman shirts every day."

"I can and I will."

Gabe shook his head. He started north toward the Galleria. "Work will love that."

"Work hasn't said a word about it."

"To you, maybe."

Loren held him up. "Wait. What have you heard?"

"Well, Myers might have mentioned—"

A plume of flame shot up in the sky before them. The ground rumbled beneath their feet, shaking every edifice for blocks. Windows shattered. Alarms blared from the massive tremor. With the cacophony, a blistering shockwave passed through the pair, sending Loren and Gabe to the ground, along with every other pedestrian in the area.

Screams arose. Cries followed. Panic filled every eye, passing along to the next and then to the next, from street to store and back again in a perpetual chain of confusion.

Loren fought to stand before rushing over to offer Gabe a hand. The kid hesitated a moment until he found the carryout bag. He snatched it close before taking Loren's waiting hand.

"You all right?"

Gabe nodded. "What was that?"

The flames flickered against the haze of the afternoon sun, like fading fireworks. Thick, black smoke trailed their path.

"An explosion," Loren said.

Gabe moved toward the door of the burger joint. He tossed the carryout bag in the trash. His steps widened, his pace increased, until he started to run toward the flames.

"What are you doing?" Loren called after him.

"What do you think I'm doing?" The stone was in the kid's hand as he waved Loren ahead. "Come on already!"

CHAPTER THREE

Loren and Gabe rushed up the Knoll. They pushed their way through frantic pedestrians and a few wayward fairies, who held phones to their ears, murmuring prayers to loved ones and checking in on those not at their side. Gabe cut across the intersection at Denmar and King's Lane to the business area of the district.

Chaos took on a whole new meaning at the explosion site. A sign near the entry steps listed the address and the name WHISTLER in dark, bold letters. Only one tenant was noted on the sign—PSI Telecom.

The building in question appeared innocuous enough—a six-story stone edifice, or at least it had been. The devastating blast had sheared off most of the front of the building along the top three floors. Papers sailed into the sky, some still flickering with flame from the bombing. Desks were collapsed, some of which rested on the street outside. The upper levels of the building had fallen into the rest of the structure, caving in on the lower floors.

Bodies littered the debris. Workers rested atop their stations or hung from the side of the building. Their eyes were glassed over, surprise permanently fused to their faces. They never saw it coming. Few did in the end.

Loren and Gabe looked on with fresh horror etched in their eyes. Alarms rang out in all directions. They came from vehicles parked along the block, some buried beneath rubble, others shattered beyond repair, but able to whine a little longer before their batteries finally gave way. Sirens joined the chorus, police and emergency crews close in proximity, but thanks to the distraught citizenry blocking every path, too far away to be of any use.

"We need to clear the road," Loren said. "Emergency crews won't be able to get here."

"We have a larger concern," Gabe said. "Look."

Hands extended through cracked and warped window frames along the first floor of the building. Screams of terror escaped the thin hatch. Cries for help were drowned out by tears. The collapsed upper floors had trapped those working below.

"Gabe…"

"They need help."

Loren agreed. His hesitation, though, centered on Gabe himself. For as much as he'd grown to trust in Gabe's abilities, ever since becoming the boy's guardian, Loren had felt a renewed sense of concern. He was responsible for Gabe's safety now—no one else.

"We can't just—"

"We have to."

No concern entered into matters for Gabe, at least, none for his own well-being. He started toward the building.

Loren's hand shot out, catching hold of Gabe's shoulder. "Don't even think about it."

"I have to help." He raced for the entrance.

"Gabe!"

The kid was already at the door. A brief glance back and then he was gone, into the black smoke and the still-shifting devastation.

Loren huffed. His hand remained in mid-air, the feeling of Gabe's jacket still coursing through his fingertips. Loren feared these situations more and more. Before, there had been a degree of separation, knowing his friends—Curtis and Nicole Dunlop, Gabe's previous wards—were in charge of the boy's day-to-day activities. They would have steered Gabe in the right direction. They would have kept him safe.

Loren only placed him in danger and that notion sat in his gut like a gigantic weight threatening to burst through with one big heave. The kid's every action left Loren with no choice but to follow and hope for the best.

"Great." Loren tucked his head deeper into his coat, hiding his mouth and nose from the smoke as much as possible. His eyes were another matter, and he struggled to see five feet in front of him upon entering the building.

A hall widened in front of him. Shadows shifted, but Loren couldn't tell what was merely smoke and what held form within the thick fog.

Snaps filled the air. Cracking plaster and shattered stone shifted with each step. A wall groaned in surrender to the mass crashing down upon it from the upper floor. It would only be a matter of time before the top floors consumed the bottom level of the Whistler Building.

"Gabe?"

"This way," a voice called from the right. Loren worked through the gloom, aided by a beam of light rising in the distance. Gabe held the Greystone high over him, the rune clear on the surface, to shine a path for Loren. He met up with the kid in front of a blocked doorway.

"Help!" Fingers stretched through the debris. A few at first, but at their arrival, more poked through and the cries repeated. "Please help!"

Loren pulled at the shattered debris. He shoved aside crumbling stone and warped plaster, digging his way to the door. Gabe joined the efforts, but a large beam angled across the collapsing door frame stymied them.

"We can't get through!" a voice cried within. Blood trickled from the man's forehead. His arm hung limply at his side. "I tried, but the wall…"

It must have happened quickly. The man had been lucky. Two more bodies lay beneath the surface, only a few appendages visible, and Loren did his best to block Gabe's view of them.

"Gabe…"

The kid stepped forward, hands beneath the beam. He heaved with all his might.

"Gabe, we can't—"

He refused to hear Loren's plea. Ripping off his jacket, Gabe took a covered breath and stepped forward once more. The stone was back in his hands. "Give me some room."

Loren nodded. "Back up, folks. We'll have you out of there in a second."

"How?"

Gabe smirked at the question. No verbal answer was necessary. They witnessed it with their own eyes as the Greystone lit up.

Every ounce of willpower poured through Gabe into the stone. The light grew brighter in intensity. The cracking and shifting no longer brought a sense of doom for the trapped innocents in the building. It was their salvation as the beam suddenly lifted back into place. The door frame, while not at its necessary height, was still usable and Loren held out a hand to the bleeding man at the front of the line.

"Come on."

The man took his hand. His eyes, though, were lost on Gabe, who continued to use the stone to hold the beam in place. "How did he—"

"Save the questions." Loren pushed the man ahead, then grabbed the woman behind him. "Let's move, people."

He prodded them through the frame one by one. Dozens took their turn; all the while, Gabe kept the beam afloat. The strain was evident on his face, but his will never wavered.

Loren's certainly did. He wanted to race from the building and never look back, but he stood his ground to help those in need. He ignored the call of the newfound parent in him, but it continued to rise in his every thought.

When the last trapped soul was released from the first floor, Loren helped them across the lobby for the exit. Loud coughs echoed through the space. A woman struggled to keep her feet because of smoke inhalation. Loren propped her up at his side, then shuffled her to the exit where he passed her along to others.

Loren held his coat to his lips. "Gabe?"

"I thought... I thought I saw something..." The kid's words were strained from the burden. Rather than let it rest, Gabe doubled down, screaming as the stone's power heaved the beam away from the door frame. It crashed across the lobby, smashing desks and chairs as it careened to the far side of the room.

"It was smoke, Gabe," Loren said. "Everyone is safe."

Gabe shook his head. He ducked below the door frame to enter the office. "There might be others."

"Ever think about us?"

"People could be trapped."

The building groaned in response. Light fixtures crashed from above, joining a rain of tiles on the floor. The entire ceiling shifted slightly, angling closer and closer to the ground. "So could we."

Gabe rounded the room hastily. He ducked under shattered

frames and around sputtering electrical lines. His travels took him to the back wall of the complex, where he sighed. "All right. Let's—"

The floor gave way beneath him. Gabe's eyes went wide, fear filling them. His hands shot up for help, but Loren was too far away.

He was gone—falling into the darkness below.

"Gabe!"

CHAPTER FOUR

Pain woke Gabe to the world. It shot through his arm like an adrenaline rush and caused him to sit up abruptly. His lungs refused to pull in fresh oxygen, his chest clenched from the fall through the floor. He wheezed for air, desperate for relief.

Lifting his right arm, Gabe winced with renewed awareness. Pure agony caused him to scream, though no sound came. Foregoing the injured extremity for his other arm, Gabe slammed his fist into his chest once, then twice. The beating sent spasms through his body until his lungs opened.

Blessed breath returned in a wave. He swallowed heaving gulps, coughing through the effort. All pain was ignored in the effort. Gabe was alive. That was all that mattered in that moment.

Unfortunately, his stomach felt differently. It lurched suddenly, and Gabe heaved the contents of his lunch all over the shattered debris beneath him. Emptied from the ordeal, Gabe swiped at his lips. "Maybe the burger wasn't a good idea after all."

"Gabe?" Loren called from above. Gabe struggled to see through the dust from his fall. The haze blocked the scant light available. Loren peered over the gaping hole, more than twenty feet above. "Are you all right?"

Why is he so high up? The fall should have brought Gabe to the basement of the building. There should have been mechanics, heating ducts and supply closets, something normal, yet Gabe had somehow dropped beyond the original structure of the building into a deeper chasm hidden beneath.

"Loren?"

"Oh, thank God."

His concern caused Gabe to grin. Struggling to sit up once again, he peered around. "I'm okay. I'm—"

He tried to stand. Using his hands for leverage, Gabe pushed up. His right side screamed from the effort, the pain back in full force. "Dammit!"

"Gabe?"

"My arm," Gabe said. He tucked it close to his chest, then shifted the debris pile until his feet found solid ground. "I must have landed on it."

"Hold tight, all right?" Loren said. "I'm getting help."

With that, Loren was gone. Gabe barely heard the shuffling steps above. He was too far down and the cracking and snapping of the entire structure continued to consume any and all other sounds within the place. Loren's departing words caused Gabe to chuckle slightly.

"Hold tight?" he asked in the darkness of the chasm. "Where the hell am I going to go?"

His sneakers slid along the floor. Cautiously, Gabe worked his way to the side of the darkened space for some idea of its size and scope. It didn't take him long to map the perimeter: a ten-by-ten space hidden beneath the building for some reason. Shattered stairs along the right-hand wall clearly led back to the proper basement of the structure, though there was no way to navigate them now. No furniture occupied the room, at least not originally. Multiple desks—broken and battered—rested along with ceiling panes in a heap on the ground.

"Couldn't have been a mattress warehouse." His laughter shook the injured arm across his chest and he winced from the discomfort.

Three walls offered the same structure as the building above. Concrete blocks, though, gave way to red brick and weeping mortar on the fourth wall. Fallen debris obscured most of the wall. It had taken the brunt of the damage in the explosion. Enough remained to give Gabe a clear image. The brick paled from age—ancient compared to the modernity of the rest of the space.

Something was noted on the brick. Even through the gloom, Gabe noticed an image imprinted on a single brick. It was gold and shimmery. He moved for a closer look when voices above stirred him from his musings.

"This way," he heard Loren say. "Hurry."

Shadows danced above. The rumblings grew louder. There was urgency in their movements, when all Gabe could do was shuffle around through the dark.

"Loren?"

His head poked through the gap in the floor above. Two others joined him. Worry filled their faces. Gabe wondered if it was for him or for their own safety.

"I'm here," Loren said. "We're going to get you out of there."

"Good," Gabe said. He shuffled against the debris, his left hand always out to catch his fall. "I've had my fill of this place. It's—"

His foot caught on something. He tried to pull loose, snarled against the object in the dark.

"Gabe?"

He ignored Loren's concerned cry. Instead, Gabe reached for his cell phone. He turned on the flashlight, something he should have thought of earlier. The beam illuminated from the small device and showered down on the debris-strewn ground. No metal snaked around his foot, causing him to stumble.

"Holy!"

"Gabe?" Loren said. "Gabe, what is it?"

It was an arm.

The light trailed along the appendage so Gabe could view the rest of the figure. Buried beneath the mound of office furniture, only the man's head was exposed. Maggots poured from the man's lips and squirmed in pools around his decayed flesh.

Dead eyes stared up at Gabe—filled with dread.

CHAPTER FIVE

"What were you thinking?" Mentor snatched Soriya's shoulders and shook her. Rage danced in his eyes. It mixed with tears that fell freely down his cheeks.

"Mentor—"

He pushed her away with a growl. "You were free!" he railed, with fists in the air. "Free of this place. Free of this burden. Eternity had no hold on you."

He knew. Somehow, Mentor always knew everything. Even from beyond the veil, her expulsion was no surprise to the man. Yet her return certainly was, and not in a good way.

His fists crashed against his sides. He beat them along his thighs once, then twice, before letting them fall limply. His shoulders slumped as the anger dissipated. Only sadness remained. "You were free, you stubborn girl. Why couldn't you let it go?"

Soriya moved for him. At her touch, Mentor reeled, but she held firm. Soft fingers raised the sleeve of his cloak from his skin. Scars became visible; deep scratches dominated his flesh, some still raw and barely scabbed over.

"What happened to you, Mentor?" she asked. "The Bypass was meant to be a place of peace—a reward for the sacrifices we've made. What has this place done to you?"

Above them, the sky crackled. The darkness split, with shadows dancing through the void. Roars reverberated across the sky. Whatever separated this version of Portents from the rest of the Bypass was collapsing. Claws scraped the heavens, ripping through the darkness for their position.

No, Soriya thought. *Mentor's position.*

"Mentor?"

"It's nothing, little one." He brushed the sleeve down along his arm to hide his battle wounds as he stumbled across the intersection. His eyes never left the sky overhead, the look of determination wavering with each roar through the night. "You don't have to concern yourself with me."

"Of course I do!" Soriya bounded to his side. "Let me help you. Let me save you."

Mentor's eyes sparked. For the first time since her arrival, Soriya saw hope in them. "Is that... Is that why you're here?"

"I..." Her arrival had come under the most selfish of needs. She'd been looking for herself—the missing piece of her soul. Not one thought had been spent on anyone else. Soriya never felt so ashamed in her life. Here was her teacher, the man who'd given her so much in life, and she never even considered rescuing him from his fate. "No, I..."

"Good," Mentor said. He sniffled hard and swiped at the last of his fallen tears. The stoic teacher returned, tall and proud against the hope she had ripped away from him in her ignorance. "You shouldn't. I'm where I belong."

"Here?" Soriya pointed to the sky filling with shadows. They appeared to be constellations given form in their size and girth. Creatures unlike anything she had ever seen formed, ripping and tearing at the microcosm they inhabited. "Against that?"

"They come in unceasing waves," Mentor said. "All those incursions into the world? This is where they start. This is how I stop them, how I can still help..."

"They are killing you."

"Every day," he confirmed. "But I come back. I rise up. This is where I belong, Soriya. What I've earned for the life I led. But you—"

"What about me? Tell me, Mentor, because I can't remember." She shook him from his position, forcing his eyes on her. "I died. I felt life slip away, and I was falling—falling forever. And then—"

Just the memory of her death at the hands of Julian Harvey, and her sacrifice at sending him into the void with her, sent a shiver down her spine. She had saved the city in that moment, using the Greystone to close the Bypass before it exploded and released the pent-up energy of the infinite on Portents. It had been a good death; one she'd been at peace with, knowing Loren would go on.

"And then the Bypass sent me back into the world. It threw me away like an unwanted toy. But not whole."

"Not whole? What do you mean?"

She groaned with frustration. "There is an emptiness inside—a hole that has left me cold and broken. My connection to the Greystone is gone. All my connections are gone, like the best part of me stayed behind."

Mentor scanned her, as if seeing her for the first time. "That's why you came."

"I had to find out about myself," Soriya said. "About what happened to me. I'm sorry."

"Don't be," he said. "If I had known…"

"How could you? Mentor, you didn't have anything to do with what happened to me."

"You're wrong, little one," he said. "This, everything you've suffered, is all because of me."

"What?"

Cupping his hands over his face, Mentor let out a guttural scream. "Damn me for a fool. Why? Why didn't I see it?"

"See what?"

He shook his head, unable to look at her clearly.

Soriya's soft grip squeezed his withered hands lightly. "Mentor, what did you do?"

"I… I made a deal," he said. "I saved you, Soriya. I gave you a second chance at life."

Joy rested on his face, the pleasure of the memory and the decision he'd made. Soriya could offer nothing like it in return.

Her hands fell away. "This isn't life, Mentor."

The elation vanished. "I should have known… should have realized. The cost would always be too high."

"Who?" Soriya asked, circling back to Mentor's earlier comment. "Who did you make a deal with?"

He swatted the air between them as he traveled the length of the intersection back to the building with no door. "Leave it, Soriya."

"Mentor—"

"I can't tell you, little one!" he bellowed. "Please. You should go. Try to live—however long you can. You have to go, Soriya."

"I won't," she said. "Tell me, Mentor. Who was it?"

Lightning cracked the sky. The shadows retreated into the dark at the sudden influx of light throughout the void. They feared the answer almost as much as the man at the heart of the five-point intersection.

Mentor's eyes widened, terror growing at her persistence. He pointed down the road where the streak of light met the ground.

Soriya left him behind. Slow steps took her the length of the intersection as a lone shadow stepped through the crack of light. Tattoos marked the figure's right arm. Several long pink ribbons were tied to her left wrist. They snaked up her forearm, then dangled along her side, billowing in the crosswind that blew through the void.

"You…" Soriya muttered, struggling to comprehend the woman's arrival. It had been a long time since she'd seen her friend.

"Me, kid," Kali answered with a dangerous smirk on her lips. "He's talking about me."

CHAPTER SIX

Thel fidgeted in her chair for the fifteenth time in the last ten minutes. Each adjustment scraped the metal legs against the scuffed tile flooring of the church basement. No comfort came with the change, not with the shifting of legs one over the other, or leaning forward along the edge. and definitely not sitting upright along the cold, rigid frame of the chair.

Nothing comforted Thel, especially her surroundings. Religious statues, those of prophets, angels, and the Lord Himself did little but remind the siren of her place in the world... and how small she'd become since her return.

There was also the smell, like a thousand cigarettes had been put out in an ash-tray and left to rot. It followed her everywhere in the room, from the circle of chairs to the podium at the head of the room, and even the small folding table with a cold pot of coffee and a still-wrapped tray of homemade pastries. It reeked of old flame; she imagined the fire waited for her everywhere she turned.

All served as a distraction from Thel's true distaste—the meeting itself. She had been forced to attend them in the aftermath of her "incident." The notion of such a word summing up the beating she'd received at the hands of a dozen masked cretins agitated her to no end. Her anxiety caused her to remove a small object from her pocket. Soft purple fur ran along her fingertips as she stroked the rabbit's foot. Squeezing the charm brought her little relief, but it was all she could manage against her spiraling thoughts.

The group was small, no more than ten in the room during any given meeting. The members all came from different walks of life—mothers, sisters, husbands, children. Every circumstance was unique to some degree, but all were based on the same criteria. They had suffered cruelty beyond measure. Victims of abuse and violence, they shared their experiences to break through the pain that came with them.

Thel couldn't. Whatever peace those around her found in their sharing only brought her more pain. She hated them for their ability to bond—to look past the "incident," when she continued to live in that terrible moment every waking second.

Jackie was the worst of the group. They called her the talker, happy to share her smile and flaunt her perfect hair and body. There were scars, of course. They ran down her arms like track marks from where her abuser had pierced her flesh, but they didn't bother her in the least. Not anymore.

Thel needled the purple rabbit's foot between her fingers more. Peace came easily to the jubilant Jackie, yet remained elusive to Thel.

"The whole time I kept hearing his words in my head," Jackie said, the story almost rote with its constant repetition. "How I deserved what was happening. How I've never amounted to anything and wouldn't drag him down with me."

Thel's anxiety spiked. Whenever she listened to those around her, it happened. She felt the hands on her, the kicks against her gut. Hate filled their masked eyes, yet not all of them had remained hidden from view. That was what made it worse for Thel.

She knew one of them.

David Yardin was a fellow officer at the Central Precinct, one she had hoped to be something more after a few flirtatious conversations. His hate, however, made that impossible. She could still see his fury as he led the assault against her. She felt each blow as if the struggle was still happening.

Jackie failed to notice Thel's unease, her smile washing over the crowd in the church basement. "I believed that, for so long, my worthlessness... it justified the beatings. It normalized them."

"And now?" Doctor Bridget Grace asked. Thel rolled her eyes at the question. They had gone through the motions for so long, but the good doctor—as if Grace was her real name—continued to feed Jackie's ego.

"Now?" Jackie repeated. "Now I see who was worthless. Who didn't deserve any of my love through his actions."

Claps echoed throughout the room. Jackie wiped away a pair of select tears as she stepped down from the podium to rejoin the circle. She squeezed the doctor's hand lightly, then took her seat.

"Thank you for sharing."

"Hear, hear," Kenneth cheered. He sidled closer to Jackie, his hand on her arm a little too long from Thel's point-of-view, but the young woman with the radiant smile failed to care in the slightest.

Doctor Grace edged her chair to the center of the circle. "I think we can end for today. Unless someone else would like an opportunity to share?"

The request wasn't subtle in the least. Grace stared directly at Thel, the lone holdout of the meeting. She always did. Six sessions in and Thel had failed to discuss one second of her experience with Yardin and the others. How could they possibly understand her terror? The pain of being on the receiving end of such hate?

They couldn't.

The assault had been publicized, though, which made her a celebrity of sorts. Everyone knew about the siren detective who fell at the hands of a mob of masked bigots. Every person in the room wanted to hear more. They wanted to revel in her pain, not wash it away.

Thel hated them for it. She dropped her gaze to the small charm in her hand.

Grace read the reaction clearly. Standing, she looked around the room. "I will see you all on Thursday."

Thel bolted from the seat without a second's hesitation. Her coat was on before she rounded her chair, wheeling away from the group for the coffeepot. Taking a disposable cup from the pile, she poured the frigid liquid.

Fingers dug beneath the wrapping of the pastry dish. She held up the snack, round with some form of jelly in the middle and a glaze that stuck to her skin like glue, smelled it, then returned the treat to the tray.

Kenneth made a beeline for her position. Thel ducked her head lower, one hand on her coffee and the other locked on the rabbit's foot. She squeezed harder as she pushed through the man for the exit.

A sorrowful look trailed her, but she did her best to block it out. Sympathy was the last thing she required. In truth, Thel didn't know what she needed. Everything hurt. Everything scared her.

Peace remained elusive.

Daylight temporarily blinded her. Cars zoomed in all directions. The endless sea of humanity used to inspire Thel. She loved being part of their world, loved observing their ambition as well as their laziness when it came to existence. Now, all Thel felt was fear, and it disgusted her to no end. Her apartment had turned into her refuge, the city little more than a nightmare waiting to pull her back into the shadows… where the monsters waited for her.

Thel let out a long breath. She circled the church for the parking lot. A single sip of the coffee was all she could stomach before she tossed it in the nearby receptacle.

At the front of the lot, a car parked across two handicapped spots. A woman leaned against the hood, a bag from a local bakery in her grip.

"Sam?"

Samantha Myers held the bag out at Thel's arrival. "I brought donuts. I might even be willing to share."

Thel grinned.

Myers cocked her head down the block. "Walk with me."

CHAPTER SEVEN

They barely made it to the bus stop on the corner before Thel snatched the bag of donuts from Myers. She tore into it without a word. Not that Myers required a thank you. She had come out of concern for her partner.

With good reason, it seemed. Thel, despite the grin on her face, was wary of everyone and everything around them. Every squeal of a tire, every clang of a door, or shout from one friend to another, rattled her. Her body shook; the dread over what happened to her locked her down. With each one, she lowered the donut from her lips and squeezed the purple rabbit's foot, a balm to her terrified form.

"Still carrying that thing around?"

Thel tucked the charm away at its mention. "I like it."

"So do I," Myers said. "That's why I bought it for you."

"I thought it was to ease your guilt at forgetting to bring me flowers at the hospital."

"You tell it your way and I'll tell it mine," Myers replied with a laugh. She missed this. Thel had always been the one to call her out on her crap at work. She'd been a great partner and an even better friend. Since the assault, though, the distance had grown between them. Myers sought to change their trajectory. The gift of the good luck charm served as a reminder of what Thel brought to the table. If only she saw things that way…

Thel focused on her donut. Three quick bites caused the delicious jelly-filled pastry to vanish. "Appreciate the pick-me-up."

"You sure?" Myers commented at the speed of her friend's eating. "I'm glad to see your appetite is back."

"The food in there is crap," Thel said, cocking her head back toward the church. A pair from within caught her attention and waved. She turned away rather than reciprocate.

Myers offered her own, then leaned in close to her friend. "How about the conversation?"

Thel's hand lingered before the bag of donuts. She fell away, standing from the bench. "Sam…"

"Have you mentioned anything to the group?" Myers said. "Maybe something you want to share with the woman who supplied you with your sugar fix for the day?"

The rabbit's foot was back out. Thel hardly realized her nervous tick was on display. There was more to it and Myers used the silence to look her friend over. Thel had certainly lost weight since the assault. Her bruises remained a fixture, the swelling along her left cheek still slightly present. Appearance aside, Thel's wariness to be out in the world frightened Myers. Her friend appeared ready to jump at every shadow and collapse at the merest touch.

"Thanks for the treat, Sam," Thel said. "I should—"

"Hold up." Myers jumped to her feet, cutting Thel off. "Where are you going?"

"Home."

"Big plans?" Myers asked knowingly. "Any plans at all?"

"I don't—"

"When are you coming back to work?" Myers pressed. "It's too quiet in the office. No one tells me when I screw something up."

Thel smirked. "You hated when I did that."

Myers nudged her friend lightly on the shoulder. "I hate it less right now."

"I…"

The silence returned. Myers could tell she was losing Thel. Her friend's fear won out over any rational behavior. The assault lingered and nothing could make it fade. Not until Thel was ready to tell her story.

Myers had done her best to proceed with the investigation. There had been no other witnesses to the beating. Thel's only luck had been in the timely arrival of the police, who drove away her masked attackers. With no leads and no suspects to pursue, Myers had been in a holding pattern ever since.

Thel's absence tore at Myers. She knew the rest of the department felt the same. With a snap of her fingers, Myers sidled up to the despondent siren with a smile on her face. "Yardin visited yesterday. With big-puppy-dog eyes. Asking about you."

At the mention of her admirer, Thel squeezed the small talisman. Her gaze fell to the sidewalk. "I'm not ready, Sam."

"I get it, Thel, I—"

"You don't," Thel seethed through clenched teeth. "You can't."

"Then help me," Myers pleaded with open hands. "Tell me what happened. Tell me who has you so scared that—"

"Stop," Thel snapped. "Just stop."

"Thel…"

The siren jammed the purple charm away, then looked at her watch. "I have to go."

"I'll come with you," Myers immediately shot back.

"No," Thel said. She read the shock on Myers' face. "Please don't, Sam. I… I'm fine. Really. Thanks again for the food and the talk. I—"

The ground quaked beneath them. Windows cracked and shattered, showering glass down on the pavement. The entire world trembled while flames rose in the distance. Myers staggered along the sidewalk, swiping the air for Thel. The panicked siren ducked her head down, her hands wrapped tight around the armrest of the bus stop bench. As they found their footing once more, Myers moved for her friend.

Thel continued to hold the bench; both hands blanched against the metal. Her eyes shook, barely able to open. "What the hell was that?"

Myers' phone dinged in response. She retrieved the device to read the notification. Her eyes widened. "An explosion. Some business on the Knoll."

"Sam…"

"You'll be okay?" Myers inquired. "I can give you a lift home."

"Go."

"Thel," Myers said. Her friend was still shaken, struggling to sit comfortably on the bench. The last thing she needed was another shock. "You're going to be all right."

"Will you?" Thel said. She shook her head. "Go, Sam."

Myers nodded. Hurried steps carried her away from the bus stop and her friend, but her thoughts lingered on Thel. She wanted to help her. No, she wanted to solve her like a damn case.

Unfortunately, Myers had a new one to handle.

CHAPTER EIGHT

At first glance, Kali appeared exactly how Soriya remembered her. Tight clothes and all attitude, even her stance showcased her brash behavior. The ribbons running down her left side brought solemn memories back to the wayward warrior. She'd once carried the same ribbons—the gift from the great goddess a constant reminder of their friendship and the adventure they had shared.

God, how Soriya missed those days. Everything had been clearer, not that she had taken time to appreciate it. Back then, things were chaotic and overwhelming. The burden of the Greystone weighed on her constantly.

Kali helped push those thoughts away for a time. She'd befriended Soriya and showed her the joy in the mission. Kicking ass didn't have to be complicated. No angst was required to fulfill the job—only the wind in her hair, the snapping sound of the ribbon at her side, and the crunching of cartilage under her fist with the fall of an enemy.

Nothing was simple now. Not even Kali, it seemed, for although her appearance matched Soriya's memory upon her arrival, there was more to the goddess. Her image fragmented as she approached. Echoes stepped in tune with her. Each aspect carried the same bravado, but all were unique from the rest. More than a few displayed a fury that gave Soriya pause and caused her to back up a step.

"It's good to see you, kid," Kali said, a smirk on her face. The image to her right matched her expression. The one on the left, however, shook with anger.

"Kill her," the echo announced. "Rip her throat out."

The echo to the right cleared her throat. She stood upright and proud. "Quiet. Show some decorum."

Soriya looked at them in turn. The argument shifted down the line. Anger was countered with patience, just as calls for physical violence were tempered by negotiation. The ten images spread before Soriya debated every word. She found it impossible to track their progress.

"Kali?" Soriya finally said, confused at her friend's dilemma.

"It's me, Soriya," Kali replied. She cocked her thumbs at her compatriots. "All of me, unfortunately."

"I'll see her burn!" the echo to her left raged. "Then the world!"

"Be at peace," the aspect at Kali's direct right said. "We certainly won't."

"Kali?" Soriya questioned again, hoping for more than a simple greeting.

The goddess sighed. "I was dying, remember? About to change into my next aspect."

The memory surprised Soriya with its clarity. Since her rebirth, she had been denied access to her past, except for the strongest connections. Somehow, though, her time with Kali remained crystal clear.

They had taken Shiva down together. The battle required Kali to make the ultimate sacrifice and absorb the evil Shiva had unleashed on Portents. Her physical form couldn't handle the influx of power. She had been on the verge of death but staved it off for one last night with her friends.

"Say hello to the rest of me," Kali remarked. She didn't sound impressed, though the others at her sides puffed out their chests with renewed strength. "Try to ignore them. I do."

"You went into the Bypass," Soriya said.

"You've heard Miss I-Want-to-Burn-the-World over here," Kali answered, nodding to her left. "I had to save everyone that pain."

"It would have been glorious!" Kali's evil aspect pronounced. Another debate sparked between the other echoes.

Kali shook her head, distancing herself from them as much as possible. "Before I left, Christopher asked me for a favor."

Soriya spun toward Mentor. His hood hid his features, but his thin gaze penetrated the dark. "You said you had saved me. You asked Kali to save me."

A nod escaped him, though he failed to look at her directly.

"That means…" Soriya took a sharp breath. "You knew. You knew what was coming."

"The Bypass showed me."

Soriya launched at him. The world blurred in her anger. "You knew and said nothing? About Evans? About the Charon? The Luminary and the Circle of Shadows?"

"No," Mentor said, reeling away from her approach. He raised a hand to separate them. "No, you have to listen."

Soriya batted the hand aside. She grabbed him by the cloak and ripped the hood off his head. "Tell me. Quickly."

"I glimpsed your death, but not the struggles that led to it." Mentor's eyes widened. His hands fell to her shoulders and squeezed. "I had to save you, little one."

Soriya pushed him away. "At a cost. Is that right, Kali?"

The goddess shrugged. "Everything comes at a cost."

"And you didn't think about that for a second, did you?" Soriya seethed at Mentor.

"If I had known..." He shook his head. "No, even still. I couldn't let you die. Not like that. Not after everything you had been through."

Fingers grazed her cheek. His heartfelt gaze lifted hers. The fury melted and she hugged him close. The decisions were in the past, the outcome standing before them. There was only the path forward. It was a lesson Soriya had learned long ago, and one that carried her away from her teacher and back to Kali.

"Who was it?"

"I'm sorry?" Kali asked in confusion.

"Who else did you promise salvation to?" Soriya snapped. "Was that the cost? A promise kept for someone else, someone who just happened to pull me along with them when they escaped the Bypass?"

Kali's brow furrowed. She shot a glance toward her aspects. All fell silent at the accusation. "I don't—"

"A name," Soriya said. She grabbed Kali by the collar and lifted her. "Who was it?"

The echo to the right bowed her head. "Stand down, child."

"Destroy her," the aspect to Kali's left demanded. Teeth turned into fangs, ready to strike. "Make her beg for mercy, then snuff her out."

Kali's eyes pleaded for understanding. "Let go, Soriya. This won't solve matters."

Soriya hesitated. She yearned for the fight, odds be damned.

There was something visceral in her need. It brought back her previous concerns, the ones that had prompted her return to the Bypass for answers.

She let loose Kali's collar and stepped away. A nod of apology passed between them.

"Thank you." Kali straightened out her shirt as she circled Soriya. "I wasn't aware of anyone else escaping eternity. I offered no other free passage from their fate in this place. If I had, I would happily tell you."

"Then how?"

"That is a very interesting question," Kali said. She leaned close. "For someone to hitch a ride on your return? They must be quite powerful, or…"

Soriya waited impatiently for the rest of the sentence. When none came, she pressed, "Or?"

Kali wasn't looking at Soriya, though. She shifted her gaze to Mentor with a knowing stare. "Or they must be deeply connected to you in some way."

"Impossible," Mentor said.

Soriya pushed through the goddess for her teacher. "What is Kali talking about? Do you know?"

"No. No, I—"

Kali cleared her throat. "The cost you spoke of, Soriya? It was a piece of your soul."

All thought of the shadow and its escape disappeared. "What?"

Kali approached with open hands. "Your whole life was full of struggle and pain. I couldn't let that continue—not through eternity and not in a second chance at life. I took a part of you, the spark at your core, and granted it peace."

"Peace?" Soriya chuckled in disbelief. "You call this peace? Kali, this is as far from peace as you can get."

"For you, perhaps," Kali said. "But for her? It very much is."

Kali pointed behind Soriya, causing the young woman to turn. In a snap of light, the Bypass changed. Mentor remained, but the entire intersection vanished. The trio no longer stood outside, but within the confines of what appeared to be a classroom.

Students sat casually, waiting for the day's lesson to begin. In their frivolity, they mingled, laughing as if they held not a single care in the world. Everything was just beginning for them and not the smallest hint of responsibility had been thrust on them from the outside world.

Amid a small gathering of friends sat a young woman with raven-black hair that ran down the back of her neck in a thick ponytail. Gone were the ripped-up jeans and purple blouse. She wore a sweatshirt, the school's mascot emblazoned across the front. Dark slacks and flat shoes completed the ensemble.

"That's…" No pain rested in the woman's eyes. She bore no scars from battle and carried no burden from the responsibility of protecting the city from threats unimaginable. She was free. Soriya stared at the young woman, unable to reconcile the differences between them. "That's me."

CHAPTER NINE

The media was all over Alejo Ruiz the second he arrived. A terrified glance shot his way from his driver, a young officer named Gomez, who had drawn the short straw on escorting the commissioner to the crime scene. Ruiz had asked for a quiet arrival. Gomez must have misheard him.

The damage done, Ruiz turned to face the swarm of flashbulbs and recording devices. No less than six reporters barred any forward movement to the still smoldering structure. Their makeup was set, their questions already formed. Ruiz, however, carried none of their preparation and looked as if he had been up all-night working, which, of course, he had been.

"Commissioner! Commissioner!" The cries rose all around him. Ruiz pushed through the initial throng, fighting for some breathing room.

"Do you have a statement about the bombing?" Nicki Dryden from WKPO-TV asked.

Before Ruiz could form a response, another question shot his way, this time from Jason Phelps, a correspondent with Channel Four. "Has anyone claimed responsibility?"

Mary at the Chronicle spoke up next. "Why was this site selected?"

"Was this a terrorist attack?" Nicki chimed in, unwilling to lose her place at Ruiz's side.

Ruiz struggled to breathe in the chaos. Honestly, he held little information at the moment. The fact offered no comfort to anyone.

The tremor was the great signifier. It woke the city to the entire situation and brought everyone to the party. What it meant for any of them was a question only the maniac behind the event could answer. Not that the press cared about that. They wanted a soundbite to play on the evening news or stretched across the front page of a newspaper.

From the corner of his eye, Ruiz noticed Myers arrive. She skirted away from the crowds—ducking around fire engines dispatched from the local company. Her head bowed low so as not to catch anyone's attention.

Ruiz sighed, wishing he had done the same.

The questions continued during his distraction. They repeated, begging for a reply. A few steps from the widening cordon, Ruiz turned to face the throng.

"Please!" he bellowed over the rush of queries. "Please!"

A hush fell over them. Pictures continued to snap, catching the burning building in the background. Ruiz could already see it causing more than a little grumble from the mayor during their upcoming conference call.

He let out a long breath. "We are working the scene as quickly and efficiently as we can. There will be a briefing at the Rath Building in two hours."

Gomez caught the instruction and moved for his radio to inform Janet at the Rath. Ruiz's personal secretary would not be pleased with the short notice, but the details would be handled in a timely manner. She was nothing if not diligent in the tasks he laid out for her, even the ones he typically forgot to mention. How he had been lucky enough to hire her was as much of a mystery as the reason for the bombing in his fair city.

Unfortunately, the press cared little about anything else at the moment.

"But Commissioner—"

"Commissioner," Mary shouted over the crowd. "Does this relate to the rise in violence in the city?"

Ruiz stopped his departure. He turned to greet the question head on. She touched on something he'd struggled to curb during his tenure as commissioner. Violence on the streets was at an all-time high. There were attacks almost daily, people assaulted on the way home from shopping or work. It was the work of hate-filled fools who sought to stamp out anything different from them.

Nicki stepped forward once more, microphone in hand. "Did the monsters do this, Commissioner?"

He stared at her in disbelief. Instead of looking to promote solidarity, they hoped to divide—to cast blame for something none of them understood. Not as things stood, at any rate.

Ruiz shook his head, then moved to the cordon. "Two hours. At the Rath. Thank you."

He passed the cordon before the rush of questions and flashbulbs started again. Officers halted the approach of the reporters. They backed away, the soundbite more than enough to set the ball rolling on their own narratives—facts be damned.

Ruiz tried to catch his breath. His chest was heavy. The sight of so many dead and even more injured in the face of the heinous act unnerved him more than he cared to say.

They wanted to blame the monsters—the myths and legends in their city. Some of it was warranted. How many times had something unearthly struck out at their home? But this? Four horns and laser beams for eyes weren't required for a bombing, yet the answer remained the same in Ruiz's book.

"Of course, a monster did this," he muttered.

A voice nearby caught him off-guard. "You handled that well."

Ruiz turned, shaken by the presence next to him. His eyes widened. Leslie Gates stood reserved, with head held high and hands behind her back. "Leslie?"

A member of the City Council, Leslie worked to rebuild Portents after the series of tragedies that had plagued it over the last few years. She appeared earnest in her efforts, yet held a deeper understanding of what was truly occurring to their home than even Ruiz did. She'd approached him during the last calamity, when the entire city had faced destruction thanks to a doomsday device buried beneath them. Her warning had come too late, but that it had come at all—from her, of all people—alarmed Ruiz, to say the least.

"It's good to see you, Commissioner. Despite the circumstances."

Ruiz grabbed at her arm and forced her behind the nearest patrol car. "Where the hell have you been?"

"Working," Leslie replied. "The Restoration Project—"

Ruiz shook his head. "Don't feed me a line. You've been avoiding me for weeks. Every call. Every visit. You came to me. Told me about Marsh and how I can help the city. Then nothing."

"I…" Leslie stopped herself. She bit her lower lip. "The others needed convincing."

"Others?"

Everything about Leslie set Ruiz off. Everything was a secret. Secrets came at a price, and Ruiz wondered who would end up paying for them.

"Trust is in short supply," Leslie continued. "Especially on a day like this."

"What does that mean?" He read the look in her eyes. Fear rested behind tired irises. Ruiz pressed, "What do you know about this?"

She hesitated only a moment, then reached out for his hand. "Come with me, Ruiz. There's something you should see."

CHAPTER TEN

The conversation with Thel hung over Myers like a shroud. She wanted to help her partner, to pull her out of her doldrums. More than anything, she wanted to solve the mystery of who assaulted her. Was that why she continued to fail at both? Were her priorities too focused on the job and not enough on the person at the heart of the matter?

Myers' dour emotional state certainly fit the scene in the Knoll. The dead were still being counted as they were brought out of the building. Fire crews worked to suppress any flareups along the upper floors. The building continued to creak and groan. Subtle shifts caused stony ash to shower the air.

Most kept their distance. EMTs treated injuries from half a dozen ambulances on site, their vehicles parked along the opposite side of the road. Traffic was diverted four blocks away, with cordons set up at every intersection to help clear paths in and out.

Myers looked on at Ruiz's impromptu press conference. She could practically hear his teeth grinding from across the street. The media storm was the last place she wanted to find herself, and she pitied her boss for having to handle it without a clue as to the situation.

The truth was *no one* knew anything. Myers had tried to pry some intel from the precinct during the trip over. Not one call had come in taking credit. Not one complaint indicated the impetus for such an act. The bombing was a mystery, another one to add to Myers' already full plate.

Looking through the ambulances as she passed, Myers tried to find someone that might bring more insight into the affair. Someone had to have seen something out of place or heard an angry call between employees or managers. Some clue had to come to light to appease not only the masses but Myers' own swirling gut.

Eyes widened as she passed the third pair of EMTs. Loren sat in the back of the ambulance. Technicians worked to secure a sleeve over Gabe's right arm.

"Hey!" Myers exclaimed at finding them.

"Myers?"

Gabe chuckled. "Hey yourself."

Loren threw the kid a glare, fire in his eyes.

"What?" Gabe said with a shrug. The motion caused a wince to spread across his face.

"What are you doing here?" Myers stepped up to the back of the ambulance, hands on her hips. "Gabe? What happened?"

"Nothing," the kid replied. "I'm fine."

"You're not fine," Loren snapped. He swatted at the EMT at his side. "Tell him he's not fine."

"It's a minor sprain," the technician answered, shifting away from Loren.

"See? Minor," Gabe said. "I fell."

"He could have died."

Gabe rolled his eyes. "I didn't. Loren, I'm fine."

Loren climbed down from the vehicle to the street. A grumble escaped his lips.

"What are you doing here?" Myers repeated.

"We came for the same reason you did," he said, pointing to the shattered business.

"Morbid curiosity?" Myers chided. A smirk broke through the surface, one quickly removed when Loren glanced back at his battered ward. Myers locked her arm under his. "Care to walk me through it?"

Gabe offered a thumbs up at the reprieve. Myers winked back.

Loren took one step toward the building, then paused. "Taking him back for additional testing? X-rays? Casts? Anything?"

The EMT shook his head. "It's a sprain. Promise."

"I'm fine, Loren," Gabe declared. "I can help—"

"You've done enough," Loren interrupted. "I've got this."

"But—"

Loren turned to the EMT. "Anything he should do while he's healing?"

"Just take it easy," the tech said. "Rest. Keep the arm elevated. Icing it will help ease the pain, and the compression sleeve will minimize the swelling."

Loren waited for more. "That's it?"

The tech shrugged. "That's it."

"Good."

"Right?" Gabe said with enthusiasm. "So, I can—"

"Head on home."

Gabe's face dropped. "What?"

"You have school tomorrow."

"So, I skip a day," Gabe shot back. "No one will care. I can—"

"Do what I say. For once." Loren let out a deep breath. "You say you're fine, so you're going to school tomorrow. Probably be more restful there than anywhere else."

"But the bombing?"

"I'll keep you in the loop," Loren said.

"Promise?"

Loren nodded. "Get moving."

Gabe looked to the EMT, who gestured his approval. The boy exited the ambulance carefully, then hesitated at the cordon. He wanted to say more, but he held his tongue. He headed down the Knoll for their apartment.

Myers watched the entire exchange with a smile on her face. Her arms crossed her chest, waiting for Loren to unclench and to stop staring after the boy. Slowly, with only a small amount of prodding, Loren started for the crime scene.

His hands fell to his hips and he shook his head. "So much for a relaxing afternoon."

"You should know better than to expect one."

"True," Loren said.

"What happened to him?" Myers asked. "He said he fell?"

"Through the first floor of the building." Loren shifted toward the entrance, Myers at his side. "He managed to clear out over a dozen people trapped inside. When he went looking for more, the ground gave way."

"Can we take a closer look? See if we can—"

"No," Loren said. "It's too risky to let anyone else back in there right now."

"So, we have nothing to go on? Not a clue as to what the hell this was all about?"

"I wouldn't say that."

He led her around the mass of humanity and the parking lot of cars that blocked any view of the structure from those on the other side of the cordon line. Bodies were tucked away in thick black bags, ten to a row and far too many rows to ignore. Myers paused beside the dead.

"I didn't realize," Myers said. "This... This is..."

"I know," Loren said. He took her hand and squeezed. "We'll figure this out, Sam."

"Loren, I..."

He dropped her hand, then nodded for the end of the last row. "It's here."

"What is?"

Loren crouched next to the body in question. He pulled the zipper down to reveal the dead man within. "Gabe found him in some kind of subbasement."

"Subbasement? I thought the blast originated on the third floor?"

"That's what the experts are saying." Loren held a hand over his nose and mouth. "I hope you have a strong stomach."

"What do you—Oh."

No scorch marks marred the body. There was no evidence at all it had been in the blast radius of the explosion at all. Instead, Myers witnessed a decayed corpse far beyond its expiration date. His flesh was almost translucent, if present at all. Insects had already snacked on the juicy bits.

"He was in there?" Myers asked. "How did he—"

Loren lowered the body bag zipper further. A clear entry wound presented along the left side of the victim's abdomen. It appeared jagged, leaving deep scoring along the now visible bones.

"A stab wound?"

"The explosion didn't kill this man," Loren said, standing away from the body.

Myers' hand fell along her brow. "Dammit. This whole thing was meant to cover up a murder."

CHAPTER ELEVEN

Like walking through a dream, Soriya entered the classroom, invisible to everyone. Pure joy radiated from her other self. The Soriya seated at the table, with books before her and a coffee in her hand, was unlike anything the stone bearer had ever envisioned. She laughed with her friends, told jokes and stories that weren't centered around unspeakable monsters in the dark or the horrors encountered during her nightly patrol.

Everything was normal. Everything was peaceful.

It stirred a memory in Soriya, one she'd fought to forget for the pain it brought her. She had been trapped in a dream like this once before, a blissful illusion where she had been happy and free from the burden of the Greystone. There had been friends, like the ones currently surrounding her other self. There had been joy.

None of it had been real. A Baku had created the dream, intending to feed on her spirit. At her realization, a nightmare took hold, shattering all the hope she had once carried for finding her perfect life with her perfect family.

Dreams had always been in rare supply after that. What encircled her now, though, wasn't that simple. There was no sense of manipulation at work, only the world as it stood if Soriya's life had followed a different path. Soriya didn't know what was more torturous: seeing the dream erode the way it had with the Baku or watching it unfold from the sideline like a spectator.

"What is this, Kali?"

Her friend stood at her side. The two distanced themselves from the rest of the class, eyes on everyone in the room. No one noticed their presence. No one cared to as they focused on the happiness permeating the entire scene.

Kali smirked. "It's a life, kid. A beautiful life without pain and without suffering. The way it could have been for you."

"It's a lie, little one," Mentor interjected. He stumbled through the room, stepping through tables and students like a ghost to split Soriya from Kali. "Listen to me. Look away from this place. Leave it behind. None of this is you."

The world cracked with his arrival. A hole opened in the classroom's wall, a window back to the intersection. The darkness waited for Mentor. When Soriya peered toward her teacher, she heard the slashes against the shadows, the tears in the sky splitting wider and wider.

Mentor shook her from the dark. "You can still go back. The Bypass has no hold on you. Be in the real world. Live your own life."

It made sense. His every word struck her as true. She saw nothing of herself in the classroom where laughter and joy held everyone together, only the illusion of hope. Something gnawed at her, however. There was more to observe, more to understand. Mentor stood against that for some reason. He appeared unwilling to hear her concerns.

"I can't, Mentor," she said. "What I went back to? The rage in my heart? That wasn't a life anyone should want. I…"

"Leave her, Christopher," Kali interrupted. Her form shifted with each movement, but she did her best to keep her aspects tucked inside to prevent dissension in the ranks. "She needs to see what could be. She needs to see the choices available."

Mentor reared up against the goddess. "Dammit, Kali, don't do this! She shouldn't—"

Rage filled Kali. Her exuberance for life shifted to hate. She swiped at the air. "Leave us!"

Mentor swung to block her blow. His arm deflected to the side and her fist connected solidly with his chest. His feet left the ground from the force, eyes wide with a terror the likes of which Soriya had never seen in her teacher before. He soared across the classroom for the hole back to the intersection. The darkness welcomed him with open arms and then closed an instant later. Mentor's hands still reached for salvation when he vanished from view.

Soriya, her fist in the air, wheeled toward Kali. "What did you do?"

"Do not push me, child, or suffer his fate!" Kali shouted, struggling to calm her aspects.

Heat billowed from the goddess in her wrath. Soriya fell to one knee from the force emitted, barely able to see through the blinding light of her former friend. Slowly, she lowered her fist.

Kali took the sign and relaxed. The light faded, and she let out a calming breath. "I returned him to his place in the Bypass. He has a role to play."

"What role?"

"He told you," Kali said. "The incursions from the Bypass have to be held at bay."

"Alone?" Soriya recalled the number of threats waiting in the dark. "Why can't you—"

"He made his choices in life," Kali replied. "That's why the task belongs to him."

"And me?" Soriya said. "What am I supposed to do here?"

Kali grinned. "Here? Enjoy your reward, Soriya. Don't you think you've earned it?"

The classroom took hold once more. The sounds of the world flooded her senses, overwhelming her from the amount of light and laughter surrounding her. Soriya stepped around the tables until she was face-to-face with her missing soul, the piece she had come to find. She stared into bright eyes that carried no sense of pain or struggle.

"I'm what, exactly?"

"A teacher's assistant at Portents University," Kali said, standing over her. "For the very man who taught you so much."

The door shut soundly. At his arrival, every student in the class quieted. A man in a brown suede jacket and corduroy pants moved toward the desk at the front of the room. A thin beard marked his chin and cheeks. No scars disfigured his face, and no tattered cloak covered his head. Mentor, the man who had once been Christopher Eckhart, was whole.

"He's so young," Soriya observed with awe. He walked with confidence, the pain in his right leg non-existent. "So healthy and alive."

"He's at peace because you're at peace," Kali said.

The door opened once more. A young man slipped inside, scurried around the table, then sat beside Soriya's other self. He took her hand in his and squeezed. She blew him a kiss before turning back to the waiting professor.

Soriya shifted toward the young man. Her eyes blazed with

recognition. "Is that... Vlad?"

The bite from a werewolf had forever changed his life. His family had shunned him because of the abilities passed on through the monster's bite. Vlad had sought his own kind, only to find more disappointment waiting. They'd desired violence and bloodshed, where he wanted nothing but peace. He ran and hid—both from his own kind and the world at large.

Until Portents. Until Soriya.

Their adventures had always been a joyful diversion from the responsibility of her role as the Greystone. She never appreciated him as much as she should have and felt nothing but regret at his passing.

Kali's hand fell to Soriya's shoulder. "That, kid, is love."

Soriya laughed at the thought. Something so simple in the world, yet so completely unattainable for someone like her. She was the Greystone. Nothing else ever entered into it. Yet, it could have. She could have had much more.

Kali patted Soriya's shoulder, then turned away. With a wave of her hand, the classroom disappeared from view. In its place, the pair stood before a small, two-story home with a dark brick exterior. Two cars sat in the driveway. A swing set, worn from use, occupied the backyard.

"What's this now?"

"Home," Kali answered.

"Home? You mean..." Shadows shifted behind the hanging drapes covering the window. Two of them. Anticipation filled Soriya. "My parents."

CHAPTER TWELVE

Leslie led Ruiz away from the bomb site. They headed outside the cordon and through the throng of curious onlookers. No one questioned their presence. No one bothered to look in their direction. They were focused on the chaos of the act, the savagery and the confusion that came with it.

Ruiz's confusion centered on Leslie. The way she constantly held the answers to questions no one else had even conceived irritated Ruiz. Her knowledge threatened his role and the way he conducted his work in the city. Her secrets were dangerous. This was clearly another one.

At the corner, Ruiz stopped. He pulled Leslie back. "That's enough," he snapped. "I'm sick of these games, Leslie. I want answers and I want them now."

She waited, an eye to the tight grip along her arm. When he released her, Leslie started once more down the sidewalk. They circled behind the smoldering Whistler Building until they came to an empty storefront, barred and gated from use.

"Through here."

A key unlocked the gate, and she raised it above the door. The same key fell into the lock. With a twist, the slab fell free to reveal a darkened hallway inside. Leslie stepped away, a hand to the shadows waiting for them.

Ruiz shook his head. "No."

"No?"

"Talk to me," Ruiz said. "Right here. Right now."

Leslie sighed. She peered around the area, her voice low to keep from being overheard. "The explosion wasn't random. It was targeted."

"Against PSI Telecom? Why?"

"PSI might have been the current occupant of the building, but they weren't the first," Leslie said.

"What are you—"

She held up a hand, stopping the question. Leslie reached into her breast pocket to retrieve a single slip of paper. She passed it along. "I received this with my morning newspaper."

Ruiz took the note in hand. Random letters, clipped from magazines and books, were glued across the entire piece. It read:

IT IS TIME TO BRING THE PAST TO LIGHT.
THE HIDDEN TREASURES BELONG TO ALL.

Ruiz's brow furrowed. "I don't understand."

"You will," Leslie replied. She entered the building without another word.

Ruiz hesitated at the door, the letter clutched in his hand. Was it truly a clue or a distraction? He certainly didn't need one, not with his people dealing with the collapsed building and the dead inside. Yet, here he was chasing ghosts, hoping to understand.

Stepping inside the narrow hallway, Ruiz noted the entrance to the abandoned storefront to his left. Mannequins littered the floor. Heavy cloths covered various displays. Signs rested along the walls, denoting sales and brands. Everything was set for the place to take off, yet all had been discarded and forgotten like so much trash.

The clearing of Leslie's throat pulled Ruiz back to the narrow corridor. She was at the top of a flight of stairs, ready to head down. "It's this way."

Ruiz tapped lightly on the door frame. A groan of frustration left him and he joined her. "How does this building relate to the attack?"

She started their descent, a hand to the railing as little light penetrated so deeply into the building. "My organization bought this place decades ago. In secret, we quietly connected the two structures. The bomber, thankfully, didn't know this."

Ruiz raised an eyebrow. "You keep alluding to your organization. Who the hell are you, Leslie?"

She peered back, eyes wide and glowing in the dim light. "Just who I've always said. A friend. To the city and to you."

"That's not an answer."

"No," Leslie said. "This is."

They reached the basement level of the building. Dust kicked up from their footfalls. Leslie retrieved her cellphone and turned on the flashlight. A long tunnel extended toward the bombing site. She led him forward, away from the semi-modern storefront, until deep red brick and thick mortar surrounded them.

At the end of the tunnel, they stopped. A wall barred their entry and offered no door through which to travel. Leslie waved the cellphone over the bricks until it fell on a single tile of gold. Emblazoned on the piece was a torch with a small flame rising from its depths.

"That symbol..." Ruiz pushed ahead of Leslie, a hand on the golden icon. "I've seen that symbol before. But that means... You're..."

Leslie nodded. "A Luminary. Yes."

A Luminary? Here? Now? After Karen Winters, Ruiz never wanted to hear about the clandestine group again. Loren had explained their role in hoarding secrets, collecting knowledge and dangerous artifacts, all in the pursuit of protecting everyone else. Or so they said. Winters, though, had taken that information and twisted it for her own purposes. If the Luminaries were back, what did it mean for his city?

A hand to the sigil, Leslie pressed it into the wall until a loud click echoed throughout the corridor. With a hard twist to the right, another click caused them both to jump away from the wall.

The brick receded before them. Layer upon layer of material shifted away from the middle, tucking into the previous column and then disappearing from view. The wall faded until only a door remained.

Leslie turned the handle to open the door to a new room. She stepped back, allowing Ruiz entry.

He paused at the threshold. Artifacts surrounded him. Shelves of ancient obols and texts towered along each aisle. Displays tucked under glass showcased weapons. Maps, never seen by humanity, hung along the walls. Suits of armor guarded the corners, swords at the ready.

To the rear of the space, Ruiz noted another entry point—the clear connection to the neighboring building. He pointed ahead. "So, you're saying this place... the bomber..."

"Was after all this," Leslie confirmed, arms spread. "Someone is targeting the Luminaries."

CHAPTER THIRTEEN

"My parents are in there," Soriya repeated, taking another step toward the front door. "She—the other me—lives with them."

She shot a look at Kali, who nodded in agreement.

Soriya chuckled under her breath. "This whole thing reminds me of a dream I once had. It's all I can think about being here in this world. I went to school, with friends and loved ones, all the same pieces you've shown me. I had a home—different from this, though. And the way it ended? Well, it went badly."

"Not here," Kali said. She sidled next to Soriya, a hand to the stone bearer's arm. "Never here."

"I hadn't thought about the dream in years," Soriya said. "I thought maybe I blocked it out because of the Baku and how close I came to dying that night. But I shouldn't remember it now, should I? When I went back to the world, I lost all of it except the strongest connections. So why can I remember a silly dream so clearly now?"

"Your proximity to your missing piece."

Of course. The missing fragment of her soul was nearby. Or was it considered omnipresent with the way the Bypass worked? Soriya didn't understand the logistics of anything anymore. Every visual imprinted on her brain by Kali or the infinite energies of the Bypass made her head spin so out of control she thought she was permanently seated on a roller coaster.

She settled on the front door to the home again. It was almost within reach—the perfect life with the perfect family. Just the way she had imagined it as a child.

"She gets all this," Soriya whispered. "Everything she—*I*—ever wanted."

"The gift of happiness, kid," Kali confirmed. "Like I said before, you've earned it. Don't you think?"

"But I didn't earn it," Soriya snapped. "She did. What you took from me. She gets the life and the happiness. What's left for me?"

"That's what you have to decide." Kali nudged her slightly. "Come with me and we can—"

Soriya pulled away. "No."

"No?" Kali asked, brow furrowed. Flickers of rage formed on her face, but the goddess subdued her less than pleasant aspects for the moment. "No, what?"

"I have to see them." Soriya started for the front door. "I have to... If this is my one chance, how can I pass that up?"

A hand latched onto her arm. Kali held her up, eyes wide. "Wait, Soriya. You can't."

"What do you mean, I can't?" Soriya ripped free and bounded up the steps for the waiting door. "They're right here. After all this time, I can finally meet them. I can look them in the eye and—"

She opened the door. Kali materialized before her, blocking the hallway. "It doesn't work like that. This world is for her—your other self. This is her reward."

"I deserve it too!" Soriya shoved Kali aside. Her friend slammed into the false wall of the imaginary home and vanished from view. Soriya ran down the hallway without thinking. Everything around her fell out of focus. She noticed frames for photos lining the walls, but nothing concrete within them. No specifics came into view in her haste to reach the living room and her parents.

She rounded the corner at the end of the hall and skidded to a stop at the threshold. Two figures stood within the room. Her mother quietly paged through a book near the shelves along the back wall. She wore a striped dress, pink and purple, that flowed over her dark skin. Her father hammered a nail lightly into place near the mantle to hang another photo.

"It's really you," Soriya said breathlessly. "Mom and Dad, I..."

They turned to greet her. Soriya had waited for this moment her entire life. Her parents had been burned from her memory at the age of four. The car wreck that had ended their lives had taken her entire existence with them. She had never known them. But here, in this heaven sustained by the all-knowing Bypass, Soriya would meet them. She would learn who they were and what lives they had led before their deaths. There would be stories shared and memories offered of their short time together.

Soriya entered the room. Her mouth fell agape and her lips trembled. "No. No, it can't be."

Her parents' faces were completely blank.

CHAPTER FOURTEEN

Loren's phone dinged again. He passed the device from hand to hand while tapping his foot against the leg of the chair. Leaning forward, Loren shifted the screen to display the message. It was Gabe again. *No surprise.* The time, though, did surprise the exhausted detective, and he stifled a yawn at the late hour.

A quick glimpse through the thick blinds around the converted classroom confirmed night had fallen. Moonlight showered over the grounds of the morgue, glinting off the metal playground in the former elementary school yard.

How long had he been sitting there in silence? Far too long if the question needed asking.

Everyone else was doing something—from Anderson and his staff, who were in charge of handling the deaths from the bombing site, to the emergency crews who continued to secure the collapsed structure. Forensics sent reports with increasing frequency, the chain of evidence passing quickly through email and text.

Even Myers was busy at work. She sat across from him in the examination room, a phone to her ear for the latest from Central. She heard from a dozen different departments, all feeding her the same pat answers with no clear inclination of how a bomb could have been placed at PSI or who might have had the ability to do such a thing.

"There's more to the bombing than we're seeing," Myers muttered at the end of her latest sitrep with the stationhouse. "Our experts think they found pieces of the device on the third floor. But why there and why that corner of the structure? They could have easily taken out the entire place from a different position."

Loren said nothing. The logic was flawless, and he had little to add to her theory. His gaze fell on the body in the room—the one

Gabe found when he'd fallen. *When he'd hurt himself, rushing into danger like a fool instead of living his life like the kid he should have been.*

Spiraling thoughts caused Loren to squeeze the phone tightly in his grip. The device dinged once more and he groaned in response.

"How many does that make?" Myers asked.

Loren tucked the phone deep into his pocket, then settled on his chair. "Hmm?"

"The texts?"

"Six."

Myers nodded. "Answer any of them?"

"I will," Loren replied, unable to make eye contact with her. He didn't know how to reply to Gabe. The kid should have been resting, should have been taking it easy after his injury. No, he should have been worrying about girls and school and more girls and maybe even college. Right? Their priorities made no sense to Loren any longer. The role of the Greystone was all-consuming.

"Loren," Myers called out to him. "If you need to go home—"

Loren sat up straighter. "I'm fine."

The door opened with his statement. The head coroner, a man named Anderson, entered the room. He carried a thick pile of notes—test results taken from the victim, including toxicology reports, prints, and a dozen other things. He had been busy. What the hell had Loren been doing?

"You sure?" Myers said.

The door closed. Anderson rounded the slab with the deceased. He lowered the reports onto the desk, then set to work on his laptop. The tapping boomed through the room and caused Loren's jaw to tighten.

"Yeah," he said. "Just tired of waiting."

Anderson's fingers stopped dancing along the keyboard. He pushed away from the desk. Thin strands of hair decorated the man's head, too few to cover the massive bald spot in the middle, yet he tried his best. Bulbous eyes glowered at Loren, and a hand fell to his chest with false dismay. "Oh," Anderson said. "Was that a comment about me?"

Loren rolled his eyes.

Myers cleared her throat and stood. "Anderson, if you could please—"

"What? Hurry with the dead man?" The coroner was back at the body, circling the slab for the instruments waiting on the far side. "Rush and miss a critical detail that may solve a murder?"

Loren's arms crossed over his chest. He nodded to Myers, who found her seat once again. They both settled in for a long night.

"Point made," Loren said.

"I should hope so." Anderson nodded at the body, scalpel in hand. "Would you like to see his stomach contents?"

Myers covered her mouth. "Can we get to the good stuff already?" When Anderson moved to make his incision, she raised a hand. "Not the stomach contents."

"I thought you came to see a show," the Head Coroner said with a gleam in his eye. He settled the instrument on the table beside the dead man.

Loren joined the man at the slab. "Do you have a time of death?"

Anderson started for the desk and the jar set upon the surface. Shaking it lightly, he held the small specimen out to Loren. The former detective backed away, happy to keep the contents in the hands of someone else entirely.

"Long enough for these little critters to take root in the flesh." Anderson eyed the maggots within the jar with morbid curiosity. "Decomposition, as you can see, has taken much from the man, but these buggers offered enough evidence to put the time of death at approximately two weeks ago."

"Two weeks? So this—"

Loren interjected, "Then why set the explosion?"

Myers' brow furrowed. "I don't think they're related. How could they be?"

"A dead body in the building that happens to be targeted like this? How could they not be?" Loren shot back.

Anderson stepped between them. "All excellent questions. But they aren't what you should be asking at this moment."

"No? Then what—"

Loren shook his head. "You know who this guy is."

Anderson snapped his fingers. "Ah, I've missed you, Loren. The dullards here offer me nothing."

Myers grumbled. "This dullard will offer you a swift kick in the ass if you don't tell her what you know."

"Drum roll, please," Anderson announced. Neither took the bait, leaving him with silence. "No love for the dramatic? Very well." He passed along the report, which Myers snatched from him.

"Our friend here is Michael Hennessey."

The name wiped away Loren's exhaustion. "Hennessey?"

"That's right," Anderson continued. "He is the direct descendant of Patrick Hennessey."

"One of the founders of Portents."

Nothing was ever as simple as murder in Portents. History always played a part in matters, clouding everything and sparking a million new questions to be asked. Loren immediately realized the truth. The key to their current crisis rested with the dead body in the room.

The Hennessey name meant too much to Portents to be a coincidence.

CHAPTER FIFTEEN

The sounds of the city were worse at night. Cars no longer screeched, but boomed through the canyons of downtown. Every voice was a shout against the shadows that seemed to take on a life of their own.

Thel hated every one of them. They used to soothe her after a long day at the precinct—a chorus in an endless symphony. They stood for life, something she hadn't felt since the assault.

Since David Yardin.

Just the thought of his name drove daggers through her. Every ounce of her spirit, what little remained after being submerged for so long in the quagmire of memory, wanted to scream and rail against what the pissant officer had stolen from her.

Television offered no distraction. The stories were endless dramas that hit a little too close to home. Somehow, everything connected to the beating, from the background set dressing to the gravelly voice of a killer. Everything brought her back to that day.

Turning away from the set, Thel rested against the back of the couch. Her couch. In her apartment. Her second chance at life had come with such promise. She had made so many plans to live the rich life she had been denied in her previous existence. Her sisters had driven her to take rather than experience anything organically, to tear down others instead of building everyone up as equals. This had been her chance to move away from that—the life of hate and vengeance—and be a better person.

It was gone. So was any hope of getting it back. Even the apartment failed to inspire feelings of safety and security. The place was merely a series of walls, confining her and constricting her. How much longer would it be before they closed in on her completely and swallowed her whole?

The view helped in the beginning. She peered outside with renewed frequency. Where once she saw beauty in the street, the way the lights beamed off the closed storefronts or the hum of neon from the bar at the corner, now only shadows waited to seize her at the earliest opportunity.

Still, she stared out into the oppressing night, wishing for something better. The sounds caused her to shake against the couch cushion. The rising black smoke across the sky reminded her of the explosion from earlier. There were bigger concerns than a silly girl afraid of the world, yet that was all she had left to her. Her fear had taken away any will to reach out and any trust that things might improve.

There was only David Yardin and his hate.

A shadow shifted across the street. Out of the alley between buildings, a figure stood at attention. Their black outfit obscured much of their body, but the mask on their face made their intentions clear.

It was the same mask David and the others had worn the day of the attack.

"No," Thel gasped. Hands covered her eyes. She fell soundly against the cushion. "It isn't real. It isn't real. It can't be. Not again. Please."

Her mutterings continued for what felt like minutes. Her heart raced in her chest. She rocked back and forth, hands still protecting her from the world. When the words failed her, when there was no recourse but the truth, Thel shifted once more toward the window.

The figure was gone.

Others had taken its place. People rushed up and down the block, living life with boisterous enthusiasm. They laughed and fought and cried and howled, but they lived each moment. Thel saw none of that, though. She was too lost on the darkness each one carried and the pain they prepared to inflict on anyone and anything different from them.

She should have turned Yardin in, should have told the truth to Myers about what had happened to her. Thel couldn't, though. Every time she thought about speaking out, her terror took over. Would she be believed? Yardin was a cop. They protected their own, even in the face of the vilest of offenses. And who was Thel, exactly? A freak. A monster. No one would side with her.

The consequences of telling Myers—of telling anyone—were

too great. The threat of reprisal was more than enough to ensure Thel's silence.

Her anxiety rose with each labored breath. Unable to think through the fear, Thel closed the curtains over the window. She snatched the pillow from her side and clutched it over her heaving chest.

"Tomorrow will be better," she whispered. "Tomorrow has to be better."

The lie of it all echoed in her thoughts, though. Nothing would get better. Not the way things stood. Not until something changed.

CHAPTER SIXTEEN

The hours fell away like the stacks of reports from Myers' desk. Loren shuffled sheet after sheet to the floor, lost in the sea of so-called progress. Nothing added up, especially the dead man at the morgue.

Hennessey.

The Founders continued to plague him. Everywhere Loren looked there were signs of Patrick Hennessey, Wilbur Caldwell, and Nathaniel Evans, though the city knew him better as William Rath. Portents' entire history was nothing more than fiction thanks to the horrors inflicted by the true founder of the city. Hennessey and Caldwell, however, had been real, and their accomplishments remained in place through various buildings, landmarks, and institutions.

How did Hennessey's descendant fit into the picture? The question clouded Loren's thinking. Every avenue of investigation had become gummed up thanks to the inclusion of the dead man in the subbasement.

The distraction ate up the night. Midnight came and went, vanishing beneath the reports and the theories and the all-too encompassing confusion of the entire event. When his phone began ringing, Loren nearly fell from his seat.

Myers stirred from her own exhaustion. She pawed at a report at Thel's desk, content to give Loren her workstation for the duration.

"Who is it?"

Loren glanced at the screen, though it was unnecessary. "Guess."

"You should—"

He ignored the call and placed the phone at his side once more.

Barely a minute passed before the loud ding of a notification echoed through the room. The text message was in large bold letters, all of which conveyed nothing but mounting frustration. Loren was getting used to the feeling. Why shouldn't everyone else?

"How pissed is he?" Myers reached down for the thermos on the floor. Opening it up, she poured two more cups of coffee, though neither recalled finishing the previous set.

Loren took the cup in hand. Setting it down, he lifted the phone. A few quick taps of the screen and the message was sent. "I told him to get some sleep."

Myers huffed. "I'm sure that's what he wanted to hear. Tell him what's going on."

"He's a kid."

She cocked an eyebrow at him. "He's more than that, Loren."

He knew it to be true. Hell, he had said the same damn thing on multiple occasions over the last year. Yet, when he tried to rationalize letting Gabe into the current crisis, he kept seeing him fall through the floor of the Whistler Building. His heart seized on that moment, driving spikes through him with each remembrance.

"I'm trying to protect him."

"How's that working out for you so far?"

Loren sighed. "Know what we ended up doing last weekend? We tracked down a rogue nest of harpies in the coves. I have scratches in places you wouldn't believe."

Myers chuckled, sipping at her coffee. "Not exactly a family picnic or a trip to the beach."

"He wants to be the Greystone. I get it," Loren said, his voice low. "But can't he have more in life? More than—"

"More than what we have?"

He hated the sense of sadness that came with her words. The truth in them lingered. "Exactly."

Her hand fell on his. "You can't make that choice for him."

"I can try," he shot back. "I have to try, don't I?"

"It won't end well." She patted his hand twice, then stepped away. Returning to her desk, Myers sat and let out a long breath. In the silence of the office, a smile cracked along her lips, followed by a quiet chuckle.

"What's so funny?"

Myers shook her head, lowering her coffee beside the reports. "I'd say you with a kid, but it's not funny. It's... You're trying,

Loren. That's a hell of a thing, considering who we are. The lives we lead. I'm... Well..."

"What?"

Her gaze fell away. "Nothing."

"Myers..."

"Go home," she said, pointing to the door. "Get some rest. The case isn't going anywhere."

He hated to do it. Something about Hennessey's involvement screamed for his attention, yet nothing connected to PSI Telecom or the bombing. They appeared to be nothing more than a coincidence. A decade of experience dealing with the bizarre had taught Loren better. He just couldn't see the connection. Not yet, anyway.

Pushing away from the desk, Loren reached for his coat. He slipped it on, then finished the still steaming cup of coffee. "You plan on doing the same?"

"In a few," Myers said without looking up from her work.

"Myers..."

She dropped the report and waved. "I will. Now go."

Loren nodded. He started for the door, his hand on the knob before she called to him once more.

"Loren," she said, eyes gleaming under the overhead lights. "You'll find your answers. It takes time."

"Thanks."

He exited the office and closed the door. The pounding of feet and the shouts of humanity filled the air. Every soul in Central worked toward the same goal. They felt the pressure with each passing minute, knowing someone was out there with the ability to strike with such devastation, and with only the touch of a button. He wanted to cheer them on, to help in any and every way possible, but Myers' words stuck with him.

He needed answers, all right, and hoped the light of day provided some. Not only for his situation with Gabe, but for the case.

CHAPTER SEVENTEEN

Myers lingered by the door. Loren's shadow hesitated outside the glass for a long moment. She wondered if he would return, if he wanted to say more or even could considering so much vied for their attention with the case and the Hennessey murder. She wondered too much and for too long, so that by the time she blinked again, Loren's shadow was gone.

The office felt colder with his departure.

Myers hated the feeling. More than that, she disliked the way Loren's presence affected her. It was the kind of confusion she'd always avoided in the past. Her secrets had made it necessary, so afraid of being found out as the fraud she was—the cop who was nothing more than a crook at heart.

Daddy issues, some would have said. Not Myers, though. Her strength had come from the man. Her survival skills as well. She needed them now more than ever. Not for fear of being discovered. Those fears had long since been extinguished. No, Myers feared a different type of discovery, one she wasn't sure she was ready for.

Especially with someone like Greg Loren.

A groan of frustration escaped her. She settled in on her pile of reports and the cooling coffee atop them, then paused. It was Thel's desk, the surface much cleaner than Myers ever left her own. She missed her partner, her impact on the work even more evident with Loren's involvement. Thel had been easier to work with. Everything had been clearer with the centuries-old siren somehow, like the rules were simpler in a way.

Loren clouded matters almost as much as the dead man found in the telecom office's basement. Michael Hennessey, age forty-three. No wife. No kids. His death was a tragedy, no doubt, but did it actually mean anything?

Myers wasn't so sure. Loren, though, believed the history of Portents always demanded a place in an investigation. His experience with matters certainly attested to that line of thinking, but for all his theories about Hennessey, none connected to the bombing in any meaningful way.

It was a distraction neither of them needed. They had enough on their plates.

Pushing aside the dead man and over a century of history, Myers pried loose the preliminary report from the explosive device used at PSI Telecom. Designs had been worked up, sketches of the probable device used. Multiple angles were displayed, hand-drawn with exquisite detail. Each piece was labeled, but how they correlated with the actual bomb remained a mystery to Myers.

Every word offered no real insight into anything other than the weapon used, not the maniac behind it. Myers couldn't work like that. She needed to get inside the madman's head. Tech had never been her strong suit. She barely knew how to operate her damn phone, let alone wire an explosive to the correct yield to lay waste to a building.

Myers paged through the device analysis until she located a name at the top of the back sheet. The technician's name was Haya Cho.

The frantic detective nearly spilled her coffee as she reached for her phone. Dialing quickly, the line rang twice, and she spoke over the greeting of the desk sergeant on duty. "I need a location on Sergeant Haya Cho."

"The bomb nerd?" the sergeant replied.

Myers smiled. "Know her?"

"Yeah," he said, grumbling through the line. "I mean, as much as you can with someone like that. Not exactly up on her social graces."

"Got a location with that bevy of intel?" Myers asked.

"The Seventh." The soft tapping of a keyboard filled the line. "Yep," the officer confirmed. "She's still there. Got a whole wing to herself last I heard."

"Thanks."

Myers dropped the line without another word. The receiver clattered into place. She finished what remained of her coffee, then gathered up the bombing reports. Loren was in the past, a distraction neither of them needed, not with everything else going on.

Myers happily left him behind. She finally had a starting point for the case.

CHAPTER EIGHTEEN

Blank faces stared back at Soriya.

"Why can't I see them?" She rushed between the figures of her parents. They remained oblivious to her presence, statues in the room of her perfect life. With each glimpse, more and more details faded from view. Her mother's dress turned into an amorphous splotch of color, no longer the striped design from seconds earlier. Her father lost his hammer in her frantic movements through the living space. Fingers melded together so she couldn't tell if they were calloused from the life of a laborer or smooth from a privileged existence.

The details mattered. These were her parents, and she was losing them by inches, never to nail down who they were or how much they had loved her. Her past had never been further from her.

Anger seeped through Soriya's body. She spun toward Kali, who waited patiently at the doorway. "Why the hell can't I see them?"

"Why would you?"

The casual dismissal of her question drove Soriya across the room. She sent her fist flying behind a scream of pure rage. Before the blow came close to landing, Kali waved her hand before her.

Soriya's entire body left the ground, struck by the concussive force of Kali's simple movement. She flew through the living room as if slapped across the face by a bear. Her shoulder crunched through photos of faceless parents, the details all but lost to smeared colors and fading light. Soriya settled against the ground, halfway through the plasterboard of the false home.

"Kali?"

Her friend stepped closer, a hand out to help. "I didn't want to have to do that."

"Sure seemed like you did." Soriya swatted the hand away. She worked her way to her feet, shuffling her hair from her face. When she turned back to the wall, the destruction was gone and the photos were back in place. "What is happening?"

"This isn't your world, kid," Kali said. "It's hers."

"She's me!" Soriya exclaimed. "I am her. If she can have this, why can't I?"

"Is that what you want?"

"What?"

"You came to find yourself, but that comes with a choice." Kali circled the lost parents. "You can stay here, reclaim your missing soul, and live in peace."

"Or?"

Kali remained quiet.

"I can't stay here, Kali," Soriya snapped. "Portents needs me. I told Loren—"

"Then this life will never be for you."

Soriya's hand slipped into the pouch at her hip. The Greystone filled her palm, and she held it before her. "The hell it can't."

"Don't, Soriya," Kali warned. "Put it down."

"No. Not after everything I have been through." Soriya looked at her fading parents. "I deserve to know who they are."

"Not like this."

Soriya closed her eyes. She channeled her will into the stone, begging the mysterious weapon for a response. "If my memories are stronger here, maybe my connection to the stone is as well."

Light beamed from the surface. Her thoughts centered on Ansuz, a revealing truth, for the answers she sought. When she opened her eyes, though, the light on the surface revealed nothing. No rune took hold, just an uncontrollable presence that grew with every rapid breath.

Holding out the stone, Soriya tried to block the light. It shone through her fingers. As it washed over the room, the world cracked. Walls shredded at the merest touch. Her parents were ripped from the space.

Everything changed. The serenity of the living space—the peace of the life Kali had offered—was gone. In its place, darkness filtered through. The stone flickered within her hands until nothing remained but the dull hue of the gray surface, icy to the touch.

"It didn't work," she whispered.

The room and her life, every hope and dream of a child, shifted to shadows. They moved along the periphery of her vision, the feel of their icy breath sending chills down her spine. Creatures took form, crawling out of the darkness as if birthed by her use of the Greystone.

"What have I done?" Soriya looked to her friend for guidance.

Kali backed away slowly, a shrug along her shoulders. "You were a guest, kid. You overstayed your welcome."

The goddess turned away from her and started for the deepening black. Soriya moved to catch up. At her approach, the creatures fell loose from the shadows they'd inhabited. Claws scratched against the false earth. They screeched with pain—or the joy of creating such a feeling. Soriya wasn't sure and definitely didn't want to find out.

"Kali!" Soriya called. "You have to help me."

"Not with this," Kali replied. "Only one person can help you."

She snapped her fingers. The world split. Soriya found herself in a long hallway. On one side was her perfect home. Her parents waited for her inside; their hands extended to welcome her into their embrace. On the other was the five-point intersection with scorching lightning in the sky and danger all around. Mentor stood in the center, his face cloaked and his fists clenched, ready for the never-ending fight to begin again.

Soriya–locked between both worlds—peered desperately for a sensible solution to her dilemma. The way to Mentor was clear, while growing hordes of shadow creatures barred her vision of heaven.

"No!" Soriya shouted. She swung out at the first wave, beating them back. "I won't leave. Not when I'm so close."

"Then you'll die," Kali admitted. "Here and now. Without any answers. Is that what you want?"

"The answers are right there!" Soriya yelled. "I had them. Let me have them!"

"That is the easy path," Kali said. "That's never been your path."

"Why not?" Claws swiped along her skin. Soriya felt a cold burrow within her spirit, as if another chunk of her soul was lost in the attack. She kicked the beast away. "Why can't I have it easy just this once? Why can't I be happy? They were my parents! They know who I was! Who I was supposed to be!"

"They aren't the answers you seek," Kali said. "They mean death for you, kid. No more revival. No more Portents. No more Loren. Only the end. Is that what you want?"

Part of her wanted to shout, *Yes. Please. Anything to stop this pain.* That wasn't the truth, though. That wasn't who Soriya had been in life. Nothing had ever been easy, not the lessons learned from Mentor or the battles waged in the streets of her city. Everything had been a struggle. Everything had been suffering. All had made the triumphs worthwhile.

"Is that what you want, Soriya?" Kali repeated.

"No." Soriya lowered her fists. The moment she did, the creatures receded. The vision of heaven turned white, then faded to nothing. Soriya turned away from her disappearing parents until only the intersection remained in view. She took one step away from her everlasting peace, and the hallway vanished.

The intersection spread out before her. Mentor stood in the middle, turned away from her with head bowed and covered.

"What now?" Soriya asked. "Kali?"

The goddess vanished, but her voice carried on the air. "He has to tell you, Soriya. He has to tell you everything."

"What do you mean? Kali?" Soriya spun around for some sign of her former friend, the anger rising once more. "Kali!"

"She's ignoring you," Mentor said. He kept his back to Soriya, his shoulders slumped forward from the incredible burden of his task. Above, the skies crackled with shadows. The creatures prepared to pour through. "She's quite good at ignoring those in need."

Soriya rushed to his side. "They were there, Mentor. My parents. Why can she be with them and I can't? Why can't I ever be whole?"

He shuffled away from her, shaking his head profusely.

"Kali said he would have to tell me," Soriya said. "Do you know? Mentor, I—"

Mentor removed the hood from his head. Tears dotted his eyes and ran down his cheeks. "It's because of me."

"What?"

"Your life, little one? Everything that has happened to you? I did this to you. This is all my fault."

CHAPTER NINETEEN

Loren never came home. The thought ate at Gabe throughout the morning. His alarm failed to go off. Thankfully, his arm took over the role with a sharp stab of pain to remind him of the sprain—minor, as it was—and all the fun in store while he recovered. After a quick shower and an even quicker breakfast, Gabe headed for school.

No one wished him a good day or passed along a bagged lunch. There was only a ride from a friend down the Knoll and the usual crass comments about how Tuesday still felt like Monday, only worse. Questions arose about the way Gabe held his arm. He'd removed the sleeve provided by the EMTs, not wanting the undue attention for his act at the bombing site.

Three periods into the day and still there had been no word from Loren. His casual text of "Get some sleep" offered no insight into the case or the reason behind the explosion. What had happened to their day of bonding? Loren had called it dinner and a show, which turned into lunch and shopping, until finally morphing into Greystone time.

While Gabe loved every second of the chaos that surrounded his chosen profession, a little downtime with his adopted parent would have been nice as well. Even if it was only to discuss the case, which is what Gabe had counted on all night.

Instead, it had been radio silence. Loren was knee deep in the investigation and Gabe had been left behind. The lessons learned during their time together had been forgotten. All thought of the fail-safe Gabe had stopped was as lost as he found himself all morning at school.

Normality didn't work for him. As much as he wanted some one-on-one time with Loren, everything else could have been tossed out the window and Gabe would never have noticed. School, homework, drama, girls—okay, maybe not girls—they all amounted to disruptions to his task as the Greystone. The city needed him. He proved that at the bombing site, when he'd pulled that beam away to free those trapped innocents. Loren knew better than to shut him out, yet he had disappeared once more down the rabbit hole of a case. With Myers, of all people, when it should have been Gabe.

His partner. His…

Gabe sighed. Frustration built inside. He knew better than to let it happen. That way led to mistakes. Worse, it never availed him anything. Loren couldn't ignore him forever. Just like Gabe couldn't ignore his studies, try as he might.

The chaos of the room slowly fell into focus. So lost in his own spiraling thoughts, Gabe failed to realize the period had started. The rest of the class seemed to as well, as talking rose from every corner.

Mr. Johnson, Gabe's history teacher, was mysteriously absent, leading to the bedlam from everyone else in the room. Gabe threw a quizzical glance at his friend, Kevin, in the corner only to receive a shrug before he returned to his conversation with Heather, who he definitely had no shot with, no matter how much he believed otherwise.

When the door shot open, few noticed. A pair of studious souls sat up straight at their desks, hands folded neatly before them. No one liked to talk about those kids on a regular basis and they demonstrated why repeatedly. The rest of the class ignored the sudden arrival. Not even the six-foot-six wide frame of Principal Milton Davis was enough to snap them from their conversations.

"All right, people, all right!" he shouted, taking long strides for the teacher's desk. A strong-looking figure with black stubble trimmed tight to his dark face followed him into the room. His Stafford shirt clung to his lean physique. Sharp eyes took in the room as he stood behind the principal. "I said, settle down!"

The clamor faded between the cliques. Snapping gum echoed in the silence and rolling eyes greeted the pair of intruders to the history classroom.

Davis grumbled slightly, hands blanched along the desk in front of him. "Class, I want to introduce you to Mr. Shepherd. He'll be taking over for Mr. Johnson."

Shepherd stepped forward. "Hello, everyone."

Gabe's brow furrowed. It was December—not exactly the time to replace a teacher in the classroom, especially not one as overly enthused about the school as Mr. Johnson was. He was always the first to report in the morning and one of the last to depart when the final bell rang.

Or at least, that was what he'd told Gabe on the few times they'd met up in the halls after school. Johnson had made history come alive in a way few others would bother to attempt, not with the constant influx of responsibilities thrown at the teachers with each new school year. For all his talk of hating normality, Gabe wasn't sure how he felt about Johnson's absence. Perhaps it was the lack of answers with the bombing, but Gabe couldn't let the man's disappearance stand without scrutiny.

He raised his hand.

"Yes, Gabriel?" Davis asked.

The fact that Davis knew his name startled Gabe, but he brushed it aside as every eye in the class fell on him. "What happened to Mr. Johnson?"

The vein in the principal's forehead pulsed a little brighter for a second. He bit the inside of his cheek, holding back an initial response as he took a breath. "He was offered another position out of town."

"This far into the year?" Gabe pressed.

"That's all I know, Gabriel," Davis continued. "Mr. Shepherd will be handling things from now on." He turned to his compatriot. A hand fell on Shepherd's shoulder and patted it lightly. "Good luck."

With that, Davis exited the room. The door slammed shut behind him, leaving the new teacher to his duty. He looked to the small window at the top of the door and smiled. "Thank you, Principal Davis."

With a clap of his hands, Shepherd shifted behind his new desk. "Well, class? Why don't we get started?"

The others fell in line quickly. Most didn't care either way. One teacher was as good as the next, a never-ending array of lessons none of them would carry far into the world. Gabe, however, continued to stare off toward the door and the departed principal.

The absence of answers stung, like his entire world was spinning out of control. He needed to hear from Loren. More than that, he needed to find out what the hell was going on with everything.

CHAPTER TWENTY

He started with Gates. Ruiz should have months earlier. The second Leslie had shown up at the precinct to warn him about the events occurring at the Marsh Estate, Ruiz should have opened an investigation into the woman.

Instead, he'd stayed silent. He'd waited. Part of him knew the problem came from just cause, from a lack of manpower, and from the absence of any personal time to dig deeply into Leslie's past. Each one sounded more and more like an excuse than the rational thoughts of the Commissioner of Police for a major metropolitan city.

Since their earlier encounter at PSI Telecom, Ruiz had done little else but try to rectify his error in judgment. The time for waiting was over. He needed answers.

Leslie Gates appeared to be an open book—at least on paper. Ruiz scoured public records to find out everything he could about her. Born in Portents, her childhood had been spent in the Knoll. Education records showed an aptitude to learn, one that carried her far during her formative years. Athletics might not have been her strength, but she filled her time with plenty of other activities: debate club, student council. Leslie was nothing if not active in her school.

That same drive carried over to her community. She ran fundraisers for those in need—neighbors overwhelmed by financial hardships, or those unable to afford a proper funeral for loved ones. She took on the role of caretaker and provider for those around her.

When it came time for college, Leslie had her pick. Portents remained her home, and she commuted to the local university rather than branch out into the wider world. Maybe it had to do with a sick family member or the need of her sister to have her close when her parents perished in an accident. The information never presented, but spoke to her character all the same.

Eventually, though, the world called for her and Leslie answered. With degrees in Business Management and Law, she became a predominant force on the West Coast. Several corporations retained her services, first as an employee or independent contractor and then as a board member. She was damn good at her work, but never forgot her roots, using her fortunes to help others. Her efforts took her around the world, where she spent months at a time fighting for one cause or another.

Her career skyrocketed into the political arena. Leslie occupied seats on multiple committees, as well as the Sacramento City Council. She had the makings of a congressional representative or senator with her track record.

Family came first in the end. The death of her sister ended that rise to power.

Her sister.

Ruiz had met Kelly Gates a handful of times and never at the happiest of occasions. The poor woman had lost her only daughter, Melanie—a wonderful and dedicated officer of the law—to mental illness. There was more to the story, though he disliked even considering it. Melanie had been possessed, her body and mind taken over by a murderous spirit who called himself Alpha. Melanie's internment at Castlemere stole any chance of happiness from her mother, who died of a broken heart and far too many cigarettes soon after.

With that loss, Leslie returned to Portents. She left behind her career, her prospects, and everything she'd built over the decades. Needless to say, the City Council welcomed her with open arms. Her election victory came swiftly, despite the time away from the city.

Had Leslie's win been rigged? Had her entire ascension come from her association with the Luminaries?

Learning about their return clouded Ruiz's judgment all over again. Like the rest of Portents, his knowledge of the Luminaries came from the tragedy Karen Winters rained down upon them the previous year.

Winters' affiliation with the group had allowed her access to the inner workings of government within the city until she'd risen to the position of mayor. Her power trip had not ended there. Seeking a tighter grip for her own personal pleasure, Winters had unleashed another secret from the Luminary archives. She had woken the Heads of Cerberus from their slumber to invade the city.

Thousands had died.

Ruiz couldn't let that go. If the Luminaries were back, a similar tragedy might happen again. Nothing would stand in Ruiz's way to prevent that from happening. Nothing would stop him from finding out the truth—about Leslie, about the Luminaries, and about the bombing of the Whistler Building.

Leslie was the key to figuring out that unknown truth. Realizing who she truly was shined a new light on recent events, and Ruiz dug into them with renewed zeal.

His investigation carried him through the night and deep into the morning. His entire focus turned from Leslie's past to her future. The Restoration Project stood at the heart of her plans. Binders stacked around his table and surrounded his feet. Financial projections filled each one, including construction phases and time frames. The details were sprawling, with a hundred different approvals waiting to be heard in chambers.

The details mattered and Ruiz looked feverishly for a connection between them and Leslie's affiliation with the Luminaries. He questioned everything. Every property request offered a new link in a colossal chain.

Sites sought by the project were historical in nature. Olcott Curve. A derelict apartment complex. The Town Hall Pub at the port. They were to be restored, and a pillar erected, honoring the site as one of the first in Portents.

On paper, the entire project seemed legitimate. These were tourist destinations that would draw people back by displaying the city's rich history. To anyone else, there was nothing untoward about any of it, from the fundraising efforts or the contractor bids.

Ruiz knew better now. With every line item read, more and more he noted the hands of the Luminaries in the mix instead of the City Council. That worried him to no end, especially when their primary goal remained hidden from view.

"Janet?" Ruiz peered around for the next binder, for the next piece of the puzzle that continued to elude him. "Janet, do you have any more files regarding—"

His personal secretary entered the office, silencing the question.

She carried four overloaded binders with papers threatening to spill from their pockets. The aging woman carried them with ease, despite the way they towered over her field of vision. She stopped short of the table and dropped them to the surface with a thundering crash.

Ruiz grazed the top, a hand on the first report. "Is this it?"

Janet's eyebrow arched suspiciously. "You want more? Because I can get more."

"All for the Portents Restoration Project?"

She nodded. "Every site. Every soil survey. Every personnel file for every bid submitted to work on the project." Ruiz grinned. Janet had clearly read almost as much about the project as he had. Her diligence in handling his every whim constantly surprised him. She leaned lightly over the binders. "There is paper on it all. These people are not messing around."

Ruiz settled against the couch cushion. "Or they're trying to hide the needle in a very large haystack."

Janet twisted her lips, the eyebrow back up. "Commissioner?"

"Nothing, Janet. Thank you."

She hesitated at the door, a long glance to the binders on the table. A question rested on her lips, but she let it die before she exited without another word.

Ruiz dug into the top binder. More sites were listed in the ever-expanding project. From the Vertrum Home to several warehouses in the Southern District, the list became more and more unwieldy. How these places connected was only a small portion of the issue nagging at the back of Ruiz's thoughts. Why they were connected was more pertinent and threatened to upend any type of actual work on the day's already busy docket.

What did it all mean?

Ruiz held the top sheet of the latest binder. His eyes glossed over the details as numbers ran in thick lines, the cost projections skyrocketing into the billions, all put forth through grants and private fundraising with the minimal impact on residential taxes.

Tossing the binder aside, Ruiz stood. Sitting around, mired in research, wasn't the answer.

He slipped his coat on and started for the door.

Janet waited at her desk, surprised at his arrival. "Now, where are you going?"

"Sightseeing," Ruiz replied. Without a second glance, he moved for the elevator. "Cancel my meetings."

"For how long?"

"If I said forever?"

Janet huffed at the sarcastic response. "But Mayor Folsom—"

The elevator dinged. As soon as the doors opened, Ruiz stepped inside. "I'll get back to him!"

"When?" Janet called after him as the doors closed. "Commissioner?"

Ruiz sighed as silence took hold. Meetings were nothing but a distraction. There was work to be done. Secrets held no place in his city. He wouldn't let them.

CHAPTER TWENTY-ONE

The Seventh Precinct was rarely visited... at least, if it could be avoided. Locked in the heart of Grant Square, the stationhouse carried more graffiti than official signage. Several depictions of all manner of genitalia decorated the stoop walls, while drawings of dragons coiled around the railings.

Inside, the situation was even more dismal. Few worked the entryway, but those that did gathered in the corner with a streetwalker, showing more than a generous amount of skin despite the rapidly dropping temperatures.

Myers tried not to get caught up in the hullabaloo or note the drool running down the faces of several young officers, who should have been taking down details about the woman's situation instead of accepting her business card.

"Excuse me?" Myers called, badge in hand. "Know where I can find Haya Cho?"

Their brief glances failed to deter them from the work in front of them. The boys—definitely not men—waved toward the back stairwell that led to the upper floor. Myers waited for more and found herself on the receiving end of a blue wall, one she couldn't wait to write up the second she could.

Not every precinct met the standards of Central. The sad fact was, the twelve district precincts were little in the way of a deterrent to the crime-infested squalor of a place like Grant Square. People called it Lowtown for a reason, after all.

When resources were allocated, the best and the brightest saw an uptick in their share of the pie. The Seventh, unfortunately, did not and the quality of personnel reflected that.

The second floor contained a series of offices and classroom-sized spaces for the different divisions kept in the building. Most appeared devoid of personnel. Boxes filled with case files were stacked awkwardly throughout each room.

Bomb Disposal occupied the largest space at the far end of the corridor. Six names were noted on the placard next to the door. Five of them were scratched through, as if it was too much work to remove them completely. The only clear name rested at the bottom of the list.

Haya Cho.

Myers took the knob in hand. A deep breath filled her as she opened the door and entered the room. Caution signs hung from the ceiling, and the dozen metal shelving units stretched in wide rows throughout the room. Ticking devices littered every shelf. Most were broken open with wiring splayed out and hanging limply from their resting place. More wire sat in massive coils, waiting to be utilized.

Plastique occupied the closest shelf. Myers' gaze thinned at the sight of it. The plastique was molded—purposely shaped—in the form of what appeared to be people. Some wore glasses. Some waved with broad smiles on their faces. The last one on the shelf gave her pause. It held a handwritten sign that read: BOOM.

Myers shook her head. "And I thought Anderson kept some strange company."

She slipped under another rope of caution tape. Weaving around the shelves, Myers skidded to a halt. Mechanical wheels whirred in front of her. A tin can shaped like R2-D2 squealed loudly, robotic arms spinning frantically toward the newcomer.

"What the—"

The claw at the end of its arm snatched her leg and squeezed.

"Hey!" Myers exclaimed. She tried to pry herself free, kicking out against the robot. Sharp clangs offered her no relief and its grip tightened. "Let me go, you walking pile of recycled material."

As she reached for her service weapon, a voice called out from the far side of the room. "Wait!"

A short, stocky woman with a magnifying glass hanging over her right eye blitzed toward Myers' position. Hands flailed to stop the rising Glock. She wore a bright yellow hard hat. The spotlight attached to the front shined a beam of white in Myers' eyes, causing her to stumble backward. The claw's grip upended what little balance Myers maintained, and the detective crashed through the caution tape to the floor with a groaning thud.

"Sorry! Sorry!"

Myers grimaced. She lifted the Glock toward the bot.

Ripping the helmet and magnifying glass off her face, the woman stepped in front of the robotic mechanism. She tapped a node on the side of the tin can's frame and the claw opened. Arms retracted and the bot's whirring faded to silence.

"Sorry about that," the woman said. "Rex gets a little protective."

"Rex?"

The bot barked in confirmation. It moved to approach.

The woman stopped the bot with a raised hand. "Stand down, Rex. Priority 42."

Without another beep or bloop, the tin can rolled down the aisle and out of sight.

"Good boy." The woman grinned. Myers finally caught a clear view of her face. She was young, with full cheeks. Despite her dumpy appearance—coveralls over what was once a white shirt, supposedly—a fierce stare shot Myers' way. "English not your first language?"

"What?"

She held out a hand to help Myers to her feet. Then she pointed around the room at the caution tape. DO NOT TOUCH signs were posted in every direction. "I can write it in fourteen others, if that helps."

"No, I think I got it," Myers replied, rubbing the back of her neck. She slipped her Glock away. "I take it you're Cho?"

"Haya."

Myers shook her head. "I'll stick with Cho."

The woman shrugged. "Detective Myers, right?"

Myers nodded. A smirk escaped Cho's lips as she cocked her head toward the back of the room. "Welcome to the Seventh. Home to the castaways of the world. I was just looking over the device used on the Whistler Building."

They left the inventory shelves for the open space in the back of the room. Desks were positioned to the right and left, with a larger community table in the middle. Multiple fragments collected from the bombing spread across the surface, all safely kept atop white tarps. Bright spotlights illuminated every inch of the device.

"Where is everyone else?"

"I'm sorry?"

"There were other names listed by the door."

"And removed," Cho answered. "As cheaply as possible."

"You're it?"

"I'd say it has to do with the lack of work, but honestly, it's probably more about the constant monster attacks that send people running for the hills—or the suburbs in the case of my so-called co-workers." Cho blew a strand of hair from her face. "Or so I've been told. So yeah, I'm it."

"I didn't mean—"

"Didn't bother me either way, Detective. Just gives me more to do these days. I like to keep busy."

Myers nodded. "Understood." She took the left side of the table while Cho rounded right. The detective's tech skills were limited at best and the image of the bomb drew a perplexed stare rather than anything coherent or useful. "How much survived the explosion?"

"Not much," Cho said, showcasing the device on the table. "Enough, though. You're looking at an IED, and a pretty clever one at that. From what survived of the casing, our suspect used a gas cylinder—most likely a metal drum of some sort. They filled the body with trinitrotoluene. Nasty stuff. Dangerous, too. Once they were set, they hooked it all up to a radio detonator. A signal gets sent from outside the blast range, at a time of their choosing, and things go boom."

"Sounds complicated."

"It's not," Cho said with a sigh. "That's the problem. Any crackpot can find the schematics for a device like this. Might take time, and the risk of premature detonation due to incompetence is quite the deterrent, but anyone could have built the device."

A groan escaped Myers. She leaned along the edge of the table. "There's nothing we can use?"

"Oh, plenty." Cho immediately waved down the glimmer of hope in Myers' eyes. "Just nothing that will lead us to our mad bomber."

Myers pushed away from the table. "Leaving us what, exactly? Hoping for another one to give us some clue?"

It was the last thing anyone wanted. Yet, it remained the best option to provide Cho and the rest of the department more evidence to nail the bastard to the wall. Rather than admit the terrible truth, Cho slipped her helmet back into place.

"I'll keep looking."

"Do that." Myers reached into her pocket and removed a business card. "Stay in touch, Cho."

The technician took the card in hand. "What are you going to do?"

"Some looking of my own."

CHAPTER TWENTY-TWO

Loren never made it home.

Parked outside for half an hour, he kept circling back to the case. Patrick Hennessey's involvement, the direct correlation to a founder of the city, meant something bigger was going on in Portents.

Rather than pace the hall of his apartment and stir Gabe from what should have been a restful sleep considering his injury, Loren slipped his Impala into drive and left the Knoll behind.

Michael Hennessey lived alone in a Riverside District townhouse. His proximity to the Marsh Estate gave Loren pause for a second. When he closed his eyes sometimes, he could still feel the tremors caused by the massive tumblers hidden beneath the hedge maze on the property. Construction crews continued to repair the damage to the estate, though no sprawling caves were ever located. The end of the threat had also wiped the hidden fail-safe from existence.

Loren put it out of mind. There was enough to consider without connecting a dead man to an old case. At Hennessey's townhouse, Loren parked and waited. He held no authority to enter the premises. In the old days, those better left forgotten for so many reasons, Loren would have been the first to break protocol in his ever-obsessive quest for the truth. The subsequent citation and reaming from his superiors never deterred him from finding his answers.

These days, he found himself more reserved and more informed about the possible consequences of his actions. He sat in the parking lot, staring out at the unit while pondering the bombing from earlier. Had the explosion been used to cover up the dead man in the basement or to draw attention to the death? If so, why wait two weeks to act?

There had to be more to it. This had been planned and acted upon purposefully. The Whistler Building had been targeted for a reason, but was it the body or something else entirely? Loren hated the thought of following the wrong lead and hoped Myers understood his role in matters would never supplant her own. She was the cop now. He was... well, that was yet another question to ask, wasn't it?

Quick searches on his phone brought up several other Hennessey descendants. Michael may have had no immediate family—no wife or kids to protect in the aftermath of his demise—but the Hennessey line went far beyond a single man. There was Henry Hennessey, Michael's uncle, as well as grandkids on another branch of a very active family tree. None of them resided in Portents any longer, though. They'd moved away in the wake of the Cerberus attack like so many others.

Loren rubbed at weary eyes. He should have taken Myers' advice and gone home for some sleep. Instead, he exited his car and started down the block for some fresh air. The cold whipped through him, the days offering little in the way of a reprieve from the approaching winter season. Loren tucked his hands deeper into his pockets, pulling the coat tighter around his body for warmth. Bowing his head to fight through the wind, Loren continued up the block to the main drag of Augusta.

Diners welcomed an early lunch crowd while shops opened their doors to the public. Few roamed the block, though. The weather and the hour sent them elsewhere. Those that lingered kept to tight-knit groups. A group of three with leather jackets and wool hats stalked ahead, thin eyes on everyone and everything. Loren didn't understand the need for such outward hostility, not until he saw the object of their hate at the next intersection.

A pack of Karura, bird-like creatures that walked like men, laughed wildly. They took no notice of their surroundings, nor did they care to interact outside their group. The trio in the leather jackets moved for the pack, their intentions clear right from the start. Words passed quickly; the laughter gone the moment of their arrival.

Ever since the Night of the Lights, Loren found himself more attuned to the true city—something Soriya always called the myths and legends in Portents. He noticed the old men with the snakelike eyes and the shopkeepers tucked behind their counters to hide their hooves. They never bothered Loren. They simply tried to live their lives in peace.

Unfortunately, with the Courtyard destroyed, those stranded in the city had become part of daily life in Portents. Everyone saw the myths now. Few appreciated the appeal. Hate grew just as easily as the situation at the end of the block.

The lead in the leather jacket shoved the closest Karura aside. "Watch where you're walking, freak."

"Watch yourself," the Karura snapped, his beak sharp and pointed.

Sides drew up, both groups ready for a fight. One human—Loren used the term loosely—pulled out a small blade. "This was our neighborhood before you monsters started showing up. Get it through your freak heads. We don't want you here."

"The feeling's mutual."

More shoving broke out. A punch landed against the cheek of the lead human, dropping him to the ground. "Hey!"

The Karura raised a fist in the air. His colleagues snatched him by the arm and pulled him back before he could continue the assault. "He's not worth it."

The fallen figure in the leather coat spat on the ground. "None of you are."

"Come on," a reserved Karura muttered. "Let's go."

The bird creatures departed hurriedly. For a moment, the trio left behind thought to pursue. Murmurs rose and angry pointing trailed the fleeing figures. Shoving away his brothers, the bleeding man stomped back up the street and entered the nearby diner. His compatriots soon followed, unable to make eye contact with the watchful Loren.

It was a close call and not the first he had seen lately. More and more were popping up. Violent incidents—fights, stabbings, and the like—were happening everywhere at all hours of the day. The city stood at the precipice of something bad. Hate rested on both sides of the equation, and no one wanted to talk about it.

The bombing failed to help matters. Hate coupled with fear over the person or group responsible. It wouldn't take long to point fingers and assign blame. Then the real problems would start.

Loren let out a long breath. "This city is becoming a powder keg. That's the last thing we need."

He rounded the corner away from the diner and bumped into the massive chest of a large bull-headed beast. Bounding back, an apology on his lips, Loren noted two more bulls on either side of the beast. Heavy huffs of breath greeted him, their eyes wide and black.

"Hey there," Loren said, offering a friendly wave. "I was just looking to—"

Behind him, a van screeched to a stop at the corner. Two more bulls exited, knuckles cracking as they blocked his egress.

"Okay…" Loren peered at the growing crowd around him. "Why don't we start again? What can I do for you, fellas?"

A black bag dropped over his head and the world went dark. Hands grabbed his body, lifting him from the ground. Hot breath wafted over him.

"You'll see, Mr. Loren," one of the bulls said in a deep voice. "You'll see."

CHAPTER TWENTY-THREE

Another meeting was the last thing Thel wanted, but the constant pestering of her counselor, her union rep, and a dozen other people—Myers included—prodded the damaged siren from her apartment and back to the church.

Tuesday was not her usual group, Dr. Grace's idea of a fresh start with new faces. She had clearly read Thel's discomfort over the previous weeks. It must have been the constant silence and disdain for everyone.

Recognition from those in the room, though, came quickly. The second she sat down, all eyes turned to her. There was no anonymity in a town where news of myths and legends filled every headline. The beating of the lone siren detective on the force was enough to warrant multiple days of coverage. Grace passed off their stares as curiosity about her unique look. Purple hair was a drawback when it came to wanting your privacy, but this went beyond the normal interest.

They knew. Somehow, everyone was tuned into her suffering and they made a show of it with her every appearance. All knew her story without her having to say a damn word, which made the whole thing so much worse.

Thel took her seat around the circle, an eye to the exit for the entire hour. Voices filtered through, but were never truly heard. The stories of these victims, with their insignificant problems and their minor pains, were nothing compared to her own fears. She felt powerless and alone; the combination damned her back into silence, despite Grace's prodding.

Thel waited for another sign of Yardin—if that had been him the previous night. The shadow in the alley haunted her. Instead of rising to confront the threat, though, Thel cowered in her terror.

Now, every shift of light near an open window or passing shadow in the door frame sparked a fresh fear, a new terror, that threatened to pull her back down again.

The hour ended with the ceremonial clapping. Thel didn't bother to join in, or to get sucked into the glare passed along from her frustrated counselor. Group wasn't working. Honestly, nothing would. The one-on-one sessions were just as much a waste of time. Thel couldn't talk about her problems, didn't know how to relate to anyone, and wanted no sympathy for her plight.

She didn't know what she wanted anymore… other than to get the hell back to her apartment.

Thel shifted through the lingering crowd for the coffee. Still steaming for a change, she lifted the cup to her lips. The sting of the liquid rushed down her throat.

A shadow crept up beside her. "It doesn't help, does it?"

Thel nearly dropped the coffee. Her body shook at the sudden arrival.

"Sorry," the shadow said, a hand to her cup to steady it. "That was idiotic of me."

"No, I…" Thel lowered the cup to the table. A handsome man in a tight jacket and dark pants stood next to her. A dimple sat at the end of his smile, hidden slightly by the stubble dotting his cheeks. "What were you saying?"

"The talking," the man said. He showcased the empty circle of chairs and the podium at the head. "It does nothing for you, does it?"

"I—"

"How could it, right?" the man continued. "Most of these people were in loving relationships that went wrong. They ran from abusers who no longer knew how to react to their emotions—who hated themselves, their work, their very lives—and blamed someone else for their faults. But it stemmed from love, twisted as it may have been."

Thel hung on his every word. There was something genuine behind each one. The man's insight rang through her ears. As he spoke, they shifted away from the crowd to the corner of the room. The stares faded to the background until only the handsome figure remained.

Where had he come from? Had he been at the meeting and she never even noticed? She had been so caught up in her own problems… problems he seemed to understand intimately. It was almost as if he could read her thoughts.

"They have no idea what it's like to face pure hate," he said, hands squeezing the air before him. "And not from one person—a spouse, a lover, a family member—but from everyone. To be surrounded, to be beat upon, for the simple crime of being different. Of looking different. Of living your life next to theirs."

A small puff of breath slipped from his lips. His smile widened, and he dropped his hands to his sides. "Sorry," he said with the shake of his head. "That was a little too heavy, wasn't it? Here you are, wanting a crappy cup of coffee, and I start chewing your ear off."

He extended his hand, soft skin so inviting. "I'm Kellon, by the way."

"Thel." Her cheeks flushed as she took the offered hand. The connection lasted only a second, yet sent a wave of warmth through her body. Composing herself, Thel backed up a step and retrieved her neglected beverage. "Is that why you came? The crappy coffee?"

"No," Kellon replied with a grin. "No, this—all of this—isn't for me. I came for you."

"Me?"

"Who hasn't heard about the siren detective?"

The warmth disappeared, leaving her cold and alone once more. He knew, same as the others did. She turned for the exit. "That's not really me anymore, I'm afraid."

A hand held her up. It grazed her skin softly, then fell away. "But that's it, right?" Kellon said. "What they did—the humans? They took away your pride, your soul. Don't you want that back?"

More than anything. That was what she wanted to say. Her life—her second chance—had been perfect. A great job coupled with fantastic friends. There was nothing more she could have asked for, other than universal acceptance, but that would have come in time, wouldn't it? Or maybe none of that mattered at all, as long as she could be herself in the world… without judgment, without hate.

She couldn't, though. It had been taken in an instant. That life had been a dream, not the reality of her existence. The notion saddened her, but she pushed it away.

"And you?" she asked. "You're—"

Kellon held out his arm. He rolled up his sleeve. The tattoos on his skin became obscured at the sudden growth of dark brown hair. It sprouted in a wave out of every pore. When she peered up into his eyes, they had shifted from sky blue to bright yellow.

"Let's just say I'm not anyone's favorite when the moon is full," he chided. The shift ended and the hairs receded. His eyes returned to their previous state, yet remained intense. "I wasn't born this way. I didn't ask for this to happen to me. None of my kind did. My brothers were hunted for what they were. My pack once numbered in the hundreds. Now there are only a handful left of us, scattered and alone. We hide, even from each other, afraid of being discovered. Afraid of everything, really."

"I'm sorry, I—"

"There's more to healing than talk, Thel. These people will never understand your world. Our world. They can't. It scares them too much." Kellon opened his hand to her once more. "I can give you your life back."

Thel gazed at the handsome man. The noise of the crowd finally filtered through, breaking the hold of his charismatic offer. Lingering members from their session eyed the pair curiously. Murmurs rose between them, questioning glares offering more to their intent than she cared to realize.

She backed away from Kellon with slow, steady steps. "I'm sorry. I don't—"

Kellon stopped her, blocking her view of the others. "I know, Thel. It's a lot. Think about it." He removed a small card from his pocket and passed it along.

Thel took it in hand, reading the name and number scrawled on the back. "I... I will."

He nodded, then moved for the exit. Before slipping through the door frame, Kellon peered back. His smile caused her own to grow.

The heat from their exchange remained after his departure. It filled her cheeks and washed over her entire body. For the first time in weeks, Thel no longer felt like a perpetual victim.

She squeezed the card tighter. The offer echoed in her thoughts.

CHAPTER TWENTY-FOUR

Gabe made his way to the library during his free period. On a normal day, the time was typically wasted screwing around with his buddies and picking at the homework that ruled his evenings. There might be talk about where the party was going to be over the weekend or who had been caught making out with Kari outside the science wing during lunch.

Not today. The library was the logical choice with everything going on. Gabe needed answers and the quiet to pursue them. Taking a workstation near the back of the room, Gabe set to work immediately. He started with Mr. Johnson. Something about the man's absence irked him. Maybe it was the swift departure without a single word of farewell. His history teacher had not been the kind of man to walk away, especially from a class he continually praised for their interest in the subject.

Then again, it was entirely possible Gabe had read too much into the man—put the weight of his own expectations on someone he had only known a couple months since his transfer from the coves to School 63, or as the district labeled it, the Emerging Leaders School of Excellence. The name meant nothing, of course: just another moniker to give relevance to the number plastered all over the building.

A quick email to Mr. Johnson's personal account went out within minutes of Gabe's arrival to the workstation. His plea for a reason behind the man's sudden absence stood out in the text, but the reply would not be immediate.

Instead, Gabe went further. He accessed the local directory for listings to a C Johnson—Clay being the man's first name. His teacher's last, however, proved problematic. There were over six hundred listings for the name Johnson in Portents. Fifty-six of them carried the first initial of C, and a whopping zero used the name Clay.

Gabe sighed. Why answers were necessary bothered him more than the search itself and he put the whole affair aside for the moment. More pressing concerns required his attention.

Loren had failed to contact him. The radio silence was worse than any teacher's departure. Loren had made him a promise to keep him in the loop. They were supposed to be partners, working together to protect the city. The lack of information, or even a simple text to check on him, left Gabe feeling isolated.

He took matters into his own hands. News of the bombing filled his screen. Every major outlet reported on the situation. Each brought their own perspective on the event, yet none offered any additional insight. Ruiz's press conference carried the same vibe. The usual pat answers and procedural jargon made it clear no one knew what the hell had happened or why.

One thing remained clear, though. The target itself. Gabe eyed the images on the news sites with curiosity. Bombings weren't random, not usually. There were reasons for a specific target. What had PSI Telecom done to deserve such a blow?

Gabe reviewed the news reports and read through a dozen articles. Everyone spouted the same talking points. They offered plenty of fear, but nothing in the way of intelligent insight about the event. Nothing shed any light on the Whistler Building or its significance.

So caught up in his task, Gabe failed to notice the shadow looming at his back until it blotted out the overhead lights entirely. "Interesting read?"

Gabe wheeled around in his chair. Mr. Shepherd stood before him, a soft smile on his face. "Huh? Oh. I was just—"

Shepherd waved him down, calming his startled nerves. He took a chair from a neighboring table and pulled it in close to Gabe's workstation. "It was scary. The way the building simply collapsed. The way people screamed in terror with no idea why."

"You were there?"

"Nearby," Shepherd said with a nod. "My ears are still ringing over it... Gabriel, wasn't it?"

"Gabe."

Shepherd's smile widened. He indicated the screen. "What's your interest in the explosion?"

"Like you said, no one knows the why behind it," Gabe said. A stern look from the librarian behind her desk caused Gabe to lower his voice. He tucked closer to the computer. "There doesn't seem to be anything special about the building."

"According to the papers, sure."

Gabe's brow furrowed. "You think there is?"

"I know there is," Shepherd declared with confidence. He cocked his head to the computer. "May I?"

"Huh? Oh, sure."

Gabe gave the man room. Shepherd typed feverishly for a fresh set of pages, which filled the screen. "I grew up in Portents. This city carries such a storied history, yet few realize it. That building was one of the first in the Knoll expansion of the 1920s."

"During Prohibition?"

"Exactly," Shepherd replied, a snap to his fingers. He pushed away from the station, giving Gabe a clear view of the neighborhood during the time of its development. It was in stark contrast to the building Gabe had rushed into the previous day. "There were false walls, secret passageways, and more. So many unique aspects to every construction of the era. Including this building."

"You think something was hidden in the building?"

Shepherd shrugged. "It's definitely possible. Secrets you won't find in a news article."

"Then where?"

"I might have some reference guides on the area. I could bring them in if you'd like."

"That... That would be great." The bell rang, stirring them from their discussion. Gabe exited out of the multiple windows on the workstation. He quickly gathered his belongings and stood. "Thank you."

"My pleasure," Shepherd said with a wave.

Gabe moved for the exit and his next class. For the first time all day, Gabe felt a trace of acceptance. He also felt useful, able to contribute to the situation instead of waiting on the sidelines. More than anything, it was nice to finally talk to someone as an equal.

CHAPTER TWENTY-FIVE

"Your fault?" Soriya staggered at the admission.

"I'm sorry, little one," Mentor said. "I should have known. When you came back, I should have realized the reason behind it and stopped you."

Soriya grabbed her teacher by the collar. She lifted his weary frame from the ground. "Explain yourself, Mentor. Tell me what the hell you meant. How can all this be your fault?"

He couldn't look at her. The sad gaze of her teacher peered into the darkness beyond, almost begging for the creatures to break through for their nightly brawl. He begged for death, rather than face her and the simple question proffered.

Soriya shook him hard, squeezing the thin material of his tattered cloak. "Tell me!"

"He won't." Kali stood beside them. Her arms crossed her chest, the pink ribbon dancing in the wind around her. "It frightens him too much."

Soriya let go of her teacher. Mentor hit the ground hard and stumbled away before catching himself. Kali raised her hands at Soriya's approach. "Now, kid..."

"No," Soriya snapped. "You don't get to pull me along like a puppet. I demand—"

The threat was enough to spark the change in the goddess. All pretense of friendship disappeared in a snap and the rage-filled aspect took hold. Fire burned in her eyes and Kali stood a foot taller. "You do not get to make demands! Not here. And not to me!"

Soriya's chest heaved. Her fists remained clenched tight before her. She had faced worse in her life—gods and goddesses, creatures made from the darkest of shadows—and won. Kali, though, was a friend. Somewhere inside her, Soriya knew that to be true despite the pretense and the pain inflicted over the course of her visit inside the Bypass.

Long breaths calmed her. Soriya backed away, a slight bow of the head to denote her surrender.

Kali continued to loom. Her stature rose for a brief instant, ready to strike down everyone around her. Then she paused. Eyes burning brighter than the sun dimmed until the brown irises of her friend returned.

A hand reached out and took hold of Soriya's. A soft smile followed it up. "Kid," Kali said. "What do you want? Why did you come here?"

"To be whole," Soriya answered.

Kali nodded. With the wave of her hand, a light formed. It spun swiftly beside them, dancing in the air. "Take it, then."

Soriya circled the light. Within the shining orb, she saw the life her missing soul had been granted. There was peace in her little world, with friends and lovers and a family Soriya had never been allowed to know.

"And if I do?"

Kali smirked. "I won't keep you here, Soriya. I won't hold you back. You'll leave this place, whole and intact. Back to Portents. Back to the life you knew, protecting the city."

"And all this?" Soriya asked, pointing at the paradise written and staged for her missing soul.

"It fades to nothing," Kali said. "It's not real."

"Parts are," Soriya whispered. She gazed deeply through the surface. The room with her parents took shape, though never in enough detail. There were too many holes in the logic blocking her from the whole truth. "They're real, aren't they? Somewhere in the Bypass. Somewhere in the infinite, they have to exist."

"You never knew them. What is here is only a dream."

"That I could live in forever."

Kali nodded. "At peace."

"But not really," Soriya said. "Living some fantasy life where everyone around me is some aspect of my subconscious instead of who they actually were in life? That's not enough for me anymore, is it?"

Kali's hand fell to Soriya's shoulder. The light spun before their eyes. "Not for you, kid. Not after everything you've done. For me. For Portents."

"You weren't really offering me a choice, were you?" Soriya said.

"Of course I was," Kali replied. "Everything in life is a choice. With a word, paradise could be yours. Or you could go back. Fight the baddies waiting for you in the big city. Whoop and holler like we used to back in the glory days."

"I think you're remembering things differently," Soriya said with a laugh. She looked to the paradise. Everything was peaceful and light. Around them, the shadows grew. That was the darkness waiting for her out in the world—the endless struggle against monsters and devils. She would be whole with either option.

But not truly.

A smile spread across her lips. Soriya glanced at her battered hands, at the wounds inflicted over a lifetime as the Greystone. Everything she knew, deep down at her core, was a mask. Even her name covered up the truth of who she was, a question she had always imagined but never pursued.

A third choice—a true choice—waiting for her to accept.

"I have to know who I am," Soriya said. Kali's grin widened at the admission. The stone bearer turned away from the goddess to Mentor. "Who I really am."

He shook his head. "You are Soriya Greystone. You are—"

"No," Kali bellowed. She knocked him aside with the wave of her hand. Mentor fell to the ground, skidding toward the far side of the intersection. "The time for make-believe is over. You heard the kid. She's made her decision. Now is the time for truth."

"You'll tell me?" Hope flickered in Soriya's eyes. "Show me?"

"Is that what you want?"

Soriya nodded.

"It's the only way forward for you," Kali confirmed. "But it is for another to show you—to guide you to the answers you seek."

Kali pointed to the cowed Mentor. He remained on bended knee, unable to look at either of them in their judgment.

"Why Mentor?"

"It is his story," Kali said. "Isn't it, Christopher?"

Mentor's jaw clenched tight. Slowly, he raised his eyes to meet them, anger and terror mixed in his thin gaze. "Damn you, Kali. Yes. Yes, it is."

CHAPTER TWENTY-SIX

The accelerator hit the floor under the constant pressure of Ruiz's foot. The second he saw the structure looming near the docks, all caution left him. It was as if the air had been ripped from his lungs, like everything he thought he knew had been absolutely incorrect.

The pillar was almost complete.

Somehow, his ignorance had blinded him to the massive construction occurring in his town. Had he become so routine in his movements? Work to home and back again in an endless circuit. Taking the same damn streets and never using the RDJ to avoid the persistent snarls of traffic every morning and evening, Ruiz had lost track of the rest of his city.

When he reached the docks, his sedan halted next to a long line of vehicles. Dozens worked the site. Crews from multiple companies wore their logos across hardhats and neon vests. They mingled together, but for the most part, worked with unwavering diligence on the massive pillar.

The structure was a tower, rising into the gray sky. Fifty feet up, yet still the crews continued to build. The outer shell of the monument was almost complete. But how? Ruiz couldn't reconcile that little conundrum. All funding for the Restoration Project remained locked in committee until the next budget meeting. Even then, they were months away from being able to utilize any public funds for such an endeavor.

That was how bureaucracy worked. Yet, here he stood in the shadow of the great pillar, completely wrong.

Rounding the line of cars and trucks outside the perimeter of the complex, Ruiz stopped. Working her way from inside the site, Leslie Gates chatted with the foreman. Her words were lost under the bevy of sounds emanating from the constant construction. They didn't really matter anyway to Ruiz. He had his own words to share with the woman.

"Leslie!" he called when she left the foreman to his task.

Her smile flickered at his arrival, but she approached without hesitation. "Ah, Ruiz. I was wondering when you would visit."

Her smug attitude grated on him. "How? How is this possible?"

If this pillar was in place, what was the status of the others? How far had the Luminaries reach grown since their return to the city? Ruiz thought he had more time to figure things out, only to learn how little he truly grasped the situation. Gates shrugged at his concern.

"Hard work," she said. "A few motivational speeches."

"You know what I mean. Folsom hasn't even approved the full project. The funding is still tied up in committee. None of this should be here yet."

"Private donors," Gates replied. "They've made this possible, Ruiz. The site-work was approved long ago. You should know. You've been looking over everything, every little detail, which has been openly provided for transparency's sake, by the way."

"How could you possibly know that?" Ruiz asked. Anger surged through him. Was she watching him somehow? Was there a spy inside the department?

Gates shook her head. "We're merely getting a jump on the sites we're able to."

"Your Four Points?"

A nod confirmed his suspicion on the priority. "Their importance cannot be overstated."

"Why?"

"I've told you before—"

"No," Ruiz snapped. He dragged her away from the site, back to the line of vehicles outside the docks. "You sold me a story about restoring Portents, about welcoming people here, but we both know there is more to it. I've seen the scope of the project, Leslie. You have dozens of sites earmarked throughout the city, some historical and others left abandoned. What are you hiding from Folsom and the rest?"

"Ruiz—"

"I'll bring this to him, to the entire council, right now," Ruiz said, a finger to her chest. "Don't think I won't."

"And tell them what?" Gates said with a laugh. "This should not be your priority, Ruiz. Not with what I've told you."

"What have you told me, exactly?" Ruiz's shouting caught the attention of a passing crew. Gates quickly waved them down, and Ruiz lowered his voice. "You drop a few hints, a little ominous warning, and offer me nothing in the way of details. You've been manipulating everyone—including me—this whole time."

Leslie backed away. She let out a long breath, then watched it rise into the late-morning sky. "You're right. You deserve the truth. If you're willing to listen."

Ruiz staggered a step. Where he waited for the fight to continue, for the secrets and lies to be on full display, Gates' response surprised him. "I..."

She failed to notice his reticence as she moved for her car. Ruiz's absence woke her to his hesitancy, and she spun around to greet him. "You want to yell at me some more, or do you want the truth?"

Ruiz stood up straight, unwilling to back down. "The truth."

She opened the passenger-side door and ushered him over. "Take a ride with me, Ruiz."

CHAPTER TWENTY-SEVEN

The road worsened as they traveled. Loren felt every bump as they lifted him from his seat. Fortunately, he was locked into position in the van, not by any type of safety restraint, but by two burly bulls, one on each side. How they fit on the seat next to him was a stretch, but so was the fact that all five had joined the journey through Portents.

Little in the way of discussion illuminated their destination or their purpose. The bag on Loren's head remained in place, the canvas smell mixed with stale cigarettes that sent his old addiction into overdrive. For a moment, he wondered if he could ask for a stick of gum, then thought better of it.

Filthy habit.

Music occupied much of their traveling. Taylor Swift resounded through the van, accompanied by the humming of more than a few of the muscular bulls. One tried to pass it off as an annoyance, but his foot stamped lightly with each chorus.

Loren had hoped for some conversation, maybe a clue about what the hell was happening, but nothing came. They were too preoccupied with which single had been their favorite from the album and how much they missed Swift's country music days.

It was clear, despite their musclebound appearance, the quintet was smarter than the average abductor. They even bound Loren's hands before him, keeping his phone out of reach for the duration.

Uneven roads slowed their progress. Horns bumped the roof. The disc started to skip in the player until the music disappeared completely. All that remained was the hard thump of tires on the street and the jostled shifting of fabric against the leather seats.

When the car stopped, his two bodyguards vacated the vehicle in a hurry. A pair of hands reached for the still-seated Loren. With a yank, Loren fell from the seat and onto the road. Before he could curse at the pain from the impact, the hands pulled him to his feet. He swayed from the sudden shift, unable to find his balance with the hood over his eyes.

"Hold still," one bull grumbled.

"You're the one pulling at me," Loren replied, his words muffled through the hood.

"What did he say?"

A huff of hot air sounded behind him. "I can't understand a damn thing."

"Then take off the hood!"

"But—"

"Idiots," the deep-throated ringleader snarled. "I'll do it myself."

A large hand fell on Loren's shoulder, locking him in position. The other struggled to grasp the end of the hood and peel it cleanly from Loren's head.

"Stop fidgeting so I can get this stupid thing off." Light flooded over him. Loren struggled even with the muted gray of the day. "There."

"Where…" Loren blinked repeatedly. Everything remained a blur. His foot caught the edge of a stone and he tumbled forward.

The bull halted his descent, a tight grip on Loren's coat. "Watch your step."

Loren raised his bound hands to his brow. He squinted through the blurring effect until his eyes adjusted to the light. Beneath him, thick stone ran the length of the road. "Cobblestone."

Spinning around, Loren noted the overpass bridge on the single-lane street. A small inlet was visible, and he saw the Franklin Center within. "We're in the Old City?"

The bull on his right nodded. "Fewer eyes on us."

"Don't I feel comforted."

A hand prodded him forward. "Just walk, Detective."

"I'm not—"

The bull in front grabbed Loren's bindings and dragged him along. He tired of waiting, his breathing more and more labored with mounting frustration. Their travels took them north, under the overpass bridge and away from the Franklin Center. For as much as Loren had visited the area, he knew very little of the nooks and crannies littering the back roads of the forgotten space.

They went north for a block before tucking between two towers of stone—both weathered and broken down over the decades. Birds trailed their movements, beady eyes keeping watch over them as they traveled. Coming out the other side of the towers, Loren found himself before twin wooden doors that loomed over him.

His escorts rounded him to open the doors. The ringleader kept a tight grasp on Loren's bindings as they entered the building. Once inside, the doors closed, dropping them once more into shadow. The bull's hot breath washed over Loren. He circled the man, sharp fingernails scraping against the nearby wall, as if to sharpen them. When he returned to stand before Loren, he raised his hand. Fingers dropped rapidly and Loren cringed at the coming blow.

A snap of rope woke him to the truth. Peering down, Loren watched his bindings fall to the ground at his feet. The bull sneered, delighting in the man's fear. He stepped aside and indicated the inner door on the other side of the room.

"They're waiting for you."

"Who?"

The bull said nothing. He patted his companions and the quintet exited. They were out of sight before the doors slammed shut once more and left Loren in the dark.

He thought about following, then again about the odds of facing five bulls in a fight. Loren grabbed for his phone, his only viable option of escape. It was dead. He had forgotten to charge the damn thing again.

Tucking it away, Loren started for the inner door. The wood scraped loudly along the frame and Loren entered the chamber.

The room widened all around him. Cathedral ceilings put the space at three or four stories in height, the length matching that of a modern-day church. Holes dotted the ceiling, streams of sunlight slipping inside to illuminate the immense space.

Shifting figures welcomed him to the room. They came out of every shadow and hid in every corner. Eyes of all shapes and sizes stared warily in his direction. Hundreds of creatures stepped into the light. He recognized some of them from his time in Portents. Fairies floated above, their wings glittering when they caught the stray beams of light. Goblins and gremlins snarled with disgust. They spat at him, yet maintained a safe distance.

Loren took a long stride inside, then glanced back at the door.

It shut with a clang at the hands of another dozen entrants—their fur mangy and their scars visible on their exposed skin.

"What is this place?" Loren asked. He continued through the chamber, eyes trying to take in every detail on every face. An altar rested on the far side of the expansive room. Three steps ran up to it with three ornate chairs positioned atop. An individual occupied each, and they stood at Loren's arrival.

The one in the middle, a woman wearing a sword at her hip and black tattoos along her right cheek and down her arms, raised her hand. "Welcome, Greg Loren. We are the Council of Legends."

CHAPTER TWENTY-EIGHT

"Council of Legends?"

The crowd continued to grow. Their numbers spread from the shadows in the corner of the chamber until they spilled out onto the main floor. Ogres loomed overhead, their clubs resting at their sides or over their shoulders. Orcs joined their goblin brethren, fighting and beating on each other as they looked on with malicious curiosity.

They were creatures Loren had once feared. The thought of such myths living in his city frightened the hell out of him. He had fought against Soriya's vision of Portents for so long. It was here, though, and it was far bigger than anything Loren could have imagined.

"We are refugees," the warrior woman on the altar said in a booming voice. Her hand hovered close to the hilt of the sword at her hip. A fur-lined cloak ran down her back and a tattered bodice of crimson covered pale skin. "Trapped here in the wake of the Courtyard's destruction. Some are able to blend in. Most though…"

Loren recognized their fear and how it matched his own. Families cowered in the darkness, their skin covered in scales with eyes of the richest red. Wolves snarled, disgusted at the multitude surrounding them as they picked at the bones of their last meal. The Courtyard had offered them a home, a place where they could all belong and thrive apart from this world. Thanks to the machinations of Karen Winters, that home had been taken from them, the connection to every other world as lost as they were.

"Here they are safe," the woman continued. "Here they are with family."

Loren caught the disgruntled glares of a few passing fairies.

They matched the thin gaze of a dozen other creatures. Loren stepped forward. "You speak for them all?"

"We try," the woman said, descending to the second step of the altar. Her hand fell to her chest. "I am Liana, a Valkyrie."

Loren paused his approach. Suddenly, the sword appeared much more imposing. He had read plenty on the Valkyrie. They had once been the chosen of Odin. Their role had been to ferry the valiant dead to Valhalla, yet their task expanded over the centuries to include claiming the lives of warriors they viewed unfavorably. They were the fiercest of warriors, and the bodies left in their wake proved their fortitude in battle.

Liana read his hesitation with a grin. "Do not worry. I don't bite. Tusk, on the other hand…"

A mangy, little creature covered in deep black fur with twin horns atop his head and surrounding his snarling lips rolled from his chair, down the altar, and to Loren's side. When he leaped to his feet, his hands turned to claws. A huff of breath left him, the smell worse than the bulls from the van.

Loren glowered down at the creature. "A Korrigan, right?" Tusk grunted in confirmation. Korrigans were known for their tempers. Loren had met plenty of dwarves with similar issues, but this one seemed ready for a fight if someone so much as looked at him queerly. "Yeah. I've heard how friendly your kind can be."

Tusk rolled away without a word in his defense, letting the silence make his position clear. The third member on the altar rose from his position on the seat and stood next to Liana. At first glance, there appeared to be nothing abnormal about him. He wore a sweater and jeans. Auburn hair rested perfectly in place on top of golden skin.

"And this is Feore," Liana announced.

The young man, clearly not much older than Gabe, stepped down from the altar. He extended his hand to Loren. "A pleasure to meet you."

"Likewise, kid," Loren said. "What can you—"

"Do?" Feore smirked. His face changed in an instant. Eyes turned dusty brown and his hair lengthened and became dirty blond. Even his stature changed. He grew two inches taller, his sweater replaced by a winter jacket. Loren stared at his own reflection, who smiled widely at him. "Plenty, kid."

"Cute." Loren squeezed Feore's hand tighter. He pulled the

shifter close. "Don't do it again."

Feore laughed. It started as Loren's voice, then returned to the young man as his appearance changed back. He rejoined Liana along the steps of the altar.

Loren peered around, curious. "How many are here?"

"Thousands."

"Thousands..." It was no wonder there was so much trepidation in the city. "Thousands hiding among us."

"Surviving, Loren," Liana said, her jaw clenched tight. "The only way we can."

"People are scared." Loren approached slowly, hands before him. "If they find out about all of this? About all of you?"

"*We* are scared," Liana shot back. "We fear for our lives. Humanity has no reason to fear us, though."

"The violence in the city says otherwise," Loren said, recalling the incident earlier in the day. "So does the angry guy at your side."

Tusk rolled into a ball and charged. Fury rippled in a scream as he shot toward Loren. Before he reached his target, Liana leaped down from the altar. Her sword was in hand and gave the Korrigan pause.

"Tusk!" she shouted. "Enough!"

The dwarf stood, beady eyes burrowing into Loren. His fury remained, but he huffed and stalked off instead of pursuing.

Loren sighed. "I think he just made my point for me."

Liana sheathed her sword. "He is frustrated, Loren. We hide to preserve our way of life. For our own protection. But this is our home now. For some, it always has been. Portents must come to understand that—to understand us."

"Yeah," Loren said, rubbing the back of his neck. "Humanity isn't big on understanding."

Feore stepped forward. "We seek only peace."

"The violence—"

"Is not our doing," Liana interjected. She circled Loren, her words meant not only for him but the others in the room. "There are enclaves—smaller than this—but louder. They demand, while we only wish to talk."

Feore nodded. "Lashing out solves nothing, but it is all they know."

Factions within the legends? Loren never realized how complicated things had become in Portents. If it was true, if other groups were vying for power and stirring up trouble, any one of them could have been involved in the bombing, or worse.

None of it added up for Loren, especially his presence in the room. "What can I do?" He peered at the surrounding creatures. Most held the same question. They glowered at him, including a long-haired ape figure who loomed in the shadows. His black fur matched the tight suit he wore. Loren felt beads of sweat form along his brow just from the creature's look. He turned back to Liana. "You pulled me here for a reason, right?"

"We did," she confirmed. "You work for the Greystone."

"*With*," Loren clarified with a smirk. "She was... *is*... my partner."

"Her and her kind have saved us many times," Liana said. "Our people trust in her. And in you."

"To do what?" Loren asked, approaching the altar. "Advocate for you? I'm not well liked in my own right, Liana."

"You can help us." Her hands washed over the gathered crowd. "You can help the humans understand. Help to integrate us."

"No more hiding," Tusk grumbled from his chair.

"This is our home too," Feore said in agreement.

Liana reached out to Loren. "Help them see that."

Loren fell silent. Their request staggered him. To be a voice for a people he once feared? He wished there was a simple answer to give them. Portents was on the edge. Something dark and terrible headed their way and these legends, these neglected and misunderstood figures, were caught in the middle of it all.

They needed help like the rest, but was Loren right for the role? So much burdened him of late, not the least of which was Gabe. His injury haunted Loren, yet spoke to the responsibility he'd accepted when he'd brought the boy into his life. That was where his focus should be, shouldn't it?

"I... I can't, Liana."

"Loren—"

He raised a hand to stop her. The disappointment on her face was enough to make her point clear. It matched his own. He swallowed his fears and his own selfish burdens.

"Not right away," he said. "I need time. To figure this whole thing out. This is a complicated situation, Liana. The last thing I want to do is make things worse."

CHAPTER TWENTY-NINE

"Hennessey was one of us."

It was the first thing Gates said during their drive. They filtered through a sea of pedestrian vehicles down the Riverside District. Ruiz hated letting Gates take control. But she had been in the driver's seat the entire time, hadn't she? Even now, with the knowledge of Michael Hennessey's name in a classified murder investigation.

Ruiz cringed at the information at her disposal. "We haven't released his name to the public."

She couldn't help but grin slightly.

Ruiz groaned, hands squeezing into fists. "Dammit, Leslie. You ask for trust when you offer nothing of the kind in return."

"I came to you."

"Because you need my help," Ruiz snapped. "You feed me innuendo and half-truths and tell yourself what? That you're protecting yourself?"

"Someone is targeting the Luminaries, Ruiz."

"So, step into the light!"

Gates threw him a thin glare. "And give this maniac what they want?"

"To save lives?" Ruiz shot back. "Yes. Absolutely."

She shook her head. "We're not ready for that. Portents would suffer."

Silence fell over them. Gates shifted the car down the waterfront. Her grip tightened on the wheel, her eyes locked on the road ahead rather than her guest.

Ruiz, though, refused to let the statement rest. "Is that a threat?"

"Never. We protect—"

"Yeah, yeah," Ruiz said with a dismissive wave. She was back to the rehearsed answers of the past, instead of the reality of the present. It was what had caused him to seek information on the Council and then the Restoration Project. Whatever the Luminaries were involved in might have been the connection necessary to understand the bomber's true intentions.

He felt like he was the only one with that goal in mind. Still, he continued to sit in the car, waiting for the answers he sought.

His eyes sparked at their destination. The car turned onto a dirt road along the outskirts of Portents University. Crashing waves filled his ears. He hadn't heard the sound in years, his last visit an unpleasant memory he didn't need dredged up.

At the peak, the river rushing below them, Gates parked. "We're here."

Her door opened and she stepped outside. Ruiz, however, remained in the car, hands locked tight in his lap.

"Are you coming?" she called.

Ruiz let out a long breath. The lever snapped, and the door opened as he stepped out into the cold. The wind battered against him, slamming the passenger-side door shut. He leaned against the side of the sedan for a long moment.

Gates joined him. Her hands jammed into her pockets for warmth. "Well?"

"I'm not a big fan of this location," Ruiz said.

He recalled his last visit, a trip he'd taken to keep his daughter safe from a professor he'd believed to be a threat—one who'd haunted his nightmares for some time. Instead, the danger had come in the form of a shape-shifting fox wanting nothing more than some stupid fun. His investigation had brought too much attention to her operations, and she'd sought her revenge on Zoe. Ruiz had managed to save his daughter and survive the experience... barely.

"I ran into some trouble here once."

"The Kitsune."

Ruiz's jaw fell open. "How did you—"

Gates sighed. "The sooner you come to grips with the level of information at my disposal, the easier this relationship will be."

She waved him forward. They stalked through the blistering cold to a lonely structure near the coast. It was nothing more than a ramshackle shed, a lookout point of some kind, though whatever purpose it had served was lost to the past.

The door was unlocked and opened with a slight twist of the handle. Lights greeted them, yet the room remained empty. Leslie made her way to the back corner of the space. A small handle presented along the floor and she lifted it to reveal a hidden staircase to a lower level.

"It's never straightforward with you, is it?" Ruiz asked. *Now I know how Loren always felt working with Soriya.*

"Hiding is a necessary precaution in our line of work," Gates said.

She climbed down, Ruiz right behind her. The walls of the home shifted from wood to hard clumps of dirt. The roar of the waves breaking against the coast echoed around them. A door rested at the bottom, lights visible from beneath the frame.

"We have people everywhere, Ruiz," Gates continued, pulling him away from the sounds outside. "We don't do it out of a need for power, or greed, or petty avarice. The Luminaries work to preserve Portents and raise her up against the dark. Don't you do the same?"

"Of course, but—"

"Then work with us. As one of us."

Ruiz stopped at the bottom of the steps. "You keep saying us, yet all I see is you."

"You're not looking hard enough," Gates replied with a smile. She opened the door and ushered him inside.

Dozens of people turned at their arrival. The room was large, with multiple doors leading from the space along the three walls opposite the coastline. Lights occupied the corners, throwing shadows over a conference table that carried a series of lamps on the surface.

Renfield was the first face Ruiz noticed in the blinding light. He held out his hand. "Hello, Commissioner."

The man wasn't a surprise to Ruiz. After Gates let him in on her connection to the Luminaries, it wasn't a stretch to realize her work for the City Council was part of their operation. The council's primary task of late was to bring the Restoration Project to life—a project engineered by Stuart Renfield and his LUMOS group. The name suddenly took on a new significance, and Ruiz cursed his stupidity.

"Renfield," Ruiz said, taking the hand. He passed deeper into the room. While Renfield's presence wasn't a surprise, the woman behind him caused Ruiz to stagger back a step. "Janet?"

His personal secretary couldn't look him in the eye. "Sir."

He had been right. There had been a spy in the department. Janet's presence at his side at all times made a sick kind of sense now.

A hand settled on Ruiz's shoulder, and Gates led him to the table. "Not what you were expecting?"

"No candles?" the Commissioner chided. "No ritual altars or masks?"

Renfield grinned. "We save them for special occasions."

"The tools of the past have their place," Leslie said. "But not today."

Janet nodded. "It is time to move beyond secrets. Don't you agree?"

Ruiz wasn't sure how to answer anymore. That had been his goal in confronting Gates, yet looking around the room, he worried what the truth might entail and its ultimate cost.

"Well?" Ruiz said, looking at each member in the room in turn with a stern gaze. "Who's going to be the first to tell me what the hell is going on and how we can stop it?"

CHAPTER THIRTY

"Loren?"

Silence filled the apartment. Gabe closed the door behind him and dropped his backpack to the ground. Loren had failed to show up at pickup for the third time in the last month. Thankfully, Gabe had made a friend or two during his brief stint at school, and they'd been more than willing to provide transportation in a pinch.

The lack of response to any of Gabe's messages, though, worried him. Loren had never ignored him so completely. Something had happened, and Gabe could do nothing but wait.

He hated it—almost as much as the quiet seeping through the apartment. He'd been raised in a chaotic household. His parents had held full-time jobs, but both rotated their time telecommuting to provide a sense of stability on the home front. They had always been around to an extent, the same as his brother, Noah. Noise had been a natural element, from random music to the television in the background or the sound of cooking in the kitchen.

Gabe set to work on some dinner for himself. He made a sandwich with the ends of two loaves of bread and the last scraps of bologna. Plenty of leftovers waited in the fridge, all from Loren's constant experimentation. Gabe might have been a thrill-seeker in his role as the Greystone, but Loren's cooking was a little too risky in his book.

He picked at the bread as he set to work. He had an English paper to write, the topic of which continued to elude him. How many more ways were there to write about Shakespeare? Didn't anyone else write anything worth a damn? Persistent math problems needed to be reworked. He'd screwed up on the initial equations in his algebra assignment and had to start all over again. *Another headache.*

History had been a blank slate in terms of work. His new teacher was still getting a feel for the coursework and the student body. It left Gabe with a slight reprieve for the week. Just thinking about Shepherd brought back their earlier conversation. He wondered what other secrets were held in the bombed-out shell of the Whistler Building and how they connected with what happened. Shepherd's interest sparked a smile on Gabe's face, though he quickly let it fade at the sight of his piling workload and growing disinterest in all of it.

He downed his sandwich. Pushing aside his homework, Gabe reached for his phone. Still nothing from Loren. Sitting around and waiting wasn't Gabe's strong suit. Instead, he left behind all thought of essays and equations. He moved for his coat and the door. Stretching his arm to retrieve his fallen jacket, Gabe felt the tenderness in his shoulder. Small stabs of pain shot down his arm, the sprain still a long way from healed. He could cope—had coped all day, in fact—but it still reminded him of his screw-up at PSI Telecom.

He had to be better. Finding out what was going on was a start.

Gabe headed out after locking up. The stairs quickly fell behind him and he stepped out into the cold. The wind died down through the canyons of the Knoll, but the frigid air still stung his cheeks. Despite the chill, his walk was much more peaceful than stewing in the apartment's silence.

His right hand needled the object resting in his pocket. The Greystone went with him wherever he went, a permanent reminder of his role and his responsibility. Loren might have forgotten that in the wake of Gabe's fall, but the young man refused to allow the lapse to continue.

He made a beeline up the Knoll toward downtown. Central Precinct was the best place to start for some sign of his wayward parent. He made it two blocks before a call rose from across the street.

"Gabe?"

Spinning to greet the voice, Gabe was surprised to see Shepherd waving to him from the corner. He held tight to a bag of groceries, another at his feet.

When the light changed, Gabe hustled to meet the man. "Mr. Shepherd? What are you doing here?"

Shepherd lifted both bags of groceries, squeezing them to his chest. "I would ask the same, but I doubt I would approve of any answer at this hour."

Gabe hadn't noticed the streetlights on already. The hour was later than he'd realized, and night had settled over Portents. He shrugged. "I needed a walk."

Shepherd nodded. "Then how about some company?"

Gabe reached for one bag. "Only if I can help carry the load."

Shepherd passed along a grocery bag, a smile across his face. "That's all any of us can do, right?"

They started up the Knoll again. Shepherd kept a slow pace, his gaze wary as he scanned the street ahead and back the way they came. Gabe looked straight ahead, unafraid of the mounting shadows from the night.

"Should I ask if your parents know you're out and about?" Shepherd said, eyes to the alleyways dotting King's Lane. As he turned back to his companion, Gabe's head fell low. His silence was response enough for the teacher. "That's what I thought."

"What about you, sir?"

Shepherd's brow furrowed. "I don't follow."

Gabe lifted the grocery bag. "This is from Parkhurst's, which is quite a jaunt from here. There are two other grocery stores closer and all have a much better selection."

Surprise filled Shepherd. He paused, jostling his bag for a better grip. "You've got me there." He scanned the block up and down. "I confess I did get a little turned around."

"You're lost?"

"Not lost," Shepherd clarified. "Directionally challenged."

Gabe laughed. "I thought you grew up in Portents. The way you talked about the Whistler Building…"

"Yes. I did," Shepherd said. "Then I left. Things change over time, including certain memories. I'm still getting used to Portents, it seems."

"I can relate," Gabe admitted in a quiet voice. Only a year had passed since the loss of his parents. And Noah…

"Not a native, Gabe?" Shepherd asked, stirring him from memory.

"Hardly," he replied. "Sometimes I wonder if I'll ever get used to this place. If it will ever be home."

Shepherd nudged him lightly. "Then maybe we can look out for each other. Two strangers in the city."

Gabe nodded. "I... Yeah. I'd like that."

"Good," Shepherd said. "Now, if you can guide me back to Cambridge, I should be able to find my way from there. Of course, if I can't, I—"

A dark hand covered in thick black fur reached out of the shadows. Fingers spread wide and caught Shepherd by the arm. Pulling hard, the hand yanked Shepherd off the street and into the alley.

"Mr. Shepherd?" Gabe watched the groceries fall along the sidewalk where his teacher once stood. "Mr. Shepherd!"

CHAPTER THIRTY-ONE

Gabe rushed into the alley. He skidded to a halt within the shadows of the narrow space. Shepherd hovered in the air, caught in the grasp of the seven-foot-tall beast. Gabe squinted, unable to make out the creature in detail. He appeared to be an ape of some kind, with deep black wells for eyes. Only his snarling teeth gleamed in the darkness.

"Mr. Shepherd!"

"Gabe!" his teacher cried out, struggling against the creature's tight grip on his arm. "Run! Run before—"

The beast roared. A fist pounded against his chest. He snatched the frantic teacher's leg and lifted him high over his head.

Gabe took another step into the alley. He lowered the grocery bag to the ground. There wasn't time to call for help and there was no way in hell he was going to run—not with someone at risk and not when he didn't need to.

He was the Greystone, after all. "Put him down. Now."

"Food," the ape growled.

"I... I have plenty," Shepherd said sheepishly. He tried to point to the groceries, but every shift caused the ape to apply more pressure. "You're welcome to—"

The ape lowered Shepherd. Hot breath washed over the panicked teacher. Wide eyes swallowed up all hope. "That not food. You food."

"Not a chance, ugly."

"Gabe?" Shepherd peered back, terrified and confused. His eyes settled on the small object cradled in Gabe's palm.

He lifted the Greystone higher for the ape to see. "Close your eyes, sir. This will be over in a second."

The ape bellowed with delight. He tossed Shepherd aside, forgetting about his bountiful meal. The idea of a fight was clearly much more to his liking than some fleeting pleasure of flesh and bone.

Shepherd slammed into the brick, then slid to the ground. A moan of discomfort slipped from his lips. His eyes closed and he failed to move.

"I've had just about enough from you, pal," Gabe said. "Say—"

Before the light could take hold of the stone, the ape rushed for his position. He wore no clothing, his thick black fur more than enough to protect him against the elements. He bounded toward Gabe, arms outstretched.

"Crap," the stone bearer muttered. He should have handled things better, should have worked more efficiently, instead of spouting off the way he always did.

Gabe ducked under the sweeping arms of the ape. Whirling around the flailing beast, Gabe looked for an opening. The stone remained tight against his palm, ready to strike.

The ape, though, refused to relent. His left arm swung back in a wide arc. Gabe caught the blow along his sprained appendage. Dots filled his vision from the agony that swelled over his entire body. He soared away from the ape and crashed at the back of the alley in a pile of trash. The smell of decay and rancid meat caused him to sputter.

Gabe kicked away from the debris, wheeling back to the fight as the ape roared mightily.

"Yeah," Gabe said. "Definitely have had enough of you."

"Food."

"Yeah, yeah." Gabe raised the Greystone, using his left hand to bolster his injured right. "Open wide."

Pain left him. All thought of the fight and the oppressive odor emanating from the mound of garbage at his feet vanished. All that remained was the Greystone. Gabe channeled his will into the stone, forgetting about the world around him. Light grew upon the surface. A warmth ran up his arms and through his chest.

With a breath, the warmth exhaled through the stone. It shot out at the creature in a beam of light that ripped through the darkness of the alley for the ape.

Fear filled the creature's black eyes. It dove away from the light, but not before the beam pierced its right arm. Singed fur overtook the garbage smell, and the ape howled with fury. The beast reached for the stirring Shepherd, then stopped.

Turning, the ape ran from the alley. Gabe moved to follow, only to pause at the rising hand of his teacher.

"Gabe?"

He took the man's hand and helped him to his feet. "Are you all right?"

Shepherd peered around in confusion. He rubbed at his head, struggling to stay upright. "I think so. Thanks to you. But how?"

"It was nothing," Gabe said. Shepherd, though, wasn't looking at him anymore. His eyes were locked on the stone still held in Gabe's right hand. Gabe quickly closed his fingers around the Greystone. "Don't worry about it, sir."

"Worry about it?" Shepherd lit up, a smile across his face. "Gabe, that stone—what it did? That was incredible."

Gabe cringed at the man's enthusiasm. He had always thought the same about the Greystone. But he knew better than to flaunt the power he'd been given. Or to show it off to complete strangers if he could help it. The stone was a secret—a dangerous one, at that. If Loren found out what he'd done, there would be hell to pay.

He tucked the stone back into his pocket. "Do me a favor?"

"Anything," Shepherd said.

"Don't mention it. Ever."

His teacher slowly nodded, recognition seeping in with Gabe's words. Staggered steps brought him to the mouth of the alley and his groceries.

Gabe followed, and the pair collected the fallen items on the street, undisturbed during their struggle. With the bags back in hand, Gabe cocked his head down the Knoll.

"Come on," he said. "Let's get you to Cambridge."

CHAPTER THIRTY-TWO

"You don't have to do this."

Mentor hid behind the hood of his cloak, unable to meet Soriya's piercing gaze. He had taken over the journey from Kali, who had vanished into the infinite without so much as a goodbye. Soriya remained grateful to her friend. She had attempted to help, even with the other aspects fighting against her.

The choice was Soriya's alone in the end. The paths laid out before her were only options, never the true way forward. Kali's gift had not ended with resurrection from the Bypass. It had only been the start.

"You know I do, Mentor," Soriya said. Answers were the only solution now. They were the only way she could continue with the second life the Goddess of Death had granted her. "I have to know the truth about myself. About who I am."

"You—"

"The whole story, Mentor," Soriya said over him. "All the pieces I lost along the way. It's the only way I can go back and face the world. The only way I can reclaim the part of myself that makes me... me."

Mentor slowly nodded. "It will be painful."

Soriya sighed. "It always is."

He held out his hands and Soriya took them, clasping tight.

The world of the Bypass shifted, and the sky with the clawing creatures fighting to break through disappeared from view. The intersection was gone. Around them, the entire world spun into a blur of colors.

"Where are we going?"

Mentor closed his eyes, focused on the task at hand. "The beginning."

Buildings rose from the ground. Spires launched into a sky that brightened as if the moon had blinked into existence. The crescent-shaped satellite beamed down upon them, filling much of the night. Streets took form. Cars materialized from memory and blitzed for their position. Headlights washed over them.

"Mentor?" Soriya tried to move out of the way. Her teacher clutched her hands tighter. The car was almost upon them. "Mentor!"

Then it went through them. No horn blared. No scream rose from the occupant, who remained a shadow and nothing more. There was no face to him or her or it. They were a memory lost or never truly perceived. More traffic took hold, but Soriya and Mentor were no longer on the street. Their position shifted with the world until they found themselves atop a four-story apartment building.

In the distance, Soriya noticed the world continuing to come to life. It stretched beyond her field of vision, but all remained known to her. She had stood among these places many times over the years, looking down upon the city she protected with boundless pride.

"Portents," Soriya whispered. "It's Portents. But..."

"The past," Mentor confirmed. He let go of her hands, but stayed close. "This is Portents as it once stood. We are nothing more than observers here. The Bypass has seen to that much. Now you must see the rest."

His hand was outstretched and pointed over the ledge. Soriya stepped cautiously away from her teacher, a thousand questions on her lips. Hopping up to the ledge, Soriya looked down at the neighboring building.

Two men stood near the edge. One peered uneasily toward the street below. He wore a tan cloak, tight to his wiry frame. Thin gray eyes pierced the darkness knowingly. A neatly trimmed beard ran across his cheeks.

Her eyes widened. She recognized the man immediately, having stolen his picture from his family's wall years earlier. "That's... that's you."

Mentor nodded toward the younger version of himself. "Christopher Eckhart stood proudly, bearing none of the scars of his older self. "As I was."

"And him?" Soriya asked, pointing to the second figure on the rooftop. He was tall with skin that matched the black leather of his jacket. His sneakers were well worn and his jeans weathered from use. He leaned against the roof's chimney, arms across his chest. There was irritation in his stance, but more than that, a fire in his deep brown eyes. "Who is he?"

Mentor's gaze fell low. "My teacher."

"Your mentor," Soriya breathed. "A Greystone."

Mentor nodded. He took her hand once more, and the pair lifted from the rooftop. They hovered over the street until they landed beside the pair of men. Mentor hesitated for a brief second, then reached out to his younger self.

The second the connection was made, he faded into the man and Soriya found herself following suit. "Mentor? What's happening? What are we—"

"Watch," he said, his word echoing through the ether of the infinite. "This is how it began, Soriya. And how it all came to a terrible end."

CHAPTER THIRTY-THREE

Christopher Eckhart felt the cool wind rush through his overgrown hair. He needed a trim, but time stood against him. There was too much to do and not enough hours in the day to accomplish everything. Like so often of late, the afternoon vanished in a flurry of research and reading until night fell over the city.

It was time to go to work.

Those were the words of his teacher and the man waiting impatiently along the rooftop on Marchand, south of the Allure Marketplace. Darius was nothing if not diligent in his role as Greystone. He lived for little else, and it showed in his demeanor upon Christopher's arrival.

"You're late," Darius said, pushing from the chimney at his back.

"I came as soon as I heard."

Darius nodded, leading them across the rooftop for the neighboring street. "The Bypass Chamber?"

His teacher knew him too well, even after only working together for the last two years. There was a reason Darius had recruited Christopher from Portents University and it hadn't been his fighting ability. Though his skills had improved during their training, research remained Christopher's primary strength. He spent his time in the chamber cataloguing the threats they met nightly and discovering methods for their removal from the city.

The hours necessary for the task made living in the chamber a necessity in his eyes. He had started renovations to make the place more habitable for the pair, though Darius looked at any discussion of the matter with disdain.

"The work continues," Christopher said.

"Your addition is coming along?"

"The domicile is almost done," Christopher replied. "With a few surprises you'll like."

Darius refused to look at him. "Too cold down there. Too cut off."

"You mean safe."

Darius stopped. He turned to his student. "I mean distant. Like you."

"It keeps me focused," Christopher said, a snarl behind the words.

Darius read his anger with a smirk. "It keeps you alone, my friend. Remember, you cannot hear answers from without unless you face those within."

Christopher rolled his eyes. He didn't need another lecture. "Not this again."

"Again and again," Darius said with growing satisfaction. He lived to lord over his student. "Hiding in that dank chamber is no way to live."

"It helps me do the work," Christopher snapped. "So let's work, shall we?"

He hated the constant judgment from Darius. It was one of the few items they disagreed on. Darius continued to live in the city with his wife and daughter. When Christopher had joined his teacher's efforts, he left his own family behind. It had been the hardest thing he'd ever done in his life.

How else, though, could he face the demons in the dark? How else could he strive to make the city better for them than by keeping the danger as far away as he could?

"You're right," Darius agreed. His speed picked up into a run for the ledge. Leaping into the night, the stone bearer tucked into a roll as he landed on the adjacent structure. He was back on his feet in an instant, his momentum carrying him the length of the rooftop in seconds.

Christopher joined him, his movements slower and less precise. He had never been a natural athlete. The training helped, but moments remained when he struggled to believe he would ever be anything more than the college professor he had once been.

Darius scanned the street below. Patrol cars parked along the sidewalk, lights flashing to block the two-story home from outsiders. Officers departed, their steps heavy along the stoop. There appeared to be no sign of trouble, the danger over prior to their arrival.

So caught up on the scene, Christopher failed to see his teacher already on the move once more. Darius jumped from the building to the street below. He raced across the vacant road and away from the distracted officers until the shadows beside the home enveloped him.

Christopher sighed, then followed. He was nothing if not the diligent student, but his teacher's methods of instruction grated on him more than he cared to admit. By the time he caught up with Darius, they were at the rear of the guarded residence.

"You're sure this was them?" Christopher asked.

Darius worked the pick through the lock on the back door. It clicked under his care, and he opened the way to the kitchen. "See for yourself."

Christopher entered and immediately wished he hadn't. His hand rose to cover his mouth and nose. Two bodies lay dead inside. A middle-aged man stared blankly from his seat at the table, his throat slashed by a thick blade. A woman—his wife, presumably—lay on the floor. Blood pooled around her, dark crimson running the length of the room.

"Oh, my."

"Four dead," Darius said, taking the lead. They left the kitchen behind for the family room, where two more bodies greeted them. The victims were younger—possibly in their mid-to-late twenties. Jagged weapons had pierced their hearts multiple times. Spatters of blood ran across the wall, over picture frames and mirrors. Christopher moved to inspect them further, then stopped with Darius' raised hand. He pointed down to the corpses of two cats. "Six, if you count the pets."

Christopher shook his head, wary of his every move. "I've never seen activity like this."

"Dark elves," Darius said. Somehow, his teacher always knew what was going on in Portents. Christopher needed to be better about that.

Darius' theory was confirmed quickly. Arrows stuck to the frame of the kitchen door, the wood splintered at the impact points. Christopher moved for the evidence with growing curiosity. Darius, though, stuck with the dead. His eyes never left them.

"Dammit."

Christopher had seen this before from his teacher. The dead

always affected the man, causing the rage to swell within him. Darius hated to lose, be it the fight or the war. The death of innocents always pained him.

"Darius…"

His fists clenched tightly at his sides. "I should have been here sooner."

"It's not your fault."

"No," Darius growled. Sharp eyes met Christopher's. "It's that damn Bypass."

"You can't blame—"

He swatted the air before him, silencing Christopher. "It feeds on this chaos. You must have noticed that in your studies."

Christopher approached with a soft hand and a softer voice. "The Bypass is a guide, Darius. A tool."

"No," Darius answered coldly. "There is something else to it. A deeper mystery to why Portents is such a hotbed for so much… death." He let out a deep breath. A measure of calm returned. "We need to find these bastards, Chris."

"We will. We're closer now than we were."

Three separate incidents had occurred over the past two weeks. Nine people had been murdered, the killing stroke matching those of the fallen surrounding them. Small armaments had been found at the sites, but no leads had been produced. Nothing appeared to connect the victims.

Christopher moved for the arrow. Blood ran in a thin stream along the wood. It must have pierced one of the victims before the elves finished them. He removed a small vial from his cloak and collected a sample. He headed for the kitchen to do the same at the pool waiting within.

Darius kept watch from the family room, an eye toward the dead as much as the cops waiting for their backup outside. When Christopher entered, he stepped away from the fallen, sadness and frustration clear in his every movement.

"Have what you need?"

Christopher started to nod, then paused. Rounding Darius, he settled beside the dead woman on the couch. Something was familiar about her, something about the look in her dead eyes and the structure of her face, but he couldn't place it.

"What is it?"

He stood. "Not sure. Not yet."

Forensics arrived with another pair of patrol cars. The home was about to get crowded. Darius pulled at his student for the back of the home. "We should leave before we're seen."

They regrouped on the adjacent block. Christopher continued to needle the vials in his pocket. The open questions bothered him more than he could say. He looked at Darius. "We should get some rest and regroup. Call me if—"

"Chris," Darius called, stopping his departing student. "How do you feel about lemon chicken?"

Christopher shook his head. "I should—"

Darius' hand fell to his shoulder. "A warm meal, Chris. In a home." His grip tightened slightly. "I won't take no for an answer."

Christopher knew better than to argue with the man. He sighed. "Very well."

CHAPTER THIRTY-FOUR

By the time Loren reached his apartment building, the streets were devoid of life. Darkness permeated every square inch of the block. Even the shadows carried shadows of their own, so thick was the night. It matched Loren's thoughts completely.

The Council of Legends stuck with him. Their request for his aid continued to trouble him. It circled around every notion that ran through his exhausted brain.

Overwhelmed by the burden and fried at the consequences that branched from every possible decision he could give the thousands of creatures hiding for their safety within the Old City, Loren didn't know what to do. He couldn't act definitively, and his reluctance to accept the task put before him clearly stung those in the room.

Liana had been more understanding. She'd known the pressure placed upon him, merely grateful to have been heard in the first place. Feore, though, had failed to meet Loren's gaze afterward, his disappointment clear. As for Tusk… well, the less said about that guy, the better. They put their faith in Loren, some more than others, and he wasn't sure how he felt about any of it.

A sigh escaped Loren. His head settled against the door to his apartment. A lead weight sat in his chest. It was all too much to consider. The legends. The bombing. Hennessey's body. Myers. Gabe. Everything spun around his brain, begging for attention. When had things become so complicated in Portents?

Opening the door, Loren stepped inside. Quiet welcomed him. More darkness settled around the living space. He shut the door behind him, careful to keep any noise to a minimum. Shedding his jacket like a lump of dead weight, Loren placed it on the coat rack, only to watch it fall to the floor. He left it there, the effort too much for his tired frame.

Too many people needed his help. How could he do it all? How the hell had Soriya for so long? Somehow, she'd protected all sides of the struggle in Portents without so much as batting an eye at the incredible burden thrust upon her. He envied her strength and her unbending resolve to help anyone and everyone without asking for a second of peace in return. He wasn't sure he could do the same.

Loren certainly wasn't the best suited for the role. There had to be better candidates available—those with charisma and capable of holding a conversation without biting sarcasm. Hell, there had to be someone available who at least owned an ironed shirt and pressed pants to appear presentable to the public for the debates ahead?

And there would be debates. The violence in the city increased by the hour. Every news report led with the unrest throughout Portents. Flare-ups over jobs being taken by the influx of mythical refugees sparked fresh outrage in the population, not to mention the sudden scarcity of essentials—food, clothing, shelter—necessary to keep everyone content.

The hate grew with each passing day—out of fear of the unknown and out of prejudice against anything different. Someone would have to educate the masses while working with the city to make things better for both sides.

Loren shook his head. That wasn't him. That would never be him. He was a former cop with a nicotine addiction and a childish Superman obsession. He could barely keep himself going, let alone prop up the entire city.

Sickened by his inherent weaknesses, Loren moved for the bedrooms. He paused at his own, noticing the light still beaming from beneath Gabe's frame. *Maybe the kid knows what I should do*, he thought as he opened the door.

"Gabe?" he called, knuckles on the door in a soft knock. "You still up?"

Gabe sat at his desk in the room's corner. His head lay inside an open textbook, drool running down the page.

"Oh."

A small grin cracked along Loren's lips. He moved to stir Gabe, a hand against his back. "Come on, buddy. Bedtime for both of us."

"Loren?" Gabe said as he woke. He swiped the puddle from his lips. A wince of pain caused his brow to crease. The sudden movement of his sprained right arm reminded Loren of Gabe's fall.

"Yeah," Loren said in a whisper. "It's me."

The words woke Gabe, and he nearly toppled from his chair. "You're here?"

"Yeah," Loren answered with a chuckle. "Relax. I'm here."

Gabe nodded. He slipped from the chair to his bed. Still unmade from the previous night, Gabe pulled the comforter over him as he settled against his pillow. "You all, right? You never called."

Loren retrieved the dead cell phone from his pocket. "Forgot to charge the damn thing. Won't happen again."

"The case?"

Loren thought about telling him about Michael Hennessey and his connection to the founders of the city. Then there was the Council of Legends and their offer. So much had happened, and he'd promised to keep his partner involved.

Yet, when he looked at Gabe, all he saw was the fall at PSI Telecom and the pain inflicted upon the young man. Every shift along the bed confirmed Gabe's struggle with the injury, as if it had compounded over the last day instead of healed.

"We're still running down what little we have," Loren said, barely able to stomach the non-answer. It was clearly not what Gabe wanted to hear. Another question rose to his lips, but Loren interjected—a false smile on his face. "How's the arm?"

"Hurts," Gabe admitted. "But it's fine."

"Sure," Loren said, reading the lie as easily as Gabe had his own. "Been taking it easy, I hope? Do anything fun?"

Gabe snorted. He cocked his head to the desk. "Homework. I have a test at the end of the week. Are you sure everything is all right?"

"I'm sure," Loren said with a nod. He patted the kid's leg, then moved for the door. "Get some sleep. I'll make eggs in the morning."

Gabe winced. "Please don't."

The reaction caused Loren to laugh. He reached the hallway, a hand still on the knob when Gabe called him back.

"You'll be around for pickup tomorrow?" he asked. "I can ask someone else if—"

"I'll be there."

"You don't have to," Gabe continued. "I can—"

"I'll be there."

Gabe nodded, then settled into his pillow. His eyes closed immediately and sleep took him.

Loren closed the door. He hesitated to depart, hating to keep the kid at a distance. A silent promise to bring Gabe up to speed in the morning echoed through his mind. It joined the chorus of unending thoughts that threatened to keep him from a restful sleep.

He wondered if they would ever quiet. He wondered far too many things and none added up to anything good.

CHAPTER THIRTY-FIVE

Thel paced along the carpet. Nervous and frantic steps carried her back and forth, her head bowed low. Few occupied the sixth floor of the Rath Building. Janet sat patiently behind her desk, a curious look at Thel's constant movement. Another pair of officers stood near the elevator. They greeted visitors to the floor, ready for last-minute checks or to escort them to their destination.

None bothered to ask Thel about her purpose on the floor. The officers, noting her badge, gave her a pass. Even Janet only offered a slight bow at Thel's approach, happy to let the siren work through her business in private.

Her thoughts had been a constant presence. Non-stop concerns, agitated questions, all of which left her more drained than when she started. But they were only part of the reason she had finally shown up at the Rath after a full month away.

The shadow had shown up again.

It had stood in the same place as before, always watching her window and waiting. Masked, there was no clear sign of the person beneath, but Thel knew it was one of them. If not Yardin, it was definitely one of the bastards who had attacked her. They would never go away, never let her forget what they had done. Their hate was palpable, and she saw it everywhere she looked now in Portents.

That would never change. So, she would have to.

Moving for the door, Thel raised her hand. Before she connected with the frame, a door opened at the end of the hall. Ruiz exited the conference room in a hurry. Thel immediately dropped her hand to her side and her gaze back to the carpet.

Ruiz approached with a stack of binders in his grasp. More had been left behind on the conference room table. Stubble ran the length of his chin and cheeks, white in patches to match his hair. His eyes were tired, his tie barely hanging around his neck, and his sleeves rolled up above his wrists.

"Thel?" he said at his office door. She backed away to give him room. "You're here early. Is everything—"

"Fine, sir," Thel answered on reflex. "And you?"

Ruiz opened his office and stepped inside. He placed the binders on the coffee table to his left, then continued across the darkened space. A wave ushered for her to follow. "It was a late night. Nothing to worry about. Come on in."

For as full as the coffee table was with the addition of the binders, Ruiz's desk was in much worse shape. Not an inch of free space was available, with piles of reports angled precariously off every edge and stacked high atop his laptop.

Ruiz rounded the desk and took a seat. "All healed up?"

Thel stepped forward, eyes still locked on her feet instead of the man. "In a way."

When she peered up, Ruiz was staring at her curiously.

Thel cleared her throat. "Well, yes. Mostly, I mean. I…"

"Take your time," Ruiz said with a soft smile.

"I have," Thel replied, her voice carrying throughout the room. It surprised her, then she let it continue. "I have, sir. It hasn't made this any easier, I'm afraid."

She pulled her badge from her pocket. It glimmered under the dim light of the desk lamp. Thel held it out and placed it along Ruiz's open palm.

Sadness filled his eyes. "You've thought this through?"

She nodded. "More than you can imagine."

"Thel…"

"It's the right move, sir."

Ruiz stood. "You saved a lot of lives, Thel. Your work here has been exemplary. There's still time to work through what happened to you. I can put in an extension myself if it will help."

"What happened…" Thel closed her eyes. She wanted to scream at the turn of phrase. That's how everyone viewed it, though, like the assault was just a thing that had happened to her. There was so much more to it, and none of them understood. They couldn't.

Every time someone mentioned it, her heart stopped. She felt like she was back in that moment with the punches and the kicks and the screams of pure hatred.

Thel shook her head. "No. There's no working through it. No putting it behind me. Not if I'm here. I'm sorry, sir."

"So am I." Ruiz ran his finger over the badge, then let it settle on top of his work. Rounding the desk, he extended his hand. "Take care of yourself, Thel. If you ever need anything—anything at all—my door is always open."

Tears dotted her cheeks. "Thank you."

Thel swiped at her eyes as she moved for the exit. The light from the hallway was blinding compared to the shadowy office, and it took a moment for her to adjust. Her breath caught in her throat. The weight of her actions swelled in her chest. It was the right move—to get away from the pain her role as an officer brought—yet the pain in Ruiz's eyes haunted her. All she felt was disappointment. But had it come from him or herself?

That thought followed her down the hall. She passed Janet with the slightest of waves, then headed for the elevator. The doors opened as she approached, and a trio exited. Two men carrying cameras and video equipment shuffled out first, careful not to drop anything as they walked. A young woman with long legs and a short skirt followed. She ran a hand through thick auburn locks that flowed flawlessly to her shoulders.

Thel recognized the woman from several press conferences during her tenure at the department. Her name was Nicki Dryden, a mainstay on one of the major networks. Not that Thel watched much of the news lately.

She sidestepped the trio for the elevator, but couldn't find a clear path with the addition of the two officers escorting the news crew. Moving for the stairs, Thel heard the murmurs grow behind her. A voice called her back before she could escape.

"Hey," Nicki said. "You're that detective. The siren, right?"

Thel turned, a false smile on her face.

Nicki approached quickly, a nod to her crew to follow. "Would you mind answering a few questions?"

"About what?" Thel asked, curious.

Nicki let out a chuckle. "You're kidding, right? With the violence happening in the city—with what happened to you? You're on the front lines facing this new dynamic. Your voice could have a real impact and make both sides see the light."

"I…" The camera was already on and recording. Nicki held out her phone to capture every word of their conversation. Thel's entire body shook. Her chest clenched. What could she say? What voice did she have left? Everything had been taken from her and only her fear remained. Her gaze fell to the floor. "I don't have anything to say. Sorry."

Thel turned and opened the door to the stairs.

"If you'll just give me—"

"No." Thel slipped into the stairwell and the door slammed shut behind her. Without hesitation, Thel bounded down the steps until all thought of the news crew, Ruiz, and her decision faded into memory.

There was only one stop left. She had been dreading it the entire morning. She left the stairs at the second floor. The noise from the Detective Bureau hit her like a tidal wave. Dozens rushed by in a hurry. They passed along case files and intel as they headed in every direction. All worked to find answers to the latest crisis in Portents.

Myers stood on a chair in the bullpen. She belted out orders to everyone who so much as looked at her. "I need that report, Atley!" she bellowed. "I swear if I have to ask again, I'll—"

Her voice trailed off when she noticed Thel. Her hands fell to her side, and she rushed to greet her friend.

"Thel!"

"Hey, Sam," Thel said with sadness in her eyes. "Got a minute?"

CHAPTER THIRTY-SIX

"No."

Myers stared at Thel in disbelief. She couldn't possibly have heard what she thought she had—not from Thel, and not when the whole damn city was dealing with a larger threat.

"What do you mean, no?"

Myers slammed the office door shut and stepped around her friend. "I refuse to accept your resignation."

"Ruiz already did."

"Refused you?" Myers asked, rounding her desk. She collapsed on the seat. "Good. Glad that settles the matter."

"Sam..." A groan escaped Thel. So did a smile and Myers focused on that, hoping to keep it going. She needed that light back in her life. There had been too much darkness of late.

"It's done," Thel said. She needled the purple charm between her fingers, squeezing it like a safety blanket. All the strength left her, and Myers recalled the broken woman she had visited in the hospital the night of the beating. "I'm done."

"Why?" It was the only question left to Myers. For over a month, she had supported Thel through her ordeal. Rebuked at every turn, every lead into her case tossed aside with a dismissive wave or a murmured reply, Myers continued to fight for her friend and partner. She tired of the excuses and the silence between them.

Thel rolled her eyes. She fought against her better instincts, lost to survival mode. Whatever had happened to her had sapped her of the fire she once held for life.

Myers jumped from her seat, slamming her fist against the desk. "You want to walk away from this so badly? Tell me why."

"I..." Thel's gaze fell. "I can't."

Myers' heart broke at the admission. No matter how many

times Thel repeated the mantra, Myers always thought there was still a way to break through, a way to silence the fear in her partner, and bring her back. There had been trust between them and an honest-to-God friendship, something Myers always dreamed of having.

Circling the desk to stand beside her friend, Myers took a calming breath. She kept her voice low and controlled. A fight wasn't necessary. It had already been lost. "Thel," she said. "I'm your friend. Forget the job and the badge and everything else. Friend to friend, what happened?"

Thel smiled at her. Those pearly whites made her purple hair glow brighter. She took Myers by the hand and squeezed. "I'm going to miss you, Sam."

"Then stay," Myers replied, holding on tight. "There is nothing we can't work through."

"This…" Thel fell away. Hair drooped over her face, masking the tears in her eyes. "I need to find my own way. I'm sorry."

She started for the door. Myers wanted nothing more than to leap in front of her and tie her down to the chair until the answers spewed forth. Hell, if it came to it, the interrogation room would serve as Thel's new apartment until Myers felt satisfied with the responses. None of it was fair, not to her, and definitely not to Thel.

Her friend was broken and lost. Why she wouldn't take the helping hand upset Myers more than anything else.

Thel opened the door. The sound of a hundred footfalls boomed for a second, then silenced. Only the two of them existed in the moment, and Myers pleaded with swollen eyes for another chance to make things right.

Thel held out the rabbit's foot. "You should have this back."

Myers shook her head. "It's yours. Maybe it will bring you some luck. Like you always did for me."

"Take care of yourself, Sam." The door closed and she was gone.

Fists of frustration slammed against the desk. Paperwork flew from the surface, scattering around the room until they slowly worked their way to the floor. Myers wanted to join them, to curl into a ball.

Instead, she swiped away the pain from her eyes and pulled herself to the desk once more. Too many other priorities remained.

Too many mysteries threatened to consume her whole, and she refused to let them win. Work was all she had left and Myers started in, pulling the latest reports off the top of her pile.

Barely a second in, her gaze shifted back to the door. Her hope at seeing Thel finally back to work had been dashed. All hope, in general, joined the lost and confused siren in her departure. What the hell had happened to Thel? What could have caused her to walk away from the life she'd taken such pains to build over the last year?

Thel was wrong to quit. Myers knew from experience, isolation never worked out in the long run. It spiraled until there was nothing left to love and no one left to pick up the pieces. Isolation was a quick descent that would leave Thel in nothing but darkness.

Thel was falling and Myers couldn't do a damn thing except worry how far her friend would fall before the end.

CHAPTER THIRTY-SEVEN

Darius' home rested at the end of a small cul-de-sac off Ness. The entire area was in need of revitalization and there had been talk for years about a project to rebuild and restructure the district. Businesses languished as people shifted their interests downtown. A fair share of the homes were dilapidated, with storm doors flapping in the wind and siding peeling and cracking from years of neglect.

Compared to the rest of the area, Darius' home stood as an oasis. Flowers sprouted in the window boxes off the front. A garden occupied the back, overgrown yet thriving despite the cooling temperatures at night. Lights were on in multiple rooms, the sound of movement and laughter welcoming the pair of protectors to the domicile as the night drifted on.

The hour was late, yet Darius seemed to wake upon approach. His smile beamed at Christopher, pulling him along the steps to the front porch and the door. He pulled it open and ushered his friend inside.

Christopher hesitated. "I really should—"

"After dinner." Darius prodded his student ahead. "Try to enjoy yourself."

Christopher nodded. As they entered, Darius left him in the doorway. He tossed his jacket aside. His shoes landed next to it as he rushed through the home. At the door to the kitchen, Darius peered back. The anger and frustration from earlier sparked for a moment on his face. He forced it down, almost visibly swallowing the thoughts, as a smile spread across his lips.

It was a gift Christopher never shared with the man. The false front had never been something he'd desired to show the world. Their work was everything to him.

Darius, though, somehow maintained his life. He created a wall between the two divergent worlds pulling at his core. More than that, he allowed both sides to flourish during his tenure as the Greystone.

Christopher noted the flag hanging on the wall in the foyer. Darius' father had been killed in combat overseas. That incident had set the man's life on a clear path. Darius had enlisted the first chance available and served tours in a dozen countries. He'd always been a soldier—built for war. It certainly aided his role as protector of the city. Yet, there were times Christopher wondered if war was the true face of his friend or if he only did it to enjoy these small moments at home.

There were lines he couldn't fathom crossing. They marred his every decision, like the one that had separated him from his own family. Christopher wondered if Darius realized how lucky he was, how precious a gift a family might be in the face of their role.

Or how easily it might all shatter.

"Are you kidding?" A strong voice shouted from the kitchen. Pushing through Darius' embrace, a young woman entered the hallway. Jayla appeared as radiant as ever, even after the long day. Her hair was tied into a bun, an apron around her waist, covering her purple blouse and dark pants. She offered a quick glance at Christopher, who waved sheepishly from his position in the doorway. A groan escaped her, and she stomped back into the kitchen. "You should have called."

"Jayla," Darius called, arms outstretched. "I was working."

A thin glare shot back at her husband. "You're always working."

Christopher joined them, maintaining a safe distance in the hallway. Jayla caught herself, ready to argue more with Darius. A false grin lifted her cheekbones and softened her gaze. "It's good to see you, Chris."

He bowed with appreciation. "I hope I'm not intruding."

"*You* aren't."

All understood the inflection. Jayla tucked her arms tight to her chest rather than embrace Darius.

He shook his head at her anger. "Jayla..."

"Not in front of our company," the young woman seethed.

Darius shifted for the doorway. He pointed toward the bedrooms to the rear of the home. "You mind checking on the rugrat?"

Christopher tracked the man's gaze, then nodded. "Sure."

The argument resumed almost immediately. Heated words, a few in whispers, shot back and forth. Christopher understood them all. Strain was part of daily living in the world. Their work at night obviously grated Jayla the wrong way, most likely because she didn't understand their role at all.

It was a delicate thing, balancing life between two separate worlds. Christopher had walked away from that choice. He'd sacrificed one part of his life for the greater good. That was how he justified it. That justification helped him sleep at night... most of the time.

The delicate nature was exemplified best by the child playing joyfully in her bedroom. Darius' daughter, Marissa, raced around the room, carrying a doll over her head. The toy soared around a kingdom built from towers of blocks that took the form of castles and caves. They were littered around the room, with tiny figures dotting the landscape.

The young girl of four wore a bright gold headband and silver wristbands. A rainbow skirt and knee-high purple socks completed the look. She stopped when she noticed the man watching her through the open doorway. The doll in her hands lowered.

"Hello, Mr. Chris," Marissa said.

"Hello to you." Christopher entered the room, then kneeled on a clean square of carpet. "And who is your friend?"

"Lady."

Christopher chuckled at the imaginative name. He held out a hand. "Hello, Lady. It's nice to meet you."

Marissa looked him over. "You dress funny."

Another laugh escaped him. Christopher picked at the folds of his cloak. "It keeps me warm. I like your outfit."

Marissa's hands immediately fell to her hips. "I'm a crime fighter. I keep people safe, like my daddy."

"I feel safer already."

Steps approached and Darius entered the room. He whirled around Christopher to pick Marissa up. "Dinner, kiddo."

Laughter echoed as Darius raced his daughter down the hallway like a rocket.

Jayla groaned beside the dining room table. "Don't rile her up!"

Darius settled Marissa into her seat, then ran a hand through her hair. "A little riling is just what the doctor ordered."

A dour look rose on the girl's face at the meal before her. "What is that smell?"

"Dinner," Jayla said in an exasperated tone. She clearly knew what was coming the second she put down the platter of lemon chicken.

"I want hot dogs!"

Darius filled his daughter's plate. He cut up the meat in thin strips, then added rice on top. "Maybe there's some hidden underneath. It's a treasure hunt."

Jayla rolled her eyes. "Just eat it, Marissa." She glanced at their guest, offering the chair at the end of the table. "Chris, can I get you anything else?"

"No." He took the chair, noticing the distance between Jayla and Darius. They sat at opposite ends, Jayla close to Marissa and Darius alone on his side. Christopher cleared his throat. "This looks wonderful. Thank you again."

"It's a rare treat," Jayla said over the clanging of forks and knives on plates. "Darius hasn't been around much."

Her eyes were like daggers toward her husband. Darius met them with his own, chewing loudly.

"No?" Christopher asked in surprise.

"I told you..." Darius started through clenched teeth.

"Work," Jayla said in a cruel tone.

"Right, Chris?"

Pleading eyes carried the message to the uncomfortable guest. Christopher toyed with the food on his plate. He hated to lie. His concern for the truth almost outweighed his teacher's unspoken request. "Work? Ah, yes. Work. Always work."

"We miss you, Daddy," Marissa said, batting her rice aside with her fingers.

"I miss you too, little one."

Jayla's hands tightened against the side of the table. She pushed back and stood abruptly. "I forgot the salad."

Darius shifted to the edge of his seat. "I can—"

"I'll handle it." Jayla turned for the kitchen and muttered, "Like I do everything else."

A low breath of frustration escaped Darius. He stood slowly, a nod to his guest. Christopher said nothing, the silence acceptable to all parties. Darius left the table behind and entered the kitchen.

"Jayla..."

The argument started again. Their words were lost, their concern about being overheard clear.

Christopher did his best to ignore the situation. He lifted his spoonful of rice and chicken and imitated a rocket ship soaring through the sky. Marissa watched with wide eyes, laughing. She joined him and together they flew around their plates, eating in slow waves what remained on the spoon after their playing.

Eventually, Darius and Jayla returned. The salad made its way around the table quickly, but no more words were spoken. Stray glances passed between Christopher and the young girl of four. Rocket ships had been put away, but quiet chuckles brought the memory back to them.

Dinner ended soon enough. Jayla took Marissa back down the hall to prepare for bedtime. Christopher helped Darius bring the dishes into the kitchen, where they settled along the counter to be washed.

Songs resounded. Jayla's beautiful voice relaxed her daughter for their nightly routine. Christopher, though, heard the sadness behind the melody.

Darius ignored them completely, escorting Christopher to the front door. "I apologize for that. She doesn't understand."

"Maybe telling her would help."

"Like you did?" Darius snapped. Christopher was surprised at the anger behind the words. His teacher noted the reaction and he sighed. "I'm sorry. That wasn't..."

"You're tired," Christopher said. "Rest. Enjoy your family."

"You could stay." Darius indicated the couch in the living room and the blanket over the back. "Plenty of room for one more."

"The Bypass Chamber—"

"Is a cold and empty place. Just like that misbegotten orb." His bitterness spoke to deeper issues, and Christopher wondered if they centered on Darius' family troubles or something more.

He shook his head. "It's home for me." Christopher opened the door and stepped into the night. Darius moved to follow. "What are you doing?"

"The elves..."

"Can wait," Christopher said. "Take the night, Darius. Stay home. We'll figure this out."

"Tomorrow?"

He nodded, wondering if his teacher could wait that long. "Tomorrow."

CHAPTER THIRTY-EIGHT

Felix Carpenter enjoyed getting up with the sun. His apartment, a seventh-floor corner unit, overlooked downtown Portents. With the dawn, light beamed off the black tower at the heart of the city and showered across the spires.

The reflection radiated warmth and welcomed Felix to the start of a brand-new day. He watched the entire affair like clockwork, sipping his green tea from his balcony. The cold weather never stopped him from taking in the view. There was nothing better in the world and no better company than the serene bliss that came from the rising sun.

His peaceful tranquility followed him from home to the start of his workday. He worked for New You Advertising, a brand marketing firm built on revitalizing floundering companies with fresh takes on old products. On an average day, the company handled no less than one hundred clients, preparing campaigns, developing slogans, or pitching new and interesting ways to uncouple troubled businesses from their past mistakes.

The place was never stagnant. Each day offered new challenges to meet. Felix, a designer for the firm, enjoyed the hell out of the work. So excited to meet each day, his green tea infusion empowering an already healthy worldview, Felix always made sure to arrive at the office first in the morning.

Today was no different. He reached the office thirty minutes before the start of his shift, visions of an ad campaign locked in his brain. The early arrival was more than enthusiasm at the job. He preferred the peace that came with being first on the floor. There was no discussion, no gossip to manage or quell, just the handling of all the little things that ate into the creative mind when they piled up.

He already had a list ready when he reached the office. There were headlines to check. Never the national news, though. Felix stuck to the business section and away from the trappings of crime and politics; they were the same thing in his mind. He wondered how his stocks had been as the holiday season loomed. Then there were the emails, most of which offered nothing but junk to eat away at his time.

Felix sighed, pushing away any ill-gotten vibes. He stared up into the morning light of Portents and smiled. It was too beautiful a day to warrant any hostility or frustration at things that had never mattered much to him in the first place. It was why he didn't bother with the drama that typically came from coworkers. Work was work, but it wasn't life. He had the one he'd always wanted, and that was enough for him.

Light reflected from the windows of the office, a building that occupied the corner of Adler and Holbrook. It carried no name, only a large number stamped along the front of the edifice. The New You logo covered the windows across the entire second floor to announce their presence to the city.

Felix removed his keycard from his wallet. He held it out as his other hand reached for the waiting door. A confused look broke across his face. The security pad showed green, as if it had already accepted the card. The door opened without prompt and without the sharp click that usually accompanied entry into the building.

"Strange," he muttered. Felix stepped inside. He pulled the door shut hard until the lock engaged. Peering through the glass, he noticed the red light above the security pad, barring entry without the proper access. "I wonder what—"

A figure passed by the lobby desk on the far side of the wide-open first floor. A baseball cap and a large coat obscured their body and hid most of their features. Wide strides quickly carried them across the space.

"Hey!" Felix shouted. "You can't be here. No one's supposed to—"

The figure slammed into Felix's shoulder. The force of the blow knocked the peaceful soul aside, and he tumbled to the ground. His bag fell from his side, skidding away from him.

"Hey!" Felix brushed off the assault. He worked his way to his feet as he gathered his belongings. "What the hell is wrong with you, pal? I'm calling the police! Do you hear me?"

The figure was already out the door, which shut soundly at their departure. They hesitated barely a second before they headed down the sidewalk and out of view. No glance passed Felix's way. No acknowledgment of any kind was offered for the rude encounter, which stuck with Felix.

The young designer huffed. "Like that's going to stop me."

He moved for the lobby desk and the phone waiting on the surface. Someone had to be notified of the situation. No one was supposed to be in the building this early. Felix didn't want to be blamed for anything.

"I'll show them," Felix said, picking up the phone. He started to dial. "You can't—"

A soft ticking rose from behind the desk. Felix lowered the phone and peered over the work surface to find a device resting beneath a chair. The timer on top ticked away the seconds left, the display passing the number three as Felix's situation finally registered.

"Oh."

Light was all Felix saw in the end. One last beautiful sunrise and then it was over.

CHAPTER THIRTY-NINE

Loren rushed up the block and through the cordon to the site. He fought with the officer working the line, his ID not exactly the authority a badge would have offered. Had Pratchett still been with them there would have been no issue and, for a second, Loren found himself looking for his old friend. His absence always snuck up on Loren at the worst times.

Corroboration with the neighboring patrolman finally granted Loren access to the crime scene. He thanked the men with a nod and a wave before returning to a run toward the building.

The place was in better shape than the previous attack. No groans emanated from the structure. It appeared stable; the blast concentrated on the center of the building and little else. That had been enough, though. Glass covered the sidewalk and street. None of the windows remained intact on the first floor. The entry doors lay on the opposite side of the road from the explosive force of the detonation.

Officers worked diligently to clear the area. Patrol cars blocked most of the view. As Loren moved his way through the blockade, he noticed Myers leaning heavily against the hood of her car. She sipped her coffee in quiet misery, rubbing at bleary eyes.

"Hey," Loren called.

Myers tossed him a look, then returned to her coffee.

Loren joined her along the hood. "I got here as quick as I could."

Her silence continued. Troubled eyes flitted from the building to the surrounding area and back again, never bothering to acknowledge his presence or the situation at hand.

"Everything all right, Myers?"

"Had a rough morning." She lowered the coffee. Realizing the absence of an explanation in her statement, Myers turned to him. "Thel quit."

Loren's brow furrowed. "She quit? Why?"

"I wish I knew." She slid from the hood of her car, stretching as she stood. "One more mystery to keep me occupied."

That was just what they needed. Both were wrapped up in the case, but more continued to pummel them with every turn—Myers with her Thel dilemma and Loren with the Council of Legends. The outside world kept throwing blinders over everything, obscuring what truly mattered until nothing did. Or was it everything?

The confusion hit everyone. Loren recognized it with the officers at the cordon, as well as the EMTs and firefighters working the scene. They all staggered along, unable to understand any of it. Crowds pushed at the cordon. Their presence added to the pressure of the moment, their fear and terror infecting everyone.

Something had to give, and when it did, Loren knew without a doubt… it would end badly.

"Shall we?" Myers asked, a hand to the shattered entryway.

Loren pushed off the hood and they started. "Is the building stable enough?"

Myers nodded. "From what I've been told. My expert is working on securing the device, but she mentioned it was a lower yield than the first."

"Someone is getting better at their craft," Loren muttered upon entering the building. The lobby was a charred wreck. Nothing remained of the decor but a blackened horror show, unfit for even the scariest haunted mansion. Scorch patterns rippled along the intact columns on the outskirts of the space and across the ceiling. Light fixtures decorated the floor. More glass shattered and fused in the explosion. It crunched under their steps as they continued deeper into the structure.

A pair of EMTs lifted a body bag carefully. They passed by slowly on their way to the waiting ambulance. Myers stared coldly at the dead man found in the wreckage. "The last thing I need is for this guy to get better at his craft."

"Was that the target? Were they—"

"No," Myers interjected. "Guy was just unlucky from what we can tell. Think he might have found the device right before it blew up in his face."

"Christ."

"Yeah," Myers said with a breath. "Not the best way to go."

"So then why—"

Myers held up a hand. "This way."

She led him to the back of the building. Twin halls diverged before a bank of elevators, which were dented and damaged in the explosion. She turned left, the building directory pasted to the wall, but no longer readable.

"Place houses some advertising business called New You. They occupy most of the building."

"But they weren't the target?"

"No," Myers said. They took the stairs and headed down to the lower level. The door opened, soft steps carrying them up a narrow hall to a lone office along the right-hand side. "I had our people scan the building the second we were able. I was really hoping your dead guy at PSI was a coincidence."

"Myers?"

She opened the door to the office. "We found her waiting for us."

A woman sat at her desk. Her carotid artery had been severed at the neck, blood dried along her skin and clothes from the cut. Stab wounds marred her chest; the damage devastated the woman's torso. Each one appeared jagged and matched those found on Michael Hennessey's body.

Loren scanned the dead. He rounded the desk, always keeping her in view. This had been a violent act. Spatter patterns marked the floor and walls. The victim had been propped in her seat, the slash along her neck nothing more than insurance.

"No one saw anything?"

"If anyone did, it was our guy in the lobby, and he won't be telling us anything." Myers said, finishing her coffee. She peered around for the trash can, then thought better.

"Who is she?"

"That I can answer," Myers said. "Wendy Caldwell."

"Caldwell?" Loren recognized the name at once.

Myers did too. "Yeah. Descendant of Wilbur Caldwell. This is the Founder's Day mess all over again."

Loren thought the same. City officials had been murdered and dressed up in a black cloak post mortem. They had been calling cards for the killer's true target, a man known only as the Founder and the leader of a church of lunatics bent on resurrecting the dead. The situations were clearly different, yet something about them stuck with Loren every time he looked at the dead woman.

"Well, we both know Richard Crowne isn't involved this time," Loren said.

"That would make things much easier."

Loren turned away at the comment. Crowne had been a friend—another in a long line of dead men associated with Loren. Myers had framed Loren for the man's death, and his reaction brought sadness to her tired eyes.

"Greg, I..."

"It's okay," Loren said.

"I shouldn't have—"

"It's okay." He didn't bother to look at her. His words wouldn't be enough, not for someone like Myers. Her guilt festered. They were too alike for their own good. Instead of focusing on the past, he concentrated on the dead woman. "What was she doing here?"

"I wish I knew."

"Did she work here?"

"Everything I've managed to find on Wendy Caldwell says she was pretty well off," Myers said. Steps approached as forensics arrived at the scene. Myers cocked her head toward the door, pulling Loren away from the body. "We should give them some room."

Loren joined her without a fight. He wanted more time with the victim, not that he had a clue what it might mean. The stab wounds appeared the same as Hennessey's, yet Caldwell had been intentionally positioned. There was purpose behind their placement, like they needed the dead to be found in such a manner.

"If she was well off, what was she doing slumming it in the basement of this building?" Loren paced the corridor. Boxes of supplies filled the end. Office equipment was staggered along the other side of the hall. Mechanical rooms took up the rest of the space, locked from access. "Well, Myers? What do we have?"

Myers sighed. "Like I said, New You Advertising occupies most of the building. They work for newspapers, magazines, even the phone book, like those still exist. Wendy wasn't employed with the firm, yet a talk with one of the secretaries who worked in the lobby mentioned she was seen quite a few times over the last few months."

"Doing what?"

"Coming down here."

"They never asked?"

"She always said she was visiting," Myers replied.

"Visiting?" Loren eyed her curiously. "Who?"

"No one in particular," Myers said. "The building, she always said."

None of it made sense. There was more to the woman's presence than they could determine. The mystery galled him, and his frustration carried him back up the stairs and through the lobby.

"They find anything else?"

"Not yet."

"I don't like this."

"Who does, Loren?"

They exited the building, leaving behind the wreckage and the dead. Loren tried to settle his nerves, but with every stray glance he found a new concern to deal with. The tired faces in the crowd echoed in his mind, terrified of what might happen next.

Shoving started near the cordon. People swatted at their neighbors. Anger took over from the fear as they realized the myths and legends among them. They gaped at the devastation, as curious as anyone else about what had happened. Finger-pointing occurred immediately; the blame game caused nothing but more violence.

Officers worked to defuse the situation with little success. Loren let out a sigh. "This is the last thing Portents needs right now. People are on edge. More than just people…"

Through the crowd, Loren noticed members of the Council of Legends. They gazed at the building. There was the ape in the suit he had seen during his impromptu visit to the Old City, along with several others. Standing at the head of the line, though, was Tusk, who seethed at the scene.

"Loren?" A hand fell on his shoulder and he spun around. Myers attempted to track his gaze. "What did you see?"

When he turned back to the cordon, Tusk and the others were gone.

"Nothing." Loren angled toward the building. "Walk me through this again?"

Myers sighed. "And here I was hoping for another coffee and a bagel."

Loren smiled at her. "Let's start with some answers."

CHAPTER FORTY

Ruiz slipped the tie around his neck. He stood in front of the mirror, trying to work the damn thing into a proper knot. The fabric fought against his manipulations, and his hands struggled with the simple task. His mind was on far too many things of late, frustrating him further. He didn't have time, not with another attack—another tragedy to manage.

The break from work had been necessary, as was the trip home. He'd reeked to high heaven from another long night of investigating the Luminaries and their activities. A shower and a change of clothes were the least he could do to feel somewhat human once again.

The drive had helped. It had offered a quiet space to figure out everything he'd learned over the course of the last day. The Luminaries had brought him up to speed on many aspects of their operations, but he knew they held back just as much information.

Their role on the City Council, within the city government, on the board of directors of several high-powered firms, bought a lot of influence in how Portents did business. Of all the revelations, Janet's role unnerved him most of all. His own actions had been under a whole new level of scrutiny.

When it came to the case at hand, the group had been relatively quiet. Whispers had passed between members, theories about rogue agents who had cut ties with the group over disagreements. Pressing them for more specifics had, however, fallen flat. Ruiz had walked away with nothing—no leads of any kind on the bomber targeting his city. For all their knowledge, they were as clueless as the rest of Portents.

Before departing, Leslie had reiterated her membership offer. It stewed in the back of Ruiz's mind the entire night and throughout the morning.

To join the ranks of the Luminaries would provide him with untold access to resources beyond anything he'd been granted in his role as commissioner. There were also the secrets to consider. It was a chance to learn them all—to force them into the open. He would be part of the system, a player in the game rather than an ignorant spectator watching from the sidelines.

Their offer went unanswered. Ruiz needed time. The Luminaries played a key role in bringing light back to his home, to improving the quality of living for those who had survived the horrors brought forth by Karen Winters and her Heads of Cerberus.

Their secrets remained, however. They continued to play in the back of his mind as he wrangled his misshapen tie into the proper knot and position. He stared at his exhausted eyes in the mirror. They were black holes of darkness which matched the rest of his bleak appearance of mussed-up hair and wrinkled shirt. He wasn't fit for the job he held. Now he considered another, with more responsibility and more power than he knew how to handle.

The second explosion pressured him to act. The call had come in during his short reprieve at home. It pushed him to move faster, to forget about any thought of rest for the long day ahead. He recognized the address immediately. It matched one of several listings he'd found during his night of research on the Luminaries.

The second attack confirmed Leslie's theory. The bomber *was* targeting them. But why?

A voice from the doorway startled Ruiz. "You never came home last night."

Ruiz turned from the mirror. Michelle stood at the threshold of the bedroom. Her arms were across her chest. Tired eyes met his, sadness and anger filling them.

"What are you doing here?" Ruiz asked, surprised at her presence. He thought the house was empty with the school day in full swing.

"When I woke up and you weren't here, I called you. At the office. On your cell." She approached. Hands made their way along his tie, adjusting the knot and fixing his collar.

"I've been busy."

Her hands fell to his chest. "Too busy for a message? A simple, I love you?"

Ruiz took her hands and brought them to his lips. "I'm sorry."

She shook her head. "I wasn't fishing for an apology. An explanation would be nice, though."

"I have to get back to work."

He entered the kitchen to gather some supplies for the trip. A granola bar fell from the box onto the counter. Some fruit joined it. Moving for the exterior door, Michelle barred his path.

"No," she said in a firm tone. "We're not falling back into this routine. You've been distant since the night those tremors hit. And now these bombings?"

He refused to meet her hard gaze. "It's nothing. I..."

"We made a promise, Alejo. No more secrets between us."

Ruiz stared at his wife. When he had learned the truth about Portents, about what terrors the true city held in the dark, he had kept it from her and his children. He almost lost her because of the great divide he'd put between them. The long hours and the late nights had split them apart, threatening to break them completely. He couldn't let that happen again.

A slow nod escaped him. "You're right. Michelle, I..." He peered at the counter. "How about some coffee?"

Michelle smiled. "I'll pour. You talk."

He told her everything. From the tremors at the Marsh Estate to the tale of the five knights and their doomsday prophecy. Leslie Gates and the Luminaries' offer followed. How they connected to the bombings and the questions that continued to plague him spilled out over the course of the conversation.

Michelle took them all in stride. She sipped her coffee and listened, staying quiet until there was nothing left to tell and the secrets fell away. Settling her cup down, she took hold of his hand and squeezed. "Feel better?"

"If I said no?" He stood, taking the empty cups to put them in the sink. "It's just... The Knights. The Luminaries. So many secrets are coming to light. When did it all become so big?"

Michelle joined him. "When you tried to take it all on yourself. As usual."

"I needed to understand it—to figure out something. Anything."

"Did you?"

He shook his head. "Not enough. Never enough." He pulled her close and held her tight. "How can I keep my family safe, knowing what's out there? How can I help keep secrets, knowing the cost they bear?"

"Those aren't easy questions."

"They haven't been for a long time."

Michelle stepped back. Her hands settled along his cheeks, then rubbed the hair from his forehead. "You'll know the right choice, Alejo. When the time comes, you'll make it. And your family will be by your side. Always."

She kissed him. For a second, the rest of the world faded. He carried her love with him to the car and out into the chaos awaiting him, hoping it would make a difference in the end.

CHAPTER FORTY-ONE

Loren forgot to pick him up. Again. Gabe tried to feign surprise, but the act still stung. Coupled with the unanswered messages in the wake of the second bombing, Gabe was more than a little pissed off at the man.

He had already been at school when the explosion occurred. Rather than panic, sending thousands of children back home in the tragedy's wake, the school district went into lockdown. There had been no transitioning throughout the day, no travel in the hallways of any kind except for the occasional bathroom trip to avoid a new crisis with the student body.

Gabe had been trapped in math class. Mr. Steck had been intelligent enough, for once, to back off on the endless equations and problem-solving to realize the stressful situation. He had switched gears pretty early in the day, allowing for a movie day. Disney Animation might have been its own form of torture, but Gabe had been grateful for the reprieve. When the girls started singing about some poor slob named Bruno, however? That's when Gabe had put his head down and turned to his phone.

It offered no solace and definitely no information. The bombing took over every headline and filled every newsfeed, but no insight was offered into the event. Gabe spent hours looking for some clue, some great connection like he had with the Five Knights, but nothing made sense to him.

Loren's absence at pickup wasn't a stretch of the imagination. Gabe had no doubt he was right in the middle of things, probably with Myers and their terrible, disconnected flirting. Loren was as clueless about women as he was about keeping a promise.

A quiet chime stirred him, and Gabe retrieved his phone. The message on the screen read, ON MY WAY, as if Loren had never learned how to turn off the caps lock. Nothing else came through. No answers shot Gabe's way for the delay or the bombing or anything of value.

Loren was holding back.

Gabe did the same. Loren had asked him about the previous night, and he'd lied about staying in to work on his homework. Gabe failed to relay his encounter with the ape-thing or his time with Shepherd. His teacher had seen the Greystone in action. Gabe should have tried to hide it better, should have passed it off as a trick of the light, but for some reason had trusted the newcomer with his greatest secret.

He didn't know why. Something about the way Shepherd treated him, the way he spoke to him as an equal, made Gabe feel valuable.

Noise boomed in the gymnasium. Pickup ran differently due to the drama in the city. Parents and guardians filtered through the hall to claim their children. Students still waiting were forced against the right wall, sitting on the cold floor with nothing but their phones as companions. Most of the staff helped with the bus lines, escorting kids to the doors and the appropriate transport.

The few remaining teachers walked the gym to monitor things. Shepherd was one of them. He did his best to maintain his distance from Gabe, but the occasional glance made it clear their adventure was still fresh in his thoughts.

"Hey," a voice called from Gabe's right. He glanced up to see Kevin Delgado standing over him. "They're finally letting me go."

Kevin owned his own car, his parents more than willing to give him the responsibility fit for a kid his age. The school, though, had been worried about sending those able to drive out on the streets with everything going on. They had attempted to contact parents throughout the day. Kevin's weren't exactly easy to get ahold of normally, let alone in a crisis.

"No word from your folks?"

"Yeah, right," Kevin said with a scoff. "They probably haven't looked up from their computers all day." He gestured toward the door. "You want a lift?"

"I'm good." Gabe lifted his phone. "My ride's on his way."

Kevin nodded, waved, then headed for the exit.

Gabe sighed, staring at the phone for another message—some word from Loren. How could he have forgotten to pick him up again? "For crying out loud. Set an alert, old man."

"Gabe?" Shepherd stood next to him. He passed along the sign-out sheet to another teacher to handle and joined Gabe against the right wall of the gym. Only a handful of students remained, the numbers dwindling by the second.

"What can I do for you, Mr. Shepherd?" Gabe asked knowingly. He kept his eyes on the door.

"No ride home?"

"He's late," Gabe said with a shrug. "It's not unusual."

Shepherd nodded. "Speaking of unusual..." Gabe threw him a look, and Shepherd grinned. "I'm sorry. That was a terrible segueway. It's just..."

Gabe's head lowered. "You want to know more about the stone."

"Is that all it is?" Shepherd shifted closer. "I mean, obviously it's not, but... How does it work?"

"Mr. Shepherd..." Gabe fell silent. He didn't know what to say or how to say it. Hell, he wasn't supposed to say anything at all. Soriya had somehow kept the secret for decades and Gabe barely lasted a year as the protector before being found out.

His teacher ran his hands over his knees. "Okay. How about, why do you have it?"

Gabe lowered his phone. He replaced it with the stone. It sat along his palm, warm to the touch. "It belonged to my parents. And my brother."

"Ah," Mr. Shepherd said. He held out his hand. "May I?"

Gabe closed his fingers around the stone. "I..." Slowly, he let his grasp recede. "Sure. But you can't..."

"Gabe!"

Loren stood at the door. He waved enthusiastically, blocked by the teacher at the door. Gabe almost dropped the stone at the man's sudden arrival. He tucked it away as he stood. Shepherd joined him, his eyes locked on Gabe the entire time.

"It's about time," Gabe said as Loren made his way over.

The former detective wiped sweat from his forehead. "Sorry I'm late. I should set an alarm."

"You really should," Gabe replied.

Loren peered between Gabe and Shepherd as he caught his breath. His eyes widened, waiting for the introduction. When it didn't come, he reached out his hand to the teacher.

"Hey. Greg Loren."

Gabe sighed. "This is Mr. Shepherd. My new history teacher."

Shepherd took the hand, a beaming grin across his face. "Gabe is a gifted student, Mr. Loren. Quite gifted indeed."

Loren cocked an eyebrow at Gabe, whose cheeks flushed at the awkward silence. Reading his reaction, Loren quickly cleared his throat and smiled. "Yes, well, I've always said so." Loren let the man's hand go, then turned to Gabe. "Ready?"

Gabe collected his backpack, strapping it tight over his shoulder. "Please."

A hand fell on his arm. Shepherd nodded to him. "See you tomorrow, Gabe."

"Right," Gabe muttered. "Tomorrow."

He waved and started off. Glancing back, Shepherd continued to watch him intently.

Loren pulled the kid away from the gym for the exit. But Gabe's thoughts returned to Shepherd and his curiosity. He knew the danger of letting the secret of the Greystone out into the world, but Shepherd wasn't some monster hiding in the shadows. He only wanted to help Gabe.

Why shouldn't he share his talent with someone so interested?

CHAPTER FORTY-TWO

Traffic snarled three blocks away from the school. The bombing brought chaos throughout Portents. No one knew which way to travel or what roads were blocked or where emergency vehicles were headed, so no one moved at all through the winding canyons of the Knoll.

It made for an agonizing ride. Silence filled the cabin. Gabe played with his phone, fingers pounding angrily against the screen. Loren tried to find a way in, but his lack of communication over the course of the past few days gave the kid nothing but frustration. It was difficult to penetrate, to say the least.

"Sorry about being so late," Loren said, eyes on the bumper of the car in front of them. "I didn't mean to lose track of the time."

"It's all right," Gabe replied. He dropped his phone into his lap and turned to the window. "Mr. Shepherd kept me company."

"Yeah?" Loren nodded. "He seemed nice. Likes you, at least."

"He's a good teacher."

Loren recalled Gabe's words in the gym. "You said he was your history teacher?"

"Yeah."

"I thought that was Mr. Johnson?" Loren had spoken with the man on the phone when Gabe transferred to the school. Johnson was one of the only teachers to meet the challenge of catching Gabe up with enthusiasm, something he radiated when discussing every aspect of his chosen profession. The rest had certainly offered what help they could, but never with the amount of boundless energy as the history teacher.

Gabe shrugged. "He up and quit."

"Really?"

"Took some new job or something," Gabe said.

Loren's brow furrowed. "Just like that? No notice?"

"No," Gabe answered. "Principal Davis was pissed."

"I bet."

Quiet returned to the car. Loren shifted to the next lane, which appeared to have been moving faster, only to slam on the brake a second later. Gabe stewed in the passenger seat. His arms crossed his chest, and he sank deep into the cushion. Heavy breathing made his mood clear.

Before Loren could inquire, the question already on his lips, Gabe shot up and spoke. "How long do you want to talk about school?"

"What?" Loren exclaimed. "I'm interested."

"*You* spend all day there, then."

"Gabe…"

He spun to greet Loren, fury in his eyes. "There was another bombing. What the hell is going on out there?"

Hands clutched tighter to the steering wheel. Loren kept his focus on the traffic instead of his ward. "We're working on it."

"That's it?" Gabe asked with a scoff. "The pat answer without any elaboration?"

"What do you want from me?"

"Are you kidding me?" Gabe shot back. He slammed his hand against the dash. "How about letting me in on the situation? How about telling me what we can do and how I can help?"

A gap opened in the traffic. Loren spun the wheel. The blinker barely activated before he plunged into the next lane. He slammed on the accelerator, and the car jerked forward. With another spin, they made it to a side street, away from the main road and the snarling that twisted up King's Lane for the RDJ.

"There we go," Loren said with a laugh.

Gabe failed to see the humor in the situation. He continued to stare coldly at Loren. "That's all you've got to say? After ignoring me for the last two days—"

"I wasn't ignoring you," Loren snapped.

"It sure as hell felt like it!" Gabe threw his hands up. "No texts. No information at all from you. On any of it!"

"My phone died!"

"Yesterday!" Gabe shouted. "What's your excuse today?"

Loren made no reply. He continued to drive along the winding back roads of the Knoll for a cross-street to their apartment. Every time he came close, the traffic closed in around them. He cursed under his breath.

"You made me a promise," Gabe said. "Tell me what is going on."

"I…" Two blocks out from their apartment, with no way to get any closer, Loren pulled to the side of the road. He slammed the shifter into park. His head fell against the steering wheel. "I don't know, Gabe."

"Come on!" the kid bellowed with frustration. "How can I prove myself if you won't let me?"

"You don't have anything to prove."

"Then put me in, coach," Gabe said. "I saved the city from that lunatic knight."

Loren's jaw clenched at the reminder. His eyes turned cold. "Your recklessness almost got you killed with that knight, Gabe. Same with the first bombing." He reached out and squeezed Gabe's right arm.

"Ow! What the hell!"

"You want to jump into danger without a second thought, and you want me to be okay with that?"

"I…"

"Well, I'm not!" Loren yelled. "You're going to get yourself killed, Gabe. Is that what you want?"

Gabe settled against the seat. He rubbed his sprained arm. "What I want is to do the job Soriya gave me. The city needs the Greystone."

Loren had always believed the same. For so long, he had turned to Soriya and her incredible power to help Portents—to save it from the worst of the absolute worst. But those were fallen gods and old souls looking for revenge. They were pharaohs and demons and monsters of all sorts that desired nothing but domination and destruction.

No one understood what the current situation was about. No one knew the truth behind the hate and the animosity that filled every soul in the city.

"I don't know what this place needs anymore," Loren said. "Things are changing, Gabe, and I can't seem to stop any of it. I can't help anyone. The only thing I know I can do—that I *have* to do—is keep you safe."

Gabe reeled at the notion. "I don't need you to keep me safe. I can handle things just fine."

"Your arm says differently."

"I fell!" Gabe said with a groan. "I am fine."

"This time!" Loren shouted. His body shook, and he fought to slow the blood rushing through his veins. "You might not see it this way, but everything I do is for your benefit. To protect you. That's the truth. You'll understand why someday."

Gabe stared glumly out the window. "Doubtful."

Loren waited for more. He wanted to explain—about his fear over Gabe and about his terror at watching Portents fall into such chaos—but the words never came. He had to protect the kid. That was the only real job left to him.

Finding answers was the only way to do that.

A loud click woke Gabe from his frustration. The doors of the Impala unlocked.

"What are you doing?"

"I need to let you out here."

Gabe looked around. "I thought we were going home."

"You are," Loren said, unable to meet the kid's confused glare. "I have to check on a lead."

"And if I ask to join you?"

Loren kept his hands locked on the steering wheel. "I'll be back as soon as I can."

Gabe huffed. He pulled the handle hard to release the door, then stepped out into the cold. "Thanks for the trust."

The door slammed, and he started up the block. Loren wanted to call after him, wanted to make things better. They were partners, they truly were, but Loren's fear won out.

He fell against the driver's seat, a hand to his brow. "Dammit."

When was he ever going to get the hang of this relationship? When was he ever going to make the right decision?

Loren put the car in drive and started back the way he had traveled. He knew where he needed to start, even if it was the last place he wanted to go.

CHAPTER FORTY-THREE

"Move. We need to move."

Darius and Christopher raced across the rooftops. Their journey carried them down the Knoll to the Riverside District. No other words were necessary, yet Christopher worried about the growing silence between them. There was an edge to Darius' every movement, an agitation and mounting frustration with the world they inhabited and the roles they played.

Word had just come down from the local precinct. They'd caught the code on their scanner, a recent addition to their nightly ritual. It spoke of an attack, and a family panicked by the situation. As soon as the address hit the airwaves, Darius took off like a shot.

Both recognized the futility of their actions. It was another attack by the dark elves. Their speed and efficiency in the previous kills made any type of pursuit damn near impossible. Darius, though, pressed on like a man possessed. He needed the fight.

Worse, he wanted one.

"Darius," Christopher called after his teacher. "If the police have been notified, there's no way we can make it—"

He stopped. He jabbed a finger against Christopher's chest. "Do not tell me there's no way. With all the might we carry?"

"The stone is not a weapon," Christopher replied. He pushed the accusing finger away. "You should know that better than anyone."

Darius wheeled away, fists clenched at his sides. He didn't care to hear anything that went against his personal beliefs. The Greystone remained a sticking point between them. Its role, the power at their command, and the true purpose behind their actions, continued to be a point of contention.

Christopher sighed, pausing at the rooftop's edge. The call originated from a home on Spruce. They were still six blocks away. Each step might have brought them closer to the incident, but by the time they arrived, the damage would most certainly have been done. They needed to be quicker.

A thought sparked in Christopher's mind. He held up his teacher at the ledge of the building. "The stone may provide some assistance, though," he said. "Take my hand."

Darius hesitated. He had been the Greystone for years before recruiting Christopher. Yet, in all those years, he never pushed the limits of his knowledge of the stone. A weapon was all it was to him. To Christopher, though, there was much more to discover, and he had spent the past two years delving into the abilities locked within the stone.

"What are you thinking?" Darius asked.

Christopher smiled. "This."

The stone lit up and with it, so did the elements of the night. Wind whirled in deep currents, spinning wildly about them. A surge of force lifted the pair off the ground. Christopher took a deep breath, then held out the Greystone. They soared away from the building and out over the street.

"Whoa!"

The wind tunnel kept them confined, but carried them briskly through the Knoll and into the Riverside District.

Darius clutched tighter to his student's cloak. "I see you've been practicing on your own."

Christopher kept his eyes on the task at hand, but couldn't help a smile. "The Bypass has opened new doors for me. If you would slow down, we could explore it more."

Darius turned away, squinting through the wind tunnel.

Christopher sighed. "Are you even listening?"

"Barely."

The smile faded, replaced with a grimace. Christopher hated how obstinate the man could be, especially when the lessons were well within reach. That was the soldier in Darius, always ready for the fight instead of taking a second to find a better way forward.

"That's the house." Darius pointed toward the ground. Glass

spread across the lawn from shattered windows. No lights beamed through the home. Only the streetlamp along the sidewalk alerted them to the shadows scurrying around the property. "The elves are there!"

Without a second thought, Darius let go of Christopher. He fell out of the wind tunnel toward the ground. "Darius, wait!"

But it was too late. His teacher rolled with the impact and launched at the home without so much as a glance back at his student. Four figures raced out the back and along the narrow yard.

Their skin was putrid, their cheeks pitted with black circles that ran in thick rings. Their backs were hunched, their frames small but muscular. Weapons occupied every hand, some with arrows notched along bows and others with chipped blades of bloodied steel.

"Stone bearers!" one shouted at Darius' arrival. He wore a crooked crown, broken in three places and rusted throughout. His stature was clear in the way he carried himself among the others. He raised a sword to his enemies. "Delay them! Our work is done for the night."

"Oh, no, you don't," Darius snarled. He leaped over a swinging blade, then kicked the elf to his left in the face. "Not this time."

Arrows erupted from two more.

"Look out!" Christopher yelled. He dove into the side of his teacher and tackled him to the ground. The arrows crashed through the windows along the rear of the home. Glass fell along the sill, and on top of the pair lying in the grass.

Darius threw off Christopher, jumped to his feet, and raced after the elves. He took out his Greystone, holding it toward them. The elves had reached the back fence of the property.

The crowned leader smirked maliciously. "Too slow, stone bearer."

He dropped a black pouch to the ground. Dust spilled loose. It rose to form a wavering door of darkness against the backdrop of the property's fence. The elves slipped inside the door and vanished.

The remaining dust dropped in their absence. When the last particle fell, the door disappeared.

"Dammit!" Darius kicked at the fence. He slammed his fist into the gate, ripping it from the hinges in his anger.

Christopher joined him, cautious in his approach. He reached out to his friend. "Darius."

"Every time!" His fist arced back, ready to pummel the defenseless gate again. Christopher caught him by the wrist and held firm. A stony glare met Darius. Slowly, he halted, his chest still heaving with frustration.

A nod to the front of the home apprised Darius of their situation. The police had arrived. Christopher let his teacher go and started across the yard. He indicated the shattered second-floor window, not from an arrow attack but from the departure of the dark elves.

Darius followed closely. He took the hint, and the pair jumped to the patio roof to clamber through the window in question.

Both found themselves in a bedroom. Blood marred the doorway; the crimson ran in a broad sweep as if painted on by someone's hand. The dead attested to who had been responsible for the defacement of the white paint on the door frame. She lay half on the bed, with the other half leaning against the frame. A sword jutted from her back.

Her wide eyes caught Christopher's, forcing him to look away.

Darius, though, continued forward. He slipped into the hallway and immediately returned. "More dead. Always more dead."

"Your anger won't help them," Christopher said. Darius wanted nothing more than the fight, one that had been stolen from him. "Darius—"

"You're right," he snapped. He bit into his lower lip, then let out a long breath. "You're right, Chris, I—"

"You're pushing too hard," the student pressed. "Didn't you take the night like I asked?"

"I couldn't." Darius replied. "Not with these monsters out there. I had to—"

"When was the last time you rested, my friend?"

Darius' head fell low. "It's been… difficult. Things with Jayla have been strained, to say the least."

Christopher patted the man on the shoulder. "Go home. Be with your family."

"I can't," Darius said. He peered around the room, unable to tear himself away from the horror. "The work—"

He stopped. Steps approached. Quickly, they ducked out the window and away from the room as a pair of officers took in the scene. Horror filled them at the sight of the dead woman. Quick calls back to the precinct took them from the room and back down the hall.

Christopher started in once more, then paused at the ledge. "The work will still be here after."

Darius hesitated.

"I have this," Chris insisted. "Trust me."

"I do," Darius said. "But I—"

"Go home, my friend. For me."

A slow nod escaped him. "You'll keep me informed?"

Removing an arrow from the wall, Christopher watched the blood drip from the tip. A small vial collected the remnants. "The dark elves came here—to this house—for a reason. Let me figure out why."

"How?"

Christopher knew the answer before the question had even been asked. He'd been avoiding it since joining the fight with Darius. He held up the blood sample. "By visiting the life I left behind."

CHAPTER FORTY-FOUR

A car backfired down the block. The sound, like a gunshot to the brain, caused Thel to jump from her couch. In her haste, her coffee cup slipped out of her hand. It shattered on the floor next to her area rug. Thel snapped her eyes shut at the crash. The few seconds of serenity that came with her hot cup of coffee vanished behind her returning fears.

Thel rushed for the kitchen. She returned with paper towels. Coffee spread across the already worn and warped wooden boards. The towels saturated instantly, yet did little to stem the small stream headed toward the area rug beneath her table. She threw the towels to the ground, disgusted at their ineffectiveness. As she collected the shattered remains of her favorite mug, a knock boomed against the door.

She gasped. Her entire body shook, scattering porcelain pieces in every direction.

"Thel?" a voice called from behind the door.

Her pulse sped up. Her cheeks flushed. Looking around the room, Thel dismissed the mess on the floor with a disgruntled wave and stood. Locks turned under her delicate hands; two deadbolts and a chain released, before she opened the door.

Kellon stood outside. He wore a light jacket, tight to his lean frame. The stubble on his cheeks perfectly suited his renegade appearance. He carried two coffees, the smell filling the entire hallway.

"Thank you for coming," Thel said, shifting to the side.

He entered. "Thank you for calling."

She closed the door, securing the locks immediately. Kellon watched with curiosity. When she finished, he passed along one coffee, which she accepted.

"You sounded distraught." Kellon scanned the room, sipping at his beverage. He noticed the broken cup. "Something happen?"

"Only the usual," Thel replied with a disgruntled sigh. She put her drink down on the table and pointed at the open window. "Everything makes me nervous. I jump at every shadow, every car horn, or screeching tire. This place is all I have left, and even that doesn't make me feel any safer from the world."

Kellon collected the broken shards of the coffee cup. He placed them on the table, then joined her on the couch. "Sounds more like a prison than a sanctuary." He nodded to the locks. "Looks like one too."

She couldn't argue with his comment. The locks had been installed for her protection, but what had they accomplished other than barricading her from the rest of the world? Thel thought things would be different now. She had left the police department in the hopes of a fresh start.

Nothing had changed, though. She was still stuck in place, still fearful of every bump in the night and every shifting shadow across the street. Yardin was still out there. So were his compatriots. Had she really done anything to put them in the past? Or had she merely made herself more vulnerable in her isolation?

Therapy was supposed to help. But she hadn't bothered with group since her last attempt. Nor had she answered Dr. Grace's calls, pushing all thought of another session out of her mind completely.

All that remained was her apartment. Her home. Her so-called happy place. *When was the last time it truly felt that way?* she wondered. A slow nod escaped her. "Maybe it is a prison."

Kellon reached out for her hand. "Come with me."

She pulled away in confusion. "Kellon?"

He continued to the door, unbolting the locks before throwing open the door. Thel stared at the hallway as if it were a foreign country.

"I can't," she said in a mousy voice.

His hand remained open, waiting for hers. "Trust me."

She took the offer, and he led her into the hallway. Instead of heading down to the street, Kellon started up the steps until they reached the roof. He led her into the dim glow of the afternoon sun.

The city spread out before them. From their vantage, they could see for blocks in all directions. Life poured out of shops lining the streets. Music echoed through the canyons, rising from apartments, cars, and businesses alike. Discordant in nature, yet somehow every tune seemed tailor-made for a symphony.

Kellon beamed down at her. "I know you, Thel. You thrived in this city. Against all odds. Against the constant hate and fear thrown against our kind."

Thel closed her eyes. She took a deep, cleansing breath. For a second, the world felt clearer, like it had at the start of her second chance. "I miss it," she said. "That innocence. Or was it ignorance?"

Kellon shook his head. "That's how they want you to feel. The humans. That's how they control you. They take away every choice. All hope. Until you're left isolated and broken."

"Why can't they accept us?"

He squeezed her hands tighter. "We have to make them accept us."

"How?"

Kellon stepped closer, pulling her hands to his chest. She could feel the beat of his heart pounding so fast and loud. "By standing together," he said. "By showing them we have no fear and by pushing back when they bring their hate against one of our own."

His eyes widened, threatening to swallow her whole. She couldn't stop staring, lost in their beauty and the fire that sparked in them when he spoke. "Stand with us, Thel. Stand with me, and this city can be yours again. Your life can be your own again."

The city surrounded her. For too long it had been lost to her, like a separate entity—unknown and terrifying. She missed Portents. She missed herself even more. Thel rested her head against Kellon's chest.

"I'd like that," she said. "I'd like that very much."

CHAPTER FORTY-FIVE

"What the hell have you been doing?"

All eyes fell on Loren. He had bulldozed his way through the pack of bulls at the door and into the cathedral with nothing more than a hard stare and a clenched fist. Anger about the bombings, about the growing silence between him and Gabe, fueled Loren's need. Everyone else read the man's insistence and moved the hell out of his way rather than incur his wrath.

Now he stood in the center of the cathedral, surrounded by the denizens within. Hundreds stopped their chatter, including the trio in their high and mighty seats atop the altar.

Liana looked at him with confusion. "Loren? What are you talking about? We—"

"No," Loren snapped. He waved his hands wildly before him. "Don't play dumb with me." He pointed to the corner. "Except that guy." An ogre held his leg up, trying to pick his nose with his big toe. "I don't think he's playing."

Loren left the image behind, pushing through the throng of creatures in the room for the steps to the altar. His eyes leveled on the Korrigan. "Why was your muscle-bound dwarf at my crime scene today?"

Tusk huffed in defiance. "I go where I want."

"Is that how it is?" Loren shouted for all to hear. "Do you *do* what you want as well? No matter the collateral damage?"

Liana cut him off from approaching Tusk any further. "Loren, we—"

"Tell me, Liana. How many of your people are involved in these attacks?"

Tusk leaped from his chair. He rolled across the altar, then bounded at Loren's leg with claws at the ready. "You dare accuse me?"

Loren met the threat with an icy stare. "I double-dog dare you, you—"

"That's quite enough from both of you." Liana shoved them away from each other. Tusk rushed at her once more, unafraid. She batted him aside. "Tusk. Stop."

The Korrigan huffed. Slow steps carried him away from the conflict and back to his seat. Loren took a satisfied breath, brushing off his shoulders. "Yeah. I don't much care for you either, pal."

"Loren," Liana said calmly.

"He was there," the former detective said. The anger swelled once more; memories of the violence erupting and the blame game roiling through the city permanently seared into his brain. "Which means you're involved somehow."

"We're not."

Loren caught her shifting gaze. He shook his head. "How am I supposed to help you when you won't be honest with me?"

Feore shifted to their side, a soft smile on his face. "He's right. Tell him, or I will."

"No threats, Feore." She moved back to her seat on the altar. "We were investigating the bombings. Same as you."

"You expect me to believe—"

"Tusk," Liana interjected. "Tell him about the building."

The Korrigan grumbled. He snarled his dissatisfaction at their human company. Liana pressed the issue, eyes narrowing on the beast. "Tell him."

A huff of breath escaped his nostrils. He pushed from his chair. "There was a hidden room in the basement. Just like the first site."

"We never found any—"

"There are secrets in this city, Loren," Liana said in a firm voice. "You more than most know that. Both buildings held such secrets."

"How did you find it?"

Tusk scoffed at the man's question. "You think I can't see the truth? You think Tusk is—"

"Our people are quite capable at their tasks," Liana said, cutting off the beast's tirade. "Infiltration is a skill Tusk knows very well."

"You mean breaking into crime scenes?" Loren replied in a low voice. "You could have tainted the entire place with your antics."

"Antics?" Tusk grumbled. "Such a human. Always want to cast

blame instead of learning the truth for yourself."

"What truth is that?"

Liana stepped forward, reaching for Loren. "A golden icon barred the hidden room. When he slipped through the first, Tusk found it to be full of artifacts, both of this world and not."

"Stored like a museum," Tusk said with a grunt. "Weapons even. To be used against our kind."

Each word slammed into Loren. He reeled with each revelation. "You've seen this?"

Tusk nodded.

"Crap."

"You know what this is about?" Feore asked.

"I'm starting to." Loren pinched the bridge of his nose. Just when he thought things were already too complicated, another layer unfolded. "You need to stay here. Out of sight."

"No," Tusk growled. "We have for too long."

"It isn't safe—"

The crowd shifted closer. Anger mounted. Fear, the same held by the human population in Portents, presented in every one of the myths and legends tucked away in their secret alcove.

"It never will be," Liana said. "We asked for your help. Will you give it?"

Loren studied them all. They weren't the only ones to feel terrified over what was happening in the city. Fear burrowed deep beneath his skin—caused by their expectations and his failure to live up to them.

"I can't. Not like this."

"Then we—"

"I need time," Loren pleaded. "This is bigger than you can imagine. Something else is at work here. Give me time. We can figure this out."

"We will," Liana said. "Without you, it seems."

"Liana—"

She turned away, no longer willing to hear his pleas. The Valkyrie wasn't the only one, though. Everyone in the space refused to meet his gaze. They ignored him completely; their previous conversations and mutterings drowned him out.

Tusk grunted happily at the turn of events. His followers did the same, the crew that had been at the scene that morning ready to escort the intruder from the premises.

Before they could, Feore blocked them. "Thank you for trying, Loren."

"I am, Feore. Make them see that."

"I wish I had that gift," the shifter said. "Their pain is too great. Their concerns—"

"Will damn us all." The young man led Loren to the door. He heaved the slab open and the first glimmers of the evening filtered into the space. "I need time."

"They have none left to give."

"Try," Loren said. "The hidden rooms… This is much bigger than we realized."

Feore nodded.

Loren stepped out into the night, a new destination in mind. His thoughts followed him, wondering about the secrets held at the bombing sites. And how much worse things were about to get…

CHAPTER FORTY-SIX

Loren slipped through the cordon. He kept to the shadows of the building as night fell over the city. The area was vacant of pedestrians. Few officers remained at the site. Most had been shifted to the second bombing. Those still on duty were forced to pace impatiently along the barricade. They appeared exhausted from the long shift and the boredom of their task.

With their backs turned to the building, Loren ducked inside. The floor groaned upon his arrival. Warning signs posted outside had done little to deter him, but the sudden shift beneath his feet gave him pause. Glass crunched under his heel and he scurried across the lobby toward the office space he and Gabe had visited. Once away from the entrance, Loren pulled out a small flashlight.

The hole Gabe had fallen through remained. There was no fixing something like that. A ladder, though, had been placed along the edge to allow better access for the open investigation into Michael Hennessey's murder.

Loren climbed down, dropping atop the shattered remains of desks and office equipment. His feet slid from beneath him, but he maintained his balance until the ground stopped shaking. Loren could still picture Gabe, so far down in the hole—lost to the dark—and the body at his side. He tried to push the image aside, the body not weighing into his current concerns. A new wrinkle had been added to the affair, thanks to a Korrigan's involvement. Loren continued down from the refuse to the wall at the rear of the space.

Steps suddenly approached from above. A patrol worked its way through the premises. Loren crept behind some standing debris and turned off his light.

The two officers worked in silence. They scanned the area for signs of life, passing the hole in the floor. One peered inside, running his light throughout the space. Loren held his breath and pressed against the corner to avoid being seen. The other officer nudged his comrade.

"Come on, man," he said. "I don't want the floor to give."

"Lay off the donuts, then," his buddy replied with a laugh.

"Seriously?"

"All right," the man grumbled. "Let's go."

After they rounded the corner, Loren left his cover to resume his search. The back wall was blocked for the most part. A small hole had been dug near the base, just large enough to fit the furry Korrigan.

With Tusk's presence corroborated, Loren set to work. He pulled away the debris, careful not to attract too much attention. He lowered each piece softly to the floor until the wall was finally exposed. Aged brick came into view. Most were almost faded to black, except for a single icon in the middle. A golden image marked the square.

It was of a torch with a flame rising above.

Loren had seen the image on several occasions over the years. Each time had brought nothing but pain and suffering. He groaned at the revelation.

"Why did it have to be them?"

Having seen Soriya interact with the image, Loren knew how to handle the golden glyph. He pushed on the icon and the square settled into the wall. It fell deeper into shadow until a loud click notified Loren of its completion. At the sound, he turned the image of the torch upside down until another click resounded through the subbasement.

The second click triggered an immediate change in the wall. The brick separated, spinning wildly on wheel-covered tracks. Each segment turned inward, then split away from the middle. Behind it, the true wall stood revealed, with the same golden symbol on each side of a lone door.

Loren lowered the handle and pushed. The door gave way, and he entered the hidden space.

The room spread out as far as he could see. Like a massive warehouse, lights came to life at his arrival, snapping on with every step forward. No fail-safes greeted him. No weapons activated at his intrusion. He had visited the library enough over the years to know what to look for and proceeded cautiously.

His caution, though, was unnecessary. Instead of staring at ancient artifacts and shelves filled with otherworldly tomes of knowledge—the collected secrets of centuries—Loren found nothing at all.

Emptiness surrounded him. Scrapes on the floor made it clear there had been something inside recently. A quick departure had stolen away all the treasures hidden inside the space, but by whom and for what reason sparked new questions in Loren. None troubled him as much as the one he'd carried since his visit to the Council of Legends.

"Why did it have to be the Luminaries?"

CHAPTER FORTY-SEVEN

Myers' coat fell to the floor inside the doorway. Her keys jingled loose from the lock, and she tossed them onto the end table next to her. The clattering was louder than she intended, causing her to wince at the sudden sound. Pushing the door closed behind her, the weary detective let out a long breath.

The double shift had taken a toll. Tragedy after tragedy slammed into her in a never-ending train of defeat. Thel. The bombing. Another dead body. Another damn mystery yet to be explained. It was all too much.

She wanted a bath. Her clothes smelled of ash from the advertising firm explosion. Her time at the morgue certainly hadn't helped in that regard. Every time she breathed, there was a mix of death and decay with an unhealthy dose of charred paint. She might as well have taken up smoking. Things probably would have felt the same.

The bath, while more than a tempting reprieve from the world, was too much work. Hot water was a precious commodity in her building. The pipes were a disaster in the winter months, and she couldn't handle another disappointment.

Instead, Myers wandered the single room apartment while looking at her phone. She rounded the bed to the tune of multiple notifications filling her screen. Calls had come through during her trek home. She'd turned off the damnable device for a moment's peace. Why she bothered escaped her, since now she had to review everything she'd missed.

Accessing her voicemail, Myers waited for the robotic voice to drone through the number and length which seemed to carry on for decades rather than seconds. During the span, she removed a pair of beers from the fridge and an opener from the neighboring drawer. Both caps flipped off to the floor below as Haya Cho's voice filled her ear.

The words were lost behind the young woman's enthusiasm. The device at New You had been intact—more so than the previous crime scene. Cho, clearly in her element, listed the components collected so far and how they connected. Everything went over Myers' head. The technician still had plenty of work ahead of her, and enough caffeine in her bloodstream to handle it. Myers deleted the message, knowing the information would most likely be repeated word-for-word the next time they spoke.

She moved for the couch and settled on the cushion. Myers instantly regretted passing along her stench to the fabric. Too exhausted to stand back up, she took a long swig from the first beer, placing the second on the table beside her keys. There were no more messages waiting for her, but other calls had come through.

Loren's name topped the list.

Myers started to dial him immediately. Before the first ring, she stopped herself and ended the call. "What am I doing?"

Their time together as partners had been so limited—her fault—and this was a second chance to do it right. That was reason enough for the callback, wasn't it? To share information about the case? But that wasn't the whole reason, and she realized it the second she let the phone fall away from her ear.

He made her better somehow. Something about having him back in her life, on the job again, made her want to be more... and to have more.

The emptiness of her apartment surrounded her. Bullet holes still filled the wall near the small balcony. A few dotted her bed frame as well. The television was old, a tube-style on its last legs. Everything was minimal and easily abandoned, the same way she had always looked at the world.

It was the only way she knew how to live. Even with Ruiz's trust in her as Head Detective, and after everything she had been through during her time in Portents, Myers still waited for her world to crash down around her. She wondered if it would be today that the government would burst through her door to take her away for her past crimes. Or if it would be someone closer to home.

Myers took a long swig of her beer. She swiped the remnants away from her lips, then settled into the cushion of the couch.

Those days were supposed to be behind her. Those thoughts, and the life she had known, were only memories now. They weren't who she wanted to be.

She wanted a life.

The notion brought a smile to her face. Life was for other people. Myers understood that better than most. Life was not something she deserved for what she had done, for the lies and the duplicity, yet she yearned for it all the same.

And for some reason—another mystery, to be sure—Loren was the cause.

CHAPTER FORTY-EIGHT

Machines hummed in the background. Christopher set to work analyzing the blood samples taken from the crime scenes involving the dark elves. There was something to their targets, some connection they had yet to stumble upon, and he knew the blood was the key to unlocking those answers.

Darius had been no help in that regard. If he couldn't punch the problem away, he offered little in the way of solutions. He saw the dark elves as nothing more than a pestilence to be wiped from existence instead of a mystery to solve.

There was more to the man's impatience, though, and it stuck with Christopher. His teacher was floundering. The pressures of his role against the burden of his family started to develop cracks that would only widen. He hoped Darius would take his advice as well as some time to reconnect with Jayla. Marissa rated that much, at least. The four-year-old deserved a childhood away from the monsters in the dark and the craziness that came with the Greystone.

If only Darius had walked away like Christopher had.

It wasn't that simple, though, was it? No matter how much a person ran from their life, it was always right there waiting. The past sat in the rearview mirror, always looking on and ready to chime in during the quiet that dominated the late hours of the night.

How else could he explain his return to Portents University? It had been a rational solution to their need—a space where Christopher could work with the blood samples to find the connection needed and end the threat of the dark elves once and for all. Yet, even in the confines of the lab, with the equipment whirring behind him and the lecture hall spread before him, Christopher felt like he had never truly left at all.

The classroom was not his own, and the lab equipment was certainly not something he had any familiarity with, but the lecture hall pulled him right back into the past. He could hear the shuffling of feet, the paging of books and the scratching of chalk on the board. Questions rose from the audience, always intelligent observations, because he had always demanded the best from those in his class. So many fond memories permeated the lecture hall, so many days spent educating and reveling in the attainment of knowledge.

A loud beeping brought him back to his work. He left behind the rows of desks and the spirit of days long since passed for the lab equipment. The humming faded behind the alert, a red light beaming at his approach. Christopher opened the centrifuge to read the error message on the screen. The vials were still intact but rattled around within the confines of the device. He plucked them clear, then attempted to restart the process.

Buttons clicked under his fingers. None, though, activated the device. Only the beeping returned, this time louder and brighter, as if his every move went against the machine's wishes.

Christopher took a step back, fists ready to unleash hell on the centrifuge. It wasn't the device's fault, but his own. He should have reached out and asked for help. There were plenty he could have turned to in his previous life. Now, though, he stood alone. He carried the weight of his task without aid and without complaint. It was better that way... for everyone.

He carefully approached the centrifuge once more. Steady hands inserted the vials into their proper alignment. He activated the device only to have the machine hum once before silencing. His fist shot up, all patience gone from the long night.

Behind him, the lights of the lecture hall clicked on. The door closed and steps cautiously approached.

"Hello?" a voice called out.

Christopher ducked into the shadows. The figure took the stairs of the lecture hall slowly. Wary eyes peered into the blackness of the lab at the rear of the expansive room. The eyes looked older than Christopher remembered. So did the man himself—tired and exhausted.

Time had not been kind to Henry Erikson.

"Is someone there?" his old colleague asked. He clutched his bag like a weapon.

Christopher raised his hands and stepped into the light. "Hello, Henry."

CHAPTER FORTY-NINE

Astonishment filled Henry's face. He rushed down the remaining steps, his bag clattering against his side. He reached the front desk and slammed his belongings on the surface. Weary eyes scanned the intruder in the room, but held no animosity at the intrusion, only an elation that came from memory.

"It is you," Henry said. "I thought my eyes were playing tricks on me."

Their past beamed from every stray glance and every smile. They had been the closest of friends at one time, sharing meals on campus and discussing the intricacies of university politics. Enthusiasm for the curriculum and the student body had made the relationship easy, one of the few that ever felt that way to Christopher. He had been sad to let it slip away when he left his previous life behind.

"It's good to see you, Henry."

Age defined the man's appearance. Only two years had passed, yet for Henry, they had clearly been unkind. Deep wells swallowed the light from his eyes and his skin appeared pale. The man's smile, though, was exactly as Christopher always remembered it.

"I sincerely doubt that," Henry replied. He wagged a finger at the man, scanning his work area with mounting curiosity. "If you truly wanted to see me, you wouldn't be skulking through my little kingdom here. What are you working on?"

Christopher chuckled. "Just like that?"

"Better to help than have you wreck my equipment," Henry said. "There won't be a replacement the way the budget keeps shrinking around here."

Christopher led him to the lab in the back of the room. He removed the blood samples from the centrifuge and passed them over. Henry eyed the vials carefully.

"A blood comparison," Christopher explained. "I need to know if there are any similarities."

"I won't even ask where they came from. How's that for service?"

Henry set to work without another word. He bypassed the centrifuge completely, the device incorrect for the task at hand. A smug comment sat on his lips, but he kept it to himself. Under delicate hands, an entirely different series of machines came to life. No alerts sounded. No errors registered. The humming of flow cytometers and hematology analyzers took over. A readout ran along the computer screens attached, processing the results from the machines.

"You look well," Christopher said, retreating to the lecture hall.

Henry, his task completed for the moment, joined him. "Another lie. I could do the same, but you haven't changed a bit. Dog-tired and determined to a fault." He rested his hands on the desk, letting his fingers spread wide. He let out a long breath. "This is about the stone, isn't it?"

"Yes."

"And Lynn?" Henry asked. "What does she have to say about it all?"

Christopher's gaze fell away from his friend. "I haven't seen... I left, Henry. I haven't seen Lynn in some time."

Sad eyes met his. Henry reached out and patted the man's arm lightly. "I'm sorry to hear that."

Christopher cleared his throat, swallowing the sorrow of the past. "There are larger concerns at the moment."

"Of course," Henry said. He let go of his friend and shuffled away from the desk. "I'll check on the samples."

"Thank you."

Henry entered the lab. Christopher let the silence fill the room. He pushed from the desk, rounding it in a large loop through the lecture hall. All the old questions came back on him. His choices. His sacrifices.

Darius had approached him in a room like this to handle a troublesome case—a monster which had woken in the city. The lore was in Christopher's wheelhouse, as the situation centered on a literary ghost of some renown.

A misguided student had discovered an original draft of Shakespeare's *A Midsummer Night's Dream* and reawakened the spirit of the actual Puck. Instead of a mischievous sprite, the fairy had turned his vengeful eye toward murder.

Christopher had joined in the hunt and learned of a new world as a result, one far bigger than any the professor had ever imagined. The true city revealed itself. And when his investigation led to finding a Greystone of his own?

He took out the stone. The ancient item held so many questions, the answers still elusive after all this time. They were the mysteries of the universe—of life itself. Christopher was sure of it and took to the role wholeheartedly.

There was no looking back after that.

He continued to do so, however. His time at the university meant something, too. The lives he'd impacted mattered, even if it hadn't felt like it every day. There had been joy and pain and longing and wonder. So many emotions mixed up and swirling with every inhalation of the past.

When he rounded the room for the desk once more, Henry was waiting. Pensively, he watched Christopher move across the open space. "Remembering better days?"

"I don't know if I would call them better. Simply different."

"You miss it?" He approached slowly, pointing to the stone in Christopher's grasp. "Not as much as you would the stone. I see that. It..."

Henry reached for the stone. Before he could touch it, Christopher pulled it away. "Henry..."

He gaped at the obol with exuberant eyes. "I can almost feel the energy inside—that glow I only saw for a split-second once. If I could just analyze it..."

"No, Henry," the former professor said. He tucked the Greystone in his cloak. "The stone can be a burden. And a terrible danger."

"Of course, I—" A beep interrupted Henry's apology. His eyes remained locked on Christopher's pocket for a long moment, then he shook his head. The smile returned, and he nodded toward the back of the room. "That would be your results."

Quick steps led them to the waiting devices. Printer paper flew free as the results shot out into the resting tray beneath. Henry retrieved the documents. He passed them along without a single glance.

Christopher took them in hand. His eyes scanned the blood analysis and widened with each word read. "I knew it."

"Christopher?"

He tucked the printout away. A gentle hand reached out to Henry and squeezed the man's shoulder. "It was good to see you."

"Chris—"

He was already at the steps, moving for the door. "Take care of yourself."

"I will," Henry called after him. "But you—"

The lights clicked off. Henry rushed to the second set behind his workstation. When the lights returned, the lecture hall was empty.

Christopher hid in the darkened hall, his body pressed against the back of the door. He wanted to linger, to hold on to the memory of the past with his dear friend, for only a moment longer.

The blood analysis overpowered all nostalgia. The past would only hold him back.

His hand grazed the door before he started out into the night. "Goodbye, old friend."

CHAPTER FIFTY

An eerie silence filled the block around New You Advertising. Stationed patrols had been given a break, their replacements held up by last-minute changes. All had been directed by Ruiz to allow him access to the building. He needed answers, to see the situation clearly without the lies and deflection offered so far. His company, though, was reticent to join him on his scavenger hunt.

"We shouldn't be here," Leslie said, trailing him to the cordon. "If we're seen—"

"The site is empty for the next hour," Ruiz replied without looking. He refused to slow down. "I made sure of it."

"You still don't believe me, Ruiz?"

"I'd like to see it for myself." His eyes narrowed on her. He slipped through the barricade, a hand waving her forward. "You coming or not, Leslie?"

She grumbled under her breath. Reaching the building, she took the lead. The lobby fell behind them quickly, as did the steps to the basement. No damage was visible from their position outside the lone office, and Ruiz looked around curiously.

"The blast seems to have been contained upstairs," he said as Leslie continued down the corridor. "Like they weren't even trying to hide the body."

"Maybe they weren't. But they were trying to hide this."

She stood before the back wall. Boxes surrounded her, but a narrow path was available that ended before the off-white plaster. In the right corner, centered on the wall, was the Luminary glyph in gold. Leslie pushed it deep into the recesses of the structure until it clicked.

The wall lifted. Like an overhead door, with tracks on the sides and wheels attached, the false front vanished above them until the actual wall stood revealed. It was red brick, with two matching glyphs around a single door. She opened it and stepped inside.

"This way." Stairs unfolded below. They wound deep into the thick black. Ruiz removed a flashlight from his pocket to light the way. Leslie didn't bother, this time waving *him* along.

Their journey brought them down multiple levels, another hidden subbasement like that of the Whistler Building. How had the Luminaries been able to accomplish so much without anyone knowing? The arrogance behind their secrets galled Ruiz. He couldn't stand the joy he perceived from Leslie with each new twist and turn.

At the bottom of the stairs, another door waited. Leslie turned the knob and pushed it loose. A hallway opened up for them. Lifted tiles, each one marked with a unique symbol, spread across the floor. All led to an archway at the opposite end, shrouded in darkness.

"Watch your step." Leslie entered the hall slowly. She skipped the first row of tiles for the second.

"Why?" Ruiz asked, not watching her movements. He was too busy scanning the walls with his flashlight. "There's no evidence our bomber was even here. This place doesn't appear any worse for wear and—"

The floor gave way beneath his foot. Ruiz fell through, dropping his flashlight into the pit beneath him.

"Whoa!"

His hands caught the edge of the tile. The hole widened as the floor continued to collapse, and his right hand slipped into the open air. He shifted for a better grip, panic in his eyes. Below, the flashlight whirled around in the darkness during its descent. With every rotation, metal glinted below. Spikes rose from the true floor of the corridor.

"What the hell?" Ruiz muttered, struggling to pull himself up. *A death trap in an advertising firm? Great.*

"I told you, Ruiz," Leslie said, reaching down to him. She grabbed his hand and lifted him to the safety of the neighboring tile. "Watch your step."

Relief filled him when he felt solid ground again, though he took that with a grain of salt, considering what he had just seen. Ruiz made his way to his feet and dusted off his clothes.

"How about we forgo the ominous warnings and speak plainly

from now on?"

Leslie smirked. She held up a finger. "Stay here, then."

"Leslie—"

Her hand pressed against his chest when he started to follow. "Stay. Here."

Ruiz relented. He watched her move through the corridor. Methodical steps took her along the right-hand wall for one tile, then back to the left for another in a jumping game until she reached the end. The shadows dominating the far side of the corridor enveloped her. A loud crash echoed around him, and he moved to cover his ears.

Leslie returned to the light. "There," she said, moving without concern. "It should be safe now."

Ruiz stared at his feet. "Should be?"

"It is," Leslie shot back in exasperation. "Come on."

He slid his foot onto the next tile and let it settle for a long moment. When the floor failed to give way beneath him, he continued, each advancement progressively quicker than the last until he joined her. She led him down the corridor and through the archway. To the right was the switch she had thrown to deactivate the trap. Beyond that, a door lay along the ground, shattered and broken.

"What?" Ruiz passed over the door into the wide room on the other side. The space opened up in every direction. Everything was charred. Shelves were blasted against the outer walls. Books upon them were scorched tatters, pieces of which still wafted through the air like leaves in the wind. Fused glass crunched beneath their steps—the display cases and contents all destroyed.

Nothing had survived.

"What happened here?"

"A second device," Leslie explained. "The one above was a distraction to hide the true target."

"What was in here?" Ruiz circled the space. His steps were guarded, not wanting a repeat of the death trap he'd barely escaped.

"Historical records," Leslie said, following him closely. "Rare artifacts, never to be seen again in this world."

Nothing escaped undamaged. Pieces of history—singular in nature—had been utterly destroyed.

"Still don't believe us?"

"I believe you," Ruiz said with a slow nod. "I believe you."

"We considered this one of our safe houses." Leslie lifted a charred and twisted piece of metal, then let it fall away with a clang. "That term should obviously be revised."

"How many others?" Ruiz asked, staring at the damage wrought. "How many more places like this are out there? How many more potential targets do we need to worry about?"

"More than a dozen. All substantially larger and more important than this one." Sadness filled her every word. What surrounded them might have appeared to be nothing more than secrets to Ruiz, but to Leslie it had been the work of a lifetime—probably several considering the storied history of the Luminaries. "We need to move everything. Hide it until the bomber is caught and the danger is passed."

"*We*," Ruiz said, mockingly. "You mean me."

"This maniac knows us," Leslie snapped with frustration.

Ruiz nodded. "You think an outsider might trip him up."

"I do."

"I'm sure it helps to have the Police Commissioner coordinating and securing your goods."

Leslie grinned. "The thought may have crossed my mind."

He glared at her. "I don't appreciate being used."

"I don't appreciate seeing unique treasures destroyed out of some senseless game," Leslie shot back.

"If that's what it is. This seems more personal and much better planned."

"Which only increases our urgency."

Ruiz scanned the devastation. More than a dozen more targets were littered throughout his city, all waiting for their chance to add to the chaos already spreading in Portents. Something had to be done. "I'll prepare security arrangements. It will be a small, tight loop. Only a few people involved to keep word from leaking out."

"My people will gather everything we can for transport." Leslie started for the door.

Ruiz grabbed her arm. "It will take time. A few days."

Cold eyes stared back at him. "You have three, Ruiz. I won't risk any longer. Not with what's at stake."

It didn't leave him much time. He wished Michelle was with them, someone who might make the situation clearer. Yet all he saw was chaos. There was only one way to stop it from getting worse.

Reluctantly, Ruiz agreed. "Three days."

CHAPTER FIFTY-ONE

Thel stood before a two-story building on the Upper West Side. The roar of downtown rang out, the proximity to the Red-Light District close enough to smell the booze in the air. The wafting scent of cigarette smoke carried on the breeze.

Though only a few blocks away, there was peace along the street. Few pedestrians wandered as the hour grew late, the old rules still influencing at least some of the citizenry.

A FOR SALE sign sat on the front lawn. It was faded from age, the grass overgrown and crawling up the wooden post to the base of the sign. Toys were strewn across the lawn and up the narrow driveway. Pallets and a rusted-out mower were tucked close to the home.

Shutters beat against the siding. Windows were covered from the inside, the glass cracked in multiple places. The weakest breeze brought out the creaks and groans of the porch, the wood all but rotted through.

"This is it?" Thel asked, suddenly worried about her decision to join Kellon.

He smirked. "What were you expecting?"

She didn't know. There were no rules for clandestine meetings with strange men and their groupies. Thel, though, had pictured a cool hideout with fancy chandeliers and goth dress—music blaring throughout and the revelry of freedom in everyone's actions.

Kellon nudged her forward, then started for the side door. "We can't exactly own property, Thel. Most of us are freaks and monsters, unable to even step foot in the workplace without causing chaos. So, signing a rental agreement is kind of tough for us."

"So, you're squatters?"

"Unfortunately," Kellon said with a shrug. "We've found several properties throughout the city. Portents has been a mess since the Cerberus attack, so we've been lucky to find some homes with working water, even cable in some cases. None of them are the Ritz, but they serve our needs. This is the one we picked for tonight."

He opened the door, holding the screen for her. Thel hesitated at the threshold.

Kellon read the look on her face. "This next step has to be yours, Thel. No one can give you your life back. You have to be willing to take it. Can you do that?"

"I want to."

"Show me," Kellon said. He entered the home, then turned back. He offered no hand inside, only a watchful eye.

Thel stared at him and the darkness beyond. She lifted her foot until it settled on the step. The door slammed shut behind her the second Thel entered the home.

Kellon led her down the corridor. Dirty clothes and flattened boxes occupied the floor along the walls. Cleaning supplies, long past their expiration dates, rested on shelves leading to the basement. Kellon took her down the hall and into the kitchen on the first floor. Shadows danced beneath the door frame; her host's guests were clearly present and waiting for their arrival.

"We don't like to gather like this most of the time," Kellon said. "Too much of a target. But I've asked some friends to stop by and say hello." He opened the door and ushered her through. "Let me introduce you."

Dozens were crammed in the tight quarters of the living space. They bled out into what must have been a dining room at one point, but had been turned into a wasteland of secondhand furniture. The second the door opened, every shift on the floor ended. All eyes fell on Thel.

Two men with ram horns and golden eyes stood beside a group of women covered head-to-toe in black feathers. Their sharp beaks pecked at the small scraps of food they carried. Everywhere Thel gazed, there was a new myth to view. Monsters of old—a Cyclops who towered over the rest of them—mingled with the more brazen cat creatures, who licked themselves delicately in the corner.

"There are so many," Thel breathed.

Kellon nodded. "And more every day. Most can't walk the streets like we can. Their origins isolate them from the world.

We're going to change that."

Demons brushed by, followed by their angel brethren. Or so they appeared. Thel had little in the way of knowledge when it came to the otherworldly legends in Portents. Her encounters had been limited to the criminal class, yet had they truly been criminals or merely downtrodden and broken as she had become?

Each of them wanted nothing more than respect among their peers—a chance to live in peace as Thel had wanted. She beamed at Kellon with wishful eyes. "You make it sound so easy."

He took her hand, leading her through the crowd. "Together, we can change everything. Thel, you can change everything."

"Me?" Hopeful stares followed her every step. They saw something more in her, something she no longer understood. "I... I haven't felt that way since..."

"I know," Kellon said. He grinned at the others. They slowly backed away, creating a sizeable gap in the center of the room where a lone chair sat, empty. "That's why I have a gift for you."

"A gift?"

The back door opened. Filling the frame stood an ape-man in a tight suit. The floor groaned under his weight.

Kellon moved for the newcomer. "This is Shin."

The ape bowed. "A pleasure."

"Do you have him?" Kellon asked. Shin nodded, teeth protruding from his lips. Kellon clapped loudly. "Excellent. Bring him in."

The ape departed immediately, but the door remained open. Outside, the wind howled. It called to Thel, but she remained locked in place. The rabbit's foot made its way into her hand, and she rubbed the small toy between her fingers.

"Kellon, I don't understand," she said in a low voice. The hopeful stares of their company grew ravenous. Their presence made her uncomfortable.

"You will." Kellon sidled next to her and squeezed her nervous fingers. "Trust me."

Shin returned a second later. Caught in his enormous hands was a man, bound and wearing a black hood over his head. The ape prodded the captive forward, then settled him roughly upon the chair. When the man fought against the seat, Shin's hands slammed against his shoulders to lock him in place.

"Kellon?" Thel stared at the figure, struggling in the seat.

Her host's gaze grew wide with excitement. "Take off the

hood."

Shin obeyed without a word. The hood fell to the floor. Sitting in the chair was a gagged and frightened David Yardin.

CHAPTER FIFTY-TWO

Yardin screamed through the gag. He kicked at the ground, shuffling the chair between the front and back legs. Shin kept him locked in position, his hands tightening against the officer's shoulder. Yardin wore his uniform, though blood now stained the collar. Smears of crimson ran across the badge on his chest.

The thick cloth wedged between his lips muted his cries. Thel, though, heard them clearly. She spun toward Kellon, ripping her hand free from him. "What is this? Kellon, what did you do?"

"We know what he did to you."

Yardin tried to stand, his defiance palpable. Shin pulled him back to the chair. A low growl escaped the ape. Sweat mixed with a spray of saliva from the beast, and Yardin relented.

"How?" Thel asked. "I haven't told anyone. How did you—"

"He had friends," Kellon explained. "Shin heard some of them bragging about it. They won't be bragging anymore."

Shin's teeth glinted in the dim light of the room.

Kellon stepped in front of him. He reached for Thel, but she reeled away, barely able to look at him. All she saw was Yardin. All she heard was his hate. Fear rippled through her. And now, to know more had been injured at Shin's hands? She worried about reprisals, the shadow on the street always present in her mind.

"Kellon..."

"He beat you, Thel," the wolfen seethed. Hair sprouted from his pores, and soft eyes of blue turned cold and yellow. The beast took over from the handsome man, yet his words still carried the same influence. "He took away the life you spent months building. All because of his fear. Because of a hatred his kind will never overcome. Not until they are made to see the cost of such hate."

Thel paced the confines of the room. The others in the room

surrounded her every move. They were nothing but spectators, but all pressed for her to face the man in the chair—the man who had stood in the way of her happiness. They prodded her along, urging her to act as if they couldn't until she did.

She shook her head at them all. The consequences of their actions weighed her down and the old terror filled her. She clutched her rabbit's foot, wishing Sam stood at her side... wishing she had told her partner the truth.

"I..."

"You don't have to be afraid anymore," Kellon said. "Reclaim what was always yours and never his."

"Kellon, I..."

"Face him, Thel," Kellon pressed. "You have to face him."

She took a sharp breath. Her entire body shook with each step across the room until she stood before the chair and the bound officer. Her hand carefully removed the gag from his mouth. She dropped it to the floor.

"David," Thel said in a weak voice.

"Well?" Yardin called. He pounded against the chair. "What are you doing? Let me go."

Thel backed away from him. His voice echoed in her thoughts. His hatred filled every word, his disgust at who she was—or at least, who she had been—dripping like bile from his tongue.

"Untie me, Thel," he continued. "We can forget what happened. We can forget—"

"Forget?" she said, eyes shaking. "How can I forget? It's all I think about."

She turned away from him.

The others in the room shifted closer. At their approach, Yardin lifted from the chair. He was immediately sent back against the wood by Shin's immense hands.

"Let me go, you freaks!" Yardin wailed. "None of you belong here. This isn't your city!"

"It will be," Shin replied, his growl only a whisper, yet boomed through the room.

"Right, Thel?" Kellon asked. "This is our chance. This is your chance."

Thel took a deep breath. A slow nod escaped her.

Kellon held out a hand. A long-handled knife rested against his palm. "Show him."

Thel squeezed her rabbit's foot. She closed her eyes, listening to the beat of her heart as it pounded in her ears. It was joined by the thrumming of every foot within the room.

All waited for her to act. Their anticipation was palpable. As was their hope. They dreamed of the start of a new day—no longer forced to hide from the world.

Yardin laughed. "What can she show me? She's nothing. Nothing but a scared—"

A scream erupted from Thel. She tossed the rabbit's foot away—her connection to her former life lost in an instant—and took hold of the knife with both hands. The steel beamed under the lights, reflecting her wild eyes back at her.

She raised the knife and brought it down on the bound Yardin. It sliced into his chest, buried to the hilt. Ripping it out, Thel drove the blade into the shocked Yardin again and again. Steel cut through his uniform and deep into his flesh. With each release, blood spurted over her hands and across her jacket. Crimson sprayed her face, obscuring her vision. With a sharp scream, Thel buried the knife into the man's heart and held it there.

A gurgle escaped Yardin. Dead eyes greeted Thel. He tried to fall from the chair, but Shin kept him there, mesmerized by her assault.

Slowly, Thel pulled the blade from the dead man. Blood ran in a long stream from the steel. Kellon took it from her and passed it along to another near the kitchen door.

Thel's chest heaved. A tingling sensation shot through her body like electricity. Yardin was dead by her hand. She had crossed a line, one she hadn't since her return to the world. Everything crystalized around her. She saw it in the faces of the myths surrounding her and the charged stares of Kellon and Shin.

Stepping away from Yardin's body, Thel looked at Kellon with fresh eyes. For the first time in what felt like forever, they were wide awake.

"That power? That's freedom," Kellon said, pointing to the dead man in the chair. "How does it feel, Thel?"

"Good," she said. "Really good."

CHAPTER FIFTY-THREE

"The blood was the key."

Christopher circled his teacher on the cold rooftop in downtown Portents. His cloak billowed around him with each movement, his hands dancing before him as he spoke. A long day of research had come to a head at last.

"The victims belong to the same bloodline. The second I understood that, I knew where I had to go. I started with the first victim—Frederick Jannik. He had lived alone, the place locked up tight. Everyone said he'd been reclusive, almost afraid. When I went back to look at the scene more deeply, I found out why."

Christopher removed the journal from his cloak. He held it before him. Darius made no move for it, lost on the city below.

"He wrote about the encounter," Christopher continued. "During a hunt, Frederick stumbled into a cave in Rose Riley Forest. Seeking shelter from a storm, he moved deeper into the structure, only to find a second exit. This one did not reveal any storm at all, only the peace of the evening. He had crossed realms, a hidden door to another place. The trees were black, the flowers glowing like stars. They hung like vines from their stalks, and Frederick had to brush through them to see the path ahead clearly.

"In his confusion, he had forgotten about the rifle in his grasp. When he came upon one of the residents of the realm unexpectedly, he cried out. The weapon went off, killing the creature that had startled him. A dark elf."

Christopher's words grew stronger as the story left him faster and faster. "He had been in Svartalfheim, the land of the dark elves. And his victim had not been some random elf. Why would it ever be that simple? The elf Frederick killed had been royalty in one form or another. His crown fell when he did and rolled into the hands of his son.

"Darius, the king's son had been with him.

"Frederick fled, but not before the boy had seen him. Not before he'd looked into that child's eyes and knew, without a doubt, he had just condemned himself to death.

"Frederick returned to the cave and his life, but it was never the same. He never told anyone, not his family, not his friends. He simply cut himself off. The boy, however, never forgot. He's come through the cave or some other door, and is unleashing hell on Frederick's entire bloodline. Cousins, children, and grandchildren. All have been hunted down and slaughtered.

"The elves have been seeking revenge."

Darius continued to loom over the ledge, staring down at the street. "Haven't we all?"

Christopher joined him. Below, restaurants dominated the block. The hour was still early enough to see a crowd of pedestrians walking to and from the establishments, the sweet aroma of food permeating the air. The former professor eyed the area with curiosity, all directed toward his silent companion.

"Darius?" he called. "Are you all right? Did you get any sleep?"

His eyes were bloodshot. His knuckles were bruised and raw. The stench of sweat wafted from him. "Couldn't," Darius said. "Wandered the city."

Christopher showcased the man's injuries. "Looking for trouble?"

"Looking for peace," his teacher snapped. He shifted away, across the length of the building to the corner. "I found none."

"Is that why we're here?"

"No," Darius replied coldly. "We're here for answers."

He stepped off the rooftop and dropped to the street below. Christopher rushed to the spot, alarms blaring in his mind. Darius fell like a comet into the alley, where he landed without a sound.

Christopher peered down the lane. Time was moving against them. They needed to act soon, or the vengeful elves would claim more victims. Once Frederick's family fell, would the violence truly end? Could revenge satisfy the hole left in the wake of the father's death? Or would the son lash out at another family in the city and then another, unable to quell the anger in his heart?

Christopher hated the truth he knew to be so clear in the way the victims had been laid out—slaughtered wholesale without mercy. He sighed, then followed Darius into the dark.

By the time he landed, Darius was already gone. He walked through the pedestrians, across the street, where he stopped before the large picture window of an Italian restaurant named Decanter.

"Darius..." Christopher kept his voice low and calm. "I gave you the answer. We know where the elves will strike next. It is the last of the bloodline. A family of four. They live on Witmer, not far from here. We should head there before—"

"We will," Darius interrupted without looking. He watched the innocents enjoying their meal. Then, just as abruptly, Darius snatched Christopher by the arm and dragged him away from the window and down to the end of the building.

Christopher freed himself from the tight grip, aghast. "What has gotten into you?"

A grimace spread across the face of his teacher. "I saw her leave," he snarled. "The neighbor was watching Marissa, and she... I had to know."

"What?" Christopher asked, confused. "What do you—"

Darius ducked into the alley behind the restaurant, once more pulling Christopher along.

"Hey!"

"Quiet." Darius tucked close to the wall, his hand locking his student in place beside him.

Two shadows passed the alley. They held hands, their laughter carefree and boisterous. The woman tucked close to the man's side, head nestled against his arm.

They headed for the end of the block. Darius moved to watch them depart. "I had to know... and now I do."

"Jayla," Christopher said, head bowed in shame.

Darius nodded. "With another man."

CHAPTER FIFTY-FOUR

"I have to stop this."

Darius took one step toward his wife and her lover. Christopher grabbed the man's arm and yanked him back into the alley.

"Darius…"

He spun around, reeling from Christopher's touch. Leading with his arm, Darius slammed his student against the alley wall. With each frenzied breath, Darius pressed tighter and tighter. He seethed with anger. "She's my wife."

"Accosting them in the street is not how to handle this. Talking things out with Jayla—"

"My wife, Chris." His eyes weren't even on his student. His every thought was on the pair departing the street. Darius' wife with another man. With each thought of them, the broken husband took out his rage by pushing harder on Christopher's chest. "How can you not understand?"

"I understand only too well," Christopher said. He attempted to work his way free, the brick digging into his back. At the effort, Darius' eyes went wide. He lowered the arm across Christopher's chest and raised his fist, ready for the fight he had been searching for all day. His chest heaved and sweat dripped along his brow.

Christopher opened his hands, head lowered in submission. "I'm not going to fight you."

Darius hesitated, his fist hovering in the air. Then he let it fall. His shoulders slumped, and he started once more for the mouth of the alleyway.

Christopher rubbed at his chest as he settled along the concrete. He had never seen Darius so lost before. He was nothing like the man he had come to know—the warrior, the protector. Now, Darius was just a man looking to fix something that had shattered long, long ago.

Cautiously, Christopher moved toward his teacher. "We chose this life over all others. We set the path, and only we can be made to walk it. I knew the cost. Now you do, too."

It was a hard thing to say. Truthfully, it was harder to watch. For so long, Christopher wondered if he'd made the right choice in walking away from his life. He had been happy with Lynn, and then, when his daughter arrived, things only became better. His family was the light of his world. They tempered the storm clouding his thoughts in the dark, the swirling chaos always begging him to do more or be more.

When the opportunity came, though, Christopher took it. Darius had opened his eyes to another world within their own. Lynn wouldn't have understood. She couldn't. Her life was about movie nights and family dinners—vacations and sporting events. Their two paths diverged at that moment. Perhaps they always had, yet he'd fought against it for the sense of normality he'd believed necessary to live a full and meaningful life.

The darkness never suited their lives. Christopher refused to allow it in, not at the risk of losing his wife and daughter to some beast, some killer he had not been prepared to face. Walking away was the only answer.

Maybe it was always the only answer.

The Greystone made any level of connection impossible. Constant pain and death, murder and mayhem, threatened Portents. There would always be some new monster in the night to worry about; some fight would always bring a level of concern about the loved ones kept at home. Christopher couldn't let anything happen to Lynn or Julie. He had to leave, to free them from the burden he had taken on.

Darius was finally waking to that burden—and the pain it caused.

"I..." He shuffled forward a step. His hand jutted out to the brick wall at his side for support. Christopher was right there to help. Sad eyes met him. "I have to go."

"Darius..." Christopher stopped himself. "I wish you could."

"I need to—"

An icy stare washed over his broken teacher. "The elves are on the move," he said in a firm voice. "More innocents will die if we don't stop them. This is what we signed up for, Darius."

He stared down the block for a glimpse of his long-departed wife. There was more to say, more to endure. The work, however, took precedence. Christopher understood that very well. The work always came first.

"Let's go," Darius said, straightening. His knuckles cracked loudly. "I could use the distraction."

CHAPTER FIFTY-FIVE

The front door to 167 Witmer crashed to the floor. The glass within the frame shattered as the elves stormed the home. Screams raged from the occupants at the sudden intrusion.

Christopher stopped short along the sidewalk at the chaos unfolding. They had arrived just in time. The home stretched deep to the rear of the property, two floors with entry points in front, on the side, and at the rear. The elves crowded through the front, bows at the ready and blades in the air. They didn't care about witnesses to their carnage. Their bellows were righteous, demanding vengeance for the fallen.

Darius didn't hesitate or care about the odds against them. Barreling forward, he leaped over the porch railing, bounded off the covered furniture set aside for the winter, and crashed through the picture window into the living room of the home.

Christopher pondered the rashness of the act. They had no plan, no strategy with which to deal with the elves rationally. Darius was still locked on his own pain, one he couldn't wait to dole out to anyone and everyone in the home.

"Wonderful," Christopher muttered. He removed the Greystone from his cloak pocket and held it tight. He hated the idea of using it in such a confined space. The risk to others was too great. Three steps toward the front door, he stopped.

Shadows shifted on the second floor. Frantic cries and slamming doors woke him to the innocents stuck inside. Christopher grabbed hold of a low branch on the tree sidled up to the porch and climbed. Reaching the roof, he ascended to the window overlooking the front of the property.

Inside, two kids held each other close. The younger of the two—a boy, no older than eight—sobbed into his sister's shoulder.

She looked on, crying all the same, but quieter. Her eyes stared at the door and the thundering sounds just beyond the frame.

Christopher lightly tapped the glass.

The sister let go of her brother. Confused and curious, she started for the window. Christopher pointed to the lock at the top of the sash. She released it and he raised the window.

"Come this way." Both children hesitated at his direction. He held out his hand. "Hurry."

A nod escaped the sister. She turned to her sibling, then ushered him toward the window and their rescuer. "What about our parents?"

"They're next on my list," Christopher said with a soft smile. "Promise."

The boy stepped out onto the roof. His sister joined him shortly thereafter. No questions were asked about the situation or the growing cacophony rising from the first floor. The rending of furniture and the shattering of keepsakes and electronics failed to slow them.

Christopher helped them to the lower branch and then to the ground. They hesitated at the sidewalk.

"Where should we go?"

"Around the block," Christopher said. "There is a shop on the corner. Stay there until your parents arrive."

The sister understood immediately. The boy, though, appeared lost, the fight finally drawing his attention. She grabbed his hand and they raced away.

Christopher let out a relieved breath and entered the home. Before he reached the bedroom door, it swung open. A woman holding a baseball bat rushed at him.

"Where are my children?" she yelled. "What have you done?"

"Nothing," Christopher struggled to explain. He caught the swinging bat, and gently tossed the woman onto the bed. "They are safe. I can show you where to go, if you would—"

The woman's kicks and screams overshadowed his words. So lost in helping her, Christopher failed to notice the shadow running behind them. A click woke him to the situation. Turning to greet the sound, the woman's husband stood before him with a rifle in his hands.

"Get away from her!" the man screamed. Christopher moved from the bed, hands in the air. "What the hell is happening here?"

"Please," Christopher said. "Your children need you. Listen to me."

"The kids?" he asked, hands shaking wildly. "What did he do to the kids?"

His wife shook her head. She retrieved her bat, gripping it tightly. "I don't know. They were here and now..."

"I helped them out of the house," Christopher said. "Let me do the same for you. Please."

"Who are you freaks?" The rifle pointed at Christopher's head. "What the hell is going on?"

"The legacy of past sins," the stone bearer answered. Confusion rippled through the pair. Of course, they wouldn't know. Frederick never told a soul about his error in judgment. He carried the burden of his mistake his entire life, not realizing the pain he had spread through multiple generations—all sharing his bloodline. It was not the legacy anyone would want to pass on. "I can help you. But you have to let me."

"I..."

The door slammed open once more. An elf, skin as dark and thick as tar, snarled at them. He leveled his arrow at the husband, satisfaction on his lips.

"No!" Christopher raised his Greystone. Without pause, he channeled his will into the ancient weapon.

Wind swept through the open window. It battered the woman back to the bed. The husband and elf took the brunt of the gale—the unintended consequence of the confined space. Hands tight to his rifle, the husband slammed into the closet and the bifold doors broke under his weight.

The elf, though, was pushed back into the hall. Christopher pursued, the stone still held high. He clutched the weapon with all his strength. A stiff breeze increased to a tempest. The elf hit the far end of the corridor. The creature dropped the bow and arrow in its grasp. Hands clawed at the wall for leverage, but the gust held him in place.

When Christopher was close enough, he lowered the stone. The elf fell to the floor. He bent to retrieve his weapon, but Christopher leaped at him before he could reach it. He took hold of the elf's shoulder and flipped him over the landing, down the flight of stairs to the first floor. The creature hollered in pain, then silenced at the impact at the base of the steps.

Christopher stomped on the bow at his feet, shattering the delicate instrument. He rushed back to the bedroom.

The woman was on her feet, her bat all but forgotten on the bed. Her only concern was her husband, whom she helped out of the closet. The second he was free, he turned to Christopher. The rifle returned, leveled at his chest.

Christopher grimaced. He snatched the rifle from the man and tossed it aside. "Run. Now."

The woman moved for the window and their freedom. The husband was slow to act, his confusion caught between Christopher and his rifle.

"Who are you?"

Christopher's firm hand prodded the man toward the window and his waiting wife. "Someone trying to help."

"And the children?"

"Down the block." Christopher pointed north. "The shop on the corner."

She nodded and started down the tree. The husband followed, his steps shuffling and his body swaying.

Once they were gone, Christopher moved for the hallway once more. He took to the stairs, stepping over the fallen elf at the bottom.

The entire first floor was a war zone. Arrows marked the walls. Blood ran in thick, black streams among them and across the carpet. Furniture had been upturned, with tables smashed and lamps broken. The television lay shattered, the body of an elf still resting within the confines of the device.

"Well, we were supposed to be helping, at any rate," Christopher murmured. "What have you done, Darius?"

Four elves surrounded his teacher, yet he showed no sign of fear. An angry snarl on his lips, Darius' fists flew without care and without restraint. He saw blood and nothing else. The frustration of his private life poured through every movement. Each blow was struck not with the face of the elf at the end of it, but at the man who had taken his wife from him.

Christopher looked on in horror. The elves swiped at their target. They cried out for the vengeance they sought, swinging their blades toward the spiraling Darius. None landed. He was too quick and too efficient.

They were battered back, each in turn. One hit the plaster and settled in the chasm left by the broken wall. Another's nose crunched under a punch, black smears of blood soaring across the room until he landed in a heap in the corner.

"We have earned this blood!" the crowned elf bellowed. He rushed for Darius, who caught the creature by the throat and lifted him high. "They murdered our own. They took my father from me!"

Darius didn't listen. He couldn't hear the cry of the elf or the struggle of the creature as it fought to breathe. His hand tightened, squeezing the life out of the elf. For all it had done, nothing would save the creature from Darius' unchecked wrath.

Christopher realized in that moment nothing remained of his teacher. Darius exuded none of the wonder present when they'd met, or the compassion he had passed along during their adventures over the past two years. There was only fury.

"Stop!" Christopher called from the stairs. "Put him down!"

"Have to… stop them," Darius replied through clenched jaw. The elf's eyes fell back into his skull as consciousness left him. A sharp snap and his body fell limp. Darius dropped the creature to the floor. The cracked crown slipped from the dead elf's head. It rolled around his twisted body until it settled before them.

"No!" Another leaped from the corner. Sword in the air, it swung hard.

Christopher jumped in to intercede. He lifted the Greystone high above his head. "Look out, Darius!"

Light erupted throughout the room. The elf screamed and dropped its blade in a panic over the brightness surrounding him. Darius failed to budge, staring into the white as if it held no power over him—as if nothing could affect him any longer.

Christopher's momentum carried him to Darius' side. He shoved him out of harm's way. Darius staggered to the left a short distance before he righted himself. As the light dimmed and the room fell into view once more, he pounded over the debris beneath him for the still-standing elf.

"I have this, Chris," Darius snapped. He batted the elf away with a sharp blow. The creature cried out, slammed into the wall, then settled to the floor. "I don't need your help."

"Could've fooled me," Christopher said, looking at the carnage of the home. Darius failed to even mention the innocents and where they might have been throughout the struggle. He cared only about the blood on his knuckles and the enemy at his feet. He searched for another opponent, someone to pummel, someone to hurt.

Satisfaction filled him when a portal opened across the room. The last elf's cry must have called to them across the realms. Four more dark elves stepped through a black doorway.

Darius pulled out his Greystone. He thrilled at the renewed battle. Waiting until they cleared the portal and for the doorway to close, Darius lifted the stone.

Fire spread quickly all around them. It bounded from the shattered furniture and the sparking wires and everywhere else there was the slightest hint of danger. The blood of their brethren served as more kindling to the rising flames, which nipped at the newly arrived threat.

The elves stared at each other in terror. They tried to create another portal, another means of escape, but the shadows were lost in the fire. Every egress, be it a door, window, or otherworldly portal, fell out of reach. They burned, consumed by the fire, their screams echoing like embers in the air.

"What are you doing?" Christopher wheeled Darius away from the slaughter.

The man's eyes were manic. "What I should have from the start. No mercy."

"At what cost?" Christopher spread his arms wide. The home was all but destroyed in the melee. The fire jumped from the living room, trailing up the steps to the upper level. It consumed everything. There would be no home to return to for the family of four.

Darius clung to the Greystone, letting the fire rage.

"Stop!" Christopher shouted. "I said—"

Darius snatched Christopher's hand. The Greystone dimmed, but the fire remained, both without and within. "Back off!"

He flung Christopher away. The student soared across the room. His shoulder slammed into the door frame leading to the kitchen. He kept his feet, but the fire cut him off from Darius.

The fury disappeared. Darius watched Christopher rub his wounded shoulder, pain in his eyes. "Chris? Chris, I..."

Darius surveyed the room. The dead burned, consumed by the fire. He stopped at the images that had survived the carnage. All contained the family of four, living their lives—happy and smiling.

He ran off, rushing through the fire to the front door and out into the street. Christopher staggered after him, then reeled at the blaze consuming the room. His feet caught on something along the carpet. It was the fallen crown. The legacy of one man's sin had brought about so much pain and bloodshed. How much more would it cause before the end?

Christopher kicked the crown away. He called after his teacher, "Darius, wait. Let me..."

But Darius was gone.

With the fire raging out of control, Christopher retreated through the kitchen and out the rear door of the home. He didn't stop until the shadows took hold and he could breathe again. He glanced back at the shattered home—burning brightly against the night sky.

"Let me help you, Darius," Christopher whispered against the crackle of the flames. "Before it's too late."

CHAPTER FIFTY-SIX

A pounding stirred Myers from her work. Work might have been a stretch, of course. She had been distracted by a cat video on the web, one where the cat worked through a maze of plastic wrap to find her way to freedom. Why people didn't view it as torture for the animal, Myers didn't understand. She certainly empathized with the four-legged feline, viewing the maze of reports on her desk, Thel's former desk, the floor, the windowsill, and everywhere in between.

Myers stood from the desk when the pounding resumed. "Yeah, yeah. Just open the damn thing already."

The door opened as Myers reached for it. She reeled back to avoid a collision with an over-excited Haya Cho. The bomb technician carried a pile of her own notes, flailing her hands before her as she wound her way into the office.

"There you are." Cho circled the space, taking in the environment for the first time. On her second loop through the disaster of a workspace, she stopped. "I've been waiting downstairs for an hour."

"Why?"

"To see you."

"No," Myers said. "Why were you waiting? I've been here."

"They said you didn't want to be disturbed."

Myers rolled her eyes. She had said that... ten hours ago. She headed for her phone and lifted the receiver. "Yeah. It's Myers. I can see people again. If I have to."

A grumble rose from the desk sergeant. "There was a crazy person looking for you. Choi or something. Would not stop talking."

"Thanks for letting her sneak through, then," Myers said, smiling at the woman in her office. "Hate to have you distracted."

"She said she had to use the bathroom."

"A full bladder. The weakness in our security plan," Myers chided. "Who knew?"

Myers hung up before the excuses started flying. She didn't much care, her previous edict as easily forgotten as her current one. She blinked hard to wake herself up. How had another night passed without her realizing? Her quick shower at home had been the extent of her time away from the office. She had immediately returned to the precinct only to find herself stymied at every turn. No answers presented.

Cho thought differently. She held out her notes. "Ta-da!"

Myers took the notes in hand. She rounded her desk, settling against the side. Her coffee cup was empty; the contents were a memory she no longer carried, like so many others of late. She stared blankly at the scribbled writing. "What am I looking at?"

"How we're going to find this guy," Cho replied with a grin. "See?"

She tapped the paper repeatedly, pressing hard against the lone image at the top. Myers squinted through Cho's fingers. "A pin?"

"Not *a* pin. This pin."

She removed the item from her pocket. It sat within an evidence bag. Myers' brow furrowed, still completely in the dark. She lowered the report and waited for the bag to replace it. Cho passed it over, nearly bouncing during the exchange.

"What does it do?"

"Do you really want to know?" Cho asked. "Because I can tell you. I'd love to, in fact. How it moderates the electrical exchange to the detonator fuse, so that when triggered, the entire device will—"

Myers raised her hand, a headache mounting. "Okay. That's enough."

Cho's arms crossed over her chest. "I didn't think you wanted to know."

Myers finally took a seat, still staring at the pin. "This didn't survive the first explosion?"

Cho shook her head. "The higher yield decimated the device."

"And the building," Myers remarked.

Cho leaned closer, excitement in her every word. "The refinement of the second device—not a compliment, merely an observation—left more components intact."

"Like the pin."

"Which is a specialized piece," Cho said. "It's military-grade, in fact. Our guy probably has some training in this area. Luckily, only a few places stock something like this."

Myers leaned back in her chair. She waited for the rest. When Cho fell quiet, she rolled her finger. "And?"

"And I've already contacted them," Cho said. "I should hear back soon."

Myers scratched her chin. She leaned over her desk, the pin settling along the top of her work. Cho's shadow loomed over her.

"I thought that would be better news."

Myers shook her head. "It is." Cho's dissatisfaction remained. "It is, Cho, trust me. Now if we can get some solid answers and a few less distractions around here—"

A knock at the door stopped Myers. She huffed at the sound and stood. The door opened before she could make it from behind her desk. A young man in blue smirked at the women. He held a report in his hand.

"Detective Myers?"

Myers grimaced. "Oh, I jinxed myself, didn't I?"

"Ma'am?"

"No," Myers said. "No ma'ams here." She sighed. "What is it?"

He passed the report along. "Call came in. They asked for you specifically."

The second the paper was out of his hands, the young man left the room. Cho leaned close, clearly reading the look on Myers' face.

"What's wrong?"

"There's been a murder," Myers said. She crumpled the note. "Not just any murder, either."

"Who?"

Myers grabbed her coat and slipped it on. "One of ours."

CHAPTER FIFTY-SEVEN

Photos snapped around her. Every flash of light took in the details that surrounded Myers. A man was dead. Worse, a cop. She wasn't close to David Yardin, knew very little about him on a personal level in fact, but he wore the badge and that still meant something.

He was strapped to a chair, with multiple stab wounds through his chest. Blood stained his clothes and spattered around the floor. No one should have met their end in such a fashion: bound, tortured, and utterly alone.

She looked over the scene in silence. Forensics arrived in slow waves, the photographers merely the first of many to attend to the room. More officers lingered outside in their search for evidence. Her job remained with the body, though she struggled to put aside everything else that was going on around them.

What the hell is happening to this city?

Gloves in place, she set to work. Before she could even search the victim, a shadow filled the doorway at the back of the room. Loren stepped inside. He appeared as exhausted as she felt, their lives one endless case file.

"I heard the news at Central," he said, joining her. "Is this—"

"David Yardin," she confirmed with a nod.

"Did you know him well?"

"Not at all," she said.

Loren circled the body. It always amazed her how he worked a scene. He saw things much more clearly than she ever had. He stopped at her side. "Wait. Yardin? Wasn't he the one who—"

"Had it bad for Thel? Yeah."

"Have you told her?"

Myers jumped to her feet. She stomped away from the body,

hands in the air. "Tell her what? I don't know anything, Loren!" Her pacing took her the length of the room, her frantic words driving all others from the space. "I have bombings and dead descendants of founders and violence on the streets—like *every* goddamn street—and I have no clue how any of it fits. If it fits. And now this."

His hand settled along her arm. "It's been a lot."

She seethed at his gentle approach. "Oh, I hate it that you're the rational one here."

Loren chuckled. "I think I've always been the rational one."

"You know who thinks they're the rational person in the relationship?" Myers asked, hands on her hips.

Loren rolled his eyes. "Let me guess. The crazy person?"

"Bingo." Myers paused. Her eyes shot wide. She ran her hands over her face with realization. "Oh, no. I'm the crazy one. Listen to me."

"I'm trying to," Loren said with a laugh. "But it's getting a little intense." She joined him, forcing a laugh to keep from losing what little was left of her sanity. Loren shifted closer, his voice calm. "Myers, take a step back. Forget the rest of the city. Focus on the room. Focus on Yardin."

"You're right," Myers replied, shaking away her anxiety. She glared at him. "Ooo, I hate that you're right. Right and rational. When did that happen?"

Loren pulled at the ratty t-shirt exposed by his open coat. An imp wearing a bowler hat offered a thumbs up, its name spelled backward across the top. "At least I haven't learned how to dress like an adult." [1]

"True."

"Now focus," Loren said, pointing to the body. "For my sake."

Myers rounded Yardin, taking in the details she had noticed earlier. "Multiple stab wounds. Cuts are all over his chest."

"The killer was angry," Loren said confidently.

"At a cop?" Myers stated. "Not a surprise."

"What else?"

She gestured to the floor. "Blood spatter on the floor and walls confirms Yardin was killed here."

"In this room," Loren said. "Cut off from the world."

Myers followed his train of thought, running her fingers together. "You're right. He could have been here for days. But he hasn't been. Someone called this in."

"Do we have the recording?"

"I'll get it." Myers moved for the door, then stopped. The lead was slim, but it was more than she'd had a second earlier. "Someone wanted Yardin found like this. They wanted his murder known."

"This is a statement."

Worse, Myers thought. *They had asked for me to handle the scene specifically. Why?*

The question stayed with her, and she found herself back in the heart of the room, looking around. "I... What am I going to tell Thel? After all she's been through? She'll never feel safe in this city. She'll never want to leave her apartment... again..."

Her eyes settled on the corner. Deep in the shadows, away from the body, a small object lay along the floorboards. Myers shuffled closer, crouching low. The metallic keyring glinted in the dark. Myers picked up the item, letting it rest across her palm. Her eyes widened at the purple rabbit's foot.

Thel had been in the room.

CHAPTER FIFTY-EIGHT

"Myers?"

She had trailed off, her worries about Thel still lingering in the air. Loren's focus remained on the body, happy to have been some help to the case and to Myers. The pressures of late had been too much for anyone to handle alone. With Yardin's death, those pressures threatened to boil over—and the entire city would pay the price.

Loren turned away from the victim, curious. Myers crouched in the corner. She bagged something up, then tucked it away.

"Did you find something?"

"Huh?" Myers said, leaping to her feet. She shook her head. "No. Nothing."

Loren eyed the bag in her pocket. When she caught his gaze, her hand shoved the item deep and out of sight. "You sure?"

"Yeah," she said, pushing through him. "Thought it might be the murder weapon. Trick of the light."

At the door, Myers waved in the forensics team. Loren wanted more time with the body. Something about the scene disturbed him, but it easily could have been the dead man in the chair or the lack of sleep over the last few days. He stood and joined her.

"I'll reach out to dispatch for a copy of the call," Myers said.

Loren shrugged. It was a long shot, but what hadn't been of late? "Maybe it can tell us more about what happened here."

"Maybe." Myers stared off. They exited the home, and she started for her car.

Loren held her up. "You sure everything is all right?"

She ducked her head low, continuing on.

Loren sped up to cut her off from the car. "Hey. Talk to me."

A false smile spread across her face. "I'm fine," she said. "Shaken up, I guess. Like you said before, it's been a lot."

"Thel will get better," Loren said. "She needs time."

"Sure," Myers replied, looking away.

Loren thought about questioning her reaction. Something had changed for her in the last few minutes, yet she refused to come out with it on her own. The last thing he wanted was to antagonize her, not with everything against them. They needed to back each other up—to trust each other through the growing nightmare.

Her past sins remained, though. He couldn't help but recall her betrayal, when the so-called trust of their partnership only ran in one direction.

Loren shook his head. Those days were long behind them. They were in a better place now, working for a common goal instead of at cross purposes. Weren't they?

"Do you think this was related to Thel's attack? Someone who knew about the two of them? Could be an escalation."

"Could be," Myers said. Her head fell low, her voice distant and uninterested in his theories. It was unlike the bull-headed detective he had come to respect.

"Of course," Loren started, a grin on his lips. "It might just be aliens out to conquer the planet."

"That's a thought."

Loren huffed loudly. "Myers…"

She peered around, then stopped. "Wait. Did you say aliens?"

"Thanks for listening," Loren said with a laugh. "Make your calls. We can meet up—"

The ground rumbled beneath their feet. Buildings shook as the world boomed and the very air snapped. A plume of smoke rose in the distance, blotting out the sunlight filtering through the clouds. Loren reached out for Myers, taking her by the arm to keep them both steady.

"Was that—"

Loren's eyes widened. "Not again."

It was worse, though. Before they had even moved an inch, a second explosion echoed around them. Alarms blared. Cars screeched to a grinding halt. Windows shattered and chaos erupted. Screams filled the air. Loren took a step toward the second explosion when another rippled at his back.

He spun around, terror in his eyes. The entire block shook, the earth cracking from the high-yield detonation. He pulled Myers close as the force of the explosion shot them into the sedan at their side. His elbow crunched against the door, his head whipping away at the last second before impacting the window. They struggled to maintain their balance as the pavement split beneath them.

Flames sparked along the skyline. Everywhere he looked was another disaster, another burning building, and another catastrophe requiring their attention.

Myers stared at him, begging for direction. Neither one moved, though. They both stood paralyzed, unsure of where to go or what to do.

CHAPTER FIFTY-NINE

Time froze. Nothing moved. The panic of the moment stretched out one second, then two, and on and on, all around Loren. The devastation was clear immediately. Crumbling masonry, the shattering of windows, and the cracking of the very ground where they stood—everywhere Loren peered, there was some additional aspect to the horror.

Myers clutched tight to his side and to the roof of the car. Her gaze flitted from one tragedy to the next, watching the rising plumes of smoke and the flames licking the skyline in multiple directions. Terror struck her, as it did everyone around them. No one acted. No one could even think.

Loren stared ahead. The flames were close, so close he felt the heat rising compared to the chill in the winter air. He moved away from the car, his feet sliding along the ground, afraid to lose touch with the tactile connection to the city. He took another, held back by a hand.

"Loren?" Myers asked, her voice shaking and her eyes unable to focus. "What are you doing?"

He pointed toward the Red-Light District. "That last explosion. It was close."

"We don't—" Myers nodded to the house and the dead man within. They had come from one tragedy and found themselves neck-deep in the next without a single reprieve. There was no downtime, no time for pondering, and certainly no answers.

Loren said nothing. The pull of the explosion turned his shuffling into a brisk walk, which picked up into a run. Myers hesitated, then joined him. She stuck close, as if afraid of being left behind. He led her to the intersection down Westgate toward the Red-Light District. He shot down Evans, passing Night Owls and a dozen other bars. Patrons scrambled along the sidewalks, pointing at the smoke. Their fear was palpable, powerless in the face of such unexpected terror.

Loren pushed through them. He rushed between trapped cars locked in the rush-hour traffic settling into the area. Delays would last for hours. The cell towers were most likely already flooded with emergency calls, making things more congested as people sought their loved ones in the wake of the latest attack.

Chaos took hold of everyone and everything. Pure chaos.

"Loren…" Myers' voice was weak, lost behind the blaring horns. Loren forced his way through the wall of vehicles on the road. He didn't offer apologies to the drivers or even bother to look in their direction. His eyes were locked on the flames, the same as the rest, but his were wide open and aware.

"The Vertrum Home," he said as they arrived. Fire consumed the entire first floor and flickered out the windows of the second. Every piece of history contained within the building was lost.

Thanks to Soriya, Loren knew the place better than most. It was a holding of the Luminaries. History had always been their bread and butter. They owned multiple properties throughout the city. From the Whistler Building, Loren realized they were the true targets of the attacks, but he had been unable to formulate a plan to utilize that vital information. His inaction had led to this—another site burned from the world.

"Why is this happening?" Myers ran her hands through her hair. "First singular events and now this?"

The truth slammed into Loren like a freight train. Her words echoed on him as he looked at the traffic, at the absolute pandemonium of the moment. "You're right."

"Loren?"

He closed his eyes, a hand to stop any further questions. "Give me a second."

"How can you even think over all the sirens?"

"The sirens…" Loren forced a nod. The traffic and the cell towers. Even the pedestrians rushing around. Everyone searched for answers and found nothing but fear and terror. Loren spun around toward Myers. "That's it, isn't it? The sirens. Every emergency crew in the city—every cop—is rushing to deal with these bombings."

"Of course," Myers replied. "It's our top priority."

"And the bomber knows it," Loren continued. "One bomb might have been too small, but spread out a bunch at the same time? Have them go off as rush hour is starting when the roadways are already clogged with delayed construction projects?"

Myers' eyes widened. "This could take hours to clean up."

"Even with every available hand at these sites."

"And only these sites," Myers said, realizing the same truth.

Loren stared at the burning Vertrum Home. "This is all a distraction."

Myers joined him, asking the only question left to them. "But from what?"

CHAPTER SIXTY

They had finally finished. After six hours spent coordinating the transfer of every artifact, every tome, and every secret hidden away in over a dozen sites, the Luminaries' treasures had been safely tucked into the truck. Trips had been made to the library in the interim, the last two sites now secure on their final load.

The massive moving truck bounced along the uneven pavement, deep in the Grove. Surrounding it were two unmarked police sedans. Ruiz sat in the lead car, his hand along the dash and his eyes narrowed on the road ahead.

Renfield said nothing about the contents of each site. Ruiz had hoped for more insight into what needed safeguarding. Before he had even stepped foot in the Luminary strongholds, everything had been packed up in crates. Serial numbers marked each one, the contents still a secret, despite Ruiz's offer to help.

Every time Ruiz tried to learn more about the Luminaries and their operations, digging through the shifting goods and the powerful obols in their collection, Renfield blocked him.

Excuses were made. It had been done to save time. It had been for their protection. None were valid in the eyes of the commissioner, but he let the justifications lie, unwilling to press the issue with so much working against them. There would be plenty of time for answers once they reached the library. Once everything was safe from harm.

At the thought, Ruiz's phone rang. He let go of the dash and settled along the passenger seat. He lifted the phone to his ear. "Ruiz."

"Where are you?" Gates asked through the line. It was difficult to hear her. Screams rose in the background.

"Leaving the Grove now," Ruiz said. "We're heading your

way."

"Good," Gates said.

"Worried?" Ruiz smiled at the notion. For their entire relationship, Gates had known everything—holding her secrets from him, only to parse them out when they became necessary. Her concern made her sound almost human.

The truth was much worse. "They've struck again."

"Where?" Ruiz asked, eyes suddenly awake to the world. He glanced out his window, a look toward the sky. Smoke filtered from the east, thick and black, over the downtown area.

"The Vertrum Home. Our facility on Westborough. The bookstore in Traveler's Cove."

"My God." Ruiz nearly dropped his phone. Three at once? The sites were scattered across entirely different districts. The attacks were escalating, but why? Better still, why now, after those locations had already been cleared of artifacts?

"Get here, Ruiz," Gates said. "Fast as you can."

He nodded to Gomez behind the wheel. The kid had obviously heard every word of the conversation. The accelerator dipped under the weight of his foot, propelling the sedan ahead to the RDJ.

Ruiz leaned closer to his window, eyes back on the smoke. "I still don't like this, Leslie. Putting everything in one very large basket?"

"It's not forever," Gates replied. "Just until the crisis is over."

"I'd still feel better knowing what I'm protecting."

Leslie sighed. "You will. I promise."

The sirens rose behind her words. There was no point in arguing with her, not with everything else going on.

"Sit tight," Ruiz said. "We're almost to the expressway. We'll be at the library as soon as we can."

The line clicked over and she was gone. Ruiz tucked the phone away. He ran his hand across his chin.

"We're almost there, sir," Gomez said.

Ruiz nodded at the kid's words. "I wish it felt that way to me."

Gomez read the man's intentions and pushed ahead. The convoy behind them followed close.

Picking up his radio, Ruiz turned the device on and held it to his ear. "Renfield? You doing all right back there?"

"We have a problem," the man said. Ruiz caught his reflection in the passenger-side mirror. Renfield sat in the cab of the moving truck. He looked tiny behind the wheel, unwilling to share the ride with anyone—not even his trusted compatriots in the Luminaries.

"What now?"

"Looks like there's a snag up ahead," Renfield said. "Construction."

"He's right, sir." Gomez pointed ahead. "I could have sworn they finished this damn project already."

"Not your fault, Gomez," Ruiz said. There was enough pressure on the kid. His involvement required secrets to be held, not the best way to acclimate yourself to the department or your fellow officers. He lifted the radio to his lips. "Ideas?"

"Legacy is on your left," Renfield responded, the line crackling. "We'll use that to cut across to the next ramp."

Ruiz peered at his driver. Gomez nodded in agreement. "All right. I'll notify Atley about the change."

The rear car took the instruction, and all three vehicles settled on their new course. Ruiz kept his gaze on the barriers erected at the ramp to their south. Few signs indicated any work occurring, yet a single cordon barred the ramp itself from use.

"Construction…" Ruiz muttered. Gomez had been right. The project had been on the docket earlier in the year. He recalled passing it during a trip to Castlemere in the fall. The entire ramp had been updated, the road paved, and the walls reinforced. What else was there to work on?

The questions lingered during their turn onto Legacy. The street wasn't ideal for their use—a single lane nightmare, locked in a residential neighborhood. Cars lined the block, the residents always complaining about the lack of parking in the area despite the garages on adjacent blocks.

Renfield struggled to make the turn, almost battering the SUV parked near the corner. The moving truck cleared the vehicle by inches, then settled on the road behind the unmarked sedan.

Parked cars surrounded them, confining them to the center of the lane. No traffic approached from the far end. If it had, they would be in some serious trouble making it through with the truck, yet Ruiz's concerns grew with every second they spent on Legacy.

"I don't like this," he grumbled under his breath. Gomez kept his eyes on the road, hands tightening along the wheel in agreement with Ruiz's assessment. The commissioner lifted the radio once more. "Renfield? We should back up and find another route."

Ruiz's eyes narrowed. A shadow stood in the road.

"Is that—"

The figure came into view. He stood before a motorbike and wore all black, including the helmet that covered his face. He raised his right hand, a bright red button clear on the device he cradled.

Ruiz reached for the dash. "Oh, hell."

A finger fell against the button. Every car around them exploded. Gomez cried out; the sedan was no longer on the road but spiraling in the air. Colors blurred as the world spun around them.

Until the crash. Then everything went dark.

CHAPTER SIXTY-ONE

Ruiz woke to pain along his shoulder and down his arm. Intense heat rose all around him, flames flickering along the periphery of his blurred vision. He was upside down, locked in place by his seatbelt.

"Gomez?" Ruiz said over the crunching of glass and the creaking of the cruiser's battered frame. He tried to fight for the belt lock, but agony restrained him more than the strap against his chest. "Gomez, are you—"

The recent recruit lay against the steering wheel. A piece of jagged metal jutted out from his neck, blood running in a thick stream down his face. Drips pooled beneath them.

Ruiz struggled to breathe. He wanted to cry out, to scream for the dead kid at his side—a kid he had requested for the job. He knew Gomez, knew he had a mother and father who loved him and worried about him. When bringing him on at Central six months earlier, Ruiz had given them a tour. How proud they had been. How excited Gomez had been.

Death was his only reward. A cheap death at that, blindsided by a maniac with a damn detonator.

Ruiz tried to find their attacker through the cracked windshield without success. The world was nothing but branches of light to him, with no sign of coalescing into anything concrete.

Except the radio. It remained tucked tight to his side, stuck between his leg and the door to the cruiser. Ruiz lifted it, a hand on the dial. "Does... Does anyone have eyes on him?"

Static filled the line. No response came. Maybe they were all dead. Maybe he was. It certainly felt like the end to him. Whose fault was that? No one knew about his task because he had withheld the information. Only Michelle had been aware, yet that brought him no comfort. The thought of her caused tears to well in his eyes.

A hand fell on the door beside him. It ripped open, but all Ruiz could see were torn pants and bloodied pale skin. The figure crouched to eye level.

"Commissioner?" Atley reached inside, careful to unlatch the belt while maintaining a grip on his commanding officer. "Are you all right?"

Ruiz made no reply. Clearly not all right, that he was still breathing at all was some kind of blessing. The belt slipped off. Atley lowered Ruiz to the ground, then helped him from the burning wreck of the vehicle.

The light blinded Ruiz. He preferred that to what he saw when the world finally fell into view. A dozen cars burned on the sides of the road. Some had been unended and now rested beside the front stoops of homes. Alarms blared in discord, most little more than a whining drone in the air.

The rear cruiser was much like the front—upside down and battered by the explosive force used to box them in. The moving truck remained upright. Cars leaned against its immense frame, but no damage had been inflicted on their precious cargo.

"Ruiz," Atley said, hair wild and smeared with blood. "Are you all right?"

"I'm okay." Ruiz settled along the curb. He patted the man's shoulder, grateful for the rescue. "I'm okay. But… Atley, look out!"

The biker grabbed Atley by the back of the throat and lifted him from Ruiz. He held him off the ground for a moment, as if scanning his entire person. His other hand encircled Atley's head. With a swift jerk, he snapped the man's neck.

Atley fell into a heap along the pavement.

"No!" Ruiz bellowed. His cry went unanswered. The masked figure didn't bother to glance in his direction. He moved for the front cab of the truck.

Whipping open the driver's-side door, he pulled Renfield out. The contractor was bruised and battered from the explosions, but still in one piece. He cradled a metal case, which he held tight to his chest as he skidded across the road.

The masked biker loomed over Renfield. His voice boomed through a speaker in the helmet. "Give it to me."

Renfield reeled away, a hand atop the case at all times. "You can't."

"I'm afraid I must," the man said. "I have need of it."

Renfield continued to backpedal, unable to find his feet. He connected with the side of the nearest burning car, the heat searing him at the merest touch. As he bounded away, the biker approached.

He ripped the case loose from Renfield. "Please! You don't understand—"

"Oh, I do," the figure replied in a cold voice. "Much more than you can imagine."

A small knife settled into his hand. He swiped wide and caught Renfield across the throat with the blow. The man tried to cover the sudden river of blood that poured from the cut. Panic filled his eyes. Then they went cold and empty. He fell to his side and didn't move.

The masked figure tucked the blade away. Retrieving his fallen prize, he held it over Renfield's corpse with pride. "Don't worry. It's in excellent hands."

"You bastard!" Ruiz cried. He struggled for his feet, the world spinning before him. Black dots filled his periphery, but he fought through them and the immense pain each movement caused. His sidearm was in his hand, shaky but aimed toward his attacker. "Hands in the air! Hands in the fucking air!"

The madman chuckled softly. He opened the case, removed the object within, then obeyed the directive. "As you wish."

His fingers receded from the object caught in his grasp. Ruiz's eyes widened with recognition as it lit up before him.

"A Greystone."

R

A gale force wind ripped from the heavens. It drove Ruiz off his feet. He flew through the air, dropping his pistol at the sudden cyclone. He was upside down again, and the world was nothing more than a blur. His head slammed into the side of a burning car, and he crashed against the steps of the home behind him.

Ruiz spit blood to the cement. He tried to push himself back up on his hands, but everything fought against him. Pain wracked his body and darkness filled his vision. He flipped onto his back. Staring up at the sky, the thick smoke seemed to grow with each passing moment.

The biker stood over him, the stone still in his hand. "You didn't know, did you? No. They kept the contents hidden from you. Just like they do with everything. They need their secrets."

Ruiz's eyes widened at the Greystone. He tried to reach for a weapon of his own. His movements, though, were clumsy and broken, like the rest of him.

His attacker halted any attempt; a boot blocked Ruiz's path. "You look at me as if I'm a threat." He shook his head, crouching at Ruiz's side. "I'm not. I'm here to save you."

"Tell that to the men you just killed."

"A necessary evil, Commissioner," the man said. "The Luminaries would damn us all to protect their power."

"And what will you do?"

"I seek no power," the man said. Laughter filled his words. "Well, perhaps some. But not to hoard. To save us all. You'll see. Soon enough."

The man stood and walked away. He headed for the moving truck and slipped inside. The door slammed shut behind him and the engine roared back to life. He coasted along, pushing the upended sedan out of the way until the road was clear.

The bomber waved as he departed with his prizes

Ruiz could do nothing but watch him leave. He pulled himself up along the railing of the stoop. His feet felt like they were a million miles away. The darkness enveloped his every sense. He slipped from the steps, crashing to the ground with a thud. He had nothing left to give and unconsciousness finally swept over him.

CHAPTER SIXTY-TWO

The midnight hour tolled when Christopher reached Darius' home. The front was steeped in darkness, the family name on the mailbox in shadows as Christopher moved for the door. It sat ajar, resting along the frame rather than closed and locked as it should have been.

He hesitated at the threshold, his concern growing by the second. A sharp breath lingered in his chest and he pushed through to the corridor. His previous visit had been anything but pleasant, but there had still been the trappings of a home.

The differences this time around were clear from the moment of his arrival. Coats and shoes were missing from the rack to his right. Photos had been removed from the wall along his left. Even in the thick darkness settling through the home, Christopher noticed how cold everything had become.

Creaking woke him to a presence in the home. At the end of the hall, a shadow lingered in Marissa's room.

Darius stood with shoulders slumped. His gaze was low, not on the floor, but focused on a single sheet of paper clutched tight before him.

Christopher left the light off, letting streams of moonlight illuminate the room. Scanning the space, he realized the absence of several of the toys that had been present during his last visit. There were fewer blocks, fewer stuffed animals, and no doll. Drawers remained open from the dresser, a few shirts and pants left behind in haste from the looks of them.

"Darius?" Christopher called into the dark. "Darius, what's happened?"

He didn't move, didn't so much as bat an eye in Christopher's direction. He squeezed the paper in front of him, fighting through the emotions it brought up. A tear ran down his cheek. "She left."

Darius passed along the note. Christopher took it from the man, but felt no compulsion to read the rapid scrawling. Jayla's name at the bottom was enough to know exactly what it said.

"She knew," Darius said. "Saw us tonight outside the restaurant and made up her mind. She took Marissa and left."

"Darius, I…" Christopher placed the letter down on the empty bed where Darius' child once slept. He imagined Julie and the pain such a situation might bring up. He honestly didn't know how Darius was still standing. "We'll figure this out. We—"

"She took my family away!" Darius roared. His fists lashed out, swinging wildly at the room. The dresser tipped in his anger and he drove a punch through the pink desk in the corner. His screams echoed across the room as he unleashed hell on the world he had spent so long building.

Christopher retreated from the tantrum, unsure how to act or what to say. The pain was inevitable. The constant pull between their disparate worlds was too much for those caught in their wake. None of it was what Darius wanted to hear. If he could bother to hear anything at all.

The man's chest heaved and his fists fell to his sides. Christopher approached, a slow hand reaching for his friend. "Darius," he said in a quiet voice. "You have to calm down."

Fury sparked in the man's eyes. "No. Never again. After all I've sacrificed? For my home, my country, my family…" Pounding steps carried him from the room. As he traveled down the corridor, Darius ripped the memories—those that remained—from the walls. He tore at photos and mementos left by his wife in her swift retreat from their home. Glass shattered with broken frames, crunching under the weight of his heavy boots as he smashed the memories away.

"I fought for them!" he bellowed. "And they walked away. Turned their backs on me!"

"Darius, stop," Christopher said, keeping his distance. "We can face this. We've faced worse."

Darius swatted the air between them. "And lost!" His fists clenched tight before him, seething with anger. "Every fight has been meaningless. To save what? This place? Let it burn. To protect the Bypass? It is nothing but a prison, holding back its secrets. It takes and takes, leaving us with nothing. I am nothing. Not without them."

Christopher's hands grasped the man's fists and lowered them. "You are the Greystone."

Darius met his concerned gaze. He shook his head repeatedly, backing away. Within the confines of the dining room, he cradled the Greystone before him, lost to the memories the weapon—and the task—spurred. Tears crashed down the man's cheeks and his grip tightened.

He shoved the stone away from his body, pointing to the floor. A light grew along the surface of the Greystone.

"Darius…"

Flames sparked from every corner of the room. They spread quickly, catching the bottom of the curtains until the entire perimeter was consumed.

"I won't let them leave me," Darius said. "I won't let her do this to me."

Christopher approached, hands in the air. "Please don't walk this path."

He needed to save his friend. He couldn't imagine continuing without him, not after everything they had been through. They had faced the monsters in the dark, yet never had Christopher seen the man so defeated and lost. The soldier was gone; the hero and protector vanished behind the broken rage of a betrayed husband.

Light remained on the stone, summoning fire throughout the domicile. Marissa's room was lost to a wall of flame. Sparks erupted in the kitchen. Everything was being burned away.

"Please…"

When Christopher was close enough, Darius snatched his wrist. Christopher flipped through the air, crashing soundly against the dining room table.

"How I tire of your preaching. You were nothing before me." Darius spat at his student. "Truth be told, you're still nothing."

He started for the corridor and the exit. No flames touched him, as if they feared his reprisal.

Christopher nursed his wrist. He leaped from the table. His body soared over his departing teacher and landed in the doorway.

"Get out of my way," Darius snapped.

"I'm sorry, Darius," Christopher said. He raised his fists before him, legs braced for a fight. "I can't do that."

CHAPTER SIXTY-THREE

A punch sailed by Christopher's head. He sidestepped the blow at the last instant, backpedaling for more distance. His travels took him into the corridor and away from the flames.

Darius was on him immediately. His anger bled out in screams. Punches flew, never connecting with anything other than the walls and furniture in the home. Tables shattered and chairs sailed away from them.

"We don't do this for ourselves," Christopher said. "We don't do it to empower ourselves. Our task is bigger than that. It is a privilege. But the reward?"

Darius scoffed. "For everyone else. To hell with them. To hell with you."

The Greystone was back in his hand. Before he could channel his will into the weapon, Christopher launched at him. He tried to pull the stone loose, but Darius was too quick. He grabbed Christopher by the arms and flipped him back to the burning dining room, the flames dancing all around them.

Barely back on his feet, Christopher caught sight of Darius just in time to avoid a follow-up strike. His teacher's fist crashed down, smashing through a chair Christopher used as a shield. The wood splintered in multiple directions.

A rune sparked across the surface of Darius' stone. Christopher recognized the rune as Uruz, the strength coursing through his teacher's body all the evidence he needed.

Christopher kicked out. He caught Darius in the chest, but the blow was weak. The man staggered back a step, then bounded at Christopher the next instant. He lifted his student from the floor and slammed him down on the dining table. It cracked in two, but locked Christopher against the bottom half, leaning along the floor at an angle.

"Jayla made her choice," Christopher said. Darius' hands closed around his throat and he tried to pry them loose. "If you let your pride go, you would see why."

"I loved her!" Darius screamed. His eyes were frenzied, the power overwhelming all sense of control. He was a wild animal, not the man Christopher once called friend. "I gave her a home, a daughter!"

He raised his fist. The second he loosened his grip on his target's throat, Christopher knocked the other hand away and dove out of range. The table broke upon impact, a crumbling memory like everything else in the home. It served as little more than kindling for the rising flames that continued to climb the walls.

"There was laughter and joy!" Darius continued to bellow. He didn't see what he was doing to their home. He couldn't see anything except the pain Jayla's betrayal caused.

Christopher leaped at him. He wrapped his arms around his friend, trying to restrain him. "Because you blinded yourself to her pain. Jayla wasn't happy. Can you honestly say you were, Darius?"

"How dare you?" The strength from the stone proved too much for Christopher. Darius spread his arms out, knocking his student away. The second he was free, his fist flew through the air and connected with Christopher's cheek.

Driven back, Christopher struggled to keep his balance. Darius refused to let up. He pummeled his student without remorse. Each blow crashed into Christopher's guts, along his side, and across his face.

"You. Smug. Arrogant. Wretch!"

Christopher had no defense against the assault. His only recourse was to use the Greystone, a last resort if ever he saw one. Darius was in pain, hurting and reeling from the loss of his family. He needed time to realize the truth of his situation. Christopher wanted nothing more than to pull his friend back from the brink, only to watch him sail completely over the edge.

Another blow slammed into his right cheek. He dropped to the floor, blood splattering across the room in a wide spray. It merely added fuel to the pyre.

Christopher couldn't feel his body any longer. His hands struggled to steady himself, yet were unable to lift him from the ground. A shadow towered over him.

"Don't get up, Chris," Darius spat. "It's over."

He turned to meet his friend. Christopher wiped the blood from his lips. "It's never over. Not with the life we've chosen. You've forgotten that."

The Greystone lit up, a look of surprise replacing the rage on Darius's face.

R

Wind crashed into Darius. He sailed across the room through the hallway wall. The impact shattered the wooden frame, already weakened by the fight. As Darius struggled to remove himself from the plaster, the last moans of the burning home caused the entire structure to shake. The ceiling collapsed at the doorway to the dining room.

Darius was lost behind the debris, but his words cut through. "They are all I have, Chris. I've worked too hard to lose them now. I wish you could understand that. But you never had anything to lose, did you?"

Christopher offered no response. Darius never required one anyway.

He looked around at the collapsed ceiling, mere inches from his position in the dining room. There was no way to dig his way through. Not with the smoke filling the space and the continued groan of the upper floor. With every move Christopher made, he met an obstacle. Debris barred him from the kitchen. Rising flames acted as a wall in front of the windows.

He was trapped.

Darius' steps faded, but his final words echoed as he departed. "I'm sorry it had to end this way. I truly am."

CHAPTER SIXTY-FOUR

Smoke filled Christopher's lungs. He kept low to the floor, struggling to find a clear path out of the room. The windows were blocked, the flames from the curtains a wall of oppressive heat that shoved him back with the merest approach. Debris barred the doorway. Even the kitchen was inaccessible thanks to the raging fire.

Time was running out. Any delay might cause him to pass out. If that happened, there would be no escape. No one was coming to rescue him. No one would help.

He had to act.

Raising the Greystone, Christopher channeled every last ounce of strength into the ancient weapon. He closed his eyes, holding the breath in his lungs, and prayed.

It started slowly. A snap of metal gave rise to the crashing pipes from the bathroom down the hall and the sink in the kitchen. They flowed beneath his feet before breaking through the floorboards, sparking to life at his direction.

Water sprayed from every side. The sudden deluge pounded against the burning flames until the room was nothing more than a massive cloud of steam. The kitchen did the same. A wave of water drove the fire from the room.

Christopher didn't hesitate. He fought for his feet and rushed for the window. As the ceiling above gave way, he leaped. The home collapsed behind him as he crashed through the pane of glass and onto the front lawn of the home.

He reeled away from the property. Eyes, wide with horror, caught the last heave of the domicile as the second floor surrendered to the damage caused by the fight.

No, not the fight. The destruction of the home had been caused by Darius.

He had gone too far in his attempt to destroy the past and to kill his friend for standing in his way. Darius had gone much too far.

Christopher watched the house burn. His efforts had only done enough to save his own skin, not the entire contents of a lifetime buried in the rubble of the once-proud home. Everything lay shattered and destroyed. So much work. So much love. Gone.

If only there had been some way to stop Darius, some way to bring him back, but Christopher knew the truth. The warning signs had been present for quite some time. Darius was all rage and no rational thought. He wanted to take what he believed belonged to him, no matter the destruction caught in his wake.

Neighbors peered from open windows at the fire. Some stood on their porches, pointing and gasping at the horror of the scene. Sirens rang out in the distance. They were too late, though.

Darius wouldn't stop with destroying his home. Jayla and Marissa were now at risk. Nothing would deter the broken husband from reclaiming his family, no matter the cost, no matter the sacrifice.

Christopher couldn't let anything happen to them. He lifted himself from the grass until he reached the sidewalk. The Greystone rested in his hand to utilize its power once more.

He had been practicing of late. With a small piece of his spirit, he worked to heal the wounds left by Darius during their struggle. Immediate relief flooded along his right cheek and his swollen lip. It would take time, though, the one luxury he could no longer afford.

Figures approached. Hands shot out, followed by shouts. Some were out of concern, but the majority set the blame on the fire without any evidence. Christopher turned toward the dead end and raced for the shadows. Explanations would serve no one. None would be believed.

He could barely believe the truth himself. He had to save his friend.

The first step was to locate Jayla. Christopher had to find her... before it was too late.

CHAPTER SIXTY-FIVE

The Grove was a massive tangle of humanity. It took two hours for Loren and Myers to work their way through the crowds until they reached the scene on Legacy Street. The fires were out, crews doing what they could with few resources available and the limited space afforded by the cramped quarters created by the explosions.

Loren stared in awe at the catastrophe around them. It defied belief. So much of the city was in flames, so much chaos and death, and for what? The question still lingered, but Loren knew without a doubt the heart of the issue lay on Legacy.

Myers tried to talk him through everything on the way. The constant interruptions from her cell phone, the radio, and all around them made any conversation almost impossible. Loren didn't know how to interact, anyway. His thoughts spiraled, cascading into a never-ending sea of information with few connections and far too many gaps in logic.

All faded to nothing at the sight of Ruiz resting along the stoop near the end of the block. An EMT bandaged up the man's arm as the Commissioner held tight to an ice pack along his forehead. His clothes were torn in several places, scorch marks along his sleeves and legs. He was bruised and bloodied from the affair, one that left his hands shaking.

"Ruiz!" Loren yelled. He rushed from the passenger-side of Myers' car for his friend. Myers tried to follow, but was forced to park down a narrow driveway to keep the road clear. "Ruiz!"

At his approach, Ruiz offered a half-hearted wave. He winced in pain at the movement. "Could you bring it down a couple hundred decibels?"

The EMT smirked at Loren. "He has a concussion. He'll be okay, but he needs—"

Loren ignored the technician, pushing past him for his friend. "What happened here?"

The EMT reached for Loren's sleeve. His eyes thinned, his anger clear. His job came first. So did Ruiz's health. Loren, however, couldn't think about anything of the sort. He continued to scan up and down the block at the wrecks left behind from the explosions, the skid marks in the road from a large truck, and the dead men covered in tarps.

"Sir, if you would—"

"It's okay," Ruiz said, barely able to open his eyes. "Give us a few."

"But—"

"Please."

The EMT silently agreed. He pushed through Loren, a jab to the man's side making his statement for him. The young man continued to his next patient and the countless hours of work left to him from the tragedy.

Loren sat beside Ruiz. "We looked into the resources available for the bombings downtown and noticed a pair of units pulled, but no reason other than security arrangements. What were you doing here?"

The Commissioner remained silent, unable or unwilling to lift his head to meet the question.

Myers arrived, hands on her hips. "We're going to need an answer, Chief."

"Don't call me—"

"Ruiz," Loren interrupted. "He attacked you, didn't he? Everything else was a distraction. You were the target. Why?"

Ruiz sighed. He pressed the ice pack tight to his forehead. "We were transporting dangerous cargo to a secure location."

Loren's brow furrowed. "What kind of dangerous cargo?"

"I don't know."

"From where, sir?" Myers pressed.

He met them with a hard gaze. "The bomber was targeting specific buildings. We couldn't let their contents fall into his hands or risk their destruction."

"We?" Loren slowly stood. Ruiz knew about the locations. He knew… "Oh. Oh, Ruiz."

Myers didn't follow. She shifted closer. "The Vertrum Home, sir? The place on Westborough? Some bookstore in the coves?

How many others?"

"Over a dozen," Ruiz confirmed.

"And you knew," Loren snapped, his voice rising. "What the hell were you thinking?"

Loren raised his fist. The EMT rushed back, hands before him. "Hey! That man—"

"Is due another concussion," Loren yelled. "Maybe it will screw his head on straight."

Myers blocked the EMT, a calm hand between them. It gave Loren a moment to do the same. He shuffled away from the stoop. When he circled back, Myers joined him, but his focus was locked on Ruiz, who waited for the inevitable question. It was right in front of him, the final connection he needed, though he continued to struggle with the realization.

"How long?" Loren asked. "How long have you been working with the Luminaries?"

"You know about—"

"Wait," Myers interjected, stepping between them. "Luminaries? Like Karen Winters? That kind of Luminaries?"

"Yes."

"No," Ruiz shot back. "Not like that, Greg. They are trying to help."

"How?" Loren railed. He spread his arms wide. "Have you looked around? If they would have said something—*anything*—we could have secured the sites, set up a trap, and ended this madness long ago. They keep secrets and we pay the price."

A hand fell on his sleeve. Myers nodded away from the stoop, dragging him with her. At the curb, she stopped. "How long have *you* known about them? As long as we're condemning people for keeping secrets."

"I…" Loren paused. She was right, of course. Ever since his encounter with the Council of Legends, the lead had been in his lap and he had told no one. "Not long."

"How?"

Another secret. How many had he kept from her? From Gabe and everyone else? Here he was condemning Ruiz, but how was he any better? He pushed through the question, unwilling to take the blame. "It doesn't matter."

Myers huffed. "Not exactly the open line of communication you're trying to convey to the Commissioner, are you?"

"He was working with them!" Loren bellowed, pointing at the man—his best friend. He spun toward Ruiz. "Why? After everything we've been through, why would you do that?"

Ruiz's head fell low. "I was trying to protect the city."

"From what? Do you even know?" Ruiz shook his head. "And the cargo? What does this guy have at his disposal now?"

"I don't know."

Loren was inches from Ruiz's face. "You don't—"

"They didn't tell me, all right!" Ruiz shouted. He shifted off the seat, his body shaking with the sudden movement. He struggled to stand. A clear wave of dizziness took him and he settled back to the stoop, his head close to his knees. "They didn't tell me."

Loren's gaze washed over the man. They had fought together, bled together, almost died together so many times, yet here they stood alone and isolated. Part of him wanted to continue screaming. The other wanted nothing more than to nurse his friend back to health—to be there for someone who had obviously made a mistake.

His anger kept him from the latter. He pushed from the stoop, hands to his hips. "This is what he wanted. All those attacks sent the Luminaries scurrying to collect their secrets and put them all in one convenient place. This was his plan all along."

"Why?"

"I'm almost afraid to find out," Loren said.

"He..." Ruiz looked at him, eyes bloodshot and wet with pained tears. "I did see one thing, Greg. A Greystone. The Luminaries had one."

A Greystone? How did that connect with everything else? And what the hell were the Luminaries doing with such a powerful tool in their possession?

"They..." Loren trailed off. Was the Greystone the goal all along? What did it all mean? He buried the questions away, a deep sigh of regret escaping him. "You should have trusted us, Ruiz."

"I was trying to protect you," he said, his words weak and distant. "To protect all of us."

The words echoed through Loren, repeating his own lecture to Gabe. "Shit. So that's what that sounds like to someone else."

Loren moved for the car, leaving behind the chaos and the secrets.

Myers called after him. "Where are you going?"

"Home." Loren pointed to Ruiz without looking. "He can clean up his own mess."

Pounding feet rushed over to him. Myers cut him off, hands to his chest. He tried to work around her, but she shoved him back. "Hey! This is not the time for this crap. You both kept secrets. Move on. We need to work together to put a stop to this. We fall apart and this bastard wins."

From down the street, a small figure exited a silver sedan. She waved her hands in the air. "Myers?"

The detective ignored the newcomer, eyes locked on Loren. "This city needs us. It needs all of us right now, more than ever. It's time to come together, the only way we can. To rally and put an end to this maniac before he can use whatever he stole to—"

The short, stocky woman jumped up and down at the curb, hands in the air. "Detective Myers!"

Myers groaned with frustration. "What? What do you want, Cho? I was making my best damn speech ever and you killed the moment!"

Cho halted at their side. Her cheeks flushed. "Oh. Sorry. Should I come back?"

Loren shook his head fervently.

Myers sighed and held out her hand. "What have you got?"

"Phones are down everywhere," Cho said, leading them back to the stoop and a curious Ruiz. "Took forever to track you down."

"Cho," Myers said, eyebrows raised. "The intel?"

"I found him," Cho announced with pride. "I found the bomber."

CHAPTER SIXTY-SIX

Thel stood outside the WKPO office. Through the glass doors, she witnessed people dashing around, papers flying as rapidly as orders from editors and producers. Everyone was caught up in the day, the news writing itself thanks to the tragedies littered throughout the city.

She hesitated at the doors, butterflies dancing in her chest. Thel struggled to catch her breath. Her heart beat so quickly, she could scarcely think. She wanted to turn around, the old fears returning.

When she backed away from the door, a hand fell on her shoulder.

Kellon beamed at her. "You've got this."

"It should be you," Thel said. "You've given me so much. What you could do for everyone else…"

He shook his head. "Is for you to give. Thel, you've seen the power we hold. You are the strongest of us. The city will listen to you. Tell them your truth."

"Come with me?"

Kellon squeezed her shoulder, then fell back a step. "Not this time."

Thel needed to stand on her own. She saw that now. He pulled her close for a kiss, then started down the block. Thel watched him depart, her guts churning with dread and excitement.

When Kellon had suggested the move, there had been nothing but confusion. His words, though, inspired her to act. She had reclaimed her power with the death of David Yardin. So much pain had vanished in that moment. It was time to pass that healing to others—to reach out and be the voice the city needed in its time of crisis.

She pushed through the doors onto the main floor of the television studio. The noise surrounded her in a large wave. Only a day ago, such a cacophony would have sent her running to her apartment. Now it emboldened her, and she stepped up to the front desk with confidence.

The receptionist threw on a false smile at her approach, her irritation clear from the tapping fake nails on her desk. "Can I help you?"

"I'm looking for Nicki Dryden," Thel said, scanning the room.

"She's—"

Thel noticed the woman at the back of the bullpen. She wore heels and a black dress, her coat hanging off one arm. Auburn hair fell to her shoulders, ruby lips spread across her face. Thel pushed from the desk. "I see her. Thanks."

"You can't—"

Thel ignored the cry from the receptionist. Working her way through the room, she called, "Nicki!"

The reporter ended her conversation, a curious look on her face. "The siren detective."

"Thel."

Nicki lowered the coat along the half-wall at her side. She towered over Thel, eyes wide and ravenous. "What can I do for you, Thel?"

"I know what I want to say now," the siren said. Her whole body felt ready to shake apart. That was the fear talking. She was better than that now. "If you want to hear it."

Nicki ran her tongue over her teeth. She looked the siren up and down, reading her entire body with a single glance. With the cock of her head, Nicki led Thel across the newsroom to an open studio off to the right. "Step into my office."

As they traveled around the rushing masses in the bullpen, Nicki signaled the young man who had been with her at the Rath Building days earlier. "Ronnie," she called. "Grab your gear."

All thought to his own work vanished. He dropped the papers in his hand, even the coffee, which spilled along his work surface and down his pants. Frantically, he joined Nicki, camera at the ready.

The trio exited the newsroom and stepped into a darkened studio. The news desk sat on the sound stage. Nicki led Thel over as Ronnie started for the lighting equipment, flicking switches and bringing the room to life.

Nicki took a seat behind the desk. Reaching under, she removed a compact and opened the makeup kit. She scrubbed blush to her cheeks, precise with each delicate stroke.

"What changed your mind?" she asked, smirking at her reflection.

"A friend," Thel replied. Yardin's screams echoed through her thoughts. She felt the pain melt away with each stab against her victim. She carried so much power now, like she had been reborn in that moment. The memory sent a chill up her spine. "He helped open my eyes."

Nicki snapped the compact shut. She gazed up at her companion. "Ready?"

"Whenever you are," Ronnie confirmed. He tweaked the lighting, locking the pair into the frame, then nodded. A red light illuminated on the camera.

"Ready?" Nicki whispered, a hand to Thel. A silent affirmation passed. Nicki's voice shifted from subtle and reserved to loud and full of life. "We're here with Thel, a detective with—"

"Former detective," Thel clarified.

Nicki paused, recomposing herself. Nothing fazed her for long. She was born to be in front of the camera. "A former detective at the Central Precinct." Nicki turned to her subject. "You carry a unique gift, don't you?"

"I'm a siren," Thel said, leaning close to the news desk. "But that's not what I want to talk about."

"Okay," Nicki said, drawing out the word. She held out a hand, giving Thel the floor.

Thel turned toward the camera. "I'm here to stand up for those who can't. For those afraid of reprisals because of who or what they are." With each word, she grew stronger. All the weakness of the past month was gone. No more terror remained. She refused to live that way any longer. No one should have to. And it was time to let them know that.

"The violence against us must end," Thel declared. "We will not live in fear—beaten and broken—because we're misunderstood and hated."

Nicki tapped along the desk. "What do you say to the humans afraid of your kind? That fear for their jobs, their neighborhoods, and their very lives?"

"Fear and hate have always been an excuse to lash out," Thel answered. "It is humanity's natural reaction. What do I say to it? We won't stand for it. Myths and legends live among you. Welcome us as the neighbors we are. Threaten us and we will retaliate."

The warm glow from Nicki faded. Curiosity shifted to confusion. "Retaliate? Thel, that sounds like—"

"Like we won't back down? Good," Thel said. Her cold stare locked on the camera. "We have the power here. We don't have the desire to use it. But if pushed, we will."

CHAPTER SIXTY-SEVEN

The door crashed open. Gabe rushed into the apartment. He whipped his backpack from his shoulder. The force caused the coat rack to tip over and slam to the floor. Rather than pick up the mess, or close the door, Gabe continued through the living area, eyes frantically searching the place.

"Loren?" he called. "Loren, are you here?"

He paused at the window. Smoke rose in the distance. The city continued to feel the effects of the downtown explosion. Gabe witnessed the terror on everyone's faces during his slow trek home. Their cries echoed in his thoughts, panic-stricken with concern over their loved ones and the endless terror that seemed to grow daily in Portents.

No one understood the attacks. There was no one to lash out against, to direct their anger toward, so they spread it to those around them. With each block traveled, Gabe had witnessed more violence.

People were dying on the streets and no bomber was to blame. This was far bigger than a lone terrorist in Portents. It made Gabe feel so small and powerless.

He left behind the window and the burning city for the kitchen. At the emptiness within, he backtracked toward the bedrooms.

"Kev gave me a lift," Gabe said, his voice filling the silence. "With everything going on, traffic was a nightmare."

The bedroom was devoid of life. So was the bathroom. Gabe stood in the corridor's solitude, shoulders slumped and hands buried in his pockets.

"Which is probably why you're not here."

Gabe circled back to the door and closed it. The couch welcomed him as he collapsed against the cushion. A hand ran through his hair and a deep sigh left him. "Sure, Gabe. Tell yourself Loren is out there, sitting in his car, stuck in some gridlock. Like you don't know exactly where he is right now."

Loren was never caught on the sideline. Somehow, he always found his way into the middle of every dangerous situation that cropped up. Gabe hated being left behind, hated the overwhelming sense of loss that came with not having his partner by his side. They were a team, weren't they? When was the last time Loren remembered that? Would he ever again?

Frustration slipped from Gabe in a loud groan. His homework waited in his bag, but rather than face another impossible task, he reached for the television remote instead. The device came to life at the press of a button and he settled against the couch cushion for a much-needed distraction.

Surprise greeted him as Thel's image filled the screen. "We have the power here. We don't have the desire to use it. But if pushed, we will."

It was from a pre-recorded interview. Gabe leaned closer. He changed the channel, only to find the same remarks repeated on every newscast. Commentary arose between pundits in the aftermath as images of the explosions took over from Thel's speech. They tried to connect the two events without a shred of evidence to back up their wild theories.

Gabe rubbed his eyes. "Well, that's not great," he muttered. "What else could go wrong?"

In answer, a knock arose from the hallway. The hard patter against the door shook Gabe from the couch.

Cautious fingers hovered over his pocket and the stone tucked within. He approached slowly, reaching for the knob. "Hello?"

"Oh, thank God," a voice rang out. "You're all right."

Gabe opened the door to see his teacher standing in the hall. "Mr. Shepherd?"

He pushed into the apartment. His clothes were ashen, his face dirt-laden and caked with dried sweat. "I was worried with everything going on."

"Worried?" Gabe said, closing the door behind him. "About me?"

"Of course about you," Shepherd said. "I went by the school, but you were already gone."

Gabe's brow furrowed. "Where were you? I mean, you weren't

in class today."

"I had some errands. Nothing terribly exciting," Shepherd said. His gaze turned to the window and the thick black smoke. "At least, it wasn't until that happened."

Gabe kept his hand on the knob. "Well, thanks for checking on me, but I'm fine."

Shepherd shook his head. He stood his ground near the window. "Gabe. You see what's happening out there?"

"Yeah," Gabe replied. He nodded to the television set. "I was just—"

Shepherd approached, hands reaching for him. "People are scared. There has to be a way to stop this. To help everyone."

"I..."

"That stone," Shepherd continued. "Can it help? Can it find the monster doing this to Portents?"

"The stone?" Gabe shifted away from the door. His hand fell over his pocket, and he took out the ancient weapon. Returning to the window, Gabe stared out over the city. He watched the anarchy unfolding and listened to the cries echoing through the streets.

He should have been helping those who couldn't help themselves. He should have been doing something, but what could the stone do against the nightmare that had enveloped Portents? *Not enough.* "Not on its own."

"What do you mean?" Shepherd asked.

Gabe pushed away from the sill, shaking his head. "Nothing. Forget I said it, Mr. Shepherd."

"I can't, Gabe," Shepherd said. "Not with people suffering on the streets. If there was a way I could end this, I would do everything in my power to make that happen. Wouldn't you?"

"Yeah," Gabe answered. "Of course, but..."

"Gabe. Portents needs you."

He wanted to prove himself. That's what he had told Loren. For so long, he had felt alone and powerless. Shepherd offered him what his own partner had failed to—an opportunity. One that set them on equal footing.

Gabe squeezed the stone. "It's called the Bypass."

"A place?"

"Sorta," Gabe said, unsure how to describe the power held in the underground chamber. "It's complicated. And dangerous."

"We have to try, don't we?"

"We…"

"You're not alone in this, Gabe. If anyone can help put an end to this nightmare, it's you."

Loren wasn't coming. He was out there, fighting with Myers and Ruiz and who knew how many others to end the threat. How could Gabe do any less? He was the Greystone, after all.

"All right," Gabe said. "Let's go."

CHAPTER SIXTY-EIGHT

It had taken two nights to find them. Christopher had spent the first night recuperating from the fight. Time slipped away from him, but it had been necessary. He had been in no shape to walk, much less run or fight.

He'd used the time wisely, though. While he recovered from his injuries, Christopher returned to the restaurant where they had witnessed Jayla with another man. Some pointed questions—a few directed at him and the still-visible wounds on his arms and face, which were dismissed without explanation—gave Christopher a starting point.

Willis Robbins was the man's name. He had been a regular at the eatery for many years, and the establishment always treated him like family. Christopher had thanked them for the information and to keep it from anyone else. They understood immediately. His injuries had helped make the point clear to them.

Tracking Willis down had required little in the way of effort. He'd been listed in the phone book, his address easily gleaned.

Christopher waited until nightfall to approach. Willis rented an apartment in the Riverside District in the Cooper Complex, a quieter neighborhood tucked along the bay. Christopher wound through the maze of buildings, keeping to the shadows and away from the lights scattered across the parking lot until he reached the building in question. He climbed to the second floor; the windows gave him a clear view of the property.

Willis worked diligently in the kitchen. He stirred a pan, adding spices and humming a tune quite different from the one playing on the small radio set upon the fridge. There was joy in his step and a smile on his face. He was in his mid-thirties and wore a sweater over khakis. An apron covered much of him with a picture of Superman's chest across the front.

Christopher left the man to his cooking. He skirted around the building, jumping from sill to sill until he settled outside a bedroom. A bright lamp illuminated the space. Two figures sat on the floor. Jayla and Marissa played with blocks. Jayla built a tower from the set, one quickly destroyed by Marissa, who roared like a dinosaur while stomping through the blocks.

Laughter rose with each destructive act. Jayla cradled her daughter, tickling her into submission. They paused their fun when Willis entered. A question was asked, unheard by the witness outside, but it pulled Marissa from the room. She bounded into the hall with Willis' hand tight around hers.

Jayla sat alone in the bedroom. She picked at the surrounding blocks, then let them fall back to the carpet. Thoughts consumed her, the joy from before lost without her daughter to bring it out.

Christopher took a heavy breath. He hated to interfere, yet knew with each passing moment, time stood against him. His hand lifted the sash, and he slipped into the room.

"Jayla," he called in a soft voice.

The woman nearly leaped out of her skin. She spun around, eyes in shock at the sudden arrival. "Chris? You—"

"I apologize for the abrupt arrival," Christopher said, hands before him. "We don't have much time."

Jayla retreated from him. She shook her head. "No."

"Pardon me?"

"Whatever this is, whatever you think you're doing here, I'm not going back."

Her rising voice brought back company. Willis rushed into the room, Marissa following close.

"Jay? Everything okay?" Willis asked in confusion. That feeling left him the second he saw the intruder in the bedroom. He pounced at Christopher. "Hey!"

Christopher caught the clumsy blow. He forced the man against the wall, restraining his arm behind his back. "Please."

Willis struggled but couldn't move. "Get out of my—"

Christopher pressed tighter. He kept his voice soft and calm. "I'm not here to fight." He turned to Jayla. "Or to force you to do anything. Do you understand?"

She slowly nodded.

Willis stopped struggling. The moment he did, Christopher let him go. As he returned to Jayla's side, he rubbed his arm lightly.

Marissa stepped forward. She smiled at the cloaked figure. "Hello, Mr. Chris."

He chuckled, crouching to greet her. "Hello, Marissa. You look lovely, as always."

Jayla patted the child's shoulder. "Go play with Uncle Willis for a few, okay, sweetie?"

The girl shrugged. "Okay, Momma."

Willis hesitated at the door. "You sure—"

"I'm fine," Jayla said. Another glare cut her way. "I am."

They headed out. The sound of the dinosaur's roar echoed around them as did the false fear from Willis as their play carried them away.

Jayla settled along the edge of the mattress. She rubbed her hands along her legs, eyes low and distant. "I read about the fire in the paper. Did Darius—"

Christopher confirmed her suspicions with only a nod.

Tears dripped down her cheeks. "What am I going to do?"

He joined her on the mattress. Her head settled along his shoulder. "What happened, Jayla? What changed?"

"He did," she said, swiping at her cheeks. "The late nights got later. The anger grew to hatred. The stone was all that mattered. He would sit up late into the night with that damn thing on his lap. I would catch him nodding, like it was talking to him."

She pushed away from the bed. Arms clasped tight across her chest to keep her warm. Christopher closed the window, cutting off the cool air. An appreciative glance passed his way, but it soured as the memories overtook her once more.

"That stone brought nothing but darkness into his life," she said. "Into our lives. I couldn't live with that. Not with Marissa in the house. I... I didn't mean for this to happen. Willis... He's an old friend. He listened. He cared, and I..."

Christopher reached out to her. He squeezed her hand. "It's okay."

"I wish it were," Jayla replied. "But if you found us, he will too. Won't he?"

They both knew the answer. It was only a matter of time.

"The city isn't safe."

Jayla stared into the darkness outside the window. "It never was. Now, though?"

Christopher moved to her side. "I'll do everything I can to protect your family, Jayla. I promise."

It meant moving quickly. Without delay, the plans started to form between them. There was only one option left to avoid confrontation.

They had to escape Portents.

CHAPTER SIXTY-NINE

Tires screeched to a halt. Patrol cars bounded over curbs, stopping short on the narrow sidewalk before a townhouse on Whitehaven. Their journey had been treacherous, to say the least. Demonstrations had broken out at the Rath and City Hall. Riots worked through the streets in Riverside. Fires burned in all districts, some from the madness of a lone bomber while others erupted at the whims of the growing mob mentality overtaking Portents.

Few from the precincts could be pulled from their mounting task of maintaining order. Two patrols surrounded Myers' cruiser as they parked before the well-maintained and innocuous building at the end of the block. No violence surrounded the area. In fact, the street seemed eerily quiet compared to the rest of the city, as if by design.

Officers took up positions outside the home. They circled the perimeter, hands shaking and eyes flitting around frantically for signs of life. Everyone was on edge. The collective sanity of the city rested solely on the success of their task.

Loren exited the cruiser with Cho in tow. Cho was dressed in tactical gear from head to toe. Her helmet slid awkwardly to one side. She fought to readjust it as she led them to the front door.

"I tracked the sale of the pin to this address. A number of other sales pointed here as well."

Loren nodded. The clip from his borrowed pistol snapped free. He confirmed the full complement of bullets within, then jammed it back into place. He took a series of quick breaths to steady his nerves. "You ready, Myers?" Peering behind him, Loren was startled to see Myers still lingering near her car. He backpedaled from the steps to her position, brow furrowed in confusion. "Myers?

What is it?"

She stared off, lost to the home and their situation. Wherever she was, it wasn't on the task at hand. Loren reached for her and she shot back at his touch.

Myers shook her head. "Nothing. It's nothing."

When she pushed ahead, Loren held her up. "Hey," he called, a hand to her arm. "You were right before. About keeping secrets. I was wrong not to tell you about the Luminaries."

A slow nod escaped her.

Loren leaned closer. "So... if you have something you want to share..."

"I'm worried about Thel. That's all."

"You want to go to her," Loren said. "Go."

"What?"

"I can—"

Myers brushed him off and started toward Cho. "No."

"Myers..."

"I will, Loren," she snapped, gun at the ready. "But if he's here?"

"Right."

Cho held them up at the door. She removed a small kit from one of the many pouches along her vest. "I'll take the lead," she announced. "Can't have anyone else going boom."

Loren cocked his head to the side, eyebrow raised. "Is that a concern?"

"How is it not a concern?" Myers replied. "Come on, Loren."

A sudden awareness filled him. He had taken part in dozens of sieges during his career. There was always an element of danger involved, but never a thought of triggering an explosive device. Somehow, bullets sounded mundane by comparison—easily brushed off. The spark of a bomb opened a whole new terror in the man, but he fought through it.

Cho worked the lock, snapping the knob clean off. The door creaked open, held tight under her careful approach. Crouching, Cho set a mini-camera through the opening. The attached screen displayed the contents within, though Loren struggled to see anything through the darkness inside.

The monitor switched settings to night-vision. A quick scan gave them a glimpse of the place. Nothing jumped out at them. No triggers appeared to be in place, just an open room with the usual trappings of home.

Cho pulled the camera out and tucked it away. "We're clear. No tripwires."

She remained in the lead, nonetheless. No one told her any differently. No arguments were necessary or warranted. Opening the door, all three entered. Loren and Myers crept right and left, leaving a wide swath down the middle for the expert.

The hallway stretched to a kitchen in the back. The living room and dining area branched off from the front of the property. Both rooms no longer carried the standard furniture found in most homes. Couches and tables had been replaced with metal racks and workbenches. Equipment tucked tight to walls and shelves dominated both rooms, crowded with wires and casings.

"This is definitely the place," Cho whispered. She showcased the nearest shelf and the bundle of wire hanging off the side. "Look at this stuff. And I do mean look. Don't touch anything."

Loren and Myers took her meaning at once. They had both been through enough during their tenure in Portents to realize the danger that came with touching the wrong object. No other prompting was needed, and the pair went about their search quickly and efficiently.

Myers nodded to the stairs and started up. Loren crept down the hall to the kitchen, securing the half-bath on his right before proceeding. The sink was clear of dishes, the cupboards full and the fridge packed. Cleaning supplies were in abundance, organized and labeled. The drying rack carried a single plate. Utensils rested next to it, enough for a lone individual who appeared quite disciplined about their eating habits. No frills. No extravagance. Like the task was necessary, but required no pomp or pageantry.

The back door remained secure. As one of the circling patrols passed by, Loren opened the door and stuck his head outside. "Anything?"

The officers shook their heads.

"Check the fence and neighboring properties. They might be close."

The pair started immediately. They radioed the other officers on site, while Loren started back toward the foyer.

"Any sign of this guy?" Myers asked, bounding down the steps.

"No." Loren let out a frustrated groan. "He's not here."

"Someone is," Myers said, eyes to the upper level.

Cho waved them on, content to go through the workstations on the first floor alone. Loren took her approval and joined Myers. They reached the second-floor landing to see two bedrooms branching on either side. A full bath occupied the end of the hall. Myers shuffled them to the room on the right.

The smell hit Loren at once. He covered his nose and mouth, leaving his vision clear to take in the dead man centered on the bed. The victim stared up at the ceiling, arms at his sides. His flesh peeled in places, with bone protruding along his cheeks and hands.

"How long?"

"Long enough to rule him out as a suspect." Myers wheeled away from the room, hands on her hips. "Dammit."

Loren stayed with the dead. The body had been positioned on the bed. There was a clear stab wound through his chest, the likely cause of death. Loren inspected the wound further. Decomposition made it difficult, but the entry was smooth compared to the jagged edges of the blade used in the deaths of Caldwell and Hennessey.

Slow steps carried Loren through the room. Photos lined the dresser. The man in the images—taken from family occasions and vacations and a dozen other events over the years—looked nothing like the decayed corpse. He appeared vibrant and alive. Loren looked at them all curiously, hoping and failing to piece together his identity.

"Myers?"

"There's a sleeping bag in the other room. The guy just slept here, like there wasn't a dead man across the hall." Myers closed her eyes and shook her head. "He used the guy's shower. Ate the man's food. Who the hell is this lunatic?"

"We'll find him," Loren said.

"I..." Myers glanced at her phone. The call she needed to make hung over her every thought.

Loren inched closer. "Go."

She glared at him. "What?"

"Go," he said again. "Thel should hear about Yardin from you."

"Loren, I can't. I should—"

"The bomber's not here."

"He might come back."

"Put the units outside on it," he said in a soft voice. "They can watch the place. Cho and I can secure the components. We've got this."

Myers mulled over her options. Worry filled her every glance, lost not only to the dead man in the next room but Yardin's open case. Her concern for Thel followed her everywhere she went, apparent in her every move.

Slowly, she nodded. "Thanks. I…" She reached for his hand. Her fingers grazed his, then fell away. There was more to be said, but she swallowed it down and started for the stairs. "Yeah. Thanks."

Her orders carried in the air before she hopped back into the car and left the scene. Reticent steps brought Loren back to the first floor, where Cho continued to work diligently to identify and catalog the warehouse of equipment.

"Cho?"

She wheeled around. A magnifying glass hung over her right eye. She cradled a large metal disc with various input ports throughout. "Yes?"

"Secure the site," Loren said. "Call Anderson. We need him here as soon as possible."

"Sure. I'll call him now."

Loren held tight to the wooden railing along the steps. His gaze trailed down the hall. A framed diploma hung on the wall at his side. Loren scanned the name scrawled across it, eyes widening with terror.

"Cho!"

She stuck her head out of the living room, phone to her ear. "Yeah?"

"You never said the man's name," Loren said, unable to tear himself away from the diploma. "Who owns this place?"

"It's all in the file." She cocked her head toward the door. Her pack with the information rested inside.

She disappeared to complete her call while Loren bent to grab the dossier. He rummaged through the scribbles of notes until he came to the property owner's information.

Everything fell into place. The bombings, the distractions, and the theft of the Greystone from the Luminaries had all been for one thing.

Worse, for one person.

CHAPTER SEVENTY

"Did you hear something?" Gabe peered back down the C-Line, scanning the shadows for signs of life. Rats skirted the periphery, the squeaks lost behind the rumbling of the subway.

Shepherd stuck close to him. A flashlight in his right hand guided their way. Somehow, he remained poised and confident in the face of pure insanity. Gabe, on the other hand, was ready to jump out of his skin. His comfort with their destination was minimal, to say the least.

"It's nothing, Gabe," Shepherd reassured him, patting his shoulder. "We've made it this far…"

His teacher was right. The trip hadn't been without its own danger. They had circumvented the protesters down Evans by cutting through Heaven's Gate Park. While the violence broke out between people and the myths they sought to blame for their troubles, Shepherd found the nearest subway access and they'd left the streets behind for the dismal dark below.

The trains continued to run. It was one of the few avenues of travel left to those wanting to actually reach their destination. Gabe led Shepherd down the platform and across the rails for a hidden walkway. It took them to the discarded and forgotten junctions of the past. He had only made the trek once before, the journey unwarranted and unnecessary, but curiosity had won out over common sense.

"I followed Loren here," Gabe said, his nerves causing his body to shake with each step. He wasn't supposed to know about the chamber or its location. It was another secret Loren held back from him, like so many others of late.

Soriya had been with Loren. Gabe had hidden out of sight, watching them approach the junction with the large red door. He'd studied their every move, listening to every word, as if prepping for an exam. He was glad he had.

"It's down here," Gabe said. They moved away from the web-covered doors close to the platform, then rounded their way into the depths of the city. When he reached the red door, equidistant between two blinking lights, Gabe stopped.

Shepherd approached from behind. He shined his flashlight upon the door, curiously scanning the hatch. "Here?"

"This is where I saw Loren go, yeah."

Shepherd chuckled lightly. "I find it strange you call him Loren. Dad never sounded right?"

"He's not my—"

"Ah," Shepherd said, a hand up in surrender. "Right. Sorry, Gabe. I didn't mean to pry."

"No, it's okay," Gabe said with a sigh. "Loren has done all right by me. He just…"

"Sees a kid instead of a young man."

Gabe nodded. "Yeah."

Shepherd pointed to the door. "So, this chamber you mentioned is here?"

"Yeah."

Shepherd stepped forward. "Then let's—"

Gabe grabbed the man's arm and pulled him back. "Wait."

"What is it?"

"The door is protected." Gabe took out the Greystone. He raised the ancient item ahead. Light grew upon the surface.

Runes appeared on the door. How they had been hidden was only one of the many mysteries created by the Greystone and its power. Shepherd staggered away from the hatch, eyes wide with wonder.

"How did you—"

"You're going to be asking that question a lot, sir." Gabe kept the stone before him, eyes taking in every sigil marking the door.

"How do we get through it?" Shepherd asked.

"I don't know if we should," Gabe said. Soriya had placed the protection for a reason and asked Loren to do the same in her absence. The Bypass was to be safeguarded at all costs and here was Gabe, trying to break into the damn place. He should have told Loren, should have attempted to explain his actions. Yet, there hadn't been time, had there? "Sir, this place…"

Shepherd's hand fell on Gabe's shoulder. A beaming smile greeted him. "It might hold the answer. You can save the city, Gabe. I know you can."

Gabe shifted closer to the door and the symbols littering the red hatch. It was a cipher, Soriya had explained—a secret message, not because of what had been written, but because of the rune intentionally omitted.

Gabe closed his eyes. Runes had never been his strong suit, but he recalled the one Loren had muttered at Soriya's insistence.

"Ansuz," he whispered.

The Greystone burned brightly. The revealing light of the stone showered over the door. All at once, the other sigils spun wildly, blurring in a grand spiral. They wrapped around the hatch, causing it to twist until a loud clanking sound echoed.

The rune dimmed as the other symbols faded to nothingness. Carefully, Gabe grabbed hold of the wheel. He struggled against the significant weight still left in place by the door. Shepherd joined him, offering his strength to the cause.

"Pull, Gabe," Shepherd said. "You've got this. Pull!"

The door gave way, groaning open until it slammed against the wall of the service tunnel. Gabe and Shepherd peered down the long metal staircase before them. A green light flickered below; a soft hum filled the air.

It beckoned them forward.

Gabe peered at Shepherd, then back to the stairs. He took his first step forward, his teacher right behind him the whole way.

"That's a good man," Shepherd said. "Lead the way."

CHAPTER SEVENTY-ONE

Dawn had yet to break. A hazy sea of deep purple remained over the skyline, casting shadows in every direction. Parked against the curb, the van was crammed with belongings. Clothes, dishes, provisions for the trip, and so many other small packages ate at the space at the rear of the vehicle until nothing was left to load but the people themselves.

Willis made repeated trips back to his home. How a man could come to be so understanding in this world staggered Christopher, yet his compassion knew no bounds. To keep Jayla and Marissa safe, there was nothing the man wasn't willing to do. He jammed some sleeping bags into the trunk, fighting with the lock to make sure they—and everything else—were secured.

Jayla cradled Marissa close. The young girl of four rubbed at weary eyes. Sleep had not come easily for her in the strange apartment. Now, to ask her to wake before first light? She was less than pleased.

"I'm sleepy, Momma," she whined. Her eyes were closed, a pained look on her face from the rough night. Marissa's only comfort was Lady, her doll, held next to her.

Jayla snuggled her daughter tighter. "I know, baby." She gently lifted her into the van and the car seat set up in the middle row. Straps fought against her every movement, her hands shaking from the effort. The night had not been easy for any of them.

"Why can't we stay longer?" Marissa asked as the straps clicked into place.

Jayla tugged them for reassurance, then settled along the side of the door. She shuffled stray strands of hair from her face and threw on the widest smile possible for one so tired and so terribly afraid. "We're going to a new place. A nicer place. You'll see."

Christopher watched it all from the sidewalk. He had been present throughout the night to make sure they remained safe from harm. Part of him wanted nothing more than to resume his search for Darius, to find a way to bring him back from the cliff he so desperately wanted to jump off.

That desire came from selfishness. If Darius could be swayed, everything might go back to the way it had been. Darius would be like him, alone and unrestrained, to handle the role of the Greystone. They would be true partners this time and everything would be better for it.

He knew the truth, however. There was no going back. There was only the path forward—one that would protect Jayla and Marissa from the brutal reality of their situation. Once they were safe, Darius would become the priority, but not until.

"Anything?" Willis paused at Christopher's side. He carried a thermos and three cups.

"Not that I've seen," Christopher said. Willis nodded, the answer not quite what he hoped to hear. Assurances were not something Christopher could offer, not when it came to the man who had trained him to be the Greystone. Not when it came to the soldier Darius had been before.

Jayla joined them and Christopher's gaze lowered. "Darius is much more capable than I am."

"Don't sell yourself short, Chris," Jayla said, raising his eyes to meet hers. "You're a good man. You're here for me. Helping me clean up the mess I've made."

"None of this is your fault, Jayla," Christopher replied with a smile. "Believe that."

The first specks of light dotted the sky. Deep purple softened and pink wisps formed in the distance. Willis headed for the driver's seat to tuck his belongings away. Finished, he leaned along the frame to check on Marissa.

Jayla sighed at their rapport. "She deserves a normal life."

Christopher held back his initial response. He wasn't sure a normal life existed any longer. Not for them and not in Portents. "We should go."

"Wait," Jayla said, a hand on his arm. She reached inside her coat and pulled out a small jewelry box. "I want you to take this. In case..."

Christopher didn't understand. He opened the box to find a

locket inside.

"It's for Marissa," Jayla explained. "When she's older. When…"

"You should be the one to give it to her," Christopher said. "I…"

"Chris," Jayla said, holding back tears. "I'm scared."

"I'm going to keep you safe." He held out the locket.

Jayla shook her head, closing it in his hand. "Give it to me when we're clear of the city. When this is finally over."

A slow nod of acceptance offered his only reply. He closed the box and slipped it into the pocket of his cloak, then moved for the van.

Few words passed between them as they settled in for the drive. Christopher took the seat beside Marissa, who instantly nodded off. Jayla and Willis sipped their coffee. The van rolled ahead, down the vacant streets of Portents. The early morning hour was enough to give them a modicum of privacy, and they took the opportunity to process their decisions in the silence.

Leaving the confines of the city, the roads became more and more twisted on the rise to Olcott Curve, and the lovers in the front seat grew more relaxed. They held hands, breathing easier with each mile marker passed.

Christopher, however, grew more restless. Chills ran along his skin. He peered at Marissa, content in her sleep, yet found no comfort in her ease. He leaned along the edge of the seat.

As the car reached the curve that marked the border of the city, Christopher realized the reason for his uneasiness. A shadow stood in the road, barring their path.

Darius waited for them. There would be no escape, not if he had anything to say about it.

Jayla read the fury on her husband's face. She covered her mouth with her hands. "No. Oh, no."

CHAPTER SEVENTY-TWO

Gabe stood in awe before the Bypass. The swirling green light hovered three feet above the ground. Black wisps of shadow intermingled with the light. They danced along the periphery like spirits caught in the tide. The entire room hummed from the energy, causing a chill up Gabe's spine.

He had never seen anything so magnificent before. He had always wondered about it, always dreamed of what it might look like. Sometimes in the quiet of the night, he felt like the Greystone passed along whispers from the infinite, sending visions of the secrets held within.

The entire chamber brought him the same sensation. It was like a second home—one he had never known to be missing from his life. The pillars were white and rose to the ceiling. Glyphs dominated every inch, spiraling around the granite surface in different languages, most of which Gabe had never seen before. He recognized a few of the symbols throughout. There were the runes his counterpart used with her stone and the hieroglyphs of social studies class from years prior. Most were a mystery, as so much had been since the stone came into his life.

Spiderwebs hung from the shadowy corners of the chamber. Neglect brought them out, and they spread down the walls and along the makeshift rooftop of the domicile tucked to one side of the wide space. Cots and shelves remained within the bedrooms. A fireplace filled with ash sat at the rear of the main living area.

While Gabe moved to inspect the place more thoroughly, Shepherd cleared his throat. He drew him back to the Bypass and their task. His level of comfort with the room surprised Gabe, but his insistence at approaching the Bypass must have come from a sense of urgency.

"I'm not exactly sure how this works," Gabe said. He stepped through the barrier of the four columns, which appeared to lock the energy of the Bypass inside. Small cracks grew more visible on the pillars—signs of age, most likely—and Gabe quickly ignored them. "I've never—"

"It's all right, Gabe," Shepherd said, always at his side. He maneuvered his student closer to the glowing sphere. "I imagine it takes a certain amount of concentration to access the knowledge kept inside."

"Yeah, I..." Gabe shook his head. "Yeah, I guess it does."

Shepherd nodded. "Clear your thoughts. Focus on the stone and the one question you need answered."

Gabe took a deep breath, then returned to the glowing sphere with renewed awareness. He raised the Greystone toward the swirling energy, channeling his will and the question at the heart of everyone's mind. He tried to imagine the bomber, to visualize the threat against Portents. As he did so, a piece of himself started to drift.

More images filtered through the void. He saw Loren's disappointment and felt the sting of Soriya's anger at his failure. With each spiraling thought, another piece of his spirit slipped beyond the veil. He felt dizzy and lost. He was being pulled into the infinite.

Panic broke his connection. He nearly fell over from the sensation of his spirit blasting back into his body.

"Gabe?"

Shepherd was at his side, a hand out for him. Gabe shook his head, finding his balance on his own. He threw off the effects of his previous attempt, then raised the stone again.

"You can do this, Gabe."

"I..." He thought about the question again. This time, though, it grew in the asking. Everyone counted on him. Everyone was panicked about the explosions and the violence and the hate. In the Bypass, Gabe saw them all—Loren, Myers, Ruiz, and Thel. His friends at school. Even Mr. Johnson. They all stood before him, waiting for him to handle things, to be the Greystone the way he was meant to be.

Mr. Shepherd's image overtook them. Gabe spun around to see his teacher next to him.

"Gabe..."

"I don't know how to do this, I guess," Gabe said, trying to laugh off the intense experience. The others remained on the surface of the sphere, all crying out to him. They begged for him to listen to a warning he couldn't hear. "This was a waste of time."

Shepherd held out his hand. "Would you like me to try?"

"What?"

"Let me help." Shepherd brought Gabe and the stone back to the Bypass. "Together, I'm sure we can figure this out. We can save everyone."

"I don't…"

"Two wills are better than one, right?"

Gabe hesitated. A pulse rippled through him from the stone. The faces within the Bypass screamed at him, the answer right there in front of him. All he wanted was the strength to reach out and grab hold of it. To bring them back from the pain that had eaten up so much of their lives of late.

He slowly released his grip on the stone. He extended it, waiting for Shepherd to join him.

"That's it," Shepherd said.

A pounding filled Gabe's ears. He imagined it to be the beating of his heart, raging so loud against the hum of the infinite. Only it wasn't his heart. It wasn't the Bypass or the screams of the voices within.

The pounding came from the metal stairs to the chamber. Loren bounded off the bottom step, his gun in his hand. "Stop! Gabe, don't!"

Gabe pulled away from Shepherd. "What? Loren? What are you—"

Loren leveled his weapon at Shepherd. "Not another damn step, you son of a bitch."

CHAPTER SEVENTY-THREE

"Loren? What are you doing?"

No answer came. Loren struggled for breath. The race through Portents had been frantic. When he'd found the apartment vacant, Loren knew he'd been too late. He couldn't think of where to go, what the next move might be... not until he focused on the Greystone itself. If someone wanted the stone, their goal most likely led them to what it protected.

The Bypass Chamber always stood at the heart of the stone's mission. The reason remained elusive—yet another mystery related to the insanity that cropped up with the Greystone and Portents. Gabe had to be there. That was the thought that kept Loren moving, the eternal hope that he wouldn't be too late.

Gabe looked at Loren with terrified eyes. It pained the former detective to see. But what other reaction could there be? Loren had rushed into the room, gun in the air and shouting through heaving breaths. It overwhelmed the kid, something he'd tried to avoid by protecting Gabe from the truth—by withholding information on the case from the very beginning.

He should have trusted in Gabe. Instead, he pushed him away... right into the waiting arms of the worst person.

Shepherd slid behind Gabe, his hands in the air. "I don't understand what this is about. I was trying to help Gabe. We thought—"

"Stop," Loren said, finger over the trigger.

Gabe took a step forward. "He's telling the truth."

"Get out of the way, Gabe."

The kid squeezed the stone between his hands. "Mr. Shepherd has been helping me. He's the only one willing to listen—willing to trust in me. He doesn't push me aside or chuck me away. He doesn't hide the truth."

"That's all he's done," Loren said.

"What?"

"We found Mr. Johnson." Loren tried to forget the image of the dead man positioned on his bed. "Your teacher didn't leave abruptly for another job. He was murdered."

"He—"

"Don't you see?" Loren continued, creeping closer. Gabe reeled with each approach, unsure about anything. "Shepherd did it to get close to you. He's using you, manipulating you like he's done the whole city. Gabe, he's the bomber!"

"He…" Gabe turned to the Bypass with wide eyes, as if a message had finally come through from the other side. He completed the shift, looking back at the teacher who had been by his side through the entire affair when no one else had. "You?"

"I'm afraid so," Shepherd said. He batted the Greystone away before Gabe brought it to bear. The stone skidded across the room. As Gabe turned to pursue his lost weapon, Shepherd snatched his arm. He pulled the boy in front of him, one hand restraining Gabe. With his other hand, Shepherd released the knife hidden behind his back and held it to the boy's throat.

Gabe kicked for release, but Shepherd refused to give him an inch. The kid screamed defiantly, lashing out to no avail. "How? How could I have been so wrong?"

"It's not your fault, Gabe," Shepherd whispered in his ear.

No truer words had ever been spoken by the man. The fault lay with Loren, who looked on in horror at his young ward in the hands of a lunatic. He should have trusted Gabe more—trusted himself to be able to inform and protect their livelihood at the same time. His actions had put them in this position, the danger all the more real and his protection less than nothing in the face of such terror.

Shepherd sneered. The beaming pride of the teacher was gone, replaced by a malevolent glare. "This city has become nothing but gullible fools. But I'll fix that. With the Bypass, I can fix everything."

CHAPTER SEVENTY-FOUR

"What do we do?" Willis turned to them, hands tight on the steering wheel. "Anyone? What do I do?"

Darius made no move against them. He stood, prepared to act, but in a holding pattern. Just as they were. Jayla's concern rested with Marissa, who continued to doze uncomfortably in her car seat. No one knew how to act or where to begin.

Not until Christopher reached for the door handle.

"Chris..." Jayla hesitated to continue, the name breathless and lingering. What else was there to say between them?

"I promised to protect you, Jayla," Christopher said. He pulled the door open.

Willis reached out. "Thank you."

Christopher patted the man's hand, then exited the vehicle. He tapped on the window, and Jayla rolled hers down a crack. "When you get an opening, you go. Do you hear me?"

"Without you?" Willis asked.

"Not a chance," Jayla said. "You said it yourself. Darius will—"

"Without me," Christopher interrupted. "No matter what happens. Understood?"

"Chris..."

"I keep my promises," he replied, leaving the van behind. He removed his cloak, letting the wind carry it away from the street. It landed in the mounting pile of leaves surrounding the road. They fell in waves from the sky, a rainbow of color against the darkness set before them.

Christopher approached slowly. He clutched his Greystone against his palm. A silent prayer left him. He hoped for answers, for direction from the infinite, but received nothing in return. There was only Darius and the path ahead.

"Let them go," Christopher demanded.

"Move aside, traitor," Darius snarled. There was no surprise in his eyes at Christopher's survival. Nor was there any empathy for their plight. All compassion had left his teacher, leaving nothing more than a stranger. "That's my wife in there with my daughter. I want them back and I want them now."

"Not like this." Christopher continued his approach, his steps slow. Eyes flitting across the landscape, Christopher tried to take in every advantage available and found none waiting. "Not with the anger and the fury. That's not how you'll win them back."

"You don't get to tell me what to do," Darius growled. He slammed his fist against his chest. "I am the teacher. Now, let me give you one last lesson."

Darius launched at Christopher. His fist drove forward with every ounce of strength in the man. He offered no restraint. No forgiveness either.

Christopher reeled at the man's strike. The fist sailed in front of him, barely missing. Two more followed, arms swinging wildly. Christopher did his best to maneuver away, his feet shuffling along the leaf-ridden road.

"Dammit, Darius," Christopher said, dodging a kick toward his midsection. Every attack by the man was a killing blow. He was not looking to wound Christopher any longer. He sought only to end the conflict as brutally and efficiently as he had against the dark elves. Christopher was an enemy, like the monsters they'd faced over the years. "Darius, this isn't you!"

Another near miss brushed by Christopher. He felt the edge of the blow, spun away, then leaped over the follow-up kick. He tucked his head into his chest to roll from the impact before jumping back to his feet.

Darius stood waiting behind him. His fist landed against Christopher's spine, shoving him forward and away from the road.

Christopher whirled to catch the next strike, a right cross. He used Darius' momentum, knocking him away. "Jayla told me," Christopher said against the mounting rage of his attacker. "About the late nights with the stone. What has it done to you?"

"Opened my eyes," Darius said with a sinister sneer. "Shown me truths you couldn't possibly imagine."

"You're lying. All your talk about the secrets kept by the Bypass. Why would it show you anything?"

"Who said it was the Bypass speaking to me?" Darius chuckled. "You have no idea the role we were supposed to take, Chris. The Greystone is so much more than a tool. And the Bypass? It hides the greatest treasure of all, one I will free when this is over."

Christopher leaped at the man. "You won't get the chance, Darius. I wish you would have seen the light. Now you've left me little choice."

Darius caught the weak strike from the man and squeezed. "You've left me none at all!"

He pushed Christopher back. A sharp uppercut caught Christopher in the chin. Dazed from the blow, he could do little against his teacher, who grabbed him by the collar and threw him into the brush lining the side of the road.

"Chris!" Jayla shouted from the van.

He spat at the leaves covering his face. Pushing up from the ground, Christopher struggled to right himself. Darius loomed over him, chest heaving and fists clenched tight. Christopher, though, looked past him for the waiting van.

Jayla reached for the handle, fear in her eyes. As she started to open the door, Christopher held out his hand. "No! Tell Willis to go. Now!"

The door slammed shut. The van slipped into drive and shot forward like a dart. Willis kept his eyes on the road ahead. Jayla, though, stared in terror at her husband and the man who had kept them safe from him. Her hand pressed against the glass—a final goodbye and thank you rolled into one innocuous gesture.

Darius spun toward the squealing tires. "No! I won't let them." He took out his stone. "He can't take them from me."

Christopher grabbed the man's arm. "Don't be a fool, Darius. Put the stone down before—"

"Get your hands off me!" He ripped Christopher's fingers off him. The stone leveled with the van, a light growing along the surface.

Christopher jumped in front of him. He took hold of the man's wrist and twisted the stone into the air. He caught sight of the rune in time to see electricity spike through the air.

The stray spark of lightning caught Christopher along his left temple. Searing pain ripped down his face, then cut across his cheek for his ear. His scream was agony. It did little to deter Darius, who broke his connection with the stone long enough to toss Christopher to the ground.

Blood seeped into his eye. The cut was deep and hot to the touch.

"You brought that on yourself," Darius said, stepping away from him. "Just like she did."

The stone lit once more, its goal obvious from the onset. Intent on stopping his wife, Darius held nothing back. All of his rage fueled the Greystone. The van erupted in flames. Tires squealed and spun as the vehicle careened off the road. It slammed into a large tree at the curve. The fire spread up the trunk and down the branches, causing the leaves to scorch instantly.

"Darius, no!"

Christopher knocked the stone away. All thought of his bleeding face left him. He watched the Greystone skitter across the road until it landed behind the back tire of the burning van.

His fist flew freely and without remorse. He saw nothing but the dead in the van as he pummeled his teacher. Punch after punch, he drove the man away from the scene. Blood spurted from Darius' lips. His right eye closed at the assault. Christopher refused to let up, his anger spilling from him with each strike.

"You monster! You…"

Darius fell to his knees. He raised a hand in surrender. Christopher snatched his collar, ready to kill the man who had once given him so much. Vengeance fueled him. He wanted nothing more than to embrace it, to use that power against his former teacher.

At the last second, Christopher hesitated. His fist opened and his hand dropped to his side. He let go of the man's collar, staggering away. Becoming Darius served no purpose. It did no one any good.

He turned to the burning vehicle. Tears stung his open wound as they flowed down his face. "What have you done?"

CHAPTER SEVENTY-FIVE

Christopher raced for the van. He tucked low to avoid the rising flames shooting out from the vehicle and raining down from the massive oak wrapped around its front. He pulled his shirt over his face to mute the smoke inhalation, then pushed for the passenger side.

Leaves fell in droves. The serenity of Olcott Curve was lost during the struggle and nature sought its revenge. The flickering flames marked the leaves. They were charred and cracked, like so much of late.

"No, no, no, no," Chris muttered. He reached for the door, but the handle fought against him. His skin burned at the touch. "Open, blast you."

Peering up at the window, he realized the futility of his actions. The blaze engulfed the entire front of the van. He no longer saw any sign of Jayla or Willis. Fire had consumed them.

Christopher reeled, fighting back a scream. Tears poured from his eyes as he fell to his knees in anguish. It had been his decision to leave. He had promised them peace from Darius' wrath. Instead, his actions had condemned them.

Christopher struggled to find his feet, struggled to care a whit about continuing on. What was left for him?

A cry woke him to the truth. His eyes, still filled with tears, opened wide as the cry repeated, louder this time.

"Help!"

Marissa was still alive—trapped inside the van.

Christopher jumped to his feet. He grabbed hold of the sliding door on the passenger side and tugged. It failed to move. Fear and panic rushed through him. He grabbed hold of the stone in his pocket to channel those emotions directly into the obol.

"Open!"

The handle cracked beneath his grasp. The door flew down the track and nearly ripped free from the vehicle with the strength afforded by the Greystone.

Marissa screamed at his arrival. A wall of flames that had devoured the front seats of the van sought to spread to the rest. The girl clutched tightly to Lady. She coughed loudly from the smoke penetrating everything.

"Marissa!" Christopher yelled. He dove into the van. Tucking the stone away, Christopher worked to remove the child's restraints. The buckles snapped open to release her.

"Give me your hand," he said.

"Momma!" Marissa exclaimed. "What about—"

"My hand, Marissa," he said again. The world blurred behind wet eyes. "Please."

The child took the offer, and he lifted her from the seat and the van. He carried her away from the wreck. Ten feet away, Marissa started to resist his efforts.

"Stop!" she said. "You have to stop!"

Christopher set her down on her feet. Lady remained against her chest. He kept Marissa's back to the van, the flames shooting out of the open door on the side.

"We should keep moving," he said, hands on her shoulders.

"But—" She tried to turn around, but he held her firm.

"Don't," Christopher whispered. "Don't look back."

Marissa stared at him, lost and confused. "What happened to Momma? Is she okay?"

"I…"

"You said you'd protect her," Marissa said. "You're going to keep us safe, aren't you?"

His grip tightened on her shoulders. "Look at me," he said, fighting through his tears. "Just keep looking at me. I…"

Marissa was right. He had failed them. The blame rested with no one else. If he hadn't interfered with Darius…

Thoughts of his teacher caused Christopher to whip his head around. He searched the entire length of Olcott Curve for signs of life but found none. Darius was gone.

Christopher closed his eyes. His failure was now complete.

"I am so sorry, little one."

"Where's Momma?" Marissa cried. "Where is she?"

Christopher pulled her close in a hug. "She's gone, Marissa. I tried, but she…"

She deserves a normal life.

Jayla's words haunted him. What chance was there of that now? What chance was there for any of them now?

He let Marissa go and stood. She continued to clutch Lady, confused and alone. Christopher held the Greystone before him, staring at it intently. Then he leveled it on the girl.

"I'm so sorry," he said. "What happened… You won't remember it. Any of it. Your mom wanted you to have a better life than this. That's the only promise I can still keep."

He opened his mind to the stone. Every ounce of sadness channeled into the powerful obol. He took that remorse—the guilt over what had happened—and pulled the same from the girl. With it came her memories. All the pain and all the tragedy.

Marissa deserved a second chance at life. A better life. A happy life.

Christopher used the Greystone to wipe the slate clean, hoping to give her that chance.

CHAPTER SEVENTY-SIX

"Marissa?"

Blank eyes stared back at him. Christopher didn't know if the stone had done what he willed it to, or if the tragedy of her mother's death merely overwhelmed the girl. Either way, she appeared catatonic, standing in the street, holding tight to her one lifeline in the world—her doll, Lady.

"What have I done?" He had spent so much time focused on Darius' sins, his own bore down on him in the aftermath of their struggle. Marissa was alone. Her world had been taken from her, and now Christopher had completed the crime. Her life was no more.

A second chance awaited her.

Before he could reach out to her and move her from the road, the sound of sirens filled the air. The flames must have served as beacon enough to call to them. Fire engines blitzed up Olcott Curve from the city, with an ambulance and police cruisers trailing right behind.

Christopher hesitated for only a moment. He grazed the child's cheek, then raced for the brush along the side of the road. He collected his cloak and held it close. Ducking deep into the foliage, he let his body sink beneath the curtain of leaves gathered to keep from being seen.

Firefighters made quick work of the disaster, while a pair of EMTs took care of their lone patient—the only survivor of the tragedy. Throughout their examination, Christopher watched intently. Marissa made no move against the first responders. No words were spoken to them, no tales spun over what had happened. She continued to stare off into the distance, as if lost to a past she no longer recalled.

Christopher hoped as much anyway. She deserved peace of mind. To burden a child with such terror at so young an age was a cruel punishment indeed. And to know that the cause of such destruction had been her own father? No one could live like that.

The first responders handled the scene efficiently. Throughout their work, they watched over the girl—their comments clear, even at a distance.

"She hasn't said a word. Doesn't even look at it like it's there," one of the EMTs said to his compatriot, a balding man with thin-rimmed glasses.

"You said her folks were in there?" his colleague replied, fixing his glasses to the bridge of his nose.

"Looks that way," said the first man. His voice was low, and he turned away from Marissa. "Pulled two bodies out. They'll be lucky to identify them, though."

"Road isn't even slick." Another voice entered the fray, more distant than the others. "How fast were they going to do this?"

"What were they running from?"

The first man's response caught her ear. "She doesn't know yet."

"Poor girl."

A leaf danced above her. It passed once, then twice, and her eyes began to stir. She woke as if for the first time as the leaf flew over her head to the wreck of the van.

No one else noticed her movements. They were caught up on the scene and with the circumstances that had brought them there. Marissa rushed under the rope line for the leaf, which slid under the van.

As she reached for it, her hand settled on something else entirely. Marissa stepped clear of the van, holding tight to a small stone.

Her father's Greystone.

"No," Christopher muttered under his breath. He slid deeper into the woods, tucking close to the thick trunk of a tree. He had forgotten about the stone in the aftermath, and now it rested in Marissa's tiny hand. What it meant, what he could do about it, were all questions swirling around his head, yet he simply looked on with growing interest.

Slipping his cloak on, Christopher felt the rattle of the jewelry box in his pocket. He took out the locket from within, dangling it between his fingers: Jayla's last gift for her daughter. Yet, maybe he had given her a better one. Perhaps the fresh start was the path forward for more than just Marissa.

Christopher watched the young girl stroke the stone in her hands, all thought of her doll and her previous life gone forever. Curious eyes followed her from the wreck, wondering what she might do with the stone… and if it was always meant to be hers.

CHAPTER SEVENTY-SEVEN

Thel barely felt the carpet under her feet when she entered her apartment. The door closing was lost behind the elation from her evening. From the interview with Nicki Dryden to the party with Kellon, Shin, and a few others at one of the many foreclosed properties at their disposal, the entire night had been a whirlwind.

It was also a reminder of how life used to be for her. No one would ever take that feeling from her again.

Her back slid along the closed door. Hands ran through the purple locks drooped down over her face. Her smile spread wider with each thought of her night. The joy. The companionship. She had missed it more than she'd thought.

There would be no more fear, no more restrictions, only the unbound living that had been stolen from her. Kellon promised as much.

When he spoke, Thel listened. His every word woke something inside her. The vision of their future together—standing up for those unable to in Portents—cemented their bond. She was part of something that mattered, bigger than herself, yet very much for herself at the same time. For the first time in ages, Thel was alive again, and it felt incredible.

The elation died at the sound of a throat clearing. Thel quickly scanned the room, suddenly aware of a presence in her apartment. A shadow reached for the lamp at their side and turned it on.

Myers stared at her with a thin gaze. "You're looking pretty chipper."

"Sam?" Thel asked, hand to her chest. She pushed from the door, dropping her keys on the end table next to the couch. A stiff wind blew through the room, a chill she'd failed to notice when entering. "Did you—"

Glass spread along the carpet beneath a shattered window.

"Did you break into my apartment?"

Myers huffed. "Call a cop." She kicked off the wall and approached, her cell phone extended. "No, really, go ahead. We can all have a nice chat."

Thel's brow furrowed. She moved for the window and closed the curtains to block the wind. "What are you even talking about?"

"Where have you been?" Myers said. "I called."

"I was out," Thel replied.

"New friends?"

"Yeah," the siren answered, drawing out the word. "So what?"

"What did you do? You and your new friends?" Myers rounded the room. The cell phone slipped into her pocket, but her hand lingered over her hip and the holster strapped to her belt. "Do anything interesting? Take a walk? Catch a movie? Commit murder?"

"What?"

From out of her other hand, Myers produced a small object. The purple rabbit's foot dangled between her fingers. "Found this in the same room as David Yardin's body."

Thel stared at the item. She didn't back away or shrink from the item she had so callously tossed aside.

Myers shook her head. "Yeah. He's dead. Hence my call earlier. But you don't seem too surprised to hear that. Or too broken up about it."

A million thoughts swirled through Thel's mind. She tried to come up with excuse after excuse, to place blame on someone else, or craft a narrative to calm her former partner. In the end, though, Thel knew those days were behind her. There was no need to explain her actions or justify them. She owned up to them, no matter the consequences.

"Why should I be broken up about it?"

"Did you not hear me?" Myers said. "He's dead."

"And I killed him," Thel snapped. "After what he did to me? Of course I killed him."

"What he did..." Myers reeled. She held the rabbit's foot up—the gift given to Thel in the hospital during her recovery. "He... He was the one?"

Thel sneered. "That's right, *Detective*."

Myers' gaze fell to the floor, clearly hurt by the comment. For a split second, Thel's gaze softened at the pain she'd caused her friend. Then she remembered the price to reclaim her power—to find her life again. It was not something easily surrendered.

"Why didn't you say anything? Why didn't you tell me? I could have helped. I—"

"I don't need your help!" Thel bellowed. "I don't need anyone's help. I can stand on my own!"

"Thel…"

"David got what he deserved."

Tears filled Myers' eyes. She fought against them, shaking her head. "You don't mean that. I don't know who these friends of yours are or what ideas they've put in your head, but this isn't who you wanted to be. This isn't you, Thel."

"This is exactly who I am." Thel puffed out her chest. She pulled the apartment door open. "If you can't deal with that, you should leave."

"You know I can't do that." Myers drew her gun and leveled it against Thel. "I have to bring you in."

CHAPTER SEVENTY-EIGHT

The gun shook slightly in Myers' hand, not from nerves, but from the weight of her task. Thel had been her partner. They'd been friends—close and personal in every aspect of their lives for more than a year. No matter what batshit craziness Portents threw at them, they had watched each other's backs. Nothing affected their companionship.

She couldn't abide murder, though. Even if Yardin had been behind Thel's assault, the siren had gone too far.

Myers steadied her weapon. "You have the right to remain silent…"

During her time as a cop, Myers had seen many different scenarios play out with a perpetrator staring down the barrel of her Glock. There was fear, of course. Few wanted to die in the face of their sins. Pleading was a popular option. Fight or flight became instinctual when cornered. Thel followed none of the standard rules.

Thel laughed.

It started small with a chuckle, then escalated to a full-blown fit that caused her entire body to quake and her hands to slap at her chest to catch her breath. Thel laughed over the death of their colleague, over Myers' attempt to bring her to justice, over everything that had once mattered so much to her.

Myers hardly recognized the woman behind the sound. Joy was present, but not the kind she'd once taken in her job. No, her laughter sounded vindictive and cold.

"Thel." Myers tightened her grip on the Glock. "Don't—"

"What?" Thel exclaimed, hands before her. The grin remained; the aftermath of her fit still caused her to shake. "Don't what, Sam?"

Myers couldn't find the words. She didn't know what had claimed her friend, only that she had to be stopped before it happened again.

Thel pointed at her, disbelief in her wide eyes. "You hold tight to that silly gun and think you hold power. You hold nothing. You are nothing. Let me show you power."

She opened her mouth, the first inkling of a song on her lips.

Myers grimaced. "Dammit, Thel. I didn't want this."

Lowering her gun, Myers barreled at her former partner. Her scream offset the song long enough for her to slam into Thel's side. The force drove them against the door, which crashed into the wall. The hinges snapped loose from the impact.

Thel elbowed Myers in the cheek and knocked her away as she grappled her way back to her feet. "This is exactly what you want. You're like all the rest. You're afraid of us. Afraid of what we can do."

"I'm your friend!"

Thel spat at her. "Some friend."

Myers brought the Glock up. Thel quickly swatted Myers' arm away, then followed it up with a blow across her face. Myers stumbled away, the gun almost lost in the melee. Relentless, Thel battered at Myers with reckless abandon, unable to see straight in her anger. Punch for punch, Thel forced Myers to the back of the couch, which she promptly fell over onto the cushions. She rolled her way to the floor, a curse on her lips.

Before she could stand, Thel was there. "You've never understood what it's like to be me. To be a freak. To be a monster."

She snatched Myers by the collar and lifted her off her feet. The strength displayed was unlike any she'd shown during their time together. Had she been holding back the whole time—hiding for fear of everyone's reaction? Or had something else changed in her friend?

"You're not a monster," Myers said, blood dripping from her lip. "That's never been who you are."

Thel huffed. "I couldn't see it when I came back. Thought this place had changed. That the world could grow to accept me, to be more than it had been before. I should have known better."

"What are you saying, Thel?"

"My sisters were right."

Myers' eyes flared. Thel tossed her aside like she was nothing.

Her body crashed against the television, knocking it over the table where both fell. The screen cracked under her weight, shards pricking against her exposed arms. Her gun clattered to the carpet, just out of reach.

Myers couldn't move. Pain wracked her bones, but it didn't lock her in position. It didn't keep her from acting. That came from Thel's sudden realization. For so long, the siren had seen her sisters as the villains of the story—manipulating men for their own personal pleasure. They had taken everything from their victims to prop themselves up.

Thel had always admonished their behavior. Now she admired it; she thrilled at the power in her grasp.

She truly was gone. Her friend was no more. Yet Myers couldn't let it be. As she lifted herself from the television, she tried to reach her former partner.

"Thel, please…"

"I'm sorry, Sam," Thel said. "You left me no choice."

Her song started before Myers could react. The melody resounded, the rhythmic beat enrapturing Myers instantly. On her knees, she reached for the gun at her side. Fingers slipped around the grip, then raised the Glock.

Eyes widened at the movement—completely out of her control. She tried to fight against her rising arm and the sweep of the gun to her temple. Myers failed in all regards, sweat mixing with the blood dabbing her cheeks and forehead.

"This isn't you, Thel," Myers said. Her words, though, were lost to the song, which grew stronger and stronger with each passing moment. "Don't make me do this. Thel…"

The gun pressed against her right temple. A finger settled on the trigger.

"Don't…"

Her wrist twisted at the last second. The gun went off, and the bullet passed before Myers' terrified gaze.

Her gun fell to the floor as the song ended. Tears streamed down Myers' cheeks, blurring the world and all sign of Thel.

The siren remained, tall and proud. She leaned close, her words barely a whisper over the sobs of the detective. "That's power, Sam."

She raised her hand to strike. Myers reeled, cowering in fear.

No blow came. Myers slowly lowered her arm to see Thel in the open doorway of her apartment, jacket on and keys in her hand.

"Remember, Sam," Thel said with a smirk on her face. "I let you live."

"Thel…"

"I won't next time." The siren's warning echoed as she departed. "Stay out of my way."

Myers collapsed onto the carpet. She pulled her legs in tight to her chest. The gun rested next to her, though she made no move for it. She kept hearing the gunshot and felt the searing heat of the passing bullet.

Sobs rocked her body. It was a long time before she found the strength to move again. It was even longer before the tears stopped.

CHAPTER SEVENTY-NINE

The world paused. Leaves hovered in the air, stuck in position around the entire scene at Olcott Curve. Emergency workers joked and laughed and cried; their every movement was locked in stasis. Christopher stood amid the tree line, his feet ready to depart, but his eyes forever pulled toward the small child in the road.

Soriya stepped clear of the man. Her journey was over. Every memory had led to this moment. She could no longer ride it out as a simple observer.

Mentor joined her. Standing next to his younger self, he lowered his hood. Pain rested in his eyes—agony at the memories shared and those forced to relive. So much time had passed, so many miles had left him withered compared to his younger self. His hand grazed the fresh wound. He would carry the scar for the rest of his life.

It all started here. Their journey together. Soriya hadn't realized it, though. The past had been lost to her and now it was frozen in front of her, locked in time and space by the Bypass.

She lingered at the side of Christopher Eckhart. The locket dangled from his fingers. A silver chain connected to a heart at the end. Swirls of glitter caused the jewelry to shine with the rising of the sun. Soriya wanted to touch it, to open the heart charm—a final gift from a dead woman.

The child called to her instead.

As she shifted away from the brush, Mentor reached for her. She stopped him with a thin glare. The time for hiding was over. There was no walking away from the truth.

Slow steps brought her to the street. She kept her eyes on the child the entire time. Marissa cradled the small stone in her hands, captivated by the mysterious object.

Soriya circled her. She looked to the burning van and up the charred husk of the great oak tree where the vehicle rested. Every sense worked overtime to capture the scene. She smelled fresh autumn air, tucked behind the ash of the leaves cracking beneath her feet. The sound of the sirens and the flickering flames filled her ears. She tasted the morning dew on the tip of her tongue, salty from the tears at such a tragedy.

"This was real." Soriya stopped before the girl. She bent a knee to the street, meeting the young soul face-to-face for the first time. Marissa made no motion, frozen by the Bypass' power. Soriya reached out, her hand resting on the stone. "This... this was me."

Tears stung her eyes. She swiped them away, but they replenished. Her heart ached, the burden of the truth filling her for the first time in her life. She wheeled around to see Mentor at her side.

"You took my memories—my life—from me," Soriya said. "Why?"

"To save you," her teacher replied, the words weak and filled with guilt. "I hoped to give you a life. A chance, free from the tragedy that would have defined you."

Soriya stood. She cleared her eyes with her sleeve, wiping at the snot beneath her nose. The rationale made sense, even though she hated him for it. In one dark, terrible second, she had lost so much. The nightmares would have been difficult to endure.

Yet, so had the blank slate. Her time at Saint Helena's Orphanage had not been some blessing offered by Mentor's so-called gift. It had been hell. Her lack of memory had condemned her to isolation and ridicule. Instead of others sympathizing with her plight, they'd viewed her as a freak of nature—a strange creature unable to connect with anyone because she hadn't known who she was to begin with.

It all started here. The ending, though, remained. Soriya turned down the road and pointed to the figure no longer present. One player had slipped away in the chaos.

"What happened to him?" Soriya asked. At the question, Mentor's gaze fell. The darkness within his hood swallowed him whole, and he tried his best to avoid the question. Soriya, though, pressed the issue, her words piercing and unafraid. "Mentor, what happened to Darius?"

"Please, little one," Mentor said. "You've seen enough. Let it go."

She grabbed his arm. She ripped the hood from his head, forcing him to look at her. "No. You don't get to walk away from me now. I've come this far for the truth. Show it to me. Show me the end of the story."

His shoulders slumped in surrender. He held out his hand and she took it. Olcott Curve blurred into a sea of color. The van disappeared. So did Marissa, wiped away like the leaves on the road—cracked and crumbling.

The world shifted once more. The end had finally arrived.

CHAPTER EIGHTY

The panel slid away from the wall, a false block of concrete chiseled out in the deepest shadows of the chamber. Christopher knew the stairs wouldn't be safe, not with Darius on the loose, so he crept in, careful not to make his presence known. The block rested to his right as he clambered into the room.

The green light of the Bypass washed over him. A darkness clung to the surface. It was a reflection of the figure kneeling before the sphere. Deep murmurs of prayer filled the air, the rapid whispers of the desperate.

"Darius."

The man whirled around, his entire body tensing. "Chris? How?"

Christopher's eyes flitted to the back corner of the chamber, but returned quickly. His secrets were necessary, though at one time they would have easily been shared with the man he had called friend and teacher.

Darius' appearance spoke to something else entirely now, though. His clothes were ripped, the stains of their earlier confrontation clear. His eye was still puffed up, barely able to see through the folds of skin protecting what little remained of his vision. Scraped knees and bruised knuckles completed the look.

All stood as an ever-present reminder of Christopher's task and the pain it brought him.

"I never meant for it to happen," Darius said. Tears fell, mixing with the dried blood caked to his skin. "Chris, you have to believe me. I never meant for any of this to happen."

Christopher ran his fingers along the deep cut on his cheek. "But it did, Darius. Your family is dead."

"I can fix it," the desperate man said, frantic in his every step.

"With the Bypass, we can fix everything. Fix it and make it better. For everyone."

Christopher said nothing. He kept his distance outside the four pillars of the altar. He peered at the man with disdain and hatred. Darius had betrayed everything they stood for, and instead of remorse, he tried to find solutions to put the genie back in a bottle that had been shattered and scattered to the winds.

"I can't hear it anymore," his former teacher said. "I came here hoping to find the way, to hear the voice in my head again, but the Bypass is stopping me. It's hiding the truth from me—from us!

"You see that, don't you?" he continued. "You see the truth behind the power. There is something there, something inside, waiting to come back. If we let it, we can bring the light back to the world. We can save Jayla and Marissa. I can…"

"Darius…"

"I searched for the stone," Darius said, ignoring Christopher's call. "After everything, I went back for it, but it was gone. The stone was my only connection to the voice." His eyes went cold, locked on his student. "You took it."

"You're delusional," Christopher replied.

"No," Darius snapped, the desperation gone. Anger replaced it, the same hatred from that morning. "No, I see more clearly than ever. You've always coveted what I had. My family. My life. My connection to the Bypass. It showed me the truth."

"Then look, Darius!" Christopher bellowed. He pointed to the swirling green energy whipping faster and faster along the surface. "Face what you've done!"

Shadows danced between the light. Images formed in the dark. Darius stared deep into the well. Then he turned away, shaking his head repeatedly.

"I can make it right. With the Bypass." He eyed the object in Christopher's hand. "With the Greystone."

Christopher tucked it deep into his cloak. "No. Your days with the stone are over. Your days are over, Darius."

Restraint left the man. His rage took over, and he charged at Christopher with fists raised and a scream on his lips. "You took them from me! You did, Chris. Just like you're trying to take this from me! Only I can save them all! Only I—"

His fist shot forward. Christopher let it sail by, the anger making the strike sloppy and unbalanced. He grabbed Darius' arm as it passed, whipping it up and behind the back of his former teacher.

With all the force left in him, Christopher drove the man to the pulsating sphere of energy. Darius struggled against the hold, unable to tear his bloodied and bruised body loose. His head settled against the surface of the Bypass, the energy washing over him in waves.

"You can't..." Darius pleaded.

"You killed them, Darius," Christopher said. "You killed them and nothing you say, no promises you make, will bring them back. You did it out of spite and jealousy. The Greystone was supposed to make us better. We were supposed to be better. Look what you've done to us."

"I..." Darius's eyes went wide. The shadows picked at his body, drawing him deeper and deeper into the wellspring of light. "Don't do this. Please..."

"I have to." Christopher shoved Darius into the sphere of green light. His entire body was submerged beneath the surface. With each pass of the infinite, more and more of Darius slipped away, pulled by the eternal stream running through time.

"No!"

The scream echoed in the chamber. Christopher ignored it, pushing harder. Darius fell through the veil into the Bypass. He offered one last glance of desperation before the waves washed him away from the surface into the depths of eternity. As he was swept away, his hand reached for salvation.

Christopher backed away rather than reach for it. When his teacher vanished from sight, he fell to his knees. There had been no choice. Darius had left him with only one recourse and he had taken it, knowing his actions that day—all of his actions—had damned him for all time.

CHAPTER EIGHTY-ONE

Soriya stepped out of the darkness. Christopher remained on his knees. Tears streamed down his cheeks. She circled the man and the impossible orb of energy—a representation of the space they currently occupied. She tried to find Darius through the ether, knowing he had already been lost inside and spread across eternity.

Because of Mentor.

"I did what I had to do," her teacher said. His hood was pulled back, the sadness a match with his younger self, though a lifetime had passed in between. The emotions were raw wounds that never healed, not with the guilt and pain involved.

"You killed him," Soriya said. She raised a hand to the Bypass; fingers passed through the orb like a wraith. "He was spiraling, and rather than help—to give him a chance—you killed him."

"He murdered your mother!"

"You did the same to him!" Soriya's anger threatened to take her away from the truth, from what she had been seeking this whole time. A calm breath escaped her, and she opened her hands to let the tension fall away.

Mentor nodded slowly, acknowledging her restraint. "I... I didn't see another way."

"I know," she said in a quiet voice. She stared into the eyes of Christopher Eckhart, a man broken by a single day. So much pain rested in them. So much remorse at his failure. "Just like I know this wasn't the end at all. It was only the beginning."

Everything in her life stemmed from that day. Soriya Greystone had been born here. Mentor found her in the aftermath, pulled her into his world, and offered her one of her own for the first time since the accident.

Suddenly, Mentor's fears about letting her view the Bypass during their time together made more sense. He worried she would see the man behind the shadows, lost in time. He feared his sins would somehow return someday to haunt them all over again.

Mentor had saved her, though. No matter her anger, that truth remained untarnished.

"My mistakes haunt me in this place. They always will," Mentor said. "I tried to keep you free—to save you—but condemned you all the same."

Her hand fell on his, squeezing lightly. "You can't shelter someone from pain. You can only be there to help them face it and hopefully move forward. Mentor, you did that for me more times than I can count. Maybe it stemmed from guilt over what you'd done, but it grew to be more than that. You did it out of love."

"Soriya…"

She hugged him close. "Thank you. For saving me and for showing me the truth."

When she let him go, the room was gone. Christopher Eckhart disappeared along with the rest of the chamber. No green light spun before them.

They were back at the intersection. The black sky above crackled with energy, claws ripping through the void. Mentor staggered away from her. With each step, he shored up his defenses and pushed away the pain of the moment for the fight to come—that would always come.

"We're back."

"Not for long, it seems," Soriya muttered. Mentor's eyes widened at the light growing around her. A glow wrapped around her skin, causing her entire body to tingle.

"Soriya, wait!"

She smirked. "I don't know if I have a whole lot of choice in the matter."

"Of course you do."

Kali approached. Her aspects danced behind her, ready to take over at a moment's notice. The strain to keep them subdued was clear on her face. The struggle did little to diminish the smile across her lips.

"Kali?"

"You've learned the truth, Soriya," she said. "Doesn't mean anything unless you accept it."

"I don't…"

Kali waved her hand. A figure formed in the center of the intersection. Marissa stood before them, a child of four. She held her doll close; the innocence of her former life was still very much alive in her eyes.

Soriya waited for more. When Kali backed away with a bow, Soriya took the hint and approached. She circled her former self, then stopped before her.

The little girl looked up with bright eyes. "Hello."

"Hello," Soriya said, bending a knee.

"You dress funny."

Soriya picked at the tattered purple blouse and her ripped jeans. She laughed. "Yeah. Yeah, I guess I do."

"I'm going to be a crime fighter. I'm going to keep people safe like my daddy."

Soriya peered through wet eyes. "That is a good thing to do for people. Do you think I could help you do that?"

"Sure." Marissa held out her hand. Soriya took hold, and the little girl smiled. In an instant, Marissa turned into light. The stream of brilliant luminescence surrounded Soriya, and she took hold of it, allowing it to penetrate her. With the boundless energy of her former self came every memory of the past. Lady. Jayla. Their home. The joy and the pain. The terror and the fun. All of it now belonged to Soriya.

She was whole.

Standing, the light continued to embrace Soriya. It lifted her off the ground. Before she could get far, a hand stopped her.

"Not yet, kiddo," Kali called to her.

"What more is there?"

"One last gift," Kali said. She untied a pair of ribbons from her left wrist. They snaked loose from her grasp and wound up Soriya's arm, tying tightly to her skin. "They always looked better on you, anyway."

Kali grinned, then vanished in a plume of light that scattered across the ebony sky.

Mentor reached for his student, beaming with pride. "You look different."

"I feel different." The tingling of the ribbons filled her with a longing she hadn't realized she had.

"You're whole. For the first time," Mentor said. "You'll need to be for what's coming."

"Mentor?"

He took her hand. "The Omega is coming, little one. When its light arrives, you'll have to make tougher decisions than I ever did. The Heart of Forever, Soriya. It is everything. You'll see that."

"I don't understand."

"You will." Mentor let go of her hand, and she felt herself drifting up and away from Portents.

She fought against the current for her teacher. "Come with me. I can save you."

"That's not my path," Mentor replied. "I have to stay. To hold the line as long as I can."

"This?" Soriya asked. "This place is killing you over and over again. I can't let you—"

"You must," Mentor said with finality. "Soriya, you can't save everyone. But you can save everything."

She didn't understand. Her eyes widened as she rose higher and higher away from him. "Mentor—"

His words followed her as she was lifted into the brightening light. "Make the right choice, Soriya. And know how proud I am of you. Always."

CHAPTER EIGHTY-TWO

"Dammit, Shepherd," Loren said. The knife hovered before Gabe's throat, his body a shield for his attacker. Loren tried to work around the problem. He wheeled back and forth with his gun, looking for an opening. Shepherd trailed his every movement, leaving him with little in the way of a solution. "Don't you—"

"I hold the boy," Shepherd said. "Don't make me kill him."

"What's one more life, right?" Loren asked. "You've taken enough already."

"Necessary sacrifices."

Loren scoffed at the dismissal. "I'm sure Wendy Caldwell and Michael Hennessey might have something to say about that. And God knows how many others."

"The founders?" A chuckle rose to his lips. "You still don't have a clue, do you?"

"Enlighten me."

Shepherd pulled Gabe closer. "Would you believe me if I told you I had nothing to do with their deaths?"

"Not a chance."

"I didn't." His eyes stared blankly ahead. There was no deceit in his voice, no hesitation at his declaration.

With so many others dead thanks to his actions, Atley and Renfield, the poor soul at the advertising firm, and the victims of the PSI explosion, why would he care about two more added to the final tally? What had been so special about the founders in those two instances that their passing caused the man nothing but glee at Loren's ignorance?

Shepherd grinned. "There are other forces at work here. This is much bigger than you can imagine. You don't even know all the players, much less the game."

"Yeah, well, you don't know us very well," Gabe grumbled through clenched teeth. He continued to struggle against the pull of his teacher. Frustration drove him toward recklessness with each jostle. None widened the gap between them. None gave Loren a clear shot.

All they did was cause Shepherd to tighten his grip. The knife dipped too close and sliced the faintest amount of flesh. A trickle of blood streamed down Gabe's neck.

"Let him go, Shepherd."

"I didn't want this," the man replied. "Gabe, I hope you understand that. I would have let you walk away."

"Now that I've given you what you wanted?" Gabe snapped. "How generous of you."

"You're right, of course," Shepherd said. The pride he'd shown Gabe at school and in Loren's presence disappeared behind the cold reality of their situation. Shepherd's true self revealed itself. The dark shadows of his eyes grew wide and reflected off the shine of the knife. "Killing you is a mercy at this point. Why let you live knowing how utterly useless you've been?"

"You son of a—"

Shepherd's fingers squeezed Gabe's neck. "For all the power you hold, you've chosen to do nothing."

"That's not true," Gabe said through the struggle. "That monster would have killed you if I hadn't jumped in."

"Please," Shepherd said. "Even if I hadn't arranged the attack, nothing would have come of it."

"You..."

Shepherd spat as he spoke. "You sew wounds when the infection festers at the heart of this city."

He peered at the glowing sphere. Gabe huffed. "The Bypass. This has always been about the damn Bypass."

"It's mine at last." Shepherd's hand relaxed, the knife lowering slightly. "I should thank you for handing it to me so easily."

Loren stepped forward to act, but was too slow. Shepherd shoved Gabe hard to the left. The kid flew, unbalanced, and slammed his shoulder into the closest pillar.

The few seconds Loren took to follow Gabe's movements were enough to cost him the advantage. By the time he opened fire. Shepherd was already rushing toward him. He moved like lightning, strides ahead of each bullet as they crashed into the concrete walls of the chamber.

An uppercut flew in a blur of light and collided with Loren's chin. He soared through the air. His body bounced along the cold ground. As he slid to a halt shy of the stairs, he realized his gun had fallen away. It lay across the room, out of reach. Before Loren could recover, Shepherd stood over him.

"I made a mistake a long time ago." Shepherd lifted Loren by the collar. "It cost me everything. But it also showed me the truth. The light at the heart of the Bypass is what I need—what we all need. It can save everyone."

"Not going to happen." Loren grabbed Shepherd's wrists and twisted. The grip on his collar fell away, and Loren hit the ground. He immediately swung out, but Shepherd had already backpedaled out of reach.

He delivered his own blow, the punch connecting with Loren's cheek. "As if you have a choice."

Gabe leaped onto Shepherd's back. "Leave him alone!"

Shepherd took the boy's hand and flipped him over his shoulder. Gabe slammed into the concrete, but held on for dear life. Shepherd's kick caught him in the gut, and the kid tucked into a ball and collapsed.

"I couldn't have accessed this place without you," he said over his victims. "The protection guarding this chamber locked me out. You made this possible. Remember that."

Shepherd stepped back to the altar, passing the pillars on the outskirts. From his side, he removed the Greystone he had stolen from the transport on Legacy. He pointed it toward the Bypass.

Loren struggled to stand, unable to shake off the effects of the man's attack. He reached for Gabe, and the pair helped each other to their feet. Light filled the room. It billowed out from the stone, white and endless, like a massive cloud spreading before them.

They were too far away to stop Shepherd as he reached out to touch the Bypass with his power.

"That's far enough."

The thunderous voice caused Shepherd to stagger back in surprise. The light dimmed from his stone. Through squinting eyes, Loren realized someone else had arrived, someone who had stepped through the mist of the infinite into reality.

"What?" Shepherd exclaimed. "What is this?"

Soriya Greystone dropped from the Bypass. Her fists were clenched before her—ready for a fight. "You want the Bypass? You'll have to go through me."

CHAPTER EIGHTY-THREE

The solid ground sent a chill up Soriya's spine. The air was electric and vibrant, rushing over her body as the Bypass swirled at her back. Her smirk widened as the world welcomed her back. Every sound ran together, yet she pulled them apart and enjoyed each piece of the symphony that was the city. The shaking earth of the subway lines above thrummed along. Ants scurried in the deepest corners of the chamber. The slight breeze of circulating air whipped the Ribbons of Kali along her left arm, causing them to dance at her side.

Her time away made it all so clear—all the little things she had taken for granted previously... and all the things she'd missed in her absence.

Especially the two men on the other side of the room. Loren and Gabe struggled to stand, their mouths agape at her arrival. They were bruised and battered from a fight that still continued—one started by the man before her.

Shepherd backpedaled from her, his Greystone still raised high. "You? But you—" he said. His momentary shock faded and his eyes thinned. "You're too late."

She had heard those words before, but they belonged to the past. Today was a new day. "No. Never again." Soriya approached, her own Greystone balanced against her enemy. "This place is under my protection. This is my city. You have no power here anymore."

Shepherd screamed with rage. Her defiance set him off, just as she intended. What she failed to realize was the amount of force he'd channeled into the stone. It lit up, the light almost blinding.

A force of energy shot at her. The pulse was a death sentence in a single beam. Soriya didn't bother to dodge the blast. She closed her eyes, feeling the cool surface of the stone warm up at her merest thought.

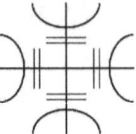

The beam deflected across the chamber. It sliced through the wall like a knife through butter. Soriya opened her eyes again, letting out a calm breath.

"Impossible."

"Nothing is impossible," Soriya said. "You should know that."

Shepherd sent wave after wave of fury at her. Light mixed with fire. Bolts rained down from above. She took them each in turn, casting them aside like the weakest of punches. Flames flickered to nothing, eaten by the wind. Light swallowed the solid shadow whole. The bolts she kept, allowing the stone to absorb the energy. Electricity ran up and down her arms. Filled with the energy, Soriya sent it back.

All of it.

Shepherd dove for cover. He raised the stone, terrified at the power rebounding back at him. It bounced off his Greystone and careened toward the pillars throughout the chamber. They took the brunt of his own assault, the one in the northeast corner slicing clean through from the energy unleashed.

The ceiling quaked. Debris crumbled from above, and the earth groaned with dissatisfaction. Even the Bypass rumbled. The great light recognized the loss of the protection that bound it to the chamber. The infinite spun madly, rising high above them. Shadows screamed within; the sound caused all to turn to view the spectacle.

"Damn you," Shepherd snapped. "Do you realize what you've done?"

The Bypass was out of his reach. That was all that mattered in her eyes. Shepherd, knowing his plan had failed, turned and fled for the stairs.

Loren barred his path. His shaky frame fought against him, but still he stood as an obstacle to the man.

It afforded them little. Shepherd shoved Loren aside; the detective's attack was nothing but a momentary delay to the fleeing villain. Gabe leaped at the man. He missed his ankles by inches and landed with a thud. The air was pried from his lungs by the impact.

Shepherd paused in front of the steps. "You've won nothing here. There is no stopping what's coming." He raised his Greystone to the ceiling. "I'm sorry you won't be able to see it."

"Wait!" Gabe shouted, the word little more than a croak.

The ceiling cracked immediately. Entire chunks of concrete, layers of earth and stone from above them suddenly descended into the forty-foot-tall room, destroying the sanctity of the Bypass Chamber once and for all.

Shepherd's laughter trailed him up the stairs. Gabe moved to follow. His anger outpaced all rational thought. He made it to the base of the steps to begin his ascension, not realizing the wall shattering next to him was ready to fall with the merest touch.

"Gabe! Don't!"

Too far away to grab him, Soriya extended her left arm. The Ribbons of Kali shot free from their moorings along her skin. They raced through the air, cutting a clear path through the falling debris. Wrapping around Gabe's arm, they retracted hard. Gabe flew back from his pursuit, launched through the air, until he landed at the foot of the platform.

The sudden movement was enough to cause the wall along the stairs to surrender. It crumbled, moving toward them in a massive wave. Loren raced from his position. He snatched his gun and the fallen Greystone, then joined Soriya and Gabe at the platform.

All around them, the chamber collapsed. Chunks of ceiling crashed down from above. The earth cried out in pain and the floor split beneath them in response.

Loren pulled Gabe to his feet. "You all right?"

Gabe reclaimed his Greystone, then glanced around the room.

The stairs were gone, lost behind a mountain of concrete. "For the moment, anyway."

Soriya smirked at them. She wanted to pull them close and never let go. Unfortunately, there were greater concerns. There always were. The pillars maintained their precarious position around the Bypass altar. They swayed, ready to give way. Once they did, the rest of the chamber would fall. Soriya needed to move quickly. She darted across the room for the domicile.

"Soriya!"

She didn't bother to reply. Her speed carried her through the common room to Mentor's bedroom. She passed the broken bookshelves and the cot for the chest hidden in the back corner. The rune, Ansuz, stared at her.

She had peered into the chest once before, in the aftermath of Mentor's death. He'd kept all her achievements from their time together—artwork and stories, dresses and gifts. His love for her had allowed her to survive that dark day. In her grief, though, Soriya had failed to notice the small box at the bottom of the chest.

Snatching it from its hiding place, Soriya rushed away from the room for the open chamber. Shards of rock shattered above. The accumulation of weight caused the domicile roof to buckle under the pressure. The second she passed the door to the chamber, the makeshift home collapsed in on itself, destroying the life her and Mentor had built together.

Loren pulled her away from the wreckage before she was lost in it as well. "What the hell was that? What were you doing?"

Soriya opened the box. The locket sat within, silver and shining, as if no time had passed. "I couldn't leave without this."

"A souvenir?" Loren asked in disbelief. "At a time like this?"

Gabe jumped between them, panic in his eyes. "There's no way out, Soriya. We're trapped."

Soriya shook her head. "There's always a way out."

She'd seen it while in the Bypass: a shadow tucked deep into the corner, one alluded to before in a memory she had failed to recall at the time. While arguing with Mentor, he had gazed at the same spot, always happy to hold the information over her until she was ready to learn it on her own.

Now's as good a time as any, she thought with a laugh.

Soriya led them to the corner. Her hands dug through the concrete, searching methodically as the world caved in around them.

Fingers settled into a groove and she felt her way around a loose piece of stone in the wall. Pulling it free, Soriya tossed the stone aside.

A tunnel opened up before her.

"How?" Loren asked, astonished.

"Do you want to question it right now?" Soriya shoved him ahead.

"Not at all."

"Didn't think so," she said. "Go."

Loren grabbed Gabe's hand and helped him into the tunnel. When it was his turn, he paused. "What about you?"

"I'm not done yet."

"Soriya..."

"I'll be right behind you," she said with a smirk. "Trust me."

"Always." Loren left without another word.

With the others safe, Soriya stepped away from the tunnel. The locket slipped into her pocket, her hand stroking the keepsake lovingly. She scanned the room—her home for so long—with quiet sadness. So much of her life had occurred here. Yet so much more remained.

The Bypass spun rapidly above her. It rose toward the ceiling. The pillars protecting it wavered from the pressure placed upon them. Struggling to maintain their hold, they snapped and began to fall.

It was all going away, everything Soriya had fought for over the years. The Bypass, though, would not escape the collapse of the chamber. If the ceiling gave way completely, the infinite would be buried along with everything else in the room. It would be lost.

"No." Soriya raised the Greystone. She aimed at the Bypass, eyes shut tight and a wish set on her lips.

The Bypass shook. The energy fought against her plea, which went from a whisper to a scream at the effort involved. The light from the stone grew brighter and spread. It swept over the Bypass, then swung back on the owner.

With a deep cry, the Bypass shrank. Pulled along the light, it crashed through the last remnants of the protective barrier and soared until just before Soriya's chest.

She opened her eyes. With one last push from the stone, the Bypass entered her body. The past, present, and future—infinite energy containing all eternity—became one with her. Runes covered her skin. Her body acted as the protection the chamber had once provided.

Soriya felt like she was boiling alive, but she buried the pain before she was buried herself. With the Bypass safe for the moment, Soriya afforded herself one last look around her home.

"Goodbye."

As the ceiling gave way with one massive heave and darkness consumed the Bypass Chamber, Soriya leaped into the tunnel.

CHAPTER EIGHTY-FOUR

The world quaked. Dust and debris filled the air. Loren crawled desperately through the tunnel, pulling himself along with his hands until the narrow escape hatch widened.

He fell clear with a thud. Coughing loudly, Loren struggled to his feet. His clothes were wrecked. No matter how hard he swiped along the fabric, the dust remained just as thick as before. The blood certainly didn't help either.

An old service station surrounded him. The C-Line most likely ran through the station before the routes shifted due to convenience or after some accident left the old line unusable. They must have been over a hundred yards from the Bypass Chamber. The tunnel would have taken months to dig by conventional means, another surprise from Soriya.

The station was a holdover from better days. A level of decadence occupied the room compared to the drab conditions of the current platforms. Fancy lighting hung limply from the ceiling, crystals spinning in uneven rotations. Railings led up the stairs to the modern junction, the path littered with spiderwebs.

A cough woke Loren to another presence in the room.

"Gabe?" he called. A sudden panic seized him. Loren spun around for a view of the kid. When he found him, Gabe was doubled over, his entire face caked with dust. Loren rushed over. "Hey. Hey, are you—"

Gabe waved him back. There were no coughs to clear his lungs. Instead, tears stung his eyes and ran down his face. "Don't. Please."

"Gabe, it's okay." Loren held out his hand and took Gabe's to lift him up. "We're okay."

Gabe shook his head. "I screwed up. I trusted him, Loren. I told him everything, and he—"

"You didn't know."

Gabe scoffed, disgusted with himself. "I should have. Maybe I am just some stupid kid. I sure as hell am no Greystone."

He took the stone from his pocket and held it out for Loren.

"You're wrong. You've earned that stone." Loren closed his fingers over the stone and pressed it tighter to Gabe's palm. "If anyone is to blame, it's me. I pushed you away. Told you I wouldn't, and I still did it. After what happened to you at the first bombing, I was so damn worried. I couldn't think straight. All I kept seeing was you... You tried to help me and when I wouldn't listen, you turned to someone who would."

Gabe returned the stone to his pocket. "Loren, I..."

Loren's hands fell on the kid's shoulders. "I was trying to protect you. You tend to do that with people you love." Surprised eyes met him and Loren laughed. "Come on, I'm man enough to say it."

"Never said you weren't."

Loren nodded. "You're my partner in this. I won't let my fears separate us again. Think you can do the same?"

"Definitely."

A loud rumble echoed through the tunnel. Concrete collapsed in droves, forcing Loren and Gabe away from their escape hatch. After it settled, he let go of his ward and moved for the tunnel once more.

"Soriya?" He quietly cursed himself when silence filled the room. He couldn't see anything in the tunnel, the dust and debris blocking his view. What the hell had he been thinking letting her stay behind? He should have stuck with her, helped her with whatever task remained with the Bypass. Frantic hands ripped crushed stone loose from the tunnel. "Soriya!"

"Why are you yelling at me?" a voice said. Hands shoved debris aside until Soriya broke through the surface. A coughing fit exploded from her lips, but the smile shined through. Loren helped her from the tunnel, and Gabe joined the effort to keep her on her feet.

"I yell because I care," Loren said, brushing the concrete from her hair.

She chuckled. "I appreciate it."

Loren looked her over. Despite the obvious need for a shower and fresh clothes, Soriya appeared stronger than when she'd left. Whatever she had been through had brought her a semblance of peace he had never seen in her before.

He pointed to the tunnel. "The chamber—"

"Gone," she confirmed. "Buried."

"But the Bypass?" Gabe asked.

She smiled at him. "It's safe."

Loren's jaw clenched. He squeezed the air before him with frustration. "When I get my hands on Shepherd—"

"He was the shadow, Loren," Soriya said, stopping his pacing. "The one in the chamber when I..."

Loren's brow furrowed. "If he... If it was him, then why didn't he strike right away? Why—"

"My arrival must have scared him off," Soriya said, clearly uncertain. "He had been in the Bypass for a long time. Maybe he was disoriented from the experience. As lost as I was before."

"Maybe..."

"There's more."

Loren grumbled, "There always is. What is it, Soriya?"

"Look." Soriya removed the locket from her pocket. Dangling between her fingers, the heart charm spun at the base of a thin chain. She let the necklace settle along Loren's palm.

He opened it slowly, careful not to damage the keepsake. The image of a woman rested inside the right half of the charm. With strong eyes and a proud face, the woman was strikingly beautiful. "Who—"

"Her name was Jayla," Soriya said. "My mother."

"Your mother?" Loren exclaimed. The mystery of Soriya's past had always remained a locked door for as long as he had known her. Those answers came to light in rapid fashion, it seemed, and with them a new problem. "Then, this must be—"

He recognized the man in the other picture immediately. Holding it out for Gabe to see, both stared in astonishment. Soriya nodded to each of them, reclaiming the locket and holding it against her chest.

"His name is Darius Shepherd. He's my father."

CHAPTER EIGHTY-FIVE
Two Days Later

When Sunday rolled around, the end of a long and unforgettable week, the city took a quiet, anxious breath of relief. The riots had dispersed with the dawn of a new day. Tensions remained, however, with everyone on high alert. Shepherd's image was passed along to every major network in quick fashion, giving the city a proper target to funnel all its aggression toward.

Questions remained. Answers, though, were something few had to offer. Without some kind of resolution, the violence would return. There was no doubt.

Thel certainly didn't help matters. Her declaration played on repeat with every newscast. Additional interviews showed the siren in a new light, one Loren couldn't help but see as harsher than anything he'd ever seen in the woman before. Trouble was on the horizon from her. The same held true for Ruiz, who had, of course, left the hospital of his own volition. Not that Loren cared at the moment. He had ducked multiple calls from the man, unsure how to deal with him after learning about his connection with the Luminaries.

The troubles would always be there, some more prevalent than Loren wished and plenty damn concerning, especially when it came to his friendship with Ruiz. Today, however, belonged to him and Gabe. They earned the reprieve, their last attempt ruined.

"Got the tickets?" Loren asked. He tucked his wallet into his back pocket. Grabbing his phone and keys, he started for the door.

Gabe waited, hand on the knob. "On my phone."

"No paper?"

Gabe shook his head. "Time to face the future, old man."

"Never." Loren ushered him into the hall, then locked the door behind them. They went down the steps and out of the building. Snow fell in small flakes, the wintry wind cutting through them as they started up the block for the local theater. Loren checked his watch. "We should have time for a bite to eat."

Gabe's eyes lit up. "Burgers?"

Loren's stomach groaned at the mention. "Again?"

"Hell, yeah."

Loren grinned at the kid's joy. He pulled Gabe close, giving him a squeeze. A nod started them off, and they headed for their new favorite restaurant. Loren kept his eye on Gabe, who struggled not to run ahead. Every glance widened the smile on Loren's face, happy to have Gabe in his life.

"You're looking at me again," Gabe said without turning his head.

"How can you tell?"

"I can."

"And I'm not allowed to do that?"

Gabe groaned. "You look like you want to have the talk again."

"The talk?"

"Not that one," Gabe immediately replied, a stern finger raised. "Never that one, understand?"

Loren laughed. "Maybe?"

Gabe sighed. "The one about trust."

"Ah," Loren said, shoving his hands into his pockets for warmth. "Do you need to hear it again?"

"Not in this lifetime," Gabe answered. He rolled his eyes in exasperation.

"You get where I was coming from?" Loren's guilt ate at him. His fears continued to haunt him. Whenever there was a wince of pain in Gabe's eyes, he recalled the terror that accompanied the kid's fall. He had been lucky to walk away with only a sprain. Next time might be much worse. It definitely would be if Loren failed to trust in those around him.

"Leaving me in the dark isn't protection," Gabe said.

"I know." Loren held Gabe up. "But everything lately? It's so much bigger than it used to be. I got scared. For you. For us. The legends aren't going to sit idly by any longer. There is going to be trouble. With them. With Thel. And…"

"Yeah…" The merest mention of Gabe's former history teacher caused his head to lower. His guilt continued to manifest. He was a good kid—a smart kid. To be used the way he had stung him much more deeply than anything Loren had perpetrated.

"Shepherd's plans are far from over."

Gabe stood tall, a sharp glance toward Loren. "We'll stop him."

The strength behind his conviction caused Loren to nod in agreement. "We will."

"Come on," Gabe said, slapping Loren lightly on the chest. "Let's get those burgers before—"

A scream cut through the air. The cry for help echoed around them. It silenced their conversation and all thought of food.

"Was that—"

Loren smirked. "Feel like a slight detour?"

Gabe lifted his Greystone. "Thought you'd never ask."

They raced along together to protect their city. The doubts and fears would never go away completely, but together they could handle them. They were finally ready to face whatever came their way.

CHAPTER EIGHTY-SIX

The rooftop offered Thel a clear view of everything in Portents. She oversaw it all, a queen looking down upon her reclaimed kingdom. For so long, she'd played the passive observer, a player in a game she never had any control over. Those days were done.

A gentle hand ran along her back. Kellon joined her, holding a pair of beer bottles. He passed one along, then toasted the moment with a clink of glass and a long swig.

The party was in full swing on the rooftop. Concerns for those below faded behind blasting music. Dozens danced the night away, drinking and laughing with their fellow freaks.

How had she come to this? Only days earlier, Thel had been lost in misery—trapped in her own personal solitary confinement. The whole world frightened her. Depressed and unable to move, she could barely function, let alone become the face of a revolution. Now, people stood with her. They listened to her and heard the message delivered repeatedly over the airwaves.

She was the voice of her people. They were legion—ready to strike out at the hate that had oppressed them for so long.

Like Myers…

Thoughts of her former partner gave Thel pause. She could still see the frightened stare, the abject terror, in Myers' face after their confrontation. Sam had tried to protect Thel, to show her the good in the city, or at least a good time while dealing with the nightmares hidden in the shadows.

There had been a genuine friendship between them. But no longer. Sam looked at Thel with the same fear the siren had once carried.

Had she truly become so frightening? Had her actions made her the villain?

Thel shook her head, dizzy from her thoughts. The old worries returned. Anxiety rushed through her veins, and she nearly toppled over the ledge of the rooftop trying to right herself.

A hand along her back settled her. Kellon was with her. So was another.

Shin sidled up to her, opposite Kellon. He raised his beer, his black fur melding with the shadows, and quietly toasted the night. His other hand rested on her back, and he stared deeply into her eyes.

The worries faded. The anxieties melted away, and all thought of Myers disappeared.

A smile spread across Thel's lips. This was her world now. No question remained about her journey. No fear existed about the path ahead. There would be challenges, but they would rise to meet them. They stood together, never apart and never alone.

Cheers rang out from the crowd. Shin started them, his voice bellowing in a growl that echoed in their ears like a deep thrumming through their very souls. It stirred them, lifting them up, and caused raucous laughter to follow.

Below, the city waited for her next move. They waited for another glimpse of her power.

I'll show them, Thel thought.

She drank her beer, an eye to the little people on the streets. They were ants to her now, petty annoyances that stood in the way of progress. It was time they saw the light. Portents was no longer home to only humans. It belonged to the freaks and the monsters.

Thel pitied anyone who thought differently.

CHAPTER EIGHTY-SEVEN

Night fell. Ruiz should have gone home hours earlier. Work, though, never ended. Not that work knew a thing about his current destination. No one did.

His car left the RDJ Expressway, winding south until residential neighborhoods disappeared. When he reached the warehouse in question, Ruiz parked in the shadows of an adjacent alley. Cautious steps carried him to the side of the building, following the instructions given to him to the letter.

Red brick dominated the wall to his right. He traveled the length of the building until he reached the center where the brick was broken up by a single golden glyph. He wiped at the surface for a better look at the rising flame at its peak.

Ruiz looked back. His doubts followed him. So did everything else that had built up over the last seventy-two hours. It had been enough time to give the city a breath, and more than enough for the lunatic fringes to put forward the worst possible solutions to quell any further unrest.

Council meetings were scheduled almost daily. Curfew was bandied about. So were special committees and protection services. New departments. It all boiled down to new problems for Ruiz. He wanted to talk to Loren about them, but the man refused to answer his calls. Ruiz's decisions had driven them apart.

Those same decisions had brought him to the library in the dead of night.

The glyph on the wall called to him. He pressed it into the structure until a click resounded, then he twisted the image hard to the right. The wall receded and the door appeared.

It was open and Gates stood inside.

"You came," she said, a satisfied grin across her face.

"I had to," Ruiz replied, rubbing his hands together nervously. They felt dirty from his entry, though he understood it went much deeper than opening a single door. He shook his doubts away. "This is too important."

"I'm glad you understand the stakes."

He did. There had been more to the bombings, more to the thefts, and more to the chaos swallowing his city whole. Portents was his home. He needed to stand as something more than a city bureaucrat—needed to be proactive against the unseen threat in the dark.

"I also understand the danger," Ruiz said, a finger raised and pointed at Gates. "Something your secrets do nothing but exacerbate."

"*Our* secrets," Gates said. "Once you do this, you own them as well."

It weighed on him, but the decision was necessary. He needed to protect his home.

"Our secrets," Ruiz confirmed.

"What we do is for Portents." Gates raised her hands. At her invitation, shadows stepped forth. A dozen figures holding candles moved before them, surrounding Ruiz in a wide circle. They wore masks of white and long, dark robes. "Always for Portents."

"Always," Ruiz muttered, a whispered prayer more for himself than those in the room.

The robes closed in. Gates reached out to receive another set from the closest member of the group. She held it out to Ruiz. He took the robe in hand, staring at the mask resting on top of it.

"Welcome to the Luminaries, Alejo Ruiz."

CHAPTER EIGHTY-EIGHT

The phone wouldn't stop ringing. Three days and the messages piled up. Work. Loren. More work. More Loren. An endless repetition of fresh cases and concerns. Myers tired of it all. She ignored them, lost to her misery.

Empty bottles covered the counter. They had been her escape, that and hours spent on the couch watching... well, she couldn't rightly say what the hell she had been watching. Shows ran in the background as she struggled to settle from her conflict with Thel.

Like a religious figure, Myers rose on the third day. She tossed aside the pity and the pain, and found fresh clothes in the mountain of laundry tucked in the corner. She slipped out of her pajamas to shower. The heat cleansed her skin, wiping away the dried tears and the blood.

Myers took to the mirror afterwards. Her clothes felt like lead weights, the badge heavy in her pocket. The bruises had diminished along her forehead and cheeks, yet were still present. Blotches of color mixed with the paleness she prided herself on during the winter months. Her *moon-tan*, she called it. A brush ran through her hair, pulling at the knots. Content with the mess, Myers moved on from the mirror.

Her holster rested on the coffee table. She reached for it, then stopped. Visions of the bullet going off just shy of her temple repeated through her memory. Thel's song echoed through the apartment. The melody drove daggers through what little remained of her sanity.

Tears welled in her eyes. She squeezed her fists tight to fight them back—struggling against the devil's chord that almost ended her life.

Defiantly, Myers ripped the Glock from the holster and held

the gun before her. She controlled the movement. It was under her authority, not at the whim of someone else. She was not a puppet and hadn't been for some time. Thel had taken away her control.

That couldn't happen again.

Myers took aim. The barrel reflected back at her in the mirror. Shaking hands clutched the grip, a finger resting on the trigger. She pulled it and the safety ratcheted loudly.

She controlled her fate. No one else.

Myers tucked the weapon away and strapped the holster around her waist. Collecting her keys and her phone, she moved for the door to face the calamities that had accumulated during her much-needed break.

More hesitation greeted her at the door. The phone chimed—work again, this time with the banner headline of URGENT on the message. She closed her eyes, wishing for help, praying for someone else to handle things. Anyone but her. The lure of another beer and binge whispered in her ear. She ripped the door open, rather than be pulled back into the misery that had swallowed her whole over the last few days.

Loren stood in the hallway, his hand raised to the door.

"Oh," Myers said. Her gaze fell to the floor immediately. "Hey, I was about to—"

"I came to—"

Both stopped talking over each other. Awkward smiles passed between them.

Loren rubbed the back of his neck. "Sorry. Go ahead."

"No, it's..." Myers retreated into the apartment. She held the door open for him. "Come in."

He followed. His eyes widened at the devastation in the single-room dwelling. Myers cringed at the reaction. She closed the door, then hurried to the counter to clear away the grief-therapy from the last few days.

"I've been..." Myers stopped. "Busy? Or something?"

"Or something?" Loren asked, unconvinced. "I've been calling."

"Yeah, I know," Myers said. Glass clattered in the garbage bag. She tied the bag off before tossing it into the corner. She moved for the bed to lift the sheet back into place. "You have. Cho has. Work has, of course, because when isn't this city going to hell, right?"

"The bomber—"

"Heard about that," Myers said. "Listened to Cho's message, at least. Her very long message."

"Myers…"

"Looks like he got away," she continued, barely able to meet the concern in his eyes. "There's still patrols in place, keeping an eye on the Johnson home, but he won't go back there."

"Sam…"

"He was Gabe's teacher?" Myers grabbed a rag from the drawer. Hands wiped feverishly to remove the stains of neglect on her furniture, on the counter, and everywhere else within reach. "This Shepherd guy?"

Loren nodded. "It's a little more complicated than that."

"When isn't it?" She scrubbed harder, finding a new focus with each breath. Anything to keep from looking at her guest. Anything to keep him from seeing her so close to the edge.

"Sam, if you would just—"

Myers tossed the rag aside. She started for the door. "Well, I'm glad you came to check on me. I should get to work and—"

Loren caught her by the hand. "What happened?"

"Hmmm? I don't—"

"Your face," Loren said. His fingers grazed her cheek. He felt warm against her skin. "The bruises?"

"Nothing."

"You went to check on Thel," Loren said. "You never said what happened. Was she all right?"

Myers' body shook at the mention. Her head fell low. "She… She's a long way from all right. Loren, she… She killed Yardin."

"What?" Loren exclaimed. "Why would she—"

She told him everything. It spilled out of her: her encounter with her former partner, the fight, and the song that continued to hum through the back of her mind. She found her hand hovering over her Glock during the retelling. Her body continued to struggle with the mental command, even after so long.

For all her lecturing about keeping secrets, about tearing each other apart rather than working together, Myers had stewed in her own silence for three days instead of reaching out and asking for help. She never went to the department with the information— never turned on Thel, even after everything her former partner had done.

Loren said nothing, simply listening to the events. Concern grew in his eyes, but he never threw the secret back at her, never interrupted and gloated, which she most likely would have done if their roles had been reversed. Myers didn't deserve his reserved approach. She didn't deserve him at all.

Tears streamed down her cheeks. The floodgates opened, and she nearly fell from the weight of it all. She had done everything to save Thel, to help her friend through the darkest of days, and now that was where she lived.

Loren was there in an instant. He held her close. "Myers—Sam—I'm... I'm so sorry."

"I have to find her," Myers said, fighting back the tears. "Help her if I can. Stop her if necessary."

"Not alone, you don't," he replied.

"Loren... I..."

She kissed him. Her lips settled along his and warmth filled her spirit. Her arms wrapped around him and he did the same, never letting go, never breaking away. They needed each other's strength. They needed each other, period. That was the only way forward.

That was the only way to survive the nightmares to come.

CHAPTER EIGHTY-NINE

Darius Shepherd rested his hands along the balcony. The cool concrete settled his nerves. It calmed the fury rising in his chest. He had been so close to success. The Bypass had been within reach, and with it, the key to saving everything.

The girl's involvement had been a surprise. Her arrival upset the delicate balance of the chamber. It had been the second time she'd had that effect on him. The first had been during his initial return to the world. He had ridden the wave through eternity, called forth by a great, unseen power to come back to the city of his birth. The stone had been waiting for him—twice the size with double the might. Yet he'd been forced to leave it behind. Her return had not only startled him but terrified him as well.

For he had seen her eyes before. They were sharp and strong. Deep brown irises carried a message from the past that rocked his present. They were the eyes of his deceased wife.

His daughter was still alive.

Christopher had lied. He had thrown their deaths in his face seconds before condemning Darius to his own. Forced into the Bypass, Darius had been ripped through time, shattered across the eddies of eternity, and lost to its unending tide. Twenty years he traveled through the infinite, listening to the whispers in the dark.

The time served him well. He learned much and saw more than anyone, all for the task ahead. Somehow, though, the identity of the Greystone had been kept secret—held back until the moment of his return like a cruel joke.

Marissa was still alive. His child was now his enemy, one who had beaten him soundly in his moment of triumph. It had not been a defeat, however, merely a setback.

Not everyone viewed it that way.

"You failed," a voice called from behind him. She stood near the door. Shadows claimed her stout frame. "All your talk. All your promises. Without the Bypass—"

"There are other ways to see my mission fulfilled," Darius said without looking. "And my promises kept."

"But if you don't—" The voice cut off. She stepped out of the darkness, eyes narrowed and finger raised. "You owe me, Shepherd!"

"I will deliver my end of the bargain." His laughter echoed in the wind. "Don't pretend you walked away empty-handed. You murdered those who stood in your way."

"Caldwell and Hennessey," she said without a tinge of regret. He had not been lying to Loren about the hand involved in those deaths. The descendants of the founders meant little to him. But to Leslie Gates? She cleared her throat, puffing out her chest. "They would have held up the Restoration Project. Their knowledge of the secrets locked in the Four Points... I couldn't let them stop me."

"Us."

Her head bowed. "Yes. Us."

"The project proceeds at pace?"

"Yes," Gates said. "With Ruiz on our side, we shouldn't run into anymore issues. You certainly helped him see the light."

"Good," Darius replied with a sneer. "Let nothing hinder our plans."

"Even her?" Gates said. "Even the Greystone?"

Darius closed his eyes. He saw Marissa, his darling child, laughing and playing. She was a memory, though. A life taken from him, never to be regained. "She has a role to play," he said in an icy tone. "Don't worry, Leslie. Nothing will stand in my way. Now go. You have work to do."

Another argument rose to her lips. She swallowed it down. A slight nod accepted her role, and she exited the balcony without a word.

The quiet barely took hold before another presence landed along the ledge. The low growl announced his arrival.

"Is the girl in position?" Darius asked, eyes watching Gates depart. When she was gone, he turned to greet his new guest.

The beast lumbered along the ledge. "Yes."

"She suspects nothing? Your control is absolute?"

A snarl answered his question. "Thel is now the voice of every myth and legend in the city."

Darius stood proudly. "A meteoric rise. Ready for a great fall. You know what to do next?"

"I do." With the task in place, the beast leaped into the night.

Darius' planning brought a malicious grin to his face. He stepped up to the ledge to look over Portents. The city was quiet for the moment, but only just. Already, pieces were moving. Players were taking their positions. The endgame was about to begin. All at his command.

Satisfied at the change to come, Darius set to his own task. He left the balcony behind and entered the storage site. Few knew it existed, tucked away in the heart of the city, right under their noses. He had quietly secreted all of his ill-gotten goods within the secret space over the last few days. None had been the wiser, not even when he'd delivered his prized possessions in the wake of his attack on Legacy Street.

He passed by shelves filled with tomes written ages earlier. The power held in their written words could raze Portents, yet they remained under lock and key rather than used. His task required more subtlety. Thanks to the Luminaries, he had the key to bringing about its success.

A locked room occupied the corner of the space. The half-glass on the door had been taken out and replaced with metal bars. Inside, a woman sat along the edge of a cot. Chains rattled before her, her wrists completely covered by the shining restraints. She had been chained within the moving truck, a secret captive held by Renfield and the Luminary inner circle.

Ruiz had thought the Greystone to be the grand prize of the heist, the reason for so much bloodshed and chaos in Portents. None could have imagined the true power held by the Luminaries.

"Feeling rested?" Darius asked, a cruel grin across his lips.

The young woman jumped to her feet. She rushed toward the door, only to be pulled back by the chains. "Let me go! You can't keep me here like this! I won't help you! I won't—"

"You don't have a choice in the matter."

Her name had been a gift from the voice in the dark. He'd witnessed her ability in her struggle with the Daughters of Salem years earlier. Since then, he had kept tabs on her, watching her abilities flourish with each use. Now her power was his.

Annabelle Waterhouse was the perfect tool for what came next.

He raised his Greystone toward her. "You work for me now, Doormaker."

Her eyes sparked with fear, and she backpedaled deeper into the cell's shadows. "No."

"You see it now, don't you, Annabelle? Just as your ancestors—the Daughters of Salem—did in the beginning. You will help me."

"I won't," she said in weak defiance.

"You will," Darius repeated, a dark gleam in his eyes. "You will help me bring about the end."

CHAPTER NINETY

Moonlight fell in thick streams over the scattered debris left behind at the Whistler Building. Through the gaping hole that encapsulated the third and fourth floor of the structure, one could see shattered desks, tangled wires hanging in strands through crumbled ceiling tiles, and a lone shadow taking it all in for the first time.

Soriya walked carefully amid the roiling building, deftly slipping around the piles of detritus left in the wake of the bombing. Sad eyes washed over the destruction, peering down the collapsed corner to the rear of the space, all the way to the ground level. So much had been lost. So much death, and all in the name of what?

The questions haunted her. Almost as much as the maniac behind the assault.

His name is Darius Shepherd. He's my father.

In her absence, her stubborn search for herself, Shepherd had wrought untold damage to Portents. Families continued to reel from the terror. Entire communities were locked away, sheltered in the night, for fear of another attack. Anger and desperation emanated down every block, echoing like a scream across her city, begging for help.

There was no more time to reflect on the past. Portents needed her.

Soriya left the remnants of PSI Telecom behind. Stepping onto the ledge of the third floor, she stared out into the night sky. The spires of Portents sparkled under the rising moon. From a distance, the clock on the Walker Complex chimed in another hour.

The passing of time was rhythmic and steady—a much different feeling than the Bypass, where everything had been stretched across the deep void of the infinite.

A smile crept along her lips. Her home was exactly as she had always remembered it. She recognized every rooftop, every alleyway, and most importantly, every shadow. They all existed at once, all trapped within the scope of her memory, and all were pristine in her recollection.

Standing in the gaping hole of the Whistler Building, the wind ripped through Soriya. It caused the ribbons down her left side to whip about her like a pink banner announcing her presence to Portents. She had forgotten the joy that came from the snapping sound, the soft cloth so delicate yet so powerful a weapon against an enemy.

For the first time in ages, Soriya felt whole. Her journey had brought her back, alive and complete. With her memories restored, her past life now merged with her current one, Soriya stood stronger than ever. Nothing would hold her back. Nothing would stop her from fulfilling her role in the city.

Not even her father.

The thought of Shepherd caused her hand to graze the locket resting against her chest. She lifted the charm at the end of the chain and opened it. Her mother's image beamed brightly, a shared smile on Soriya's lips. The other side darkened with the image of her father. His eyes were deep wells of pain. She still heard his anger echoing through her thoughts at their battle.

Their *first* battle.

Shepherd was still out there. Though she might have stymied his ambitions, his plans had yet to reach fruition. That was something a man like her father would not be able to let stand. He was waiting for the right moment to strike, to bring more darkness to her city.

The Greystone pulsed at her hip. A sigil on the surface beamed in soft white, a constant reminder of the power within her. The Bypass was locked away, for the moment, but her personal prison would only last so long.

Soriya could feel the energy building beneath her skin. It shifted through her body, carried like blood in her veins. She needed to find a haven for its power—yet hesitated at the very thought of relinquishing the turbulent energy coursing through her.

The Bypass opened her eyes wider with each breath taken. Something inside the infinite spoke to her in whispers, warning her of the danger to come and reminding her of her teacher's words as they parted company.

"The Omega is coming, little one. When its light arrives, you'll have to make tougher decisions than I ever did. The Heart of Forever, Soriya. It is everything. You'll see that."

She couldn't. Not yet. Whatever the Omega was, whatever the Heart of Forever contained, remained hidden from her. But Mentor was right. Both were coming for her—and soon.

Soriya leaped from the building into the night sky. The Ribbons of Kali snapped forward, latching onto a streetlamp in the distance. She whipped through the blustery wind, carried deeper into Portents. The fight of her life was ahead of her, and she would be ready for it.

She had to be.

ACKNOWLEDGEMENTS

This book was an immense effort. Months of blood, sweat, and (mostly) tears went into building the narrative you've hopefully enjoyed. None of it would have been possible if not for these amazing people:

Matt Patrick
Sally Hall
Sara Frandina
Paul Sardella
Vicki Wilkinson

I don't say it enough, but you make this whole endeavor worthwhile. Thank you for all that you do. From the little words of encouragement to the kick in the pants I need to keep writing, all is appreciated.

A special thank you to my lovely daughters: Parker, Samantha, and Iris. You are the only legacy I need in this life. You make me proud every single day.

ABOUT THE AUTHOR

Lou Paduano is the author of the Greystone series of urban fantasy adventures, which follow Detective Greg Loren and Soriya Greystone as they hunt myths, monsters, and legends in the city of Portents.

He is also the author of the conspiracy thriller series, The DSA, a serialized tale about a clandestine government agency trying to discover the true power behind humanity's future.

He lives in Grand Island, New York with his wife and three daughters. Sign up for his e-mail list for free content as well as updates on future releases at loupaduano.com.

THE GREYSTONE SAGA
AVAILABLE NOW

Follow the adventures of Soriya Greystone and Detective Greg Loren as they hunt dangerous myths and legends in the city of Portents.

BOOK ONE - SIGNS OF PORTENTS
BOOK TWO - TALES FROM PORTENTS
BOOK THREE - THE MEDUSA COIN
BOOK FOUR - PATHWAYS IN THE DARK
BOOK FIVE - A CIRCLE OF SHADOWS
BOOK SIX - ALPHA AND OMEGA
BOOK SEVEN - ERRANT KNIGHT

GREYSTONE-IN-TRAINING

For years, Soriya trained to become the Greystone. Follow the trials that made her the protector Portents needed to fend off the darkest of threats.

BOOK ONE - HAMMER AND ANVIL
BOOK TWO - THE GIFTS OF KALI
BOOK THREE - THE FINAL GAUNTLET

GREYSTONE LOST TALES

ARMY IN THE OBELISK
THE LAST KING

GREYSTONE CONTINUES IN...

What is the true purpose of the Greystone?

This question has plagued Soriya for years. No answer has been discovered during her tenure as protector of Portents. Now, however, she has no choice but to find the truth. To save her city from an unimaginable threat, Soriya must gather all the pieces of the Greystone and learn the secret behind its power.

Her quest brings new allies into the fight and reveals treacherous adversaries lurking in every shadow. Piecing together the stone is only the beginning of her journey. The Bypass awaits, along with the mystery that's been locked in its heart for eternity.

Soriya isn't the only one facing untold dangers. The death of a key figure sparks violence across Portents. Fear runs rampant. Called to help quell the unrest among humans and myths alike, Greg Loren finds himself in the middle of a high-stakes hostage situation. Commissioner Ruiz stands with him, but can he be trusted? Or has his allegiance to the Luminaries compromised him?

www.ingramcontent.com/pod-product-compliance
Lightning Source LLC
LaVergne TN
LVHW040037080526
838202LV00045B/3371